the

belonging

duet

CORINNE MICHAELS

THE BELONGING DUET
Copyright © 2015 Corinne Michaels
All rights reserved.
ISBN: 978-1-942834-00-7

Cover design:
Najla Qamber Designs
www.najlaqamberdesigns.com
Cover photo © Cocoa Bean Photography
www.cocoabeanphoto.com

Interior design and formatting:
Christine Borgford, Perfectly Publishable
www.perfectlypublishable.com

Editor for Beloved:
Megan Ward, Megan Ward Editing
www.meganwardediting.com

Editor for Beholden:
Lisa Christman, Adept Edits

beloved

CORINNE MICHAELS

dedication

To my husband, my anchor, my beloved.

prologue

To belong to someone.
All I've ever wanted is to be loved. I crave it—need it, desire it—more than food and water. I long for undying love and affection. The kind of love that bonds souls. The kind of love that's so deep two become one.

To be someone's beloved.

As a child I had my father, who adored and worshipped me—I was his perfect little daughter. He held me when I was sad, kissed my knee when I fell and got hurt, and read me bedtime stories. I was his princess, his daughter, his entire world.

What happens to a little girl when all of that stops? When she's no longer her father's perfect angel, but *instead* a painful reminder of his past. What happens to her when he pushes her aside and shows her he doesn't want her anymore?

"I just can't stay, Catherine. It hurts too much." *His eyes are filled with pain and regret.*

"Daddy, I love you! Please don't go. I won't cry anymore. I'll be good," I plead as I look into the dark brown eyes that mirror mine. My heart is begging for understanding from all this confusion and change. It's my ninth birthday, we finished cake and presents, and he's leaving. If only I could go back in time and change my wish. I'd forget about the silly bike and wish for him to stay.

"It's not you, baby girl. You have to understand—it's too much. Your mom and I don't love each other anymore." He looks into my eyes, unwavering, as I continue to plead.

"Don't you love me, Daddy?" I ask the man who is supposed to love me forever, the man who's supposed to never leave me.

"I do, but I have to go now. You be good. Goodbye, Catherine." He kisses the top of my head and I grab onto his leg for dear life. I know, even at this age, this will be the last time I see my father.

He pries me off his leg and turns without another word. And I watch the man who promised to always be there leave me behind without another glance.

He broke me.

He ruined me.

And he won't be the last man to do so.

chapter
one

"Ashton, I'm running over to Neil's house. I'll be back in a bit!"

Our wedding invitations arrived. They're beautiful, everything I could've hoped for. I can't wait to show him. Not that he's really into the details, but we spent a lot of time choosing these. It'll be such a relief when we finally move in together and stop all this back and forth. Ashton and I signed our lease a month before Neil proposed, so I couldn't leave and screw her out of half the rent. Though I adore my best friend, I would've loved to have lived with Neil as we planned the wedding. Thankfully, the big day is in four months and we'll finally be under one roof. I'm excited and anxious to make everything official.

"Okay. I'll be here," she says, walking toward me.

"Don't get into any trouble while I'm gone." I wink as I grab my purse and rush out the door. Once I get in the car I send him a quick text.
Me: On my way. I have a surprise!

Ten minutes later, I'm pulling into a parking space in front of his cozy two-bedroom townhome in the trendy section of Hoboken. This area is all older homes on cobblestone streets. It's a place I look forward to building a life and starting a family in. I gather my purse and the invitations and hop out, excited to share this piece of our future with him. His car is in the driveway, but the door is locked. Digging for my keys, my bag topples over, spilling all my belongings on the stairs. After collecting everything, I use my key to get into his house.

As the door opens I hear a low moan. Slowly I lift my eyes. Nothing could've prepared me for the sight before me. I freeze, watching my worst nightmare unfold.

The shock ripples through me, coming in waves of horror and pain.

And no matter how much I want to … I can't look away.

The man I love, the man I'm going to marry, is having sex with one of my friends.

Neil has Piper bent over on the couch—the couch *I* picked out—and is taking her from behind. His head is turned toward the door, his eyes are closed, and his face is pure ecstasy as he drives into her, enjoying every second of it while my world crumbles. With each thrust I feel the floor falling out from under me. I can hear them, see them, smell the sex in the air. Each slap of skin on skin, each grunt and moan tears through me like a knife slicing my veins open. I'm bleeding out, and there's no stopping it.

I close my eyes, begging for this not to be real, hoping this is a sick joke or a bad dream, praying that when I open them again, this cruel vision will fade away. When I gather the strength to look at them, I realize this isn't a joke or a dream—it's reality.

Piper's head is thrown back as she moans. "More. Harder!"

His hands grip her hips as he rears back and rams into her.

"Neil, yes!" Her loud, high-pitched voice screams out, "Oh! I'm coming. Oh. My. God. Neil! Fuck!"

Unable to control the shaking of my hands, the invitations fall to the floor. My sob breaks through the sounds of their pleasure, alerting them to my presence. The air punches through me as both their heads snap up and Neil's eyes lock on mine.

"Catherine." He stops moving, staring at me with wide eyes. "I can explain."

He grabs the blanket off the back of the couch and covers himself, hastily throwing another one at Piper.

"Explain? You can't fucking explain!" I choke out as the tears begin to flood my vision. "Oh my God! You ... you ..."

My limbs are tingling and my breathing is shallow as I try to remain standing. Everything around me is fading, but cruelly, my mind keeps the two people in front of me crystal clear. I close my eyes, hoping to give myself a reprieve.

Neil speaks as I grip the doorway for support. "Give me a minute and we can talk."

I don't want to talk. I want to pour bleach in my eyes and rip out my heart so it will stop hurting so much. Nothing he can say will erase this. Ever. My heart will never be the same. Cheating is bad enough, but for me to witness it—with one of my friends, no less—is torture.

And she was my friend, or at least I thought she was. Sure, she was never in my inner circle and we drifted apart after college but I never saw this coming. I didn't know she was even capable of such a vile betrayal. Piper was the one who introduced me to Neil. She dated one of his frat brothers and the four of us used to spend a lot of time together. I knew they broke up a few months ago, but never in a million years did I expect her to go after Neil.

When I look back up, the smug smile on Piper's face says it all. She wanted this to happen. She's enjoying my humiliation. Standing here shocked and horrified, watching her with my fiancé while she grins, obviously convinced she's won whatever game this is ... I snap.

I turn, slamming the door, and run as fast as I can. Shakily, I turn the car on and speed out of the driveway. All the good times we had, beautiful memories tarnished by his act of betrayal. As I drive the memories besiege me one by one—good and bad, love and hate, happy and sad.

Our first date ice-skating in Rockefeller Center, Neil skating backward holding my hands so I wouldn't fall. Two months later, going to the bed and breakfast on the Jersey shore and making love for the first time. He was tender and caring. The love and adoration he had in his eyes as we looked at each other during intimacy. I swipe the tears streaming down my face. It was all a lie. You can't respect someone then turn around and deceive them.

The memories keep coming.

The ride to the city, playing stupid car games and laughing until my sides hurt and Neil trying to convince me that the Jets would win the Superbowl. When he took me to Little Italy in July and got down on one knee and proposed in the middle of the street. The tears become too much. I can't see the road, so I pull over. In the confines of my car I lose it. I cry and sob for everything I saw and will never forget. I call Ashton hoping she can calm me.

"Hey, Biffle," Ash answers.

At the sound of her voice, any emotion I was holding back breaks free. A choked sound rips from my chest and the tears come faster.

"Catherine? What's wrong?" Her voice changes from singsong to concerned.

"Neil … He cheated on me! I saw it! I … I."

"What do you mean?"

"I w-went there and he was f-fucking her on the c-couch. I-I can't-t bre-athe," I stutter as the phone shakes against my wet cheek and ear.

"Okay, calm down. Where are you?" she asks.

"I d-don't know! I couldn't s-stand there and w-watch it," I cry, weeping on the side of some unknown road.

Ashton takes a deep breath before speaking. "I'm coming to get you. Where are you?"

"Why?" I croak, letting the pain take over.

"Catherine," she says, authority ringing through the phone. "Listen to me. Can you drive?"

"I g-gotta go," I say and hang up, right before I throw the phone against the dash.

I can't talk anymore. I can't even think. My head is a mess. I want to forget and stop seeing that moment of betrayal on replay.

I grip my hair, screaming in frustration as I try to form coherent thoughts through my agony.

Why? Why after all this time? Why?

Seconds, minutes, hours are lost to me. As the tears begin to ebb, even though the pain doesn't, I pull myself together enough to drive.

After driving around in circles for hours, my phone has over thirty missed calls and voicemails. I have no idea who they're from and I don't care.

There are no words of comfort anyone can give me. My life, my future, my everything— … is gone.

Somehow I find my way back to my apartment where Neil is waiting for me in the hall outside. Seeing him brings me up short. The last few hours come right back, slamming into me with the force of a thousand bricks, piling around me and threatening to bury me under their weight.

He stands there, staring at me. "Hey."

"How long have you been here?" My voice is quiet, but there's no mistaking the undertone of disgust.

"A while. Ashton wouldn't let me inside."

My eyes close of their own accord as I try to find any ounce of strength I have left to handle this. The nausea hits me full force and I hunch over, trying to keep the bile down. Looking at him, being around him again, makes me physically sick. He's destroyed every good memory we've ever had. Five years of love is gone. I want to crawl into a hole and never come out. The pain of the last few hours has left me empty.

"Catherine, please." Neil comes forward and places his hand on my back.

I snap back up, throwing his arm off me. "Do *not* touch me!"

"I didn't want you to find out this way." Neil runs his hands through his sandy blond hair as he huffs.

"Really? How would you have preferred? After the wedding maybe? Or maybe at Christmas?" I glare as moisture returns to my eyes, threatening to spill over.

The tension rolling off of him shifts and he snaps, "I wanted to talk to you weeks ago, but I couldn't do it. I didn't want this." He gestures between us, apparently indicating the "this." Gone is the apologetic man from a few moments ago. His eyes are cold and devoid of the love that once shined brightly in them.

"You think *I* did?" I scream in his face. "I don't deserve this!"

"I need more," he bites out, completely uncaring that he's ripping my heart out—again.

"More? What more do you need? I can't believe this. You cheated on me!"

He steps back, averting his hard stare at the elevator. "It's been over for a while. I think we both knew this was coming."

My eyes widen in shock and disbelief. "You're kidding me, right? Because I didn't know anything. We were getting *married*, Neil. How is that knowing this was coming? How many months of planning and building a life together shows me you were done?"

"I've been unhappy for months." He sighs, running his hands through his hair. "I didn't know what to do."

"I'll tell you what you could've done. You could have told me! You could have not slept with my friend!" I shout, but my words don't even penetrate. He stands there, completely apathetic. "So that's it? You're going to walk away after five years?"

"Why fight what we both know isn't going to work?"

I step back, shaken by his words. And then it sinks in: he's not here to make it right; he came here to end it. To further damage my beaten heart—the heart he bruised and battered with his infidelity.

"This is why you're here? To tell me this. Now?"

I ask with fear choking me.

His voice is empty as the words tumble out of his mouth. "What we have just isn't enough, Catherine. It's better this way."

Without another word he turns and walks away, ending the last five years of what I thought was the beginning of our life together. The elevator door closes and my heart shatters into a million pieces. Broken. This can't be happening. We were getting married. We were going to have children, a life, a future! *No!*

I gasp for air, trying to fill my suffocating lungs. Ashton opens the door and pulls me inside while I lose everything I ever thought mattered.

"Shhh, it's okay." She holds me close to her chest. "It's going to be okay," she murmurs quietly in my ear.

There is nothing to hold me together as I crumble to the ground in complete devastation.

Not enough.

All over again.

chapter two

Three months later

"Ever wonder what makes these people think they're going to find love on these stupid reality shows?" Ashton asks as she plops on the couch next to me.

We're watching another episode of this show where random women try to find their one true love through a series of dates with multiple people.

"No. But maybe we should sign up since the traditional route isn't working so much." I laugh, shoveling another spoonful of ice cream into my mouth.

It's a three-day weekend and we've been lazy, drinking wine and watching trashy television and movies. After spending the first month post-break-up wallowing, Ashton put her foot down and forced me to function outside of work. I believed my life was just beginning and there was a happily ever after in sight, but I should've known better. This is real life: there is no prince charming, and I'm definitely not a princess. No more illusions of fairy-tale endings. He's gone, and I'm alone.

"Could you imagine? All these girls are hot too. They're dumb, but at least they're pretty. Your company should represent them."

"I don't represent celebrities, Ash. You know

that. I like being a publicist in the business world. Way less drama dealing with companies versus people." She tries to snatch the ice cream but I move it out of her grasp. "Can we change the channel? Let's watch something about blowing people up, or shooting people! I have no desire to watch people fall in love. I'd rather pretend everyone's miserable like me," I say, grabbing for the remote as my phone vibrates with a text.

Ashton slaps my hand. "Don't change the channel. I want to see her cry and be all sad when he picks the other idiot."

"You don't want to watch the other girl be happy?"

"Are you crazy? This is better than watching someone get blown up!" Ashton sits up, animated and excited. "She's going to be all 'I thought what we had was real.' We can change it after the first girl gets dumped." She looks down at the phone and her jaw falls slack. "Neil's still texting you?"

"If so many people didn't have my number for work purposes, I'd change it." I groan and grab the phone.

For two weeks after he chose another woman, I didn't hear a word from him. Then I started getting periodic text messages. Initially I thought he was concerned, considering he broke my heart and ran over it a few times with an eighteen-wheeler. However, I figured out pretty quickly that he wanted something. His texts were usually about issues with cancelling wedding vendors. But lately, his texting has become more frequent and has focused on us exchanging belongings.

Neil: I have a few things I found of yours. Also, I think I left some stuff at your place.

I'm sure he did, but a few weeks after I found him and Piper together, I burned it. I took everything and anything I could find of his and set it on fire.

At first, I wanted to hold on to anything that was his. Even with how our breakup happened, I loved him. A part of me hoped we could reconnect, find a way to get past everything and move forward. But he never called. I held on to the false ideas of what our life was like—how we loved once and how wonderful he had been. All of those memories I latched on to so tight, hoping if I squeezed hard enough, they'd be enough. But they weren't.

"You know none of this is your fault, right? He did all of this," Ashton says while snatching the ice cream from my grasp.

"I know, I know. I want to stop thinking about him and move on, but he was my life for five years. I hate him so much, but then there's this small piece of me that won't let go."

The worst part was when I was depressed. I was barely eating, forgetting things all the time, and the tears were pretty much constant. Days were lost like that. Work was the only place I could function, the only place that wasn't tainted by memories of Neil and Piper. I could be me there, or at least some semi-normal version of me.

Now I'm in the anger stage, which is working out just fine. Every time I've had to explain why I cancelled the wedding, I've relived what he did. It's been humiliating. I'd rather deal with a hundred rabid reporters than call my family to explain how my fiancé cheated and then broke up with me because he needed "more." I remember the way he was so callous, so emotionless. The Neil I fell in love with wasn't the same person at the end.

The memory floods back, barreling through my anger, which quickly morphs into sadness as I recall the pain. A tear forms, but I swipe it away before it can descend. Crying is for the weak, and I will not let him break me again.

Ashton smiles and places her hand on mine. "I'm sure there's a part of you that will always love him. But I'll help you hold on to the hate because that's the only emotion that douchebag is worthy of." Her blue eyes are blazing.

"I know, Ash. I'm ..." I try to find the right words. The bottom line is I'm not really sure what I am anymore. At first I worked so hard to hide it all, putting it aside so I could continue on with my life, not wanting anyone to see how badly it hurt. No one wants to be the girl that was stood up at the altar—even though we never made it there, the context is the same.

Her jaw sets and she narrows her eyes, trying to ensure that I'm listening as she says, "I say the prick did you a favor. Guys like him are never content. He would've done it sooner or later."

"I'm tired. All I want is to enjoy our weekend and not think about him anymore." I sigh and lay my head in Ashton's lap. "It'll get easier, won't it?" I ask with a touch of hope.

She stares back and shakes her head. "It's already easier. One day you won't be sad or angry, you'll only feel pity for him."

"I'd like that day to be now. And I'd like him to stop texting me." I half laugh.

Ashton swipes the hair off my face with a sad smile. "Do you remember in high school when I swore I was going to marry Stephen? I thought he was perfect. I mean he was the captain of the football team, smart, funny, fucked like an animal." Her arched brow rises with amusement.

I laugh. "Yes, I remember Stephen the Stallion."

I used to laugh so hard when she would call him that. She thought she'd marry him based solely on his ability to do things to her she never knew were actually possible. He doted on her, but we later found out he had a few other girls who were also receiving the benefits of his talents.

"What I wouldn't give for another ride on that pony." She reminisces, laughing as she returns her attention to me. "I digress. My point is he was the one who lost out. I didn't cry. I punched him in the face, walked away, and found myself a better horse to ride."

"I didn't want another horse, Ash. I thought I'd finally found my white knight," I say as a flash of loneliness stabs through my heart.

Ashton isn't the wallowing type. She breaks up, moves on, and finds greener pastures. I've seen her go through her share of breakups, but she always bounces back quickly. Thing is, she doesn't know what it's like to get engaged, plan a wedding, and think you're going to spend your life with someone only to have it all taken away from you.

"Well your horse wound up being a donkey. Time to put his ass where it belongs—outside."

She's crazy, but I love her. I smile, shaking my head at another one of her off-the-wall retorts. "You and your metaphors."

"Okay, enough of this. Tonight's Gretchen's birthday. We need to get ready," Ashton says and slaps my ass. "We have dinner plans in the city."

"Crap!" I say, sitting up quickly. I haven't seen

Gretchen since my engagement party. She, Ashton, and I grew up together. We've been friends since we were eight. Gretchen lives in Manhattan and even though Ash and I work in the city, we live in New Jersey, so we barely see her.

"You better not try to back out." She glares indignantly.

I raise my hands in mock surrender. "I'm not. I forgot. I'll go get ready."

"That's my biffle!" She jumps up off the couch with a gleam in her blue eyes.

"Don't call me that around Gretchen. You know how she feels about it since 'she's our best friend for life too,'" I say, imitating Gretchen's sweet voice. She gets a little touchy when she feels we're not including her.

Ashton grins. "She'll be fine. I'll call her now and let her know we're taking a train in. Go! Move it, sister!" She grabs my hand, pulls me up, and pushes me toward my room. "We don't have time for your shenanigans. Now go take a shower. You smell!"

"You're a real bitch and I hate you," I lie.

"Well, I love your smelly ass." She giggles and runs off.

"I do not smell!" I say to her back. Then I head into my room to start getting ready.

An hour later, Ashton busts through my door looking breathtaking. She's wearing her long hair pin straight, the fiery red strands compliment the emerald top she has on. Her black eyeliner makes her blue eyes look bolder, bring out the cobalt in the depths of her irises.

I'm wearing my dark blue dress paired with my four-inch silver stilettos. At least I'll get an extra few inches on my five-foot-four, vertically challenged self. Ashton and Gretchen were both graced with being tall and slender, so I always feel tiny around them. My makeup is minimal, but I spent extra time curling my long brown hair into loose curls, which tumble down my back.

"Well hello, sexy! Where have you been hiding? You don't look like you'll be turning the big three-oh in a few months." She nudges me as she appraises my outfit.

Maybe I have been hiding, pretending things were okay while I was finding a way to be on my own. But today is a new day.

"I'll forever remain twenty-nine, thank you very much."

"Sure you will. And I'm still a virgin." She laughs and grabs the eye shadow from my bag.

My phone buzzes again.

　　Neil: I'll be around tomorrow if you can meet.

I decide to respond because he's apparently not taking the hint, no matter how hard I try.

　　Me: No. I'm busy.

"I'm changing my damn number."

Ashton grabs my phone and powers it off. "No phone. No Neil. You, my love, are beautiful and we're going to focus on that!" She places a kiss on my cheek and heads out to finish getting ready.

Dressed to the nines and excited to be going out tonight—though I'll never admit that to Ashton—I look for the finishing touches. I rifle through the beautiful mahogany jewelry box that my father gave me for my ninth birthday. I finally find my diamond studs and go to close the lid, but my eyes get caught on the light shimmering off my engagement ring snuggly sitting in the ring slot. I pull it out and look at it, remembering all the promise it once held, before putting it back in its place.

After my breakup with Neil, I started wearing a sapphire ring instead. When I took off my beautiful diamond engagement ring, my finger felt awkward, naked. Ashton convinced me that I deserved an apology gift, and since Neil and I still had a joint bank account, we went and spent a little of his money. It's a one-carat sapphire surrounded by diamonds in a platinum setting. It's vintage and beautiful. We call it the "Fuck You" ring.

"Let's go, Catherine! Dinner's in an hour and we have to get into Manhattan," Ashton yells from the hall.

I grab my clutch and rush out of the room, ready to start putting the past where it belongs.

Behind me.

"Cat?" Gretchen jumps up when she sees me walk in with Ashton.

"Hi, Gretch!" I rush over, throwing my arms around her.

God, I've missed hanging out with my friends. No matter how many years or miles there are between the three of us, we've always been constant. When everything went down with Neil, they both rallied behind me and took care of cancelling everything. I, on the other hand, have been a shitty friend. When I'm not at work, I'm at home, so I see Ashton all the time. But I always find a way to get out of any parties or anything requiring me to leave the house.

"Hello to you too!" Ashton feigns being hurt.

"Oh Ashton, always the drama queen." Gretchen giggles and pulls her into a giant hug. "Both my girls are here! Tonight's already a great night."

It's so easy to make her happy. She's a lawyer in one of the most affluent firms in New York City, and she's aiming for partner within the next two years. There was a time we didn't see her more than a few times a year because she was inundated with work, but I always understood. Work is something the three of us thrive on, always have. I'm a publicist for one of the premier companies in Manhattan, and Ashton works as an embryologist. Who would've thought the three of us would each find a career we love and excel at?

I look around the restaurant, taking in the unique design. I'm instantly in love with the old-world charm and kind of Tuscan feel it's got going on. Judging from the interior, you'd never guess it was located right in the middle of the West Village.

"Any new clients, Cat?" Gretchen asks while sipping her beer.

"I have a meeting on Tuesday with a possible new client. We're pitching against Boyce PR for this one. It's a cosmetics company looking to expand their brand. I'm really excited. If I can land it, I think I'd be up for promotion."

"That's great! I'm sure you'll get it," Ashton says, smiling.

We laugh, catching up on work and any good gossip about people from back home.

Ashton and Gretchen are babbling on about some movie they're both dying to see, so I glance around the room and take in the crowd. When I hear a boisterous laugh, I turn, searching for the source of the sound. When I see him my breath catches.

He's sitting at a table to my left with a few guys. There's something about him that's mesmerizing, something that prevents me from tearing my eyes away. His entire presence pulses with energy, demanding my attention without saying a word. He has dark hair, styled—or maybe not—in sexy disarray. His strong jaw is covered in stubble, only adding to his attraction. Though I can't see his eyes clearly from here, I can imagine the virility within them. But it's not just his looks, which are more than any man should be allowed to have. There's more ...

He's commanding even in a relaxed state: confident bordering on arrogant. Every part of him is captivating.

"Earth to Catherine!" Ashton waves her hands in front of me, breaking my trance on the sexy stranger across the room.

"Sorry ... too much wine." I laugh and grab my glass, trying to keep my attention off him.

We finish our dinner and polish off another bottle. It's been a wonderful night, filled with laughter and tons of memories of our crazy childhood. I'm glad we could spend this time together.

Gretchen clears her throat. "So ... I got a call from Piper the other day. She called the office asking if we could talk. She said she needed legal advice."

I was about to take a sip but freeze midway. My heart accelerates at the sound of her name. We all became friends with Piper during college. She was in my marketing class and also in one of Ashton's labs. Over the years, we grew apart, but until three months ago we all considered her a friend. After what happened though, no one has spoken to her again. If hateful is what I feel toward Neil, murderous is what I feel toward Piper. What she did to me is reprehensible. No woman should ever go after someone else's man. Which brings us to the burning question: Why, after three months, has she decided she needs legal advice from Gretchen?

Ashton chimes in quickly, "I hope you told her to take her fake-ass bullshit and shove it, and the only thing you'd represent is a case against her."

"Oh honey, I told her that and a whole lot more. I still can't believe she was so devious about everything. I always knew she was jealous of you and Neil, Cat, but I never believed she was capable of being so disgusting."

Air … I need air. "I'm gonna go to the bathroom. Be right back."

"Cat," Ashton calls out, empathy swimming in her eyes.

"It's fine. I'm okay." I smile and pat her arm before heading toward the bathroom.

As I'm sliding through the tiny aisle, a chair juts out and slams into me, throwing me backward. My arms shoot out in an effort to brace myself from the inevitable fall, but two arms wrap around my torso, saving me from hitting the ground. However, I'm now sitting in a stranger's lap.

"You okay?" a deep, throaty voice asks from behind me.

The sound of his rasp stills me, awakening all of my senses as it reverberates through my body. "Yes, thank you," I say, trying to calm my heart rate.

"Glad I caught you." Before I can move, his large hands grasp my hips to lift me up. His fingers wrapping around my waist may as well be flipping an internal switch inside of me. My heart kicks up, beating erratically from the warmth of his hands on my body.

I stand and turn, locking eyes with the most hypnotizing blue-green eyes I've ever seen. If I thought he was handsome from across the room, up close he redefines the word. He's rendered me speechless. My eyes devour him, my mind cataloging every feature. A dimple on his left cheek, a square jaw, and an angular nose give him a rugged, almost beautiful face. Everything about him screams masculinity.

I start to wobble on my heels and he stands, placing his hands on my shoulders to steady me. I take a deep breath, inhaling the scent of crisp linen and cologne—his scent. It fills my mind, practically overwhelming me, as I commit it to memory.

"I'm so sorry," I murmur, barely able to form words.

"No need to apologize. That asshole should've been more careful. Can't say I minded, though." His eyes crinkle in amusement.

Is he flirting with me? How sad that I don't know for sure.

"Well ..." I give a shy smile. "Thank you again for catching me."

He stares at me, looking me up and down. Something about his gaze makes me feel naked, exposed. Here I am, standing before him, fully dressed but completely bare.

"So since I saved you from a rather embarrassing moment, how about you tell me your name?" the drop-dead gorgeous man asks in that low rasp of his.

And though every part of me feels inexplicably drawn to him, something in the back of my mind, the part that knows how off-kilter he's knocked me, is telling me not to give it to him. I have no reason in the world to want this man, but I do and I can't explain it, which means it's time to walk away.

Trying to find an excuse, I look over at Gretchen and Ashton. "Sorry. I have friends waiting." I shrug.

"Well tell them to come join us."

I smile, looking at the two guys who keep volleying their eyes between him and me. "I'll let you boys get back to your dinner."

I start to walk away, but he grips my arm. His touch sends shockwaves through my system, momentarily stunning me again. "Wait. Sit. Have a drink with us. This is Nathan, that's Garrett, and I'm Jackson."

Even his name is sexy. *I'm in so much trouble.* I need to get away from him and quick, before I say or do something stupid. Oh wait. I already did. As much as I would love nothing more than to sit, I'm not ready. I know exactly where this will end up—I'll be hurt and he'll be leaving.

"It was nice meeting you, Jackson, but I have a table waiting."

"Don't you think you owe me your name at least?" Jackson asks, his eyes bright with mischief.

I look down, spotting the ring on my finger. It gives me the perfect excuse to run and avoid this bizarre encounter. "I'm getting married, but thanks again for catching me." I show Jackson my ring finger and shrug. "Sorry, I have to go," I say and turn to leave. Who knew Neil would be good for something?

"Lucky guy," I hear him say as I'm walking away.

I walk back to the table, forgoing the bathroom. There's no way I'm walking past him again.

Thankfully, Ashton and Gretchen are oblivious to what happened or they'd both be grilling me. My heart is racing and my body is tingling everywhere he touched. I slouch in the seat, feeling as though I've run a marathon. It's been so long since a man sparked any emotion or arousal within me. I feel unmistakably alive, which scares the hell out of me.

"You okay?" Ashton asks.

"Yeah, do you think we could head out? I'm not feeling so good."

I want to get away from this place and get myself under control. Unease is running through my veins. Foolishly, I look over and catch him smiling in my direction.

Deciding I'm not waiting for Ashton, I grab my bag and run out the door, away from a man who reminds me how easy it would be to fall all over again—only this time I don't think I'd survive.

chapter three

*B*ack to work today and my mask is back in place, so everyone will believe I'm the put-together Catherine Pope. My commute on the train from New Jersey into Manhattan gives me time to prepare. I've been restless since the night we went to dinner and I literally fell on that guy. Jackson. I swear I can feel his hands, hear his voice, smell his cologne everywhere I turn. Until that night, it'd been months since a man had touched me. I've not allowed myself to get caught up in any kind of relationship. Men have asked me out, but I knew I wasn't ready for that yet. Plus, there was nothing pulling me toward them. However, the other night I wasn't just pulled, I felt bound. He awakened me—my body, my emotions, my mind—and I still haven't recovered.

Shaking my head, I chastise myself. Today I have to be on my A-game. I have an important meeting across town and if it goes well, I'll be solidifying a promotion in my company. I don't have time to fantasize about a man I'll probably never see again.

Once I get into the city, I walk the four blocks to my office at CJJ Public Relations. In this building, I'm more than *enough*. My skills, my smarts, my vision, me—I'm worth something and it's well known. Instantly I'm stronger. For the last six years I've worked my ass off to become a top publicist.

I've climbed the corporate ladder fast and proven myself account after account.

I enter my office, smiling and saying hello to my assistant, Taylor. If it weren't for her, I'm pretty certain I would've lost my job by now. The first week back after things ended with Neil, I was a mess. One time I wore my shirt inside out. Taylor came over and pointed me toward the bathroom with one word: shirt. She's kind, caring, and always ensures my schedule is perfect. More than that, she's a friend. I love her. One day she'll realize she can do my job and I'll be lost. But for now, I have her and I'm thankful.

I have all my notes and I've gone over every possible scenario in my mind. Usually before we go into a meeting we know the client. We study them and learn as much as we can to gain the upper hand. In this case, we couldn't get as much information as I would've liked, but I'm confident, even with what little knowledge I've obtained, I'll come out victorious. Boyce PR is my only competition for the account, and they usually don't invest their time in research like I do. They typically send the same two reps to bid meetings, and they've only won an account over me a few times.

"All right. The meeting's in an hour and it'll probably be about a fifteen-minute cab ride to get over there." Taylor smiles and throws some lip gloss on my desk.

"Thanks, Tay. I need to print out some files I emailed myself last night."

"I found out that you're going to be dealing with two people: the assistant and another member of their team."

I seriously couldn't do this without her. "I'm

pretty sure I'm in love with you."

The people at Raven Cosmetics are anxious to get a publicist on board quickly. The more I learn about them, the more my confidence grows. I know I'd represent them well. I know this demographic. Plus, with my vast amount of contacts in this particular industry, I'd be able to get them in the spotlight easily.

Taylor turns to me, giving me the remainder of the files and presentation boards she had mocked up. Her sweet, timid voice is now firm, making sure I'm ready. "Were you able to find out any more information on the CEO?"

"No. And I despise the secrets behind this account. I asked around again. All I found out was that Mr. Cole recently took over. Whoever was running things early on left, and the interim CEO didn't want to stay on." I let out a frustrated sigh.

Taylor and I scoured the Internet and questioned all our contacts to learn anything we could about Raven Cosmetics. The company is only about four years old, but they've changed CEOs three times already. Even so, they've grown extremely fast in the industry. They have a line of natural eye products that exploded and skyrocketed them to the top.

The rumors floating around are that when the first CEO and co-owner left abruptly, someone stepped in as acting CEO. I don't know what happened with the acting CEO, but the silent partner, Mr. Cole, stepped in, apparently worried about the image of his company. As he should be. A young company needs to portray strength and consistency to its consumers and investors. That's why they decided to seek out a publicist to help clean up their chaotic, and relatively unstable, image.

"It doesn't matter, though. We're the right firm. Despite the lack of information, we'll still have the best strategies," I say. I straighten my back, gathering my confidence as I go over my notes, making sure I'm fully prepared.

"Agreed. Time to get going. Your cab's waiting. By the way, I wasn't able to find out who's representing Boyce PR. My friend said the original rep got sick and they're sending someone else in their place."

"Really?" I ask, surprised. It doesn't sit particularly well with me, but there's nothing I can do about it at this point. I collect my things and head for the elevator. "As always, you amaze me. Wish me luck!" I say over my shoulder.

"Good luck! Even though you don't need it. You'll be great!" she shouts behind me.

On the ride to the lobby, I can't stop my mind from wandering to the fact that Neil works for Boyce. Over the years, it was part of what solidified our relationship—us both working in the same field. We understood each other's need to be number one and how demanding the industry is. There was friendly competition between us, but more than anything we supported and encouraged each other, even sharing tips and ideas. It was fun talking about our day and what accounts we were working on. At least, I thought it worked well. Maybe that was why Neil did what he did. Maybe his tiny ego couldn't handle his future wife being better in business than he was. Or it could be he's just a fucking cheater.

He sent another text yesterday about needing to get a deposit back from the reception hall. Apparently, they won't refund him the money. I don't know why he thinks I care. I lost money too. If any-one should be trying to recoup their losses, it's me. I've been a bitch, then nice, then I ignored him, but the texts haven't stopped. I'm beyond irritat-ed. And, of course, my phone has been chirping all morning. Against my better judgment, I decide to check it.

Neil: We should talk. See you soon.

Me: No, Neil, I won't see you soon. Stop messaging me.

Neil: I'm sorry, Cat.

I have no idea why he's apologizing. Games—all he does is play games. I hate him for everything he's done and all he keeps doing. I'd like to put this behind me, but he continues to infiltrate my life.

The elevator dings and I walk out toward the waiting car, pushing thoughts of Neil out of my head as I get in the cab. I have a good feeling about today. I'm dressed in my favorite outfit—a black pencil skirt that ends right at my knee, my white blouse tucked into my skirt, and my favorite pearl earrings and necklace. My red heels finish off the ensemble. They're a power color, which is what I exude in the boardroom. As we near the building, I grab my purse and pull out my compact, checking one last time to make sure my makeup is flawless. The cab stops. I put my compact away, swipe my credit card, and head in to Raven Cosmetics' head-quarters.

Heading straight for the receptionist, I intro-duce myself, "Hi, I'm Catherine Pope from CJJ PR. I have a twelve o'clock meeting."

"Yes, Ms. Pope, they're expecting you. I'll bring

you right back." She smiles and walks me to the conference room.

"Thank you so much," I say as she retreats back to the reception area.

Steeling myself, I place my hand on the door handle. The scent assaulting my senses stops me dead in my tracks. I know that smell—clean soap and cologne. I'm instantly taken back to the night I fell into Jackson's lap. It's like I can feel his strong hands setting my body on fire, see his enthralling god-like face, as his eyes penetrate my soul. I shiver, trying to compose myself. I look around expecting to see him, but I don't. Someone else must wear the same cologne. I'm dreaming. That's what this is because there is no way in hell he's here. I need to focus, but it's kind of hard when my stomach is in knots. Shaking my head to release the memory, I draw a calming breath and open the door.

Entering the conference room, I look around, taking in the floor to ceiling windows, the long dark table, the small woman in a suit with short blond hair, and the two people talking over to the side near a refreshment area. All I can see of the two people is the man's back, but as he turns his head his eyes lock on mine, and the past hits me all over again.

I close my eyes and take a deep breath. *Please, God, let me get through this.* Of all the people at Boyce PR, they chose Neil to take over this account. I should've known.

He gives me a smug smile before he shifts, revealing the person behind him.

Piper.

My stomach plummets as the floor drops from beneath me.

Her eyes peruse me as a snide smile forms on her plastic face. My chest hurts. It literally hurts to breath. *I can do this.* I have to do this. It's only my ex and the woman he cheated on me with—easy day. Right. Just another meeting.

The small woman approaches with her hand extended. "Hi, I'm Danielle Masters, the assistant to the CEO of Raven Cosmetics. You must be Catherine. This is Piper Carlson. She's consulting with us. And that's Neil Mullins with Boyce PR," she says, pointing toward Neil and Piper.

If karma is paying me back for something I did in a past life, I'd like to say after this my debt is fully paid. My professional sense kicks in immediately. I straighten myself, and prepare to kick some ass. If I fail, they win, and that's not an option.

"Danielle, it's a pleasure to meet you." I extend my hand and shake hers. She has kind eyes and a brief but genuine smile.

"Nice to meet you as well. I apologize that Mr. Cole isn't able to attend. He had an emergency, which is why we called in Ms. Carlson's firm to assist us in deciding the best publicist to help us achieve our vision," she replies.

"Of course. I understand." I smile and place my bag on the table. I'm going to lose my mind before today is over. I glance up, looking at Neil and Piper, who are now standing in front of me.

"Catherine, you look lovely as ever." Neil smiles, but I know him well enough to see the underlying sarcasm.

"Neil, good to see you again so soon." I'm biting my tongue so hard I swear I'm going to taste blood. Right now I'm anything but good.

Neil turns his attention to Piper, and I have to

choke down the bile climbing up my throat. I try not to look at her. Though I knew she was an independent marketing consultant, I had no idea either of them would be at this meeting. A few years back, Piper formed her own company. Basically, she acts as neutral third party who evaluates an agency's ideas and then helps the client find the one best suited for their vision. So, of course she's here. *I can kiss this account good-bye.*

I turn to Piper and try to refrain from wrapping my hands around her neck. "Piper, I'm surprised to see you here." That's all I'm able to manage in terms of niceties.

"I wasn't aware you'd be presenting," she retorts.

Sure she wasn't. I'm sure Danielle filled her in on the details of the account and was told CJJ would be here. I guess lying comes second nature to her. Seems she and Neil have a few things in common.

Neil places his hand on her lower back and she smiles at him before walking over to stand by Danielle. Gathering my confidence and all strength I have left, I smile and mentally roll my eyes. They deserve each other. Assholes.

Danielle points to the chairs, instructing us to have a seat as she and Piper sit opposite us. "Let's begin. Who would like to go first?"

I quickly yet politely jump in to gain the upper hand. "I'm happy to go second, Neil. Since this is a last-minute meeting for you, I'm sure you have other clients that need your attention," I say in a saccharine voice, putting on my best fake smile.

"That's very considerate of you." He knows he can't argue, or he would look like an asshole. Well, more of an asshole than he already is.

Let the games begin.

Danielle steps in. "Yes, Neil, we don't want to keep you. Please begin. I'm sure Catherine and I can continue without you if you need be somewhere."

Neil takes over forty minutes to present—in my opinion—a mediocre presentation. He obviously didn't prepare as much as I have, but that's typical of him. He and Piper keep sharing tender glances, making me want to gouge my eyes out. Judging from their body language, I'd guess their relationship has progressed. Clearly they're still together. I don't want to be here and now I'm having difficulty focusing, but this is my chance and I can't blow it. He drones on and on and I've mostly tuned him out, until I notice the words he's speaking sound extremely familiar.

"The number one market segment we need to reach are the young girls starting to wear makeup. My company will use several targeted social media campaigns as well as television spots to engage these consumers. Girls between the ages of fourteen and nineteen spend at least 78% of their time..." This is *exactly* my pitch. He goes on, meeting my eyes and silently confirming that he's somehow gotten my presentation. I look over at Danielle and Piper to see how engaged they are—Piper is hanging on his every word, but Danielle doesn't seem impressed. He's cocky and condescending, talking to her as though he's above her because she's only an assistant.

My head is spinning. I can't believe this. *How* did this jackass get my files? How did he get my social media stats and all my graphics? I did everything at home and then emailed my graph and presentation to myself. There's no way he could have gotten them.

I'm trying to contain my rage and maintain my professionalism, but right now I could tear him limb from limb. I've never wanted to inflict bodily harm on someone as much as I do in this moment—hell, I could kill him with the rage coursing through me. Once again, Neil has stolen something from me and there's not a damn thing I can do about it. Thankfully, I always have a backup plan. My hands are shaking with barely contained anger as Neil finishes and sits.

Danielle turns to me. "Ms. Pope, if you would like to begin, please."

I smile, harnessing my indignation so that I can use it. "Thank you, Danielle." I gather my now useless boards and set them aside.

My eyes are sharp as I look over at Neil, and my voice is strong and steady. "Well, Neil, it sounds like you and I are in agreement for once." I stand up, moving over to the projection screen to set up the video I put together.

"Danielle, let me show you the mock-up on what CJJ would want to hit the sites with. I won't bore you with statistics and numbers—we all know this market. Instead, I've prepared a video to showcase how we'll approach the campaign." I go on explaining how I'd work with Raven's marketing people and the press to strengthen the brand and image of the company. While I talk, I try to hit on points Neil didn't mention to differentiate my presentation from his.

I finish my initial pitch, press the start button, and watch, hoping the video is enough to sway the vote to my side. It's short and raw, and it certainly isn't flawless, but it's powerful. Part of being a publicist is marketing and helping clients create a plan. Whether I secure this or not, I know that I've shown my dedication and ability to think outside the box.

As the video ends, I look at Neil with my eyebrow raised and a smile that clearly says, "Screw you, asshole."

I turn to Danielle and Piper, giving them my final pitch. "I assure you that my ability to work with the press along with my vast experience in marketing will help us skyrocket Raven to the top." I'm completely composed because, like it or not, Piper is going to have a say on whether or not I get this project. It's out of my hands now. I have faith that I did enough. If not, there's nothing I could've done differently. Neil, on the other hand, better pray for mercy—I'm going to rip him to shreds.

When Danielle speaks again, I wonder if she's more than an assistant. I can't put my finger on it, but she seems assertive, not at all intimidated by handling a big meeting like this. Taylor is one of the best assistants I've ever known, but I'd still never send her into a meeting of this magnitude. "Thank you both for your presentations. I have a contingency that Mr. Cole needs to be in agreement before we make a final decision." She looks at both of us for confirmation.

Neil cuts me off before I can speak. "Danielle, we're prepared for whatever your company needs."

"Both of your presentations were quite similar, but Piper and I will speak with Mr. Cole about our impressions. Typically, he isn't involved in these projects, but this campaign is important to him. He's aware that he needs to be the face of Raven now. We want the publicist to be available whenever necessary. That person will also need to travel on short notice at times."

I nod in agreement. "Yes, of course, that's all included in our contract. My schedule is open to Mr. Cole and the team here at Raven." My eyes don't waver from hers, which I hope assures her of my sincerity.

"Thank you both. We'll be in touch." She and Piper stand to shake our hands. "I truly appreciate your time."

Now the waiting game begins. As for Neil, he should start running because my patience has reached its max. It's about time he pays for his sins.

chapter four

I step out of Raven's building into the warm air, but a chill settles over me. I can't believe what happened in the meeting. Of all the possible scenarios I was prepared for, Neil being the other publicist and Piper being a consultant was not one of them. I heard she'd been busy with her firm, but her attempt at surprise when she saw me was complete bullshit.

Then to have my research stolen by Neil? I'm at a loss on what to do. All I know is there's no way I'll allow him to get away with this. I've never been aggressive with him—I was always the perfect girlfriend, quiet and supportive. Good thing I'm not his girlfriend anymore. I deserve an explanation for this, among many other things.

I stand off to the side of the main entrance, waiting for Neil to exit. I hear him before I see him. He's talking on his phone as he walks out, so I stand and wait. With each passing second my anger grows more and more. Who does that to someone? It's so unethical. So ... fucked-up. I'm about to lose it. He continues talking to whoever's on the other line while I stare incredulously at this man I loved with every fiber of my being. The man with warm brown eyes, a smile that could light up a room, and soft sandy brown hair, which I used to run my hands through to put him to sleep. That was then.

Right now all I see is a liar and a thief. I'm ready to get this confrontation over with. I walk over, grab his phone out of his hand, and end his call.

"What the—" Neil starts to say, whipping his head up. When he realizes it's me, his mouth quirks into a self-satisfied grin.

That's all I need to release the fury I was barely holding on to.

"How *dare* you? You son of a bitch!"

"Now Cat, you need to calm down. I'm not sure why you're so upset." A red haze begins to take over my vision.

"Not sure? Are you stupid? Oh wait! I already know the answer to that, you prick!" The scales deciding whether or not to inflict bodily harm are tipping decidedly toward inflicting. If I were on a seesaw, I'd be on the downside, heading to hell.

He looks at me as though I'm insane. I'm sure I appear to be to anyone passing us on the streets of New York City.

He raises one eyebrow and smirks. "You should really be more careful. I hear it's very easy to forget things when you're not paying attention. Like the funny way passwords save when you login on someone else's computer."

"Wow! You have some balls. You hack into my email, steal and use my presentation, and this is what you say to me? No 'I'm sorry?'" I'm trying to control myself, but each time he speaks the fight is leaving me.

"Well, love, it's not hacking if I have a password. Plus, we were going to share a life together. I didn't think you'd mind sharing a few statistics for old times' sake," he replies smugly.

That's it. I raise my hand, rear it back, and slap

him across the face, enjoying the bite as it connects. The sound reverberates, causing a few people to stop and stare. My palm stings, but it reminds me that this is real. I've hit him. Finally. I've done what I wanted to for far too long and it feels damn good. Considering I had to sit through a two-hour meeting next to his self-righteous, project-stealing ass, I've earned the right to do a lot worse.

The shock blankets his face before he recovers, rubbing his now reddened skin. "Well that wasn't very nice."

I continue forward, pure hatred flowing through my body—it's red, ugly, and can no longer be controlled. He's quick, though, and anticipates my next move. His arms wrap around my shoulders, pulling me against him. Using whatever strength I have, I punch him in the chest over and over again. I know I'm not causing any damage, but I can't stop. Each blow is a release of the pain he's inflicted on my life. The cheating, stealing, lying, and the way he makes me feel worthless expels with each fist I land.

"I hate you! Don't touch me! You *asshole!*" I scream and continue my assault. Neil grabs my arms, pinning them to my sides so that I can't hit him any more. I'm flush against his body. My brain ceases to make rational decisions as I sink into him. Memories of being in his arms surround me. I remember the strength and love they once held for me, the way they used to hold me for hours after making love, how he would wrap them around me from behind when I would do dishes. Why am I leaning into him? I close my eyes, pretending I'm his fiancé again and that the last three months were just a misunderstanding, a bad dream. As angry as I was a few minutes ago, it's gone now, morphed into pain and sadness. I wanted him to love me. I needed him. He promised to cherish me. I inhale, taking in the scent that's all Neil—cinnamon and coffee. Losing myself in the past, a tear falls from my lashes and slowly glides down my cheek to rest upon my lip.

I turn my head into his chest as his grip tightens around my arm. "You don't hate me. You're just pissed because you want me back."

The words force me to remember he's not the man I loved—this is the man who destroyed my world. He took from me and made no apologies for hurting anyone. This person has allowed me to spend my time wondering what I did wrong and why I wasn't worthy while he moved on with Piper. He's not a man—he's a coward.

Gathering the hate and anger I previously held, I shove back against him. "No, Neil, that's where you're wrong. I want to be around when karma finds you so I can sit back and watch with a big bowl of popcorn."

"You should save your energy, love. You'll need it if you think you're going to get this account," he scoffs.

I lean in close and whisper, "Let's be crystal clear, you cheating bastard. You fuck with me again, I'll ruin you, *love.*" I kiss his cheek and lift my knee straight into his balls. With him hunched over and clutching his junk, I turn and walk away before he can reply.

I start walking as adrenaline floods my system. Oh my God, I physically assaulted him. While I'm relieved that I stood up for myself, I can't believe I actually slapped him, punched him, and then kneed him where it hurts. I've never in my entire life hit someone, and I'm not sure how to handle the high I'm on right now. I need Ashton and I need a drink.

I walk another few blocks, letting my pulse return to normal, before I hail a cab. Once my hands are steady, I grab my phone and text Ashton.

Me: I swear you're never gonna believe this shit!

Ashton: You got the account???

How I wish that were the case. It would at least make this day worth it.

Me: No decision yet. Will you be home tonight?

Ashton: Be there by 6 xoxo

I call Taylor and let her know I'm going home instead of heading back to the office. I can do a few things remotely anyway. She almost goes postal when she hears Piper was in the meeting. I relay the turn of events to a stunned Taylor—everything from Neil stealing my presentation to our showdown outside the building. There are times in your life you wish there were a reset button—this is one of those times. My anxiety is starting to rise again. What if Piper's involved with the entire project? There's no way I could deal with her day in and day out, pretending she doesn't bother me. I head to the station, anxious to get home and glean some wisdom from Ash. She always knows how to talk me down.

With perfect timing, I catch the train back to Hoboken—luckily, there was one leaving in five minutes. I have a three-seat row all to myself, which almost never happens. I'm usually crammed in a middle seat, trying to avoid people touching me. However, this ride I'm going to stretch out and enjoy the peace.

The conductor's voice comes overhead, informing us the train will be delayed. Fine by me. I close my eyes and sink into the seat. I'm spent from the meeting and my confrontation with Neil. He deserved to be dealt with, even if it did cost me the account and my possible promotion. Whichever way the account goes, this day has been overwhelming. I'm going to use this time to relax, not think, and clear my mind of all the drama I just endured.

"Hello." I hear a familiar voice and open my eyes. Scanning the train car, I see him. Jackson. He's one row back, and he's staring right at me with a dimpled grin.

This day keeps getting better and better.

"I'll call you back," he says into his phone. He ends the call and stands, smiling over at me. "I thought that was you." The timbre of his voice travels straight to my core.

God, he's even more handsome than I remember. The sight of him dressed in dark blue jeans and a tight olive green T-shirt, which makes his eyes more green than blue today, causes my heart to flutter in my chest. He reaches up and grabs his bag from the rack above his head. As he moves, his shirt lifts so I can see his ripped abs.

Wow.

"Mind if I join you?" he asks, snapping me out of my dreaming.

"Ummm, sure. I have room." I scoot over to the window, looking down and allowing my hair to create a veil. If I can control my blushing, I'll be shocked. Hiding my emotions has never been something I've excelled at outside of work. Hard as I try, people usually see right through me. The last three months have given me some practice, but here I sit, red-faced and wide-eyed because of him.

"Thanks. I'm Jackson, in case you forgot." Jackson's hand extends, his eyes soft and warm as he waits to shake my hand.

"Catherine. I remember you, though," I say, placing my tiny hand in his.

My arm feels like it's been shocked—the current running from his body to mine feels as if I've grabbed a live electrical wire. I gasp and pull my hand from his. The sensation was so strong and intense that my fingers are tingling.

I look to Jackson, who is opening and closing his hand. I wonder if he felt it too.

"So you do have a name. I like it. Nice to meet you *again,* Catherine."

"Yes, what are the odds?" I seem to be on some kind of eternal karmic payback plan. Why not? Keep piling more on top of my already ridiculous day. At least if it all comes on at once, I can get a reprieve … eventually.

Jackson clears his throat, which draws my attention to his beautiful face. "Fall into any more handsome strangers' laps since I last saw you?" His grin is playful. It seems to melt any irritation I'd begun to feel over my luck.

"Who said you're handsome?"

"Lots of people. What do you think?" Jackson asks and I burst out laughing.

"I think you're … " I look around, trying to appear allusive before responding, "Funny." There. He can take that however he wants.

"You know, I'm more than just handsome and funny."

"I bet you are, but I never said handsome." I smile and shake my head.

Jackson shifts in his seat. "Yes, but you haven't said I'm not." His brow rises. "Well? Any more casualties?"

"Anyone ever tell you you're a pain in the ass?"

He shrugs and leans closer to me. "I've been called worse." His voice drops to a low rasp. "I didn't mind having your ass on me. It's not every day I get to save a beautiful woman."

"I wasn't talking about my ass. I was saying you *are* an ass."

He's an expert at twisting my words. Typically, I can banter better than most people. Sarcasm is my first language. I'm either off my game today or Jackson's thrown me—I'm not sure which.

Jackson smirks and his gravelly voice stirs the butterflies in my stomach. "I think you're afraid of how handsome I am."

"I think we can add frustrating to the list of your attributes."

Jackson clears his throat. "So where's your ring?"

"Oh, ummm, I left it home."

The train starts moving. I only have about ten more minutes with him before we arrive at my station. I'm hoping there will be another delay so I can talk to him longer, or stare—either works for me.

"So what's his name?" I scrunch my brows, confused by his question. "Your fiancé?"

"I should've said I left it home because he's not my fiancé anymore," I reply.

"Sorry to hear that, but I'm sure he's much more sorry than I am." Jackson grins, showing me that adorable dimple of his. For the first time, I get a strong whiff of his cologne. Why didn't I notice it before? Now that I have, the thought crosses my mind that I could inhale it all day and be perfectly happy.

"Thanks. I'm not so sure he's sorry at all, but I appreciate you saying that." I smile.

His face changes and his now serious gaze locks on mine. It's intense, so much so that I can't look anywhere but into his captivating eyes. "I can assure you, Catherine, if he's not sorry yet, he will be someday. Any man would be an idiot to let someone as gorgeous as you go," he says, and his eyes dart to my lips.

"Jackson," I say in a breathy whisper, unsure of whether or not I can say anything more than his name. My mind is scattered, invaded by thoughts of his lips touching mine, the feel of his mouth on mine, and all the ways I want to explore him. No one has ever confused me like this. I don't know anything about him, but I crave his touch, his words, his presence. Something about him stirs feelings deep within me. Maybe it's not something at all. Maybe it's just him.

I turn to say more, but the train stops. Shit!

"I have to go. This is my stop." I fail to keep the disappointment out of my voice.

I step past him into the aisle. As I'm about to walk away, he grabs my hand and places a kiss against my knuckles. "Until next time."

Though I only have a minute before the train leaves again, I have to say something. I go with the only reply I'm capable of. "Good-bye, Jackson."

I exit the train feeling off balance. Between Neil's antics and seeing Jackson unexpectedly, I need to talk to Ashton more than ever. I feel like I'm one of those Stretch Armstrong dolls being pulled so taut I'm about to snap. I'm digging through my bag, looking for my keys, when someone grabs my shoulder, startling me.

I gasp and turn only to be gazing back into Jackson's eyes.

"Hey." He smiles and drops his hand.

"Hi," I reply, bemused.

"Sorry, I realized you dropped your keys. Didn't want you to have another disaster." Jackson smiles warmly.

"How noble of you to save me *again*," I say, moving through the parking lot toward my car.

"I guess this is our *thing*."

"Oh, we have a thing, do we?" I ask with a smile.

"Are you asking about my thing?"

I gasp, immediately feeling my face flame red. "What? No! I never said anything about your thing."

He laughs out loud, full-on belly laughing at me. After he recovers, his voice drops as he says, "So you do want to see my *thing*." He winks and leans in close to me. So close I can smell the mint on his breath. "I wouldn't mind."

I take another step toward my car, flustered by him and my incapability to handle him. "Again I revisit the list—definitely a pain in the ass."

"You just have to ask."

My pulse is so loud I'm sure he can hear it. "I guess it's a good thing I'm not asking," I manage to reply. I wonder if I sound as frazzled as I feel.

Jackson takes a step closer to me, stalking me like I'm his prey, and I counter with another step back. Once my back hits the car door ... that's it. He has me pinned and we both know it. He raises his arms, placing them on the frame and caging me in.

His lips brush against my ear when he whispers, "Oh, but your body says otherwise." His body closes in on mine and the last remaining space between us disappears. Heat floods my core, my face, my body—my lids flutter closed and I take a shaky breath. "Open your eyes, Catherine."

I submit to his command, watching how his pupils dilate as his eyes seem to go from solid to liquid. Colors blend together in a sea of blue and green lust. He leans forward, removing one of his arms from the car and placing it on my arm. Slowly his fingers trail my bare skin. The current flowing between us is even more powerful than before. While my common sense dies a slow death, every other part of me is alive under his touch. My body and mind are at war with each other, both trying to gain the upper hand—right now my body is winning.

He licks his lips slowly, torturously, until I'm unable to take another second of this suffering. I snap, grabbing his shirt and yanking him toward me. My lips meet his with a passion that borders on hostile. He pushes us backward, pressing me against the car. The cold metal bites through my shirt, but I don't care. I can barely feel it. His tongue licks the seam of my lips, and when I grant him access, he plunges it in. With every swipe of his tongue against mine, he's igniting the lust I was smothering.

I'm losing myself in his incredibly skilled mouth, feeling lighter, as though I'm floating away. The only thing tying me to this earth is Jackson. He's taken over every part of me. All that exists are his hands and his lips and him, but I want more. I kiss him deeper and harder as he moans against me. Releasing his shirt, I run my hands down across his chest and then lower over his abs, taking in every dent and ridge. His arms pull me tighter, securing me against the front of him. I gasp at his excitement pressed against my stomach, and his mouth moves to my ear.

"Next stop Hoboken Station."

"What?" I ask breathlessly as his nips at my earlobe.

"Now arriving at Hoboken Station."

My eyes flutter open, expecting to see Jackson's sexy face, but … no. I'm on the train.

Holy shit! I was dreaming. It was so real. My palms are sweating and my pulse is racing, and if I'm being honest, I'm panting a little. But none of it happened. Oh, how I wish it had.

I gather my belongings, grab my keys out of my purse, and head out to my car. That drink is looking better and better.

chapter five

The drive back to my apartment is short thanks to the lack of traffic at this time of day. It's odd being home so early. I have about an hour until Ashton is due home, which gives me enough time to change and check my emails. Throwing my hair into a messy bun, I opt for my leggings, a gray tunic, and my mint-green lace leg warmers—cute and sassy, as Ashton would say. I can't wait to unload all the stuff going on in my messed-up brain—nothing seems to make sense.

I step out into the living room and stop dead in my tracks. This place is a mess! Papers are everywhere, mail's lying around, dirty dishes sit on the table, and clothes are strewn over the back of the couch. Between both our schedules, the house is rarely spotless, but we've never let things get this bad. I decide to skip the emails and pick up a little. We pay way too much money for this place to allow it be this out of control. Ashton and I looked for an apartment in Manhattan. We had always wanted to be like the girls on television, but once we saw the going rate for apartments and sublets we opted for New Jersey. Our high-rise is on the river, overlooking the city, so our rent is high, but it's worth it. We both make a good salary, so we decided to live comfortably and have an apartment with security.

Me: Hey. Gonna start dinner.

Ashton: K. I'll be leaving the city soon.

I look through the kitchen and realize we're out of pretty much anything edible. I can either head to the store or order in. The sensible choice would be to go to the store, but after the day I've had, I decide to say screw it.

There's a knock at the door. Weird. The doorman usually calls if we have visitors.

"Open up, Cat," a bubbly voice says. Gretchen.

With a huge grin, I throw the door open.

"What are you doing on this side of the river?" I ask.

"I had a case here in Jersey, so I figured I'd see if my two crazy-ass friends were around. And lucky me, I get you!" She grins as she walks through the apartment.

"At least it's lucky for one of us," I snort.

"Honestly, I didn't think you'd be here. What gives?" she says, assessing my outfit and facial expressions.

"I had my meeting today for that prospective new client. I finished early. Figured I'd work from home." I shrug, attempting nonchalance.

Gretchen glares, giving me her lawyer look. The one that sees through you as she weighs each word you say and interprets your tone. She does that and then she chews you up. I should've remembered who I'm dealing with. Even fielding questions from crazy reporters hasn't properly prepared me for her.

"So why do you look like shit? Why don't you tell me what's really going on, Cat? Considering I don't believe you for a second." Her voice is stern but sympathetic. She knows the nightmare I went through. I knew it would only be a matter of time until she started pushing me to talk.

We head into the kitchen and sit at the table. I look down, trying to find a way to put into words what's jumbled in my head, as my fingers trace the grain of the wood. "I'm a mess, Gretch. It's been three months since Neil cheated on me, and sometimes it feels like it happened yesterday. Sometimes it hurts so much it's hard to breathe, but I have to pretend I'm great.

"Then today I had to present against him at the client meeting I told you about. Not only was Piper there …" I trail off, looking up to see her reaction.

"What? Oh wow," she says, stunned, before recovering. "You've had quite a day, babe."

"You could say that. And then I find out he stole my presentation." My head falls to my hands and I release the flood of emotions I've been restraining. "This is the man I was supposed to marry?" I drop my hands, letting out a ragged breath. My voice trembles when I ask, "How can I still love him, Gretch?"

"Do you really love him?"

"Yes … No … I don't know. I'm so stupid! I don't understand how he could have loved me and then done such messed-up things. I thought I knew him. I trusted him, gave my heart to him—only to have it ripped out of my chest. Why did I let him do this to me?" The tears I've been fighting threaten to spill over.

"I feel like something changed about a year ago. At least that's when I noticed it. He got distant and moody and started skipping out on things."

"I remember. I noticed too. When I questioned him about it, he proposed. I figured he was nervous about taking such a big leap."

"You never really know someone. But the more you sit here and question yourself, the more you'll drive yourself bat-shit crazy. Trust me. My mother used to say this to me and I think you should hear it: love is a verb—it's an action. Can you tell me what he did to *show* you he loved you? Anyone can say the words, but they need to prove it. His choices are his choices and now you have to make yours." Gretchen grabs my hand and holds it tight.

In the beginning he did show me. He cared and did things to make sure I felt special. It was the little things that meant the most—the handholding, the stolen moments between us, an unexpected note or text—but slowly that all changed.

"I know I'm not to blame for his choices, but *his* choices affected the rest of *my* life," I reply, my voice filled with bitterness and hurt.

"That's where you're wrong, hun. What he did affects today—but *you* decide if it affects tomorrow. The only power he has is the power you give him. You know how brave and strong I think you are. Not many people could handle what you saw and dealt with. Sure, you cried, but you still went to work, kicked ass, and found a way to smile."

It's liberating finally letting it all out. With Ashton I always guard a small part of myself—the vulnerable side. Sure, we share everything, for the most part, but she's so much stronger than me. Gretchen would let me sulk and mope forever, but Ashton doesn't play that game.

"Oh, if you would have seen me, I don't think you'd be saying that." I laugh and squeeze her hand.

Gretchen smiles with warmth and love. "I did see you. I saw the mess you were, but I saw the strength behind it too. Look at you now. You had a fucked-up day, but you're not sitting here sobbing. You're surviving, and you're up for yet another promotion. Of course there are going to be bad days, but you dictate how many. I don't want to mother you, but anytime you want to talk, you know I'm here."

My phone rings, interrupting our heart-to-heart. Taylor's name flashes across the screen, which is odd because we usually text or email. She never calls, not unless it's an emergency.

"I gotta grab this."

"No worries. I have to get going anyway. I love you! Remember what I said, though." She stands, giving me a kiss on the cheek before heading to the door. I smile at how great our impromptu visit was, waving as the door closes behind her and the phone rings again.

"Hi, Tay."

"Sorry to bother you, but I thought you'd want to know immediately," she replies excitedly.

"Okay, what's going on?"

"Raven Cosmetics called. They'd like to speak with you first thing tomorrow morning. They asked if you'd be available for an 8 a.m. phone conference with the CEO. I said absolutely. I hope that's okay," she says nervously.

"Yes, of course. I hope this is a good thing."

"I'm sure it is. I'll confirm the meeting and email you the details."

"Thanks. I'll work from home in the morning and be in the office around eleven," I tell her.

"See you then. Let me know if you need anything before you come in."

"I will. Have a great night."

I hang up the phone, surprised that we're having a conference call instead of another meeting. I don't know what that means, but I need to stay positive. I did the best I could, and all in all I feel good about how I presented. Even with Piper being in my face and unwanted thoughts of her and Neil resurfacing every time I looked at them, I kept it together.

There's a part of me that still doesn't understand how it all happened. What could possibly have brought them together? Sure, she has beautiful blond hair and bright blue eyes, but I never thought Neil saw her as more than a friend. I never imagined she'd be the demise of our relationship.

I hear my phone chirp and look down, hoping it's Ash letting me know she's close.

Ashton: Hey. I got tied up at work.

Me: It's fine.

Ashton: I think I'm staying in the city tonight. You ok?

Me: I'll be fine.

Of course she's not going to come home the one time I need her to. Is anything going to go my way today? I needed my ex-fiancé to act like an adult, I needed him to leave me alone and not make an attempt to further obliterate me, and I needed my best friend to help me cope when said ex asshole ignored my needs completely and behaved like a selfish bastard. My phone starts ringing and I see Ashton's face pop up on my screen.

I smile to myself, swiping to answer. "I'm okay, Ash."

She giggles. "Liar. I can tell by your text message

that you're not. What happened today?"

"Well, let's see. First, Piper consults for Raven Cosmetics, so she was in the meeting."

"What?" she shouts. "Did you punch her in the throat? Or bitch-slap her? I wish I could've seen that."

"Yeah, Ashton, that's what I did in a client meeting. No, I didn't, although I wanted to." I take a deep breath and quickly tell her the story of my afternoon with all the sordid details and drama.

"What did you do to piss God off? I've never met anyone who has such shitty luck." Ash laughs. "No matter what happens, this will work out. If not, we'll get drunk and make fun of people."

"I still don't know why the hell I keep you around. I gotta go. I have an early phone meeting with the Raven people and I need to be prepared."

"Okay. I probably won't make it home. The new doctor is up my ass about the clinical trials he's running. I need to be in the lab in case something happens. I'm sorry I can't be home for you today, but please promise me you won't eat a pint of ice cream. Just break out the old rabbit and—"

"And that's where we hang up. Thanks for the advice. I love you."

"Love you too. Seriously, an orgasm will totally—"

I disconnect before she can finish, laughing at her ability to change my mood. There are no words for that girl. She really is my twisted sister. I decide it's time to throw myself into work.

As I sit at the table, I replay the day's events. If I were an outsider, they'd be hilarious. Since I'm the one involved, however, they're not. I have two choices: either I do my best and win the only way

I can, or I lie down and let Neil win. Right now, I'm more eager than ever to nail this phone interview and win this job. I go straight to my desk, change my email password, along with the passwords for any other account I may have logged in to from his computer, and get to work on my Raven project.

When I finally look at the clock, two hours have passed and I've accomplished a lot. I crunched numbers with an intensity I haven't felt in a long time. I'm ready for tomorrow.

As I step into my room, all the confidence I built up working over the past few hours vanishes. I look around, feeling uncomfortable and ashamed. It looks like a disaster zone in here. This isn't me. I've always been neat and organized, ready to tackle the world. But the person living here is anything but that. My side table is covered in dirty dishes, piles of clothes are scattered everywhere, the trashcan is overflowing with tissues, and empty ice cream containers and candy wrappers litter the floor. Is this what I've become?

Feeling determined to pull myself together and start rebuilding my life, I begin cleaning up my room, finding my strength through cleanliness and organization. Sometimes putting things in their rightful place is therapeutic. Right now, it's giving me some small measure of control. The hurt and pain are still there, but I need to put this behind me. I need to move on.

Today has reminded me that the life I thought I had and the man I thought I loved aren't things I should want anymore. The future I dream of doesn't look like this. It's full of devotion and happiness, not sadness and betrayal. I deserve more. Silently, I promise myself to guard my heart from now on.

Love is a gift, and I will not give it freely to anyone.

Just as I'm thinking this, I accidentally knock over a frame, which crashes to the ground. Though the glass doesn't shatter, when I pick it up I see a huge crack down the center between Neil's face and mine. Broken—like we are. It's the photo from our first anniversary. I'm clinging to his back and he's looking adoringly at me with a huge smile on his face. We were so happy and in love. It shone through our eyes as we laughed at whatever joke we shared. We were always playful and silly in the beginning—he brought that out in me. But at some point it stopped. We went from happy to comfortable, and then he made his choices.

I can't keep thinking about this. All I want is freedom from him and this idea of what our relationship was or could have been. Alone in my room, I let it all go. Silent rivers of tears stream down my face as the weight of the last three months comes crashing around me. All the lies, hurt, and infidelity, the broken promises … it's destroyed a part of me. I know that even when I'm fully over everything, there's a part of my heart that will never be repaired. There's a fissure that will always be there, a wound that will one day heal and scar over, but it will never be forgotten.

Grabbing an empty box, I start to place the pictures and the memories that accompany them away. I'll never heal if I keep pretending he'll come back. I glance at our engagement photo. It's amazing the difference between this picture and our first anniversary shot. He's not looking at me like he did in the first photo. In this one he's barely smiling—his eyes look empty, as though he's looking past me, not at me. Why didn't I ever notice that? I was so blinded by my need to be loved that I overlooked the truths that were staring at me every day.

Intent on putting things away, I eye the jewelry box that holds my engagement ring. Tentatively, I open the lid and stare at the shiny diamond nestled in the ring slot. I place it on my finger one last time, and the light creates prisms that bounce off the walls as I twist it around. Tears continue, but instead of feeling weighted by them, I feel as though each one is cleansing me. Reluctantly, I take it off my finger and tuck it back in the ring slot. Back in the box that I received from the other man in my life that I wasn't enough for. I pull out my "Fuck You" ring that I purchased for myself with Neil's money and slide it on my finger. Even though the purpose of the ring was to distract me from Neil and my empty ring finger, when I look at it now I remember Neil. I don't want to remember anymore. I take the sapphire ring off, placing it next to my engagement ring. They are a symbol of the past going where it needs to go—away.

While I'm clearing out my heart, I decide that my father's last gift and the belongings inside it need to be put to rest. These are two men who've caused me tremendous pain—their love was tainted, if it ever was love, and I have no room for it anymore.

Glancing around the room, feeling better about the way it looks, I grab the jewelry box representing my father and Neil and place it on the top shelf in my closet. Staring at the ornate box for a moment, I allow a few final tears to fall as I say good-bye. Then I close my closet door and lie in bed, noticing as I drift off to sleep how my heart feels lighter and how breathing isn't quite as hard as it has been.

chapter six

The alarm blares at six the next morning. I roll over, hit the off button, and shuffle into the kitchen to start my Keurig. It's amazing how much better I feel after having a night of restful sleep. Grabbing my cup of coffee, I head to my desk to prepare for my phone call with the people from Raven.

With coffee in hand, I fire up my laptop and get to work. The new email alert sounds off so long that it almost seems as if I've held my finger down on a keyboard for a minute or so. Great. I'm out of the office half a day and I have over one hundred new emails. I skim through and see a few new possible client assignments that look promising and one that I'd love to grab if Raven Cosmetics doesn't work out. I open the email from Taylor, which goes over the details for today's call, and see that she's attached a few files with updated sales figures for the company. They show a small decline from last month's figures but nothing too drastic.

After going through the remainder of my emails and taking care of some mundane things around the house, the conference call reminder pops up on my phone. Dialing in, I mentally prepare myself to hear Piper's and Neil's voices so I won't be blindsided by them. I hear the beep and announce my name and company.

"Hello, Ms. Pope. This is Danielle."

"Good morning, Danielle. I hope your morning is good so far."

"Yes, thank you. We appreciate you fitting us in last-minute," she replies.

"As I promised in our meeting, I haven't taken on any other accounts in hopes that you'll select CJJ to represent you," I say, projecting my strength through the phone.

"I'm glad to hear that. After we conclude our call, we have a call scheduled with Boyce PR. Mr. Cole should be on in about two minutes. We were advised by Piper of her opinion, and we want to be one hundred percent sure we choose the right person."

"I understand completely. Do you have anything you'd like me to clear up prior to Mr. Cole joining us?" I ask earnestly.

"Our questions this morning will focus on you and your company. I think either company would provide a similar approach, but we would like to know more about you since you would be the person primarily responsible for ensuring clear and consistent branding. Also, I wanted to let you know that I'm not an assistant—I'm actually the director of product development. I'm sorry I wasn't honest, but I wanted to get a feel for both you and Neil without either of you being influenced by my title."

"Honestly, Danielle, I never believed you were an assistant, but thank you for being frank." I let out a short laugh. "I assure you—"

A tone cuts me off, alerting us that someone has joined the call.

"Good morning." A deep, hoarse voice fills my ears. My body tenses and something stirs deep inside. "Danielle?" he asks.

"Yes, Mr. Cole, good morning. I have Catherine Pope on the call, sir. She's with CJJ Public Relations," Danielle informs him.

I shake my head, trying to release the tension triggered by his voice, and prepare to impress him. "Good morning, Mr. Cole. It's a pleasure."

"Ms. Pope, thank you for joining us. Danielle was impressed by your presentation. I asked to have a call with you since I was out of the area and couldn't make it to the meeting yesterday. I wanted to speak with you and the other candidate before I make my final decision." The strong, sexy timbre of his voice exudes confidence.

"I'm more than happy to go over any questions you may have."

The call continues for about thirty minutes as we discuss my professional background and the company's growth expectations. The sound of his voice pulls at me, though I can't quite place it. With each question he asks, I field and answer appropriately, reaffirming that I'm the right choice.

Mr. Cole breaks in right before we're about to wrap things up. "I'd like to know one more thing."

"Ask away." I smile, hoping it shines through the phone.

"Why should we hire you?" he asks point-blank.

I anticipated this question. It's pretty typical and I honestly love to answer it. There's no real reason other than what I always answer. "Because I'm the best. I work hard, and I don't fail. Ever," I say confidently.

His deep voice vibrates through the phone. "We'll be in touch by the end of the day with our final answer. Thank you, Catherine."

When he says my first name, a familiar feeling washes over me. Though I'd love to take the time to analyze why that is, my professionalism prevents me from dwelling. "I look forward to hearing from you. Have a wonderful day."

"Thank you, Ms. Pope," Danielle replies.

Then the line goes dead.

And I wait.

Again.

After taking a long shower, I stand in front of my closet debating what to wear. The warm water helped ease my residual anxiety from the phone call, but I need something that will make me feel sexy and strong. It's still warm out, so I opt for my navy blue empire dress and pair it with my dark crimson heals. I smile at my reflection in the mirror—I look good. I decide to take some extra time on my makeup and hair. Large barrel curls soften the ends of my dark brown hair, and I leave them hanging loosely down by back. For my makeup, I choose a really soft smoky eye, which gives me that coveted mysterious look. Not bad. This is the Catherine Pope I know and remember.

Once I arrive at the office, I settle into my desk and … feel useless. I don't know if I won the account yet and my last two clients finished last week. I cleared out most of my emails at home, so I have nothing to work on. My ambition and work ethic won't allow for me to sit around, so I decide to look at the open bids board and start mock-ups for a pitch. I have no idea if I'll get the Raven account and I don't want to waste any time getting to work on the next possible account coming in. Plus, my coworker Elle is the only other person competing with me for the upcoming promotion. I can't let her get ahead, so I need to focus and act as though I've lost this one.

I head over to the board to see what's there, and Elle looks up, grinning broadly at me. "Already looking for a new account, Cat?" Her high-pitched voice pierces through the room.

I give her a fake smile. "No, just looking to see what came in. What about you?"

"Oh, you know, I've got some new models coming in for a shoot. Atelier Clothing wants to do a tour with hot guys. You should stop by and see the eye candy I have coming in!" She's practically bouncing. I have no desire to see the "hot" guys she has lined up. She has the worst taste, especially when it comes to the way she does ads and press releases. I can only imagine what the guys will look like. I'll never understand her choices. They always seem overdone to me.

"Oh, I wish I could." I feign disappointment and stifle the comments rolling around in my mind. "I have a few things that need my attention, but I'm *sure* they're drool worthy." I can't stop myself. "You sure know how to pick 'em."

She smiles, thinking I'm complimenting her. "I know! I love the one I found today. His name is Colin, and he's just … wow!"

I smile and look back to the board. "Good luck, Elle. I gotta get back to work."

I add my name to the next best account on the board and head back to my office. When I get there, I send Taylor an email to be in my office in fifteen minutes to start research.

I hear a knock on the door and look up.

"Hey. You want to do research for a new company looking for representation?" Taylor is standing against the doorframe looking baffled.

"Yes, we can't have all our eggs in one basket," I reply and gesture for her to sit in the chair.

"Okay, but doesn't that seem hasty?" she asks tentatively. "You should hear back by the end of the day, right?"

"I don't think so. It's been over three hours since the call ended, and I haven't heard anything. For all I know they've offered Boyce the account and are waiting until they settle the deal before they call me. I can't sit here and do nothing. You know me." I shrug with a smile. "Anyway, the promotion is still up for grabs and I refuse to let Elle get a leg up. Are you ready to get to work?"

"Of course. Let's dig in." Taylor smiles and we get to work on researching the new company.

We're immersed in our iPads and computers and have completely lost track of time when I look at the clock, realizing it's almost five. I start to stretch but jump midway as the phone rings, startling me.

Taylor runs to her desk, grabs the receiver, and pokes her head around. "Cat, it's Raven. Want me to shut the door?"

"Yes. Thank you."

This is it. I grab the phone and take a deep breath before pushing the blinking button that will finally end the waiting.

"Hello, this is Catherine Pope."

"Hi, Catherine. It's Danielle. I wanted to let you know we've made our decision." Her voice is steady, giving nothing away.

"Wonderful, I hope you're calling with good news."

"Yes, we'd like CJJ to be our new PR firm. Congratulations."

I let out a huge breath and stop myself from dancing around the room. "Oh! Thank you, I'm glad you chose us. I look forward to working with you."

"Us too. We're very excited about your vision. I know this is last-minute but Mr. Cole arrived back in the city today. He would like you to meet him tonight at the office if possible," she responds hesitantly.

I've already stated I would be available for this project, and even though I want to celebrate, I can't wait to get started. There's a new feeling of determination and excitement coursing through my veins. I could probably run the forty blocks to Raven Cosmetics with all the energy I have right now, but not in these heels. I want to hit the ground running, impress him and everyone else, and then land the promotion.

"Yes, that would be fine. What time would he like to meet?"

"Can you be here around six? I have to leave the office to head to our production facility tomorrow, so I'll be heading home to pack, but I'll leave your information with security."

"Perfect. I'll be there." We say our good-byes and I can't help the smile stretched across my face. I message Taylor to come into my office.

She enters with a tentative smile, as if she wasn't listening at the door. Inside I'm doing cartwheels—I needed this. I feel strong, confident, and again—I beat Neil. Even though I don't want to think of him, I enjoy this victory and relish the fact that despite his efforts to sabotage me, I still won.

My smile widens, if that's even possible. "We got it! Oh my God, Tay! We got the account!"

"Ahhh! I knew it!" she squeals with as much

excitement as I'm feeling and rushes over, giving me a huge hug. She pulls back, keeping her arms on my shoulders. "I never doubted you! So what happens next?"

"I have to meet Mr. Cole at six. Can you call and have a cab or a car waiting? I want to make sure I'm on time." She nods and zooms back out of my office. I only have thirty minutes to get there, and it's at least a twenty-minute cab ride with the traffic at this hour.

I start to pace. The adrenaline and excitement is starting to ebb—I'm anxious because now that I have the account, I have to implement all my ideas and gain the trust of the CEO. Nervous energy fills my body and I grab my iPad to start taking notes on all the things I want to lobby for.

Taylor buzzes the intercom. "I have a cab downstairs. Good luck and congrats again. Now go kick some ass." She giggles and disconnects.

I grab my purse and rush out of the office, throwing a quick good-bye over my shoulder. Throughout the ride to Raven Cosmetics I go over my key notes, examine some of my earlier sales figures, and plan to spend the next few days really honing in on the company's core values. When I get there, I hop out of the cab, prepared to make one hell of an impression.

Entering the building, I make my way over to security. The guard hands me the badge that Danielle left for me and calls Mr. Cole, letting him know I've arrived. I'm told to head straight to the office, where he'll be waiting for me.

Luckily the elevator is empty, so I have a minute to mentally prepare. Taking a few deep breaths, I start to form some ideas on how to best sell him on my plan. I also wonder about the man himself. I've met a lot of executives, but there's something about his voice. The deep, raspy sound has me curious as to what triggered the familiarity. I haven't really had time to think about it until now. Surely I would remember if we'd met or spent any significant amount of time together. I'm pretty good at remembering people and small details; it's part of why I excel at my job. As the elevator ascends, so does my anxiety.

Before I have another second to think about it, the door opens. My eyes immediately lock on familiar blue-green ones and the breathtaking face of the man who I've dreamed of for the last week.

chapter

seven

My free hand flies to my mouth in disbelief. "Jackson," I say, barely audible.

Jackson stands there looking absolutely magnificent—he's everything I remember and more. He's wearing a crisp white dress shirt with the sleeves rolled up—the top two buttons undone—and dark gray, perfectly tailored dress pants. His hair is disheveled, like he's been running his hands through the dark brown locks. He steps forward and places his hands on the elevator doors to prevent them from closing. His eyes haven't left mine, and the cocky grin I remember is present as he processes who I am. He shakes his head back and forth in disbelief and gives a small half laugh. I look down and shift my weight, afraid to speak and unable to move forward.

He clears his throat, forcing me to look up. He finally speaks first. "You're Catherine Pope?" he asks, sounding amused as he tries to smother his grin.

I nod my head in response.

He extends his hand, inviting me to exit and reminding me that I'm still standing on the elevator. I place my hand in his and the electric current, which I've tried to convince myself I'd imagined, buzzes through my entire body, energizing every nerve from head to toe. Jackson pulls me forward, still unspeaking.

He's unbelievably sexy and try as I might, my eyes refuse to look away while he measures his next words. Jackson steps back, pulling me with him toward the office. What are the odds? I never thought I'd see this man again, and now he's standing in front of me, smiling and shaking his head, almost mirroring my own response. Of all the accounts and all the men *he* had to be Jackson Cole.

Jackson clears his throat again, breaking into my thoughts. "You're even more beautiful than I remember." He looks down at our hands and the shift in his attitude is unmistakable, as if he's considering the current relationship we now share.

I remove my hand from his and pull myself together. He's my client. I'm a professional.

"Thank you, Mr. Cole. CJJ is proud that you chose our vision to take your company forward." I smile and mentally high-five myself for saying that without stuttering.

He chuckles at my attempt at professionalism. "Oh, let me assure you, this project is quickly becoming my favorite," he says with amusement, looking me up and down. His deep, sexy voice travels straight to my core. "The more I think about it, the more I think I'm going to enjoy working with you."

I lick my lips as I stare at his mouth. I need to get it together. This is my job. He's just a man, a very sexy and fuckable man, but still—he's my client. I'm not about to be seduced by his gorgeous face or ripped abs and defined arms—nope, not going to happen.

Bring on the delusions.

I smile tentatively. "Shall we get to our meeting?"

I ask as my voice shakes, betraying my nerves.

"We're going to play it that way, are we?" He smirks, obviously amused. "Okay, Ms. Pope. Right this way," he says as he looks directly into my eyes, saying so much more with his body than with his mouth. His perfectly formed, totally kissable—

My thoughts are scattered. I want to run back into the elevator and tell him to give the account to Boyce. I don't know how I'm going to be around him for days on end. We've spent a total of five minutes together and he already has me in hyperdrive.

"Thank you," I mumble.

He extends his arm, showing me where to go. I shift my purse on my shoulder and begin walking. When he places his hand on the small of my back, I shiver inadvertently. I feel his warmth through my shirt, burning my skin. I'm mentally berating myself for acting like this.

"Are you cold?" he asks with humor in his voice, somehow aware his touch is wreaking havoc on me.

I turn and look directly in his eyes, hoping to convey my own message of strength and defiance. "No, I'm fine. Thank you." I was strong and confident this morning, but now I feel like I'm on the edge of a cliff. I smile and straighten my back, trying to walk past him as he stands in the doorway. He's left me very little room to get through, though, so I shift to the side, scooting by without touching him. Of course, it's impossible and my arm slides against his, causing goose bumps to form in the wake of our skin-to-skin contact.

His office is nothing like I would have imagined. It has a feminine feel to it. He has a glass desk table with a high-back chair. The walls are cream and the couch is a light lilac color. There are no photos, no personal touches throughout the room. I fight the urge to laugh—this is definitely not a man's office.

Jackson clears his throat again and I wonder if it's a nervous habit of his. Could he be as nervous as I am? "I just moved into this office," he begins, pausing as if carefully weighing his next words. "The person before me was obviously a female. Danielle was the acting CEO for the last ten months. I haven't had time to change anything." He closes his eyes, looking almost pained. I have the strangest urge to comfort him, but I resist.

"I understand. But for the record, purple's not your color." I sit in one of the chairs in front of his desk and start to get out my mock boards and planning sheet.

"No? And what color would you recommend, Ms. Pope?" Jackson asks, smiling.

"Hmmm, I'd say pink." I look around before returning my gaze to him. "Definitely pink."

Jackson comes around and sits in the chair next to me instead of behind the desk. His cologne assaults my senses as I inhale, breathing in all its masculinity. It's even better than I remember and so much stronger.

I open my eyes to see him staring at me with a wide smile. He shifts in his seat and props his arm on the back of mine. "Pink, huh? Well only real men wear pink, and I assure you, Catherine, I'm all the real you'll ever need."

I cough, trying to regain my focus as his eyes bore into me.

"So, fall on any more men at dinner lately?"

And there it is.

"Actually, no. Thanks for being concerned, though." I laugh while shaking my head.

"Good to know. I'd be jealous if you had."

"Anyway, I brought the mock-up and I emailed Danielle the video."

"I saw the video. It's the reason you're here now and not the other company." His compliment washes over me. He didn't hire me because he knew me, no. It was because of my vision and my plan for his company.

"I'm glad I impressed you."

Jackson shifts in his chair and crosses his leg, getting closer to me. "I'm hoping there are many ways you'll endeavor to impress me." His tone is light and joking, but his eyes suggest the truth in his words.

He can't touch me or I'll crack. I try to move back in my chair, but there's nowhere to go. I stand and start to pace. I'm nervous, wound up, and out of my element.

"Mr. Cole—"

"Jackson. You should call me Jackson. We'll be together a lot," he cuts me off. I turn to look out the window, trying to gather my thoughts.

I'm freaking out. I can't do my job and work with *him*. I can't think straight around him—he's too much. Too sexy. Too intense. Too all-consuming. How am I going to do this? I can't focus around him and if Jackson touches me, I'll crumble. On the other hand, if I walk away from this account, I'll never get the promotion. Shit. I could lose my job. Wouldn't that be the icing on Neil's cake? He would get the account and I'd be unemployed. No. No way. I can do this. I have to be strong.

I really need a vacation from my life.

I turn and he's standing so close behind me that I almost collide with him. "Mr.—Jackson, I think we should go over your company's goals and make a plan. It's getting late."

Jackson walks over behind his desk and sits in his chair. I follow, returning to the chair I was in before, thankful for the desk between us. If I can maintain distance and space with zero physical contact, then I can keep the account and my job. Let's see how long this plan will last.

"How about we grab dinner?" he casually says.

"Dinner?"

"Yes, you know that meal that comes after lunch. I haven't eaten yet and you probably haven't either." His eyes don't waver from mine.

"I can't. I have to do—"

"I'm pretty sure the stipulation was that you're available whenever I need you." He raises his brow as he taps his fingers on his desk.

"Yes, but we've yet to sign our contract." I smile sweetly, but I can't keep the exasperation out of my voice.

He stands and walks around the desk slowly. Each step is measured and deliberate. Every moment stirs something within me. My anxiety is already sky-high. I can't take much more of this tonight. When he's finally in front of me, he leans back on his desk and his voice drops when he asks, "Where's the contract?"

I reach into my bag and pull out the paperwork that will solidify the deal. This is my last chance to walk away from him. I'll have to see him, smell him, be around him, and there will be no backing out without me losing everything. Once he signs this, it's over. I hold the papers in my hand, which is visibly shaking from my poorly concealed unease. Jackson reaches out, silently asking me to hand it over.

I stand and walk toward him with the contract extended between us. He grabs it and leans on his desk, signing on the dotted line without even reading it. Jackson puts the pen down and turns back to me. Though he doesn't voice it, his expression says, "Gotcha."

"Well, Ms. Pope, there's no turning back now."

I bite my bottom lip and my stomach drops as Jackson hands me back the signed contract. Oh God, what did I just do? I'm so stupid and in so much trouble. It's as if he has some inside knowledge of what makes me tick, like he sees right through my layers of bullshit, straight to my libido. No man has ever made me this unbalanced. Even when Neil and I first started dating, I don't think I was ever this scattered. But with Jackson I'm a mess.

I stare into his beautiful eyes. They're dancing with humor. He smirks and holds my gaze, unwilling to break away first. Both of us struggle to gain the upper hand, knowing whomever breaks first is somehow showing they're weaker than the other. I hold my eyes steady and smile, hoping they aren't showing the internal war going on inside my head. I need to say something and put an end to this. "Mr. Cole, thank you for signing the contract. I really do need to go now."

"We just made a deal and I told you to call me Jackson, twice. Now, let's head to dinner," he commands, his voice leaving no room for discussion.

"Jackson, please." I take a deep breath, my eyes begging for understanding. "I really can't tonight." I have no good reason and if he pushes me, I'll cave. My only reason is he scares me. I don't trust myself around him.

He stands and walks over to my chair again. He grasps my chin between his finger and rough thumb. The feel of his skin against mine causes my pulse to race. I'm sure he can hear it. Just like the first night we met, he holds my face steady as he stares into my eyes, searching for something. "Fine, not tonight. However, I need you to meet me here Monday by 9 a.m. There are a few meetings I want you to sit in on with the production team and then we leave for Virginia on Friday."

"Virginia?" I ask, completely thrown off.

"Yes, it's a state a few states below New York." His grin grows and his dimple deepens with his taunting.

"I know where Virginia is." *Ass.* "I wasn't aware you had an office there."

"Our production plant is there. I'd like you to fly out with me this week, see some of the new products that are being developed, and tell me your ideas for future campaigns. If this one goes well, hopefully we can work together on a more permanent basis." He raises an eyebrow suggestively.

I shift in my seat and try to calm my heart, which is threatening to fly out of my chest. Future campaigns? Ugh! This would solidify my career at CJJ. There's no way I can refuse him. Damn him and his gorgeous face. "Okay, next Friday will be fine. I can meet you here Monday morning as well."

Jackson grabs my bag and offers his hand to help me stand. I take it and the contact causes heat to pool in my center, again. A simple touch is all it takes for me to become a puddle at his feet. Who am I kidding? All it took was the sound of his voice. I turn my head away, trying to hide any emotions showing on my face. He gently pulls me up. He's close, so close. It's like he's everywhere. His cologne, the warmth of his body—it's all encompassing.

Feeling overwhelmed and dizzy, I start to tilt. Jackson moves his hand to my hip to steady me. His deep voice does nothing to calm my nerves. "Easy. You don't want to fall into my arms again."

"Yes, that would be a tragedy." I blink hard, shaking my head and trying not to focus on the way my body is heating from his touch.

"I wouldn't go that far. I can think of far worse places to land. The ground for one."

I laugh and try to take a step back, but I'm stuck. "Right. I have a feeling I'm going to pay for that for a long time."

"What? Me catching you? I would've let it go if you'd stayed and had a drink with us." He smirks.

If there were ever a time I wanted the ground to open and swallow me, this is it. "If this is going to be my punishment, I almost wish you would've let me fall," I kid.

"Now where would the fun in that be?"

I nod and start to head toward the door. "I really have to go. I'll see myself out. Thank you for your time." I turn my back and exit his office.

I should have known he'd follow me. I sense him before I hear him. Deciding to ignore him and get the hell out of here, I start moving quickly, hoping he gives up and goes back to his office. I hear him chuckle behind me as if he can read my mind. Right as I reach the exit, his hand presses against the door so I can't open it.

I huff and turn with my back flush against the door and—Jackson is so close. It's like my dream, only this time I'm not at my car. The cold glass is doing nothing to help the fire burning within me.

He takes a deep breath, and neither of us speaks as his hand slides down the door until it's next to my shoulder. Ever so slowly, he lifts his left hand and caresses it down my arm, stopping at my wrist. Lifting and opening my fingers, he places something in my palm then closes my fingers back around it. Still neither of us has spoken a word, but it feels as if we've had an entire conversation. Jackson leans forward and I think he's going to kiss me. I close my eyes, silently praying that he will. Instead he uses his weight and pushes himself back upright. I feel his warmth evaporate and it takes all my strength not to wrap myself around him and get lost in his touch. Jackson smiles, looks at my hand, and turns away without saying a word.

Somehow I manage to keep myself from collapsing and make my way to the elevator. Once inside with the doors shut, I slide to the floor and close my eyes. I inhale deeply, trying to calm myself. Remembering that he placed something in my hand, I unclench my fingers and look down to find a business card. On the back, scribbled in short, precise strokes, is a message.

Catherine, this is my personal cell phone. Call anytime.

"Why didn't you ever tell me about him?" Ashton

continues to question me. She's been grilling me for the last hour.

I haven't seen her at all over the last few days. She's been staying at the lab because of the clinical trials, and the one night she was home, I had a dinner meeting with the other publicists from my office. By the time I got back, Ashton was already passed out. Needing some girl time, we decided to spend the weekend relaxing before I have to deal with Jackson again. We're now on our second bottle of wine. During our first bottle, I was a mess—trying to form words while rehashing all the details about Neil and Piper, then about Jackson. She was quiet and listened to me get it all out, constantly filling my glass and offering me silent support. However, during the consumption of bottle number two, we've moved on to complete giddiness and feeling no pain. We're now laughing over all the stuff I was upset about an hour ago. Of course, Ashton finds it highly entertaining—I find it disturbing and unfair.

"I don't know, Ashton. What the hell was I going to say? I tripped over a chair and fell on a ridiculously hot guy? I felt stupid enough. I didn't need your shit too." I laugh and gulp my wine.

"Only you! I swear this shit never happens to anyone else I know. So what are you going to do? I mean he's hot and he's obviously sexually attracted to you." She raises her eyebrow and grins.

"I'm not going to do anything. He's my client."

"So? Who says you can't service your boss?" She winks and giggles.

"I can't believe you. You would never sleep with the doctors in the lab, would you?"

"Who says I haven't? Plus, they're all ugly as shit. If there was a hot one, I'd totally play doctor and let him cure me." She lays her hand across her head in mockery.

"You have issues." I groan at the sheer ridiculousness of my situation. "What the hell am I going to do?"

"You're going to do what you always do—you'll go in there and fight all of your emotions and kick some corporate ass. Then you'll come home and wallow in your Ben & Jerry's, be miserable, and cry yourself to sleep. Eventually, you'll waste all your chances for a real connection and sabotage your own happiness." She shrugs and refuses to break eye contact.

I gasp at the cruelty—and accuracy—of her statement. "What the hell, Ashton?"

"Sorry, Cat, but it's true. You knew things were wrong with Neil, but instead of leaving him, you got engaged. Before him there was Eli. You stayed with him for years because he was safe and you thought you deserved the sheer *hell* he put you through. I'm not trying to hurt you." She scoots over and puts her arm around me, pulling me into a hug. "I'm just telling you that whether this guy was your client or not, you'd find a reason to destroy yourself over him."

My heart clenches at her words. It hurts so much coming from Ashton. I know she loves me, but I hate what she's saying. "I don't understand why every guy I meet or date lets me down."

"You need to stop looking for this perfect guy. You need to get out of your own head and start having fun. Once the product is released, who knows where you and this Jackson guy will be? Maybe you'll like him. Maybe he'll be the world's biggest piece of shit. Either way, you need to figure *you* out before you fret about all this. Monday morning, go to your meeting, be the kick-ass girl I know you are, and blow them all away." She smiles reassuringly before picking up the empty wine glasses and bottles and heading into the kitchen.

I grab a pillow and clutch it to my chest. She's right. It's not like I even know Jackson or have any connection to him, other than this crazy feeling I get when I'm around him. I need to focus on my life for once. I don't have to take anyone else into account. The realization is liberating. Now I need to figure out a way to make my body stop reacting to Jackson and all his sexiness.

chapter eight

For the third night in a row, I've slept like complete shit. I tossed and turned all night, tormented by images of Jackson and me rolling around in my bed. It was pure heaven. Then I woke up and realized none of the amazing things he just did to me were real. Now I'm all keyed up and have to go to a meeting where I'll spend the majority of my time trying not to stare at his gorgeous face. I groan and roll over, punching my pillow, wishing that I could call in sick today. But I'm no chicken shit, so I throw my covers off and head into the bathroom.

I strip out of my clothes and enter the waterfall shower, turning on the side jets. The hot water relaxes my muscles as my mind wanders to—who else?—Jackson. I need a plan on how to handle him—he makes me feel too much. He's even taken over my subconscious while I sleep. Last night's vivid dream of Jackson touching me, licking me, and claiming me rushes back, rekindling my need for relief. I close my eyes, letting the steam envelop me as I start to remember the way he played with my body, as if he'd been doing it for years.

The warm scent of my vanilla body wash relaxes me as I gently rub the soap over my curves. I lean back against the cold shower tiles and slowly move my hands to my breasts, circling the soap, imagining it's his mouth on me. My nipples harden as I tease myself. I start to gasp and moan, fantasizing that his hands and voice are coaxing me on, telling me how much he wants me. The demand to release becomes stronger as I get lost in the sensations. My hand slides down my slick skin until it finds my clit, circling the bundle of nerves, pushing me further and further into ecstasy. My muscles clench as I envision Jackson's fingers, his body covering mine and entering me. I insert one finger, climbing higher, higher, moaning and quivering. My release comes fast and hard as I increase the friction, finally erupting. I'm panting as bursts of light blur my vision.

Eventually, I come down from my euphoric state, finish my shower, and manage to dress myself without any major catastrophe. Hopefully the release will alleviate some of the tension in my body and make it easier to deal with Jackson. I make it to the train without a minute to spare, but at least it's nice and quiet. I'm hoping I can hold on to this blissful feeling all day.

Once I arrive in Manhattan, a new set of emotions overcomes me. Raw strength and determination flow through me. There's something about working in New York City. You can almost feel the power in the streets. It's a breeding ground for success. Being here, working here, living here—it's invigorating.

Standing in front of Jackson's building, I see my reflection in the glass. I certainly look the part. I have on a soft cream blouse tucked into a pair of high-waisted gray suit pants. My long hair is pin straight, my dark brown eyes look soft with only a wisp of mascara, and sheer lip gloss accentuates my lips. My black heels elongate my tiny frame, making me feel tall and bold. With my posture straight, I enter the office, heading up to face Jackson and start kicking ass.

The same sweet receptionist guides me back to the conference room where my initial meeting was held. I'm a little early, so there isn't anyone else in the room yet. I'm removing items from my bag when I hear the door click open. Jackson's voice floats through the space.

"Yes, I'm aware of your opinion on the matter. However, I've made my choice." He sounds irritated.

A second voice responds, but I can't make out what they're saying. It's a female, though, and by her tone I can tell she's trying to make him listen to her.

"I don't care or agree with you," he responds to whatever the comment was. Another long pause as I strain to hear her response. The door inches open a little more.

"Well, Ms. Carlson, it's a good thing I'm the CEO."

Shit! Piper! My blissful mood drains away.

The door opens and Jackson steps aside to let Piper come in first. She looks up and grimaces when she notices me standing here. Jackson enters. It's as if the world stops moving. His presence would cause the energy in any room to shift, but I can't help wondering if I feel it more intensely than everyone else. It's—he's—intoxicating.

He looks over at me and smiles. "Good morning, Catherine."

"Good morning, Mr. Cole." I smile and look at Piper. "Good morning, Piper. Nice to see you in a

color other than nude." The last thing I wish for her
is a good morning. However, pleasantries are necessary, and I refuse to let her to take yet another
thing from me. But I allow myself the small dig.

She snorts and rolls her eyes.

Bitch.

Jackson doesn't notice her catty behavior. He
sits at the head of the table with Piper to his left
and me in the chair on his right. He's so close. I can
feel the heat radiating from him.

"Okay, let's get started," Jackson says.

We spend the next hour debating and discuss-
ing the best way to present the soon-to-be-released
makeup line. Piper tries to undermine my opinion
at every turn, but I hold my ground. Jackson sits
back and interjects only when he feels the need. It
seems more like a volleyball game than a meeting.
After another hour, she's finally done arguing and
agrees with my vision on how to get the company
on track.

"Well, ladies, I think we're about done here. It's
been rather entertaining." Jackson chuckles and
stands, gathering his papers as he does.

Piper leans over to him, trying to keep her voice
down. "Mr. Cole, I really think we should talk pri-
vately about our options."

A flash of irritation cross his face as he gruffly
replies, "Piper, again, I'm well aware of your opinion and the answer is no." Jackson meets my eyes
and grins.

I sigh and flush with embarrassment.

"Mr. Cole—"

He raises his hand to stop me. "I asked you to
call me Jackson."

Piper stands there slack-jawed with her arms

crossed.

"Yes, sorry. Jackson, I've arranged everything for Friday's trip—"

"My secretary will send you the details. I've already arranged to have a car pick you up and take you to the airport. You won't need to worry about anything." He tucks his materials under his arm and pushes in his chair to leave. As he approaches the door he stops, turns to me, and smirks. "Expect to have dinner while we're there." He winks and exits.

Dinner. Of course. I'm never going to avoid this man. He's going to take full advantage of our time together in Virginia. There is no escaping him. If he's persistent enough, I may not be strong enough to resist him. I'm barely hanging on as it is. Except there's the small problem that he's my client, and I could lose everything I've worked for if anything happens between us.

A cough breaks me from my thoughts and I realize I've been staring at the door. I look to see Piper glaring at me. "Are you dating him?" she asks in a condescending tone.

"Excuse me?" I stand so I'm eye level with her, looking at her incredulously. Surely she isn't talking to me like that.

"I asked if you were dating Jackson Cole." She walks toward me and places her hands on the table, leaning in. She raises her eyebrows, waiting for my response.

My eyes widen at her challenge. I glare right back at her with unadulterated hate. "You're insane—and a whore, but we'll revisit that in a minute. Are you seriously talking to me right now?" I'm seething. My body is shaking at her asinine question. She slept with my fiancé and now she's going to stand here and give me shit? I don't think so.

"I'm just surprised, Catherine. Is that how you beat out Neil for this account? *His* numbers were flawless. He deserves to be here, not you," Piper states, tilting her head to the side as she narrows her eyes accusingly.

"Well I'm glad you think so because Neil stole *my* figures!" I step closer to her, radiating anger. First, she has the nerve to insinuate that I won the account because I'm sleeping with Jackson. Then she brings up Neil's stellar figures. "I seriously can't believe you have the balls to address me, let alone accuse me of something. It's none of your business—any of it—but for the record, I got this account because *I'm* the better choice!"

She huffs and rolls her eyes. "Well I guess *I* was the right choice for Neil."

"Wow, Piper, you want to go there? Good, have him! After seeing what he's capable of, I'm glad we're done." I clench my hands, desperate to punch something or someone, like the blond bitch in front of me.

Her eyes flash and venom fills her voice. "You think you're so fucking smart, don't you? You think I give a shit about what *you* think or what you're happy about?" She steps toward me, grinning. "I fucked your fiancé for four months and you had no idea."

My hand flies to my throat. "Four months?" The words slip from my mouth. My stomach plummets and I grab onto the chair for support. Four months of Neil sleeping with her and then sleeping with me? I'm such a fool. I thought it was a one-time thing, not an affair! My chin quivers as I drown in pain and betrayal, but I won't let her see me cry.

"Not so smart now, huh?" A victorious smile spreads from one cheek to the other, and I want to slap it off her arrogant face. That's all it takes for the tightly pulled thread of my control to break. What the actual fuck? Where I was upset a few moments ago, right now my blood is boiling. I won't break down any further in front of this piece of trash.

"I'm not going to stand here and listen to your shit. The only thing you should be saying to me is, 'I'm sorry,' not this bullshit. You went after a man that wasn't yours! You were my friend, or at least I thought you were. Then you try to give me crap about going after Jackson? Fuck you! I'm done here."

"Well I'm not done yet," she sneers.

There's no way this bitch is going to call the shots. "I have nothing left to say to you, and I couldn't give two shits about whatever you want." I take a step toward her and smother the urge to choke her. "I won. I got the account and you got Neil—which was the best fucking thing that could've happened to me."

She lifts her bag and turns to me, her eyes narrowed. "Just so you know, Neil came to me. Not the other way around. I didn't need to go after him. He obviously wasn't happy with what he was getting at home. I think that says something, don't you?" She raises her brow and takes a few steps toward the door. Without looking back, she says, "I wonder how long until Jackson gets bored with you." Then she shrugs and strides out of the office. I guess she couldn't resist digging the knife in a little deeper.

I'm crazy to think I have any shot with a man like Jackson, not that I'm trying for anything with him anyway. If I don't get out of here now, I'm going to break down. I know I shouldn't let her affect me, but she managed to remind me of every insecurity I've ever had in a matter of five minutes.

I grab my belongings and rush out the door only to crash into a hard chest. All my papers fly out of my bag and flutter around me. As they settle, I let out a sardonic laugh and hear a deep, familiar chuckle, letting me know I've run into Jackson yet again. Will the humiliation ever end? I look up and see his captivating eyes change as he takes me in. I haven't had a chance to school my features, so I have no idea what he's seeing right now. He's close enough that I can feel his chest rise and fall. I can feel his warmth. Neither of us has spoken. He hasn't said anything obnoxious. He's staring at me inquisitively.

"Are you okay?" he asks in a soft voice as he crouches down to collect the papers. His concern makes my heart ache. "What was that about?"

Oh God, did he hear what Piper said? I clear my throat, bend down across from him, and try to force the conversation with Piper—and all the emotions that came along with it—out of my mind. "Yes, I'm fine. It was nothing I can't handle," I say as I pick up the last paper.

His penetrating eyes lock onto mine and he cocks his head to the side, trying to determine if I'm telling the truth. Giving me a half smile, he silently hands me the papers he gathered and we both stand. I stuff them back in my bag and return my gaze to Jackson's. Deciding to break the awkward silence, I speak first. "Well, thank you for helping me. I should go."

"No thanks needed." He looks like he wants to

say more but is debating internally. Without another word, he grabs my bag off my shoulder and places his hand on the small of my back to guide me. "I'll walk you out."

When we arrive at the front desk, he hands me back my bag and smiles warmly. "I'll see you in a few days."

I grab his arm, stopping him in his tracks. I'm not sure why—I couldn't let him walk away. Quickly, I try to think of something to say to justify my behavior. "I ... I meant to ask you about ..." I stumble over my words, feeling more and more foolish. "You know what? It's fine." I smile awkwardly, hoping he lets it go.

Jackson leans forward, dropping his voice so only I can hear. His eyes give away nothing, and I can only imagine the myriad of emotions my own eyes show. "I was having a hard time walking away from you too." He leans back and grins at me as his words float into my brain.

"Yeah," I say breathlessly. Wait, what? That isn't what I wanted to say! Dammit! I had a great come back and *that* is what comes out of my mouth? Shoot me now, please.

He raises his eyebrow and gives me a full mega-watt smile, enjoying my discomfort. "This trip is going to be fun. I'll see you soon, Catherine." His voice drips with the promise of things to come.

I smother my groan and decide to try to play it smart and casual. "Good-bye, Jackson." I turn and walk to the elevator, hoping he's watching as I sway my hips a little more than normal. I look over my shoulder, smiling when I see his eyes are exactly where I want them to be.

chapter
nine

"Ugh! Where the hell is my black dress?" I yell out my bedroom door. Ashton is sitting on the couch laughing at something on TV.

"Stressed much?" she replies from the other room.

"I need your help! Get your ass off the couch!" I say in my pouty voice and stomp my feet like a twelve-year-old. I need her to calm me down and pack for me. It's been four days since I last saw Jackson. I've gotten almost nothing accomplished because every time I sit to start something, I find myself daydreaming of his face or imagining his lips leaning down to kiss me. Lost in yet another fantasy of Jackson, I sigh and hear Ashton laugh again, only this time she's in my doorway, staring at me.

"Lost in Jacksonland again, are we?" She snorts and heads into my room. "You got it bad."

"Shut up. I do not!"

"Really?" Ashton tilts her head up and taps her finger on her chin as if she's debating something. "Well if that's true, then where's his business card? I could always call him since I'm single." She shrugs, gauging my reaction.

I glare at her. "You wouldn't dare."

"Hmmm. You said he's hot though, right?" She grins before continuing, "I *really* would like to see for myself. Who knows? Maybe we'll hit it off."

"You're so full of shit. You wouldn't do that to me." I turn and look in my drawer for the damn black dress that's not in my closet.

"If you're not interested, why should it matter?" In the mirror I see her raise an eyebrow, goading me.

"I'm not interested, but that doesn't mean I want him hanging around here." I know she'll never buy it, but that's all I've got.

"I'll make sure not to bring him around. I know he's your client and all." I turn and look at her smiling face. She's waiting for me to either have an epic tantrum or call her on it.

Fine. Two can play at this game. "The card is on the dresser," I walk over to the card Jackson placed in my hand last week. "Go ahead and give him a call. I'll be right here." I hold it out to Ashton, willing her to take it, hoping she doesn't.

She grabs the card and reaches for the phone. She types the numbers and smiles the whole time as I gape at her. I can't believe she's calling him. I know what I said, but I never thought she'd actually do it. She knows me better than that. I'm about to say something when I look closer and realize she has *my* phone in her hand. I leap over the pile of clothes on the floor and lunge for the phone. She falls back on the bed, laughing hysterically as I claw my way up and rip it out of her hand. "You bitch!" I try to contain my laughter as I scroll through the call log to see if she dialed. "I'm gonna kill you! Thank God you didn't freaking call him!"

"Nope, I wouldn't call him. That would be *sooo* embarrassing." She stands and heads into my closet.

Just as I'm about to go back to packing, my phone vibrates in my hand. I look down and open the text message from a number I don't recognize.

Unknown: Can't wait to see you either.

Dread seeps through my veins as I grab the business card and check the number. Sure enough, it's Jackson. She's dead!

"Ashton! You've got to be kidding me! You texted him?" I exclaim.

She peeks her head out from the closet, smiling. "I said I didn't *call* him. Never said anything about other forms of communication." She giggles and goes back into the closet.

I take a deep breath, trying to calm down. *Okay, I can handle this.* I won't respond, and I'll play it off when I see him—although, I might be in a jail cell instead of meeting Jackson tomorrow. I think a judge would understand why I had to murder my best friend. I sink onto my bed and put my pillow over my head, groaning.

Ashton comes over and nudges my leg. I pull the pillow down and glare at her in response. "You're being a drama queen. Look at the message I sent him before you get all stabby." She starts folding clothes and putting them in my suitcase.

I look at the outgoing text message.

Me: Ready for the trip. See you at 8.

Whatever. She should have never sent him a damn text message. Now he probably thinks I sit around thinking about him. He wouldn't be far off in that assumption, but I don't exactly want him to *know* that. Damn Ashton and her stupid interfering. I look over to find her rummaging through my underwear drawer. I snap at her, "What the hell are you doing in there?" I rush over to close the drawer.

"If you're getting naked, you need proper panties." She smiles mischievously.

"There will be no naked!" I sigh and grab out a few pairs of underwear.

"Sure, Cat. Keep telling yourself that. This guy wants in your pants and you can't even try to tell me you're not dying to get in his. So embrace your inner temptress, get some cute panties, and get on it ... or under it." She winks and runs out of my room before I can throw something at her.

Not even ten seconds later she pops her head in my room, giggling. "Oh, your black dress is in the bag. You can thank me later," she says. Then she runs out again.

Sure enough, I look in the suitcase and find my black dress along with one of my negligées. Ashton!

My suitcase is bouncing noisily down the foyer stairs at our apartment complex. I'm exhausted and crabby after being completely unhappy with pretty much anything I had in my closet. Since I have absolutely no idea what we're going to be doing in Virginia, I packed for any scenario. Trying to pick the perfect travel clothes for today, I went for comfortable and cute. I'm wearing a black and white sundress with my black flats. I don't know why I thought a dress would be a good option for being on a plane and going through security, but it doesn't matter now. I'm ten minutes late and don't have time to change. As I make my way outside, my eyes widen in surprise. Jackson is in front of my building, leaning against the door of a black town car sedan and smiling at my reaction.

He walks forward, takes the handle of my bag, and leans toward me, handing me a cup of coffee. "Good morning, Catherine. You look happy to see me."

I groan and roll my eyes, taking the coffee out of his hand. He lets out a deep chuckle at my reaction and hands my bag to the driver.

"Good morning, Jackson." I turn and walk to the other side of the car, open the door, and whisper under my breath, "Yeah, oh so happy." I hear him exhale in a short burst, almost like he's laughing. I look back to see him smiling from ear to ear. Of course he heard me.

He slides his big body into the seat next to me, taking over all the space in the car. We're close. So close that his warmth radiates into me and his cologne fills my nose. He leans down, reaching for something in his bag, and his fingers brush the bare skin of my leg. Tingles shoot up my thighs at the contact. It's too much for me.

I scoot over a little more toward the window. Even though I'd love nothing more than to sit on his lap, I try to avoid touching him. My walls are going to come crumbling down really fast if I don't keep some distance. I look out the window and sip my coffee. Smiling, I glance at him, surprised that he somehow managed to make it the way I like it. I was prepared for it to be black, not light and sweet.

"How did you know?" I lift the cup.

"I have my ways." He grins and turns his attention to the file folder on his lap.

I'm sure he does. I smile reply, "Well, thanks."

"You're welcome." He doesn't glance up and I'm a little disappointed. He has this uncanny way of knowing my thoughts—maybe he's trying to keep his distance so I'm not uncomfortable?

I grab my iPhone and go through my alerts. We have about a thirty-minute drive to the airport.

I notice the voicemail that I've been avoiding—my mother's. She's called eight times, but I keep putting off returning the call. She frustrates me, and lately I don't have the patience to deal with it. I glance at Jackson. He's engrossed in whatever he's reading, so I decide to listen to it.

"Hello, Catherine. It's Mom. I hope all is well." She pauses and I can almost hear her bristle. Her voice is filled with frustration. "I've tried to call you about ten times now, but I guess you're ignoring me again. I'm not sure how to say this, so I'm just going to come out with it." She lets out a deep sigh and goes on, softer now. "I got a letter from a lawyer. They sent notice that your presence is required next week at their office. They need you to—" Another long pause. "—settle your father's estate. He passed away a week ago." She sounds sad, and I can hear her taking short breaths as if she's crying. "You were listed as his beneficiary and this was your last known address. I'm so sorry, sweetie. Please call me. I love you." The line goes dead.

I drop the phone in my lap. The emotions swarming inside of me are jumbled, all over the place. I haven't spoken to my father in almost twenty years. I don't know why I feel sad. I hate him. He walked away. He deserted me—never called, never cared—so why do I feel like I'm going to cry? What do I do now? I'm supposed to go through his affairs, settle his estate—I don't even know where the hell he's lived all this time. I drop my head in my hands and struggle to catch my breath. I'm so angry. I moved on. I forgot about him. I got over the fact that I wouldn't have someone to walk me down the aisle or dance with me at my wedding. I don't need him or want any part of him, so why do I feel such utter despair? The tightness in my chest has me gasping for air, shaking. I roll down the window frantically—I need air.

Jackson places his hand on my arm and I snap my head up. I kind of forgot about him there beside me. He's staring at me. He squeezes my arm and his eyes soften as if he can sense my panic. "Are you okay?" His voice is concerned.

I shake my head subtly up and down. I don't think I can speak. I avert my eyes, looking at my hands grasped tightly in my lap.

"Catherine," he says softly, looking alarmed by whatever emotions are showing on my face. He reaches for my hand and places his gently over mine. I can't look at him. I need to keep it together. I should have never listened to that damn voice-mail. Who tells someone their parent died on a voicemail? Another way my mother and her self-ish ways come to light. She could've called again, could've called Taylor—anything other than leave a voicemail.

I need to explain this to him. I have to say some-thing. I look over and whisper, "My father died."

His eyes widen in shock before changing to sympathy. "I'm so sorry," he says, and his sincerity breaks my carefully constructed wall.

"It's fine. I mean, we weren't close. I just—" My chin begins to tremble. I can't speak anymore.

My heart is aching. All these years, all this time—it's all over and I'll never get the answers I so desperately needed. Why did he really leave me?

Tears blur my vision. I close my eyes and try to hang on to the anger I had moments ago.

Jackson must sense I'm about to fall apart because he leans in, puts his arm around me, and pulls me to his side. I try to resist, but he's stronger and grips tighter. Not wanting to fight him, I give in, allowing myself this one moment to accept the comfort he's offering. His warmth cocoons me as I curl into his chest and slip my arm around his stomach. He holds me so snug, keeping me together while my mind spins. He does nothing to move me, just tenderly strokes the side of my arm. My heart is pounding and my breathing is shallow, both from the whirlwind of emotions and his closeness. I start to pull away, trying to put some distance between us, but Jackson refuses to relax his hold on me. I have to admit I feel so small and safe in his embrace. Closing my eyes, I lose myself in his touch. I want to cry, but the tears won't come. I focus on the steady sound of his heartbeat. So sure, so strong. The thrumming anchors me and keeps me from falling apart. We stay like this the rest of the car ride, neither of us speaking as I try to understand the numbness I'm feeling.

When we arrive at the airport, Jackson shifts slightly and I sit up. I look out the window and realize we're at Teterboro, which means we're flying on a private jet. I turn to look at Jackson, confused and embarrassed, when he puts his hand on my cheek, softly cradling it. "Are you going to be okay? We can cancel the trip if you need to."

"No!" I say loudly and he startles, dropping his hand from my face.

"I'm serious. You need to deal with—" His brows draw together before he runs his hands down his face.

"No, it's fine." I don't want to deal with any of it. I'm not going to run to take care of a man who never cared enough to take care of me. I take a deep breath and move my hand, placing it tentatively on his. "Please, I don't want to reschedule the trip. I promise, I'm really okay."

He stays quiet for a minute. I'm praying he believes me. Jackson pinches the bridge of his nose, closing his eyes. He blows out a long breath, exits the car, and walks over to speak to the driver. My heart can't take this pain. I hang my head, creating a veil with my dark brown hair so he can't see me falling apart. I need this trip. I want to escape and not go back and have to deal with my dead father who abandoned me. I put him and all the shit he did to me in a box—then I took his box and shoved it away. I have no desire to dust it off and open it again.

I hear my car door open and look up. Jackson is standing there, hand extended, with a sad smile on his face. He tilts his head toward the runway and says, "Come on, we've got a plane to catch."

I place my hand in his and allow him to help me from the car. "Thank you, Jackson." My eyes are soft and my voice is full of emotion. I remove my hand after giving his a small squeeze and head toward the trunk to collect my bag. Jackson walks silently behind me. I've probably scared him with my almost breakdown.

We both reach for my bag's handle at the same time. I giggle as he swats my hand away. I look over at him. His eyes are bright and glossy and his mouth is in a half grin. "I love your laugh."

The way he says it makes my heart feel lighter.

"Thanks," I murmur and look away.

Jackson clears his throat and says, "Now, let's head to Virginia." His smile grows as he tilts his head to the side. "You know where that is, right?" He winks and grabs my bag. There's the smug bastard I know.

"Yes, I knew where it was before too." I smile, thankful for the change in topic.

"Sure you did."

"You know I have a master's degree, right? I'm pretty sure I had a class or two where we discussed the fifty states." I huff, pretending to be irritated with him. In reality, I'm silently awed by how quickly he brought me back.

"Hey, it's not my fault you were confused the first time."

"Gah!" I throw my hands up in mock frustration.

Jackson stops at the bottom steps of the plane, shifting his weight back and forth. My eyes dart between the contemplative look on his face and the plane—I hope he's not going to cancel. As if sensing my distress, he places both hands on my shoulders and waits for me to look at him. Our eyes meet and I can't look away. My breathing stops. My heart accelerates. His eyes are clouded with emotion. For me? For my loss? I can't tell. He looks sad, and it rocks me to my core. Slowly, he pulls me toward him and wraps his arms around me. I return his embrace as he rubs my back. We stand there in each other's arms, giving and receiving comfort from one another. My news was unexpected and so was Jackson's response, but I don't mind it.

I clear my throat and I swear I feel Jackson kiss the top of my head, but it's so light I can't be sure.

We break apart and I smile. He reaches for my face but drops his hand before touching me, frowning as his eyes empty of all the emotion present just seconds before. Without a word, he turns and ascends the stairs to the plane. I take a deep breath and follow, praying I can keep it together and remain professional. The lines are blurring, so I need to redraw them and stay on the appropriate side.

chapter ten

The plane is breathtaking. It has plush leather seats and a couch against the right wall. There's a wet bar at the back wall and another room in the rear of the plane. I'm assuming it's an office or a bedroom, but I have no intention of finding out. The décor is beautiful. Done in cream and a rich blue, it's striking and regal. Very fitting for the man I'm traveling with.

Jackson walks forward from the bar area looking calm and collected. He's back to being professional. "Make yourself comfortable. It's only about a two-hour flight."

"Is this your plane?" I ask, still looking around the cabin as I sit in one of the captain chairs.

"Yes, I fly back and forth from New York to Virginia a lot. Purchasing a company jet made sense." He looks at the seat across the aisle and then turns and sits in the seat next to me. Why does he insist on sitting so damn close?

"Oh, I didn't know you visited the facility that much."

He looks up, shifting uncomfortably in his seat. "I don't. Well, I didn't. I have a second company, which is why I spent a lot of time in Virginia. Plus, I was stationed there when I was on active duty, so I get to visit the team when I'm there."

"You served?" I never would have thought he

was prior military. He looks so young. Finding out he owns a second company throws me as well.

Jackson straightens in his seat and lifts his head, his eyes locking on mine. One side of his mouth lifts revealing that adorable dimple. When he speaks, his voice is laced with pride. "Yes, I served eight years in the Navy."

I smile at this remarkable man, who's accomplished so much, and realize I know nothing about him. I guess this explains the hero complex. A small giggle escapes me, and I slap my hand over my mouth. *Crap!*

He looks at me with amusement. "Why is that funny?"

I smile. "It's not. I'm just laughing at how you seem to like to save people." Great, now I sound stupid.

He lets out a short laugh. "Yeah, well there's a lot about me you don't know." He nudges my arm.

I smirk and shake my head at him. Out of nowhere the plane jerks and I freeze. A sudden burst of anxiety hits me and I grab the arms of the chair, white-knuckling it. He notices, of course, and places a hand on my arm. "Are you afraid of flying?" he asks. His sultry voice does nothing for my nerves.

"N-No," I barely get the word out. My hands are sweating and my heart is pounding as he removes his hand. I've flown hundreds of times. I don't mind it at all, but I've never flown on a private plane. Or flown next to a man who seems to affect me so much.

He leans closer. His clean soap and cologne smell is so hypnotic, I can't stop myself from taking a deep breath. The heat from his body is everywhere, and he's not even touching me. "Don't worry, Catherine, you're safe with me. Just close your eyes."

I glance at him as the plane begins to move again. "I'll be fine. I'm being silly." How many more ways am I going to embarrass myself with this man?

"Relax and close your eyes," he says softly but with an air of authority.

"When did you get so bossy?" I close my eyes and smile, hearing a rustling before I sense him shifting closer.

"Wouldn't you like to know?" he replies, humor dancing in his voice. "Now, stop talking and just breathe."

I take a deep breath and start to sing to myself. My father used to sing this song to me at night whenever I had bad dreams. The lyrics soothed me. Throughout my life, I've always sung that song when I needed strength, even though it was associated with him. Now is no different. My father's voice, singing about me being his one and only sunshine, echoes through my ears and floods my mind. If only it'd been true.

I repeat the song over and over as Jackson's fingers graze my arm. Abruptly, the contact I'd been enjoying vanishes. I shiver from the loss, terrified to open my eyes. What if I'm alone again?

"You're safe now." His warm voice blankets over me.

I'm far from safe, but somehow during that brief moment we managed to become airborne and I didn't even notice. My lids are heavy, so I relax into my seat and think about my morning with Jackson. Within a matter of minutes he put me at ease. He cared for me when he saw my distress. How easy it would be to fall for him. To give myself to someone who looks out for others before himself. But at what cost to my heart? Somewhere before unconsciousness I realize—it's not the plane I should be afraid of, it's the man next to me.

"Catherine..."

No! I don't want to wake up. Damn Ashton and her nudging.

"Catherine." I hear a throaty chuckle. "You're adorable when you sleep."

What?

"Come on. Time to get up. We're in Virginia."

Virginia?

I groan and open my eyes to see Jackson smiling and leaning over me with both hands on the arm rests. Damn, I'd love waking up to that face every day. I rub my eyes, realizing I slept the entire flight. Between the lack of sleep last night and the events of this morning, it's no wonder I passed out. I try to move but he has me caged between his muscular arms, a huge grin on his face. I clear my throat and look at his hand, hoping my silent cue will register. However, he only seems more amused.

"Could you let me up please?"

He leans back but not enough to give me the space I need. I glare at him until he takes a step back, crosses his arms over his chest, and smiles widely at me.

Now standing, I become extremely self-conscious as he stares at me. "What? Do I have something on my face?" I wipe my face, smooth my hair, and inspect my clothes.

He inches forward, dropping his arms to his

sides. His eyes tease me as they travel the length of my body. "Did you know you talk in your sleep?" His voice is full of mischief.

No. Oh no! I'm aware of this, but I've never really thought too much about it. Though, Ashton does make fun of me all the time for the things that come out of my mouth at night. Pink paints my cheeks as I cover my face with my hands. I open my fingers a tiny bit so I can see through them. "Please tell me I didn't say anything embarrassing," I say hesitantly.

Jackson tugs at my hands, pulling them away from my face. His calloused thumbs are rubbing back and forth against my wrists. Taking a deep breath, he gives a small smile. "You said 'Daddy' a few times."

"Oh." I give a deflated huff. "I guess that makes sense ... with everything today." I look down to where he's still holding my arms. I shift my weight and stare at the floor.

Sensing my discomfort, he drops my wrists. "I'm sorry again," he says. And again, I know he is. I can hear the honesty in his voice. It's touching but disconcerting at the same time. I can't afford to form an emotional connection with this man. The physical one is bad enough.

"I know." I smile. "I'm excited to get to work and see the plant," I say in a polite tone, switching topics. I don't want to discuss my father or anything personal, and I'm not going to think about all the issues waiting for me back in New Jersey. There's business to handle while I'm on this trip, and that is going to be my priority. In the last twenty years, my father never once made me a priority—I'm not about to make him one now.

"We'll head straight there. Then we'll have

dinner, since I know you're excited for that too."

"Too?" I straighten my back and snap my eyes to his.

"You might have said something about that." He laughs. "And a few other things," he adds as an afterthought. Jackson turns and cleans up his papers.

Is he serious? I bite my lip and hesitate before asking my next question. "What are you talking about? Did I say anything else?"

He tilts his head to the side, grinning, and then shrugs. What the hell does the shrug mean? I have to know. He grabs his bag and moves past me. I'm stunned, silently praying all I did was mumble.

As he walks by, I grab his arm to stop him. I try for nonchalance, hoping that maybe his good-humored side will play along. My stomach is doing somersaults as I think of all the possible things I could've said in my sleep. In the short time we've known each other I've dreamed of him so often—if my words were anything close to sounding like the two very erotic dreams I've already had, I may die.

His eyes are playful when he looks at me. "Something you want to know?" he asks, raising one eyebrow.

"Me? No." I smile and look contrite.

"Are you sure? You look rather curious." He smirks and pushes my hair off my face.

I laugh, hoping to get him to tell me what I said. "Jackson, I thought you were into saving girls from disastrous situations. You know, a soldier and all—"

He cuts me off. "No, I was a SEAL, not a soldier. Big difference," he says as he puffs his chest out.

"Okay ... SEAL, then. Didn't know the term

meant anything." I tilt my head, smiling and batting my eyelashes. "Anyway, don't you want to tell me whatever it is you think you know?"

He smiles at my blatant attempt at persuasion. Dropping his bag, he says, "Catherine, you don't really think I'm going to give up that easy, do you?" He grins and takes a step closer. I notice his Adam's apple bobbing as he debates his next words. "I'm like a vault, and it's going to take a whole lot more than those gorgeous eyes batting at me to crack this one," he says huskily.

I take a step back and smile. "So there *is* something to spill, then?"

He laughs loudly and steps back. "Come on. We've got places to go."

"Anyone ever tell you you're a frustrating man?"

He taps his finger on his chin as if deep in thought. "Nope, most people find me endearing and charming."

I snort. "Are these people on your payroll by any chance?"

"Maybe, but then again you're on my payroll and seem to disagree with the consensus." He smiles and heads toward the cabin door.

"Good thing I don't work for you. You're just a client, so I don't have to agree."

He stops and turns toward me suggestively. "Good thing I have three days to change your mind about that, then." He winks, leaving me speechless as we exit the plane.

chapter eleven

*J*ackson and I don't speak much in the car. Both of us are looking at the new sales figures he received from his secretary when we landed. The numbers look promising and show a shift in the market. I look through a few more emails on my phone, not really paying much attention to where we're going. I shoot a quick text to Ashton, letting her know we've landed safely. About fifteen minutes later, we pull up to a large office building that's all windows.

I look over at the Cole Security Forces sign and I'm suddenly confused. Clearly, this isn't the production facility. I glance at Jackson. He's still engrossed in the figures, so he hasn't noticed we've stopped.

I clear my throat. "Jackson, where are we?"

He looks at the building and back at me. "This is my other company. I run a security force that has contracts all over the world. I need to run in and show face for about ten minutes. Would you like to come in?" His eyes shift back and forth and he sounds genuinely nervous.

Well there's a surprise. The man owns a cosmetics company and a security company—talk about polar opposites. My eyes widen at his admission and then I recover, smiling softly. "If you'd like me to, sure."

We both exit the car and head over to the entrance. Jackson places his hand on my shoulder as he opens the door. Just the small touch sends me into overdrive. I tilt my head and give him a small grin as I enter the office.

It's nothing like Raven Cosmetics. Where that office is almost feminine, this one is modern and masculine with clean lines and distinctive colors. The floors are gray concrete and the walls are cream and royal blue, which makes sense based on the décor from the plane. In the center of the room, there are two big cubicle sections that each seats five people. The left wall is taken up by four large offices with huge mahogany doors.

Jackson clears his throat as we make our way into the space. Three guys stand and smile when they see him. A few other guys stick their hands up, acknowledging his presence, but continue to work.

"Hey, Muffin!" A tall, muscular guy with long light blond hair styled back off his face says as he walks over, smiling. He's huge and his arms are covered in tattoos, which might be intimidating if he wasn't so warm and friendly.

"Hey, Mark." He looks happy to see him. The two men shake hands and clap each other on the shoulder. Mark turns his attention to me with wide eyes and a large, appraising grin. Jackson bristles. "Mark, this is Catherine. She's the new publicist for the cosmetics company," he says stiffly.

I smile and extend my hand. "Hi, Mark. Nice to meet you."

Mark shakes my hand. "Catherine, it's a pleasure. Sorry you have to work with this prick all day." He elbows Jackson in the stomach, still smiling at me.

I giggle and reply, "Interesting choice of words. Jackson describes himself a little differently."

Mark raises his eyebrows, looking intrigued by my statement. "Really? What did Muff describe himself as?"

"Muff?" I ask, completely lost.

He howls in laughter. "Yup. That's Jackson! He was always a little soft in the middle,"—he leans in—"whereas the rest of us worked out to keep our amazing physiques." He stands back up, beaming. "So we told him he had a muffin top and that stuck as his call sign."

I giggle at the nickname and glance at Jackson, who's shooting daggers at Mark. Turning back to Mark, I ask, "So what's your call sign?"

Jackson places his hand on the small of my back. "Twilight and I were both on the same team for four years."

"Twilight? Oh, I gotta hear this!" I laugh. Now it's Mark's turn to give Jackson the evil eye.

Jackson chuckles and pulls me against his side. "Notice how pale Mark is?" He asks, jutting his chin out in his direction. I nod. These two are the female versions of Ashton and me. It's comforting, considering the day I've had. "Well he's so white he could glitter in the sun. One of the guys' wives had some kind of obsession with that movie, and he kept telling him he could star in *Twilight*. So Mark here is our glittery, pale Twilight."

Mark scoffs and puffs his chest out. "I'm proud of my name. At least they aren't saying I'm a fat ass. That Edward dude had abs like a rock. Besides, I could kick your ass any day, any time," he challenges, stepping closer to me as he smiles widely.

Jackson raises his chin and addresses me. "He's

an asshole but knows his shit, so he stays—for now." He smirks at Mark. "And anyway, he knows who's in charge. Right, Mark?" I can almost smell the testosterone in the room.

Mark laughs and his eyes crinkle. "Keep thinking that, assclown. You need me too much." He puts his arm around my shoulders, taunting Jackson.

"Right, remember who signs your paycheck." Jackson raises a brow.

"Anyway, Catherine, this fucknugget gives you any problems, you call me and I'll kick his ass."

I instantly love this man. He flashes me that ever-present smile one last time before heading back over to his desk. Jackson grips my hip, grimacing and mumbling something under his breath.

Jackson guides me over to an office and flips on the light before closing the door. It's large and airy. There are photos all over the wall and I walk over to get a closer look. There are a few of Jackson, Mark, and some other guys drinking and laughing. A few of him on a boat with some friends, looking carefree and happy. My stomach clenches at the next one. He's standing in camouflage with a huge gun slung across his body, a menacing look on his face. He looks scary yet unbelievably sexy.

"You know ..." I say, turning, and then I gasp as he startles me.

I was so lost in the photos I didn't even realize he was behind me. "What?" He smiles.

Once my heart settles and I can speak again, I remember what I was going to say. "You looked pretty nice in uniform."

"Nice?" he asks, arching a brow.

"Cute."

"Cute?" Apparently this is even worse than nice.

I look back at the photo, trying to figure out what he seems bothered over. "What? Is cute not a good word?"

I feel him move in behind me, and I struggle not to lean back into him.

"Cute is for babies and puppies. I can think of at least ten other words to better describe me," he says against my ear. A shiver races over my body and I have to consciously work to steady my breathing.

I close my eyes and smother the desire burning through me. "Really?" I ask breathily.

"Hot, sexy, buff, handsome, fucking amazing, God's idea of perfect ... I could go on, but any of those would be acceptable," he says, and I can hear the smile in his voice.

I turn to face him. We're so close physically, but in any other way we're miles apart. Still, I'm battling every cell in my body not to give in to him.

"Jackson," I warn.

He takes a small step forward. "I know you're taken, but I can't stop thinking about you."

My brows furrow in confusion. "Taken?"

He looks down at my left hand and brings it up between us. "Aren't you engaged?" He looks from my eyes back down to my hand where my ring used to sit.

"Oh. Ummm, no. Not anymore. We're over and have been for a while." I don't know what to say. I can't tell him the guy was Neil. I start to feel panic rising at how ridiculously screwed-up my life is and how all of this can come crumbling so easily.

"That certainly changes things." His eyes blaze with unspoken promises.

"Changes things? No. It doesn't change the fact

that you're my client." Or how I'm a mess over the constant screw-ups from the men in my life. And it definitely doesn't change how I know with every ounce of my being that Jackson would ruin me if I let him in.

"Catherine, I can't stay away from you." His voice penetrates through my thoughts, straight to my heart, and it takes me a second to find my resolve.

He cups my face in his hands, holding me, forcing me to look at him. "Jackson, I'm not with anyone, but this isn't a good—"

Before I can finish my sentence his mouth is on mine. All at once, I'm surrounded by heat, strength, and power—all that is Jackson. The sparks I felt previously are nothing compared to the inferno raging between us right now. I close my eyes and lose myself in the feel of his mouth on mine. My chest presses against him as he pushes me back against the wall and tilts my head to the side. His tongue is against my lips, begging for entrance. I sigh, which is all the permission he needs. Our tongues swirl together as we kiss with fervor. Lifting my hands, I grip his hips and pull him closer. Wanting to touch his body, I trace my hands across the muscles of his taut back, over his hard arms, across the ridges of his abs. The way he feels against my lips, against my body, against my fingers … it's incredible. I could kiss him forever—his mouth is heaven. Never have I been kissed like this. Jackson shifts and lifts my head to gain better access, and I willingly give it to him. Pushing and pulling each other, trying to get closer and closer, I moan, causing Jackson to break the kiss.

He rests his head against my forehead as we

both struggle to catch our breath. I can feel the shift in him as he sighs loudly. "Fuck! I'm sorry." He shakes his head. "I shouldn't have kissed you." He leans back and looks over toward his desk.

I snap my head up, wounded and embarrassed by his sudden rejection. His words, the regret in his voice, and his now distant behavior has me in knots. My stomach flops and I feel sick. He kissed me, and now he's acting like it was a mistake. I don't want to want him, but I do. As much as I want to fight what I feel for him, I'm not sure I'm strong enough. But maybe I don't need to be after all. Maybe my concern was all for nothing. His aloof attitude stings, but I shove down my feelings. I can't let him know he's hurt me. I won't let another man destroy me.

I move over to the side of the room and take a deep breath. "Jackson, it's fine. I should never have crossed that line." I don't know what line I actually crossed, but I'll take the blame. He's my client, and the last thing I need is for him to fire me. Besides, it will only be a matter of time before he sees the real me and decides he's better off. My mind is spinning as the pain of his rejection swells. My God, how many times will I do this to myself? You'd think by now I'd realize that *every* man in my life leaves. They take and take and then I'm left cleaning up the pieces, praying next time will be different.

He moves toward me and stops suddenly. He swallows hard and rubs his hand over his face. He looks sad and angry. "You did nothing wrong!" he snaps and I take a step back. He lifts his head to the ceiling and shakes his head. "You've had a lot of shit happen today. I didn't mean to ..." He takes a step forward with his hands by his side, clenched into tight fists. I'm not sure why he's so angry about it. I thought he enjoyed it, but I guess not.

I put my hands up to stop him—I don't want to hear it. "Please, just stop. Let's forget about it, okay? I'm a lot stronger than you think. I've dealt with a lifetime of this." I turn away and look out the window. I don't trust myself to say any more right now.

"Catherine, please ..." he pleads. I hear him step forward but he doesn't say anything else. It feels like five minutes have passed when I feel his hands on my shoulders. I shrug him off and turn to face him. The look in his eyes stops the hostility I was feeling. He looks devastated, torn. He swallows and his voice is soft, laced with pain. "I've wanted and yet not wanted to kiss you for the last two weeks. It isn't you, I promise. I don't want to take advantage of the grief you're feeling."

I don't know what to believe. "Okay, let's just call it what it was—a mistake. It won't happen again."

"I'm not sure about that—"

"I am. It won't happen aga—"

"It won't happen again on the day you lost a parent," he says with a small smile. "Don't misunderstand what I'm saying. I've been there. I know the pain you're feeling. Okay?" He takes a deep breath and looks at the wall of pictures, staring at one in particular. There are so many, I'm not sure which one he's looking at. However, he was a SEAL—maybe he's lost friends? My heart breaks for him at the thought, and I want to soothe his pain.

"I'm sorry you've lost someone."

"That's not for today. Let's get out of here." He smiles and walks over to his desk, grabbing some papers. I walk back over to the wall, looking at the photo of Jackson—so strong and lethal. A chill runs down my spine. Jackson comes around to where I'm standing and looks at the photo. He's close enough that his arm and chest are touching my back, and I know he positioned himself there on purpose. Every time he touches me I lose the ability to think clearly. I step away from him, trying to keep some space between us.

"You done ogling my picture?" he asks.

My jaw drops at his sudden teasing. "I wasn't ogling. Maybe I was staring at Mark's picture." I lift my eyebrows and challenge him.

"I'm sure he would love that." He smirks and turns to head out of the office.

Before we can leave, Jackson's called over to handle an issue. I meet a few more people in the office as he's dealing with things. Once he finishes, we say our good-byes and Jackson assures them that he'll be back in the office a few times this trip to work over some contracts. Mark and a guy named Ski joke with him, telling him he can only come back if I come with him. He laughs and tells them he'll think about it. I'm captivated by the way he handles two companies—companies that are on such opposite spectrums. It's obvious the security company is his passion and evidently he's good at it, considering some of what I've heard here today.

Once we're back in the car, it appears all the joking and normalcy is gone. He seems distracted. I give him the quiet I assume he's seeking and try to focus on my own emotions. I press my hands to my lips. I swear I can still feel him. I can smell his cologne on my skin. The car is filled with tense energy. I want to say something but I can't. I know what his mouth tastes like, feels like. I'm fighting every part of my self-control to kiss him again. But his small rejection reminds me of the ability he has to hurt me. I don't know if I could handle that again. I promised myself I wouldn't go there until I was sure the guy was worth it. And right now I'm not sure if Jackson is.

chapter twelve

We check into the upscale Ocean View Hotel. It's chic. The concierge informs us that we both have rooms on the fifteenth floor—right next to each other. Thoughts of how close he'll be float through my mind. I enter my room and the sheer beauty of it takes my breath away. There's a four-poster king size bed that faces the ocean. It's adorned with a fluffy white down comforter and luxurious soft blue linens. However, nothing is as beautiful as the wall of windows that opens to a balcony overlooking the waves. I put my bags down and explore the rest of the room. The bathroom is contemporary but still has the beach feel to it with blue and white accents that match the bedroom area. A huge two-person shower all done in marble is on the left, and in front of it is a square white soaker tub. Everything about this hotel is picture-perfect.

The sound of the hotel phone startles me. I rush over, picking up the receiver.

"Hello," I say, a little breathless.

Jackson's rough voice meets my ear. "Hey, I know we were going to leave right away, but I had something come up at the office that I need to handle." He sounds frustrated. I picture him pacing the room and rubbing his hands over his face.

"Sure, that's fine. Take as long as you need."

"Shouldn't be more than two hours. Sorry, but I have to go," he says quickly and hangs up.

I flop onto the king size bed in my beautiful hotel room and stare at the ceiling. I'm dead tired, even after my nap. It's only 2 p.m. but I feel like it's 2 a.m. Jackson exhausts me—hell, my life exhausts me. Instead of taking yet another nap, I decide to take this time and call my mother. I'm still beyond pissed that she left a voicemail, but she's all I have left and I need some answers.

I dial her number and press the send button. After two quick rings, I hear her voice come through the line.

"Oh Cat. Hi, honey." She sounds so happy to hear from me.

"Mom." My reply is clipped and full of sadness. I'm trying to control my emotions.

She huffs. "You got my message, I assume."

"Yes, Mom, it was wonderful hearing that on a voicemail." I roll my eyes even though she can't see it. I need to keep calm. I walk over to the balcony overlooking the ocean and stare out at the horizon.

"Catherine, what was I supposed to do? Huh?" she asks and takes a deep breath. "You don't answer your phone. You don't call me back. I do the best I can with your attitude toward me. If *you* answered your damn phone, I wouldn't have to leave you messages." She sounds exasperated. I don't have an answer to that. Talking to her usually ends with one of us upset. We both argue and fight, and most of the time it's about something I'm doing wrong—according to her.

I've always felt second best to my mother. Either I wasn't smart enough, didn't try hard enough, or was too much like *him*. She would cry at night about how I was a constant reminder of my father. My father and I were pretty much identical, so I can understand how looking at me was difficult, but it was even harder having her push me away. The pain of having both parents walk out that day—one physically and one figuratively—was excruciating. I lost every idea I coveted about what my family was like the day he packed and left. He took more than just his belongings with him—he took my child-hood. All I've wanted was for her to *see* me without seeing my father.

I let out a deep sigh. "Really, Mom? A voicemail? Why didn't you call Taylor?" I'm trying to restrain my voice, but I'm growing more and more agitated with her.

"I shouldn't have to call your damn secretary!" she yells. Then her voice softens. "I'm still your mother. I don't know why you hate me. You never think of anyone but yourself. I wish just once you cared about what I'm going through."

I choke back the emotion bubbling up. Once again she makes me feel stupid, as though I've done something wrong. I know she means well, but her execution leaves a lot to be desired. "I don't hate you. God. I love you and I don't want to fight. I've been really busy with work. That's why I haven't called." *And it hurts too much.*

"Too busy to call me back? Ten times I called!" She gets frustrated again. This is her thing: she gives me guilt trips and somehow I come out feel-ing inadequate. She hasn't yet asked me how I'm doing or if I'm okay.

"I'm sorry, Mom. I will try to do better about calling." I soften my voice, knowing we're getting nowhere. I decide to get the answers I need. "So what information did you get from the lawyer?"

"I got a letter stating you're named in his will and you need to call them. I don't know much more than he died last week. Alone." She lets out a puff of air and quickly sucks in another breath as if she's upset. "I'm so sorry, baby girl." She starts sobbing.

"I don't understand why you're crying," I say in an even tone, feeling betrayed by her reaction. "Why are you upset? He left us and never looked back. He didn't love us, Mom. At least now I know he won't come around because he's dead and not just because he doesn't want to."

She cries harder. I'm shaking, trying to wrap my mind around this.

"Catherine, I loved him! I had a child with him."

I understand loving a man who doesn't love you back—hell, I know it all too well. I can't fully understand since I never had a child with Neil—thank God for that. But for once I want her to put me before my father. Sure, at some point he was a good dad, but I barely remember that because the bad memories far outweigh any good ones. There's a small part of me that understands that once you love someone there is a piece of your heart that is always theirs. But doesn't the hurt and pain that he put us through for twenty years negate that love? Don't the months where we ate macaroni and cheese every night because it's all she could afford due to his disappearance and lack of child support dampen that? My head and heart can't find common ground with her reaction. I'm angry over his death more than anything. I will never get answers. I won't know why he did these things. Did he feel remorse? Did he think about me and wonder who I became?

My blood boils as my chest tightens. "Yes, and then he left!" I remind her as the anger takes hold of me.

"He was a good father—"

All the air is pushed out of my lungs as if I've been punched in the gut. Of all the things she could say—to side with him is more hurtful than anything. "Are you kidding me?" I shriek. This is insane.

"Catherine Grace Pope, you do *not* get to yell at me! I don't give a shit how old you are."

"Mom—"

"Don't you *Mom* me. He was my husband. Yes, he left, but I made vows with him. I loved him— very much. I know you don't feel the same. I've never asked you to. But don't you *dare* try to make me feel bad for being sad that someone I shared a part of myself with is dead." She starts to hiccup-cry again. I know better than to try to speak. My hands tremble with rage as angry tears flow down my face. She composes herself and starts again. "He loved you. Maybe he didn't know what to do or how to be a father after he left, but he did love you."

Apparently she forgot all the nights I cried myself to sleep begging for him to come home. The days I sat at the top of the steps with a bag, hoping he was going to come get me for the weekend. The thousands of times I would ask if Daddy was going to call or come back. Every birthday when I would cry because I would wish for him and he'd never show. Tears fall relentlessly as anguish slices through my heart.

"That's where you're wrong, Mom." I take deep breath. "I wasn't enough. I have to go." I press end, disconnecting the call, and throw the phone on the bed. I won't listen to her tell me he loved me. If I stayed on the phone, we would've fought more and I can't handle any more of it today.

The anger evaporates and all I'm left with is nothingness. Numb. All I feel is complete numbness. I'm not angry anymore, or sad. I couldn't give a shit less about anything regarding my mother or father. I open the balcony door and sit out there, enjoying the solitude. There's something about the ocean that's soothing. I hear my phone ring a few times, but there's no way I'm getting up. I'm enjoying this small sliver of peace. The smell of the salty air, the sounds of birds and the waves crashing, and the caress of the gentle breeze overwhelm my senses. Focusing on them, I melt into the lounge chair and just breathe. Time passes and I'm content and restful.

"Well, this explains why you aren't answering my calls or the door." I leap out of my seat at the sound of an angry voice.

Jackson is standing on the balcony to my right, glaring at me. Trying to slow my rapid pulse, I place my hand over my heart. Short of breath from the rush of fear, I gasp and try to speak. "You scared the shit out of me."

He pinches the bridge of his nose and closes his eyes. "I was worried. I had no idea if you left or were lost." He opens his eyes, straining to maintain his temper. "I didn't mean to scare you, but I didn't know what to think."

His concern warms my heart. I smile and shrug. "What if I was in the bathroom?"

"For an hour?" he questions in that raspy voice of his.

"An hour?" I ask, confused. I thought it was maybe twenty minutes.

"Yes. An hour of calling and then banging on your door. I came out to my balcony to see if maybe I could see you on the beach because I was starting to panic." He shakes his head and runs his hands through his dark brown hair.

"I came out for some fresh air. I didn't even hear the door. I'm sorry you were so worried." I walk over to the edge of my balcony to get closer to him. "You should know, though, I'm not as fragile as you seem to think." I smile, trying to reassure him.

Closing his eyes, he turns his head toward the ocean and mumbles to himself. Something about women being the death of him.

Using my diversionary tactics, I clear my throat to grab his attention. "Ready to go?"

He seems to collect himself and one side of his mouth quirks up. "Yeah, I'll meet you right outside your door."

"Okay. I'll see you in a few minutes."

I head back in the room. Grabbing my phone, I look at the call list: eleven missed calls. Two are from my mother and the rest are from Jackson. No wonder he was pissed and worried. I check myself in the mirror and groan at my appearance. I look like a bus hit me. Knowing that he's waiting and already irritated, I decide not to push my luck. I pinch my cheeks for some color and flip my hair a few times, trying to bring some life back to it.

As I open the door, I can't stop the smile that forms at the sight of Jackson. He's pacing with his hands clasped behind his head. When he hears my door shut, he looks over and walks toward me. Standing face-to-face, I tilt my head to look up and try to read his mood through his eyes. They give nothing away as he stares down at me. He shakes his head, letting out a short groan as he does so. I lift my eyebrow at the noise that escapes him and Jackson returns the gesture. Then we both start laughing at each other.

The moment of humor seems to have quelled our awkwardness. He puts his arm out in a gentlemanly way and I place my hand through it. He looks down, smiling as we walk and get on the elevator. "What am I going to do with you?"

"What the hell does that mean?" I ask, narrowing my eyes as I try to decipher what exactly his question is implying.

"Just what I asked."

"Yes, but what kind of a question is that?" I drop my arm from his.

"Clearly there is something happening here." He steps closer and I take a step back.

"Nothing is happening." I straighten and take another step back, trying to put distance between us.

His jaw tics at my statement and he takes another step toward me. He's hot and then cold—I can't keep up. He kisses me—a soul-searing kiss—and then acts as though it was a mistake. Needing something to hold onto, I grip the hem of my dress. Jackson's eyes snap down as I tug on the fabric and he grins.

"Catherine—" Before he can speak, the elevator door opens allowing me to get the hell out of here.

I don't reply or acknowledge him as I practically run out of the elevator. This man manages to suck the air out of any space we share. He makes it difficult for me to focus on anything other than him. The intensity between us is crippling. I continue walking through the lobby and outside, heading over to a bench to sit. *Think, Catherine!* I need to be able to do my damn job.

He sits beside me, not saying a word. I need to tell him that this has to stop. He must have sensed my apprehension at some point, yet he continues to play whatever game this is. It's my life he's playing with. My job pays me way too much money to screw this up. I also refuse to go through another agonizing breakup—as if we're even close to that. Ha! It's too much. I have to maintain control. Yeah, like there's a shot in hell that's going to happen with a man like Jackson. Regardless, I'm going to *attempt* to keep it together.

I glance at him and my heart squeezes.

He returns my gaze as the car pulls up. "Let's get to work," he says as he stands and walks over to the car. This time he gets in the front seat.

Good. We need physical distance. We need to resume the roles of client and consultant. No matter how charming he is, no matter how handsome, he's ultimately paying me to help his company. I need to honor that agreement.

We arrive at the production facility fifteen minutes later. I used our travel time to strengthen my resolve and plan how to get back to being the strong businesswoman I am rather than the girl who can't control herself over some guy. Hell, I never acted like this with Neil. Half the fun with him was kicking his ass in the business world, not fawning and tripping over myself.

I open the door and smile at Jackson, wearing my business mask. This time he keeps his hands in his pockets.

"Welcome to Raven Cosmetics," he says as I walk past him into the building.

"Thank you. I know our main objective is the successful release of the new line you have coming out. Will we get to see that today?"

"Yes. The older products are being handled for now. The new line is really what we want you to focus on." It seems Jackson has also found his professional mask. Thank God! When he's charming and flirtatious it makes it damn near impossible to keep my mind on task.

"Perfect. Can I ask why you brought in an outside company?" The more information I have, the better.

He looks away and stops in front of a door. "Do I look like I wear makeup?" he asks, dripping with sarcasm. My breath hitches at his sudden mood shift. Jackson has never been rude or nasty. It shocks me. "Sorry. I didn't mean it like that. It's been a real shitty day." He inhales and begins to speak in an even tone. "I never had control over anything that happened with the cosmetic company. I honestly couldn't tell you the first thing about what the hell went on here. So when—" He stops abruptly and looks up before continuing, "—the former CEO departed, I knew I needed help. That's where you came in." He turns and opens the door, holding it so I can pass through.

"I understand." I nod and smile tightly as I walk past him. I stop and turn back, adding, "I'm glad you chose CJJ."

"I chose you. Not CJJ." He reaches for my hand and places it in the crook of his arm, holding it there. I stare at his beautiful eyes, biting my lower lip. "Now let me show you all the girly shit we make here." He turns and pulls me through the hall.

Our tour lasts about two hours and I'm

exhausted by the end. I've met all the people on the production team as well as a few people I'm sure I'll speak to when I start to get more involved with each product. I have a million ideas floating around about things I want to focus on. I also have a huge bag of products to sample. Jackson was friendly, funny, and playful with his employees. The rapport he had with them was amazing. Just as impressive was how obvious it was that they love him. He knew almost every person's name, which is rare in a lot of big companies nowadays. It's clear that he views them as people and not just numbers. For someone who's had little to do with the company, he's either learned fast or has been more involved than he let on.

After the tour, both of us seem to relax into our appropriate roles. Throughout the car ride, we talk a lot about what he wants regarding the company's growth and how he'll be hands-on but ultimately knows nothing about this market or how to handle the press. The amount of free reign I have on this account has me feeling confident, even a little giddy.

Once we get off the elevator at our hotel, Jackson's phone rings. He glances at the screen and grimaces. He looks at me, a frown marring his features as he takes the call. "Hi, Mark. Everything okay?" He makes a low grumbling noise in the back of his throat at whatever Mark is relaying on the phone. "Well, fix it!" he yells, clearly frustrated at the situation. "No, I don't ... fine. I'll be in the office in twenty minutes. You better have Tom, Aaron, and Dean on standby. I'm not fucking around this time." He disconnects the call and puts his phone in his pocket.

Looking over at me, he swallows and his shoulders drop. "I'm sorry, I have to go deal with this crap. I know we planned to go over some things at dinner, but ..."

Wanting to relieve whatever turmoil he's struggling with, and also understanding all too well the pressures of his position, I smile and place my hand on his arm. "No problem. I'm exhausted anyway. Today has been ... overwhelming."

His eyes look sad. "I promise I'll make it up to you." He gives me a small smile.

"No need, Jackson. Just go. What time is our meeting tomorrow?"

His eyes twinkle with mischief and his voice turns playful. "No meetings. I have other plans for us. Be ready by one o'clock."

My eyes widen and I start to twist my hands as my heart races. Do I continue to fight this? There's only one way this is going to end—badly—but I want to spend the day with him. I want to see if this is all my crazy imagination. I'm too tired to think anymore. I take a shaky breath and exhale. "Okay." My brilliant plan to keep things strictly business just went out the door. I know I should spend tomorrow working or alone, but I can't resist him.

"Good night, Catherine." And with that, he turns and walks away.

Too late to change my mind now.

chapter twelve

I slept well, considering the absolute shit day I had yesterday. Between my dead father, the earth-moving kiss with Jackson, Jackson regretting said earth-moving kiss, and the fight with my mother, I'm surprised I can even function. The worst part is I'm more upset about Jackson than any of the other things. One minute he's seducing me with his magnetic eyes, sexy grin, and that damn dimple, and the next he's pushing me away and tormenting me.

I roll over and my eyes land on the clock sitting on the nightstand. It takes a second for them to focus, but when they do ... Holy shit I slept late—it's almost noon. I've always been an up-at-seven-no-matter-what girl, but not today apparently. Groaning, I get out of the extremely comfortable bed and start getting ready for whatever Jackson has planned for me. Looking over the outfits I threw in my bag during my pissed-off packing, I realize I don't have an outfit for *"I have plans."* I have no clue what to wear or where we're going. Instead of agonizing over it, I opt for jeans and a cute pink top. Luckily I brought my favorite pair, which hug my butt perfectly and accentuate my curves. The top that Ashton threw in is not a business top, but it's perfect for our *"plans."* The one shoulder gives a little sexy, but the loose fit keeps it looking casual.

I have my hair in a loose ponytail with the ends curled. I throw on my white sneakers and hope for the best.

I've just sat in the chair and broke out my Kindle when I hear a knock on the door. Rushing over, I take two deep breaths, press the handle down, and open it. Jackson's smiling as he leans against the wall with his legs and arms crossed. My brain ceases to form rational thoughts. The sight before me takes my breath away—he's mouthwatering. I look down at the floor, trying to hide my blush and get my mind functioning again. As he uncrosses his leg and stands straight, I can't help but think that this man is going to be the death of me. My eyes slowly scan his body, absorbing as much detail as possible before I have to meet his eyes again. First thing I see are his dark blue track shorts, and above them a tight black shirt shows the ripples of his abs. My greedy perusal continues until I land on his face. That's when my knees buckle and I grip the doorjamb for support. His eyes darken. The intensity of his stare causes my stomach to clench and heat to pool in my center.

He steps forward so we're toe-to-toe and I have to tilt my head to look up at his smiling face. His six-foot-three frame towers over me and the sheer size of him has me parting and licking my lips. Jackson's expression changes as he follows my movement. He takes a deep breath and closes his eyes, letting me know I'm affecting him as much as he's affecting me. A thrill runs through me, increasing my desperation for his lips on mine. He pushes forward. Our chests are touching, my nipples pebbling at the warmth of his body and the thoughts flooding my mind of him taking me right here, right now. Jackson lifts his hands and cups my face, slowly leaning into me as we breathe each other in. He stills, our mouths almost touching, but I hold my ground. I want him to be the one to kiss me again. I need it to be his choice. I close my eyes, trying to make my intentions clear, silently begging. *Please, just kiss me!*

I feel his lips brush against mine before I hear, "Not yet, Catherine. But soon." Jackson's voice drops even lower. "The next time there won't be any mistakes."

He takes a small step back and I open my eyes, watching as his gaze darts between my eyes and my lips, as if he's battling his own desire. I can't speak. I can barely process anything he's saying. He takes a deep breath and shakes his head. "First, we have plans, okay?"

No, it's not okay! I want him to push me down to the floor or up against the wall and take me. Damn him and all his self-control. I take a step out of his grip and respond in a breathless whisper, "Sure."

"Good. Grab your stuff. We only have it reserved for an hour. I think you'll have fun today." His voice is now playful, refocused and excited by whatever plans he's made for us.

The only fun I want to have doesn't include us leaving this hotel room. I walk over and grab my purse, shoving my phone in and gritting my teeth. So much for my own self-control—I have none when it comes to him. Not even two seconds after seeing him, I'm ready to strip and let him have his way with me.

Jackson turns to walk away, taking only two steps before he stops, grabs my hand, and weaves his fingers through mine. I can't help but smile at

the small gesture. Great. Holding hands has re-
duced me to a schoolgirl.

"Oh, and Catherine?" The hair on the back of
my neck rises at the deep rasp in his voice. "Today
we're going to talk and figure this out."

I nod, praying that we can figure out whatever's happening between us before it destroys everything I've worked for. No matter what I'm feeling
for him, he needs to know that I won't sacrifice my
career for this, for him, for anything.

"Where are we going?" I ask, grabbing my driver's
license out of my wallet as he requested. We're
waiting in line to get through security.

"This is the Navy base. I thought you might have
fun doing something different," he replies, taking
my license and handing it over to a guy with a rather large gun around his chest. I'm so confused.

"Wait," I say as he starts driving forward. "Did
I miss something? Are you still in the Navy?" I narrow my eyes and he smiles over at me.

"No, but I'm a contractor, so I can still access
the base. Also, I was a SEAL, so I called ahead to my
friends and got all this cleared." His smile widens
as we pull up behind a fence.

"These are our plans?"

Jackson doesn't say anything as he parks the
truck. When he sneaks a peek at my expression, I
can see the mischief dancing in his eyes. What in
the ever-loving hell is he thinking? I'd be lying if I
said I didn't love this side of him. I've never really
enjoyed surprises, but he looks like a kid on Christmas morning and I don't want to spoil his mood.

I look around, trying to see exactly what he has planned for us on a Navy base. I can't see anything through the trees lining the fence, and my lack of information is quickly turning my excitement into anxiety. Jackson leans over the console and grips my hand. I'm both relieved and annoyed by how my panic starts to ebb at his small touch. He squeezes once and exits the car. I climb out of the cab and squint, trying to decipher what the large tree-house-looking building is.

"Ready?" I flinch, my heart accelerating at the feel of him behind me. I didn't even hear him approach.

"Stop scaring me! Jesus, don't you make noise when you move?" I ask, slightly flustered. He lets out a loud, carefree laugh as he comes around. The look on his face is priceless, and his dimpled smile melts my momentary irritation.

"I'm just stealthy."

"I have no words for you." I smile and shake my head. "Stop scaring me all the time."

"You're just skittish. Maybe you should pay closer attention to what's going on around you." He pulls me in by my hips, right up against his chest. My eyes widen and the air expels from my lungs at the sudden contact. In a flash, his expression changes. His eyes smolder and his voice is low and hoarse when he says, "Maybe soon you'll hear *all* the noises I make." I gasp as a shudder passes through me. He releases me without a word and walks toward the metal gate.

There are no words. I can't think of a single thing to say to him. Once again, Jackson renders me speechless. He's flirtatious and seductive one moment and then a smartass then next. He's unlike any man I've ever met. Shaking my head to rid the turmoil in my mind, I gather my wits and walk over to him.

"Are you ready for some fun?" he asks with an amused smirk.

I have no idea what kind of fun we're going to have in a gated, woodsy area, but for some reason I trust Jackson. I don't know if it's because of his time in the service or the fact that he owns a security company, but I don't believe he'd put me in harm's way. I take a deep breath and smile. "Ready as I'll ever be. Do you mind clueing me in to what this fun is?"

Jackson grabs my hand as we walk through the gate. What I see stops me dead in my tracks and I drop his hand absently. He's got to be kidding me! Through the clearing is a large four-story building. Long ropes stretch from the top of it to a huge pole across about a hundred feet of open air, with only a shabby-looking net under them. Off to the right are four tree trunks on their side with about a foot of space between the ground and the trenches dug beneath them. Farther down are large metal cylinders that you either climb through or over. What the hell is this place? As I continue to look around, there's more—ropes, walls, even a moat! Oh hell no! I'm in jeans—cute, expensive, skintight jeans—and a pretty pink top. He's insane. I look over to where he was standing, but he's moved about ten steps away. He's leaning casually against the gate, and judging from the look on his face, he's getting quite a kick out of my reaction.

"You're enjoying this, aren't you?" I ask him with a half laugh.

"What?" he replies innocently, a sarcastic grin

plastered to his face. "You said you were stronger than I thought. I figured maybe you'd wanna put your money where your mouth is, Ms. Pope."

"I never said I was training to become a soldier!" I huff.

Jackson walks toward me and stops about a foot away. He has one brow raised and his voice is playful. "Sailor," he reminds me. "Hmmm, maybe you're too ..."—he taps a finger on his chin—"scared?" he taunts.

My jaw falls slack as I stare wide-eyed at his comment. I'm way too competitive to let that comment slide and somehow he knows it. Yet again he's found a way to bend me to his will. Who the hell does he think he is? Screw that! "I am *not* scared! I will own this course, *Muffin.*" I glare and then soften as an idea enters my head. Giving him a taste of his own medicine, I bend and touch my toes, providing a little seduction of my own. I glide back up and cock my head to the side, pursing my lips and narrowing my eyes. "I hope you're ready to have your ass handed to you." I'm about to embarrass myself, but I will not let him beat me.

Jackson takes a small step forward. His cheeks raise and the crinkles by his eyes grow more defined. His eyes are sparkling and his voice is smooth. "Then by all means." He waves his hand toward the course. "I can't wait to have my ass handled by you."

"Handed! I said handed!" I throw my hand over my face. I fell right into this trap and now I'm going to look like an ass. If I'm going to lose, I will go down with dignity.

"Same difference." He laughs. "You should know this isn't my first time here. I also *never* lose, so if you want to back out, now's your chance," Jackson says, completely relaxed. He starts stretching, laughing at me as I glare at him.

"Nope," I say confidently. No way am I going to back out now. I'm in this—balls to the walls. I mentally roll my eyes at my false bravado. I'm so screwed.

I look over and realize I have no idea what the hell I'm supposed to do. Is there a safety harness or padding I can wear? Shit! I clear my throat and Jackson looks back with a knowing grin. "Ummm, how does this work? Do I start here or what?"

He walks me through the course, explaining whether to go under, over, through, or up. I keep shaking my head and huffing, each time earning a laugh or some other entertained reaction from Jackson. I sure hope he's enjoying himself because I'm freaking the hell out.

We end back at the starting point and he places his hands on my shoulders, brushing his thumbs across my collarbone, sending chills through my body. His finger glides up my neck, just barely touching my skin. Without permission, my head tilts into his touch, naturally gravitating toward him like a magnet. His eyes swim with emotion as I try to decipher what he's feeling. Jackson shifts forward and puts his lips to my forehead. My lids shut as I absorb the moment of intimacy. Inch by inch he backs away and I stare at him with questions floating in my head. One side of his mouth lifts and his low voice cracks through my daze. "Time starts now."

"What?"

"Clock is ticking. You're wasting precious time that you're going to need if you plan to ..." He looks pensive as he rolls his eyes up and taps his foot. "What was it? Oh I know, *handle* my ass." He leans down and whispers in my ear, "Remember, I never lose." He swats my ass and laughs.

I take off and start running, half surprised, half frustrated that his plan to get me flustered and then start the timer worked. Stupid boy and his stupid plan. I can't believe I'm actually doing this. The only thing keeping me moving is my need to win and the chance to watch Jackson run this damn course after me. I climb over the logs and then crawl through the metal tube. As I approach the huge building, I swallow nervously. Seriously? I have to climb this? Panting my way up the stairs, I make a mental note that the gym is now a daily requirement. It feels like someone's sitting on my lungs. I continue to climb but stop when I notice Jackson standing at the top, smiling. Asshat!

As I move toward the ropes, he steps forward and puts his hands on my waist. I don't have time for his stupid touch-Catherine-and-she-gets-flustered game—I have a challenge to win, dammit. "Place your hands on the rope," his deep voice commands. "Now swing your legs up and grab it with your feet."

My eyes widen and my mouth drops open. He's joking, right? There is no way I'm sliding down this rope. "Yeah, no thanks. I'll just slide down the net."

His loud guffaw reverberates in the woods around us. "Fine. Then I'll add two minutes on to your time." He shrugs as he returns to his spot against the wall.

"Yeah, that whole endearing thing is total bullshit. They lied." I narrow my eyes and then grab the rope, swinging my body forward but missing with my feet on my first try. I cast a quick glance at Jackson, who's trying to hide his smile. Bastard. I bite my lip and try again, managing to get my leg around the rope this time. I hold on for dear life and lean my head back, smirking at Jackson with an I-told-you-so look. Okay, now what?

As if hearing my mental question, Jackson walks toward the rope. I'm hanging upside down with my head still tilted backward, giving him a perfect view of my breasts. Though he seems to be trying to keep his eyes on mine, he's failing miserably as he glances more than once. A low grumble sounds from his chest and he closes his eyes. His voice is strained when he looks back at me. "Okay. Now, slide down the rope and keep your feet locked. If you fall, you lose."

I groan, slowly starting to move down the rope. There are times I truly wonder what the hell is wrong with me and why I'm being punished. I look back at him when he grabs the rope and pulls himself up. It jumps and I clench my legs tighter, letting out a high-pitched scream. "Jackson!"

"What?" he asks innocently.

I'm not buying his act.

I slide lower down the rope, getting about halfway and feeling confident I can do this, when it jerks again and I bounce up and down. He smiles widely and I let him know what's about to happen. "I swear you're going to pay for this!"

He's a dead man walking. I continue to slide until I reach the end, where I promptly let go and fall on my ass. *Awesome.* That's going to leave a mark.

Running to the finish line, I hear his throaty laugh behind me as he claps his hands. "You did it!" he yells excitedly, moving fast in my direction.

My hands are on my knees as I gasp for air, trying to catch my breath from running and hurling myself all over this stupid course. People do this for fun? He moves toward me and picks me up, throwing me over his shoulder. I gasp and squeak, "Jackson! Put me down!"

He lets out a chuckle while carrying me over to a bench near the starting line. His voice is happy. "Nope. You need to sit and see how it's really done. Time to watch the master." He plops me down and hands me his watch. I stare up at him as I realize I get to watch him run it now.

"Master? What if my time is better?"

He laughs and quickly recovers. "Should we bet?"

"Are you sure you want to chance it?" I smile, goading him.

Jackson has a huge grin on his face as he stands in front of me, blocking the sun with his muscular body. "If I win, you have to have dinner with me in New York."

"But if I win, you owe me a spa day and a new pair of jeans."

Jackson smirks as if this is the easiest bet he's ever made. "Deal. This is going to be a walk in the park."

"I wouldn't be so sure of that."

He chuckles and grabs my hand holding the watch. "Okay, that button on the right is the timer. When I say go, you press it. Got it?" He smiles as I nod in agreement. Good thing he missed my finger twitch when I pressed it a moment ago.

"Oh, Jackson?" I ask innocently.

"Yes?"

I casually lift my shoulders and press my chest

out to stretch my back, taking an agonizingly slow time with each movement. His jaw tics as he watches me roll my neck. I let out a gentle breath and drop my voice to a seductive whisper. "Did you enjoy the show?" My teeth bite on my bottom lip and I watch every moment, taking great pleasure in the way his eyes drop to my mouth and his Adam's apple bobs.

He takes a deep breath and rips his shirt off, stopping whatever game I was attempting to play. Holy fucking shit. He's standing completely still, allowing me to take him in. Each muscle in his solid body is toned and perfect. My mouth goes completely dry as I stare at his taut chest and the large tattoo covering the left side of it. It's a tribal sun that takes up the entire space over his heart. Greedily, my eyes graze lower to his rippled abs, all the way down to my favorite part of a man—the deep V. I find my way back up to his blazing eyes—the look he gives me cements me to my seat.

He takes three long strides and places his hands on the back of the bench on each side of me, staring intently into my eyes. I feel naked, the intensity of his gaze stripping me and baring my soul. I've never felt so vulnerable yet so desired at the same time. His breathing is labored and I'm completely still. Neither of us moves as my eyes start to drift, and then he makes a deep noise in his throat. My gaze quickly reverts to his turquoise eyes as they probe for something. Between the running, adrenaline, and the intensity that is Jackson I start to get dizzy.

He leans in and drops his head to the side of my neck, taking two deep breaths. I can feel the tension, the turmoil rolling through his body. I don't know what he's fighting. He runs his nose up my throat and my eyes roll back as I moan. "Keep making those noises and I'm going to get the wrong idea."

Abruptly, he's gone. He's at the start line looking back at me. "Ready for *your* show, Catherine?"

So damn sure of himself, isn't he? Leaning back, he lifts his arms over his head, which causes his shorts to drop a tiny bit. My eyes follow the indentation of his hips down to the tiny trail that leads to all things happy. My lips part and my breathing becomes erratic. I'm incredibly turned on right now. He gets in the ready position, waiting for me to tell him to go. I smile inwardly knowing that he's added about three minutes on to his time with his little seduction game. I lift the watch and yell, "Go!"

Nothing could have prepared me for watching Jackson run the course. Not only does he have a large tattoo on his front, he has one on his shoulder as well. It's black and looks like the skeleton of a frog. His body moves as if he was made for this— each leap graceful and precise, every step calculated. His body moves, his muscles tighten, and my mouth waters at the sight of him. There's no time for me to return the favor of climbing to the top of the ginormous building, so I decide to rush over to the bottom of the steps. Jackson still has a little time before he makes it over there, although with the way he's moving, it may be a lot faster than I'm anticipating. I get there before him and try to climb a couple flights, but the five-alarm fire burning in my legs prevents me from getting too far. I sit on the steps instead, trying to appear casual as Jackson starts to climb.

I lie across the step and rest my hand on my

propped-up knee. He gets to my step and stops briefly, letting out a throaty laugh. "Nice try, babe." He leaps over me and laughs the rest of the way up.

I turn and yell in his direction, "Hey! Not fair!"

I look up and see him descending a rope faster than I thought humanly possible. Somehow when he reaches the bottom, he's not even winded. He sprints to the end, finishing without breaking a sweat. Jesus!

He yells back, "Done! Press stop!" as I gingerly walk to him, trying to lessen the throbbing in my muscles. Jackson heads toward me with a huge smile on his face as I press the button.

I place the watch in my back pocket. He's not getting it until I know my time. "So, Jackson, you tell me my time and I'll tell you yours. Then we can see who the winner is." I raise my eyebrow, smiling coyly.

He reaches forward and pulls me against him. "First, dinner. I'll tell you then."

"What?" I huff. "No! I want to know now." I purse my lips and push back from him.

"Too bad. If you want it, you have to have dinner with me. Besides, you owe me anyway."

"Ugh! You don't fight fair." He drives me insane. On the other hand, I haven't had this much fun since … I can't even remember. He makes me laugh and feel special. There are worse ways to spend my evening than dinner with an extremely sexy and agile and funny and powerful and … Oh man. This is bad. He's all of those things, but he's also my client. Still, he doesn't seem to be concerned with that little fact.

His low voice halts my mental debate. "Stop overthinking. It's dinner—we can even talk business.

Plus, don't you want to know how bad you lost and if you get your spa day?"

I grab the watch, taking a picture of his final time with my phone. I clear the display and then hand it back to him. His time was outrageously long—that makes me smile. And now that I have the proof in my phone, there's no way he can deny it. "Fine. Dinner, but we talk about work. Then I'll show you just how bad you lost." I grin, walking toward the car.

chapter fourteen

I climb into the cab of the truck, laughing as I imagine his reaction when he finally sees his ridiculous time.

"What's so funny?" he asks.

"Oh, nothing. You'll see later tonight. Unless of course you're ready to share my time now?" I smile and bat my eyelashes.

He returns my smile and throws the truck in reverse. "Nice try, babe. But if I give you the time now, I'll have nothing to ensure you show up tonight."

"It's not like I can go very far." I really want him to tell me so I can watch his face fall when he sees how bad he lost. There's no way he beat me. Well, there is, just not with the amount of lead-time I added in. If he still beat me, even with the extra time, I'm not only signing up for a gym, I'm getting a personal trainer.

"No, I think I have you right where I want you." He winks and his cheek rises.

We start driving back toward the hotel, but it's a different way than how we came. When I look off to the right the shoreline is close. It's beautiful. The homes lining the street are all quaint little beach cottages with white picket fences and trees that cast shade over the road.

"This area is adorable," I muse.

Jackson looks over, smiling. "I lived on this

side when I was stationed here. It's the locals' beach on this side of the bay. You get to enjoy the ocean without the crowds."

"So if you still have your headquarters down here, do you stay in a hotel every time or do you have a home here?"

I wondered this before but wasn't sure how or if I should ask. Since he thought it would be entertaining to make me run an obstacle course, I think it's fair game. If it weren't for him, my legs wouldn't be throbbing and my arms wouldn't be numb.

"No, I sold my house when I moved up to New York. I kept the office here because it made more sense being close to the base. Plus, it gives me an excuse to come back to the beach and see friends." His hand grips the steering wheel and he puts his blinker on.

"Where are we going?" I ask, confused. The hotel isn't here, not that I know where here is. But still, there isn't anything here but trees. I look at the sign as we turn—another military base. No. No. No. I'm *not* doing this again. He's trying to kill me. "Ummm ..."

Jackson laughs but doesn't answer. He gives his ID to the guard at the gate and keeps driving forward. "Relax, this will be fun."

My hands are clenching the seat as I try to get a grip. Jackson reaches over and grabs my hand, pulling it onto the middle console as his fingers intertwine with mine. If he keeps pushing against that wall, soon enough it's going to crumble. Distance. I need distance. I try to pull away but he tightens his grip, continuing to look forward.

"I don't believe you. You said the same thing about the last base we went to."

"I had fun. Didn't you?" he asks.

"Fun? Sure, if you call aching joints, atrocious hair, and a dirt mark on my butt from falling fun. I would call it something else, but we can go with that." I smile even though I was going for sarcasm.

Jackson's loud laughter fills the truck as he parks. A little nervous and afraid to see where he's brought me, I decide to stare at him—the view is beautiful either way.

"You still look perfect even with messy hair and dirt on your ass—which I happen to be fond of." Jackson's brow raises and he shifts forward, coming so close our lips could brush. "I want to show you my favorite place in Virginia Beach, or would you rather go back?"

With his breath heating my face, I'm cognitively misfiring. He could ask me to strip and run the course again and right now, I would. "Here is fine."

His smile is brighter than the sun. "Good, let's go."

I climb, or more like hobble, out of the truck. The sea air assaults my nose and seagulls fly overhead. I look around and it's truly remarkable. The sand is a little whiter than by the hotel. There are no waves. It's calm and peaceful. But what causes my breath to catch is the huge brick lighthouse. It's very old but still perfect. The red is muted from years of wind, rain, and storms, but there she stands—steadfast and strong to guide the ships home.

I look at Jackson leaning on the hood of the truck, watching me take in the sights. He walks around and extends his hand. Instead of wavering, I eagerly give him what he wants, reveling in the way his hand engulfs mine.

"I used to come here a lot. Have you ever been to a lighthouse?" Jackson asks in a hushed tone.

"In Jersey there are tons of lighthouses. My uncle had a boat, and when I was young we used to fish right by one. I always thought they were magic." I smile and Jackson pulls me closer to him as we walk.

"Magic, huh?"

I shrug, not wanting to share too much of my heart with him. I loved the stories my uncle would tell me about sailors and the women waiting for them to return. He was a silly old man but he always made it seem so romantic, talking about how men would be lost for days until the lighthouse guided them home. And how the lighthouse keeper would ensure it was lit, helping sailors find their beacon. He used to call my aunt his light-keeper and say she was the light he'd always find his way back to. All my life I've dreamed of sharing a love like that.

We stop in front of the steps that lead inside. The wind whips my hair forward and I realize I have to climb my way to the top. I'm not going to be able to walk for a week. Maybe we can go back to the hotel where there's an elevator?

Jackson notices my body tense and rubs his thumb in small circles on the back of my hand.

I have two choices: either I suck it up and climb to the top to see the view, or I pout and go back to the car. Option two sounds like a better idea for my feet, but there's no way I want to miss this. Even back home I couldn't ever go inside the lighthouse.

I nudge Jackson as we enter the small building. "Just in case you're curious, no matter who wins the bet, you owe me a massage. And a new pair of jeans."

"Are you saying you want me to rub you down?"

I scoff and roll my eyes. "Let's go, Muffin. We have about four hundred stairs to climb." If he only knew how bad I want his hands all over me, I'd be in big trouble.

I hear him sigh deeply as I giggle to myself.

The inside is cramped and the spiral metal stairs are terrifying. I'm sure I'll have blisters all over my hands from gripping the railing so tight. My legs are quivering—not sure if it's from the previous workout or from fear of falling to my death. The only thing giving me any comfort is Jackson insisting on going behind me in case I lose my footing.

"How much farther does this go?" I ask.

Next thing I know I'm being hoisted over Jackson's shoulder.

"Stop wiggling or I'll drop you," he says with a short laugh, seeming unconcerned as he carries me up the steps.

"You're insane! You're going to drop me anyway!"

"Only if you keep moving. I'll put you down on one condition." Jackson's voice is loud and strong as he begins to lower me. He's very good at getting his way.

"What's that?"

"You let me carry you on my back."

What? No. "I can walk up the steps."

"Then you deal with being upside down," he says and starts climbing the stairs again, throwing me back over his shoulder.

Jackson climbs about ten more steps and I slap his ass, giggling. "Jackson! Put me down!"

"Nah, this is more fun," he says, gripping my

legs tighter.

I can't take another second of being hung up-side down, staring and feeling suspended over the hundreds of feet below. "Fine! I give up. You win."

For once, he doesn't make a noise but I can feel his chest bounce as if he's laughing. *Cocky bastard.* Instead of putting me down so I can climb on his back, he lowers me and scoops me in his arms. My arms naturally wrap around his neck as if it's the most normal thing to be carried like this. Nev-er once can I remember having this happen in any past relationship. His strong arms hold me close against his chest and I feel his heart racing through his shirt. I don't say a word, afraid to break the mo-ment between us. Safe and secure is the only way I can define this space in time.

Once we reach the top of the lighthouse, he sets me down. My arms fall to my sides as he leans for-ward and places a kiss on the top of my head. I swallow and try to regulate my breathing and slow my pulse.

He weaves his fingers with mine again and guides me to the windows.

"I used to come up here after my run in the mornings," he says quietly as we look out at the horizon.

"So you worked out and then climbed the stairs? By choice?" I ask with a raised brow.

His throaty laugh echoes through the building and he pulls me close. "Not all of us find exercise dumb. There are lots of activities that can be"—he coughs and smiles—"enjoyable."

Jackson's innuendo makes my cheeks flush. Him and his mouth!

"Well, only if you do it right," I say boldly.

He leans in conspiratorially. "I always do it right," he says in my ear. Then he walks past me.

"I'm sure you do," I mutter.

"What was that?"

Of course he heard me.

"Nothing. Just admiring the view," I lie and stare out the window.

We walk around the lighthouse, viewing the ocean from all angles. Times like this you realize how small you really are. Up here, looking out, I see endless seas and skies. Jackson and I are the only ones standing here, and as I take it all in I wonder who would light the way home for me?

I'm lost in thought when Jackson comes behind me, pressing against my back. His heat comforts me and I lean back a little. "Look over there," he says against my ear, pointing toward a huge bridge.

I look over but it's not the bridge that causes me to gasp. It's the huge aircraft carrier that's floating over where the bridge becomes a tunnel.

"Ships come in and out through there. You see the white?" Jackson asks.

I squint to get a better view. It looks like there's a white lining around the deck of the ship. I nod, still trying to get a closer look.

"That's called manning the rails. When a ship goes in or out of port for a deployment, they stand around the side of the ship and watch their home either go out of view or come into view," Jackson explains.

I wonder how many times he's done that. How many families have watched their loved ones leave, knowing they were about to spend countless nights alone? How many have stood waiting, anticipating their love's return, serving as lighthouses to guide them home?

In the softest whisper I say, "See. Magic."

Jackson smiles and his eyes lock on mine. "Yeah, there's magic here for sure."

"I don't know what the hell to do!" I say into the receiver. Ashton is not helping and I *need* my best friend to help me right now.

I called her shortly after we got back from the lighthouse. Jackson and I spent about a half hour up there, laughing and talking about different stuff—what it was like for him going through boot camp, a little about my college experience and Ashton and Gretchen. I was nervous and quiet in the car after we left, unsure how to proceed with him and how to process what I was thinking. Jackson, however, was relaxed and completely at ease with our silent drive back. As we were arriving back at our hotel, another call came in from his security team. All I could hear was something about an issue with the contract in Afghanistan. Jackson apologized for being on the phone again and when we arrived at our rooms, he just gave me a wave and a wink, un-locked his door, and went in.

"See why I told you to bring pretty panties?"

"You know! You're not freaking helpful." I sigh and pace around the room. After crawling and run-ning around all over today, I desperately needed a shower when we got back. But while I was enjoying the warmth and serenity, I remembered I was going to dinner with Jackson tonight. My nerves grew to the point that I had to do some deep breathing ex-ercises to avoid an anxiety attack.

"Look, you like him, right?"

"Yes … I think. I don't really know him. He could be a complete asshole."

"Or he could be perfect for you," she quickly replies.

"Again with the helping." I huff and continue to pace. "You're supposed to be on my side. Where is *my* best friend?"

She makes an obnoxious sound—a mix between a grunt and a snort. "I really hope you're kidding me, twunt. I *am* helping. You just refuse to listen to what I'm saying."

"Twunt?" I ask. "Seriously, did you make that word up?"

"Yes. Be jealous of my superior intelligence."

I laugh. "Wow, you *can* make up stupid curse words."

"Whatever." I can almost picture her rolling her eyes. "Let's get back to the issue at hand. He wants dinner. You're on a business trip. Go to dinner with your sex-on-a-stick boss. And if you didn't pack the right stuff, just go commando."

"The problem isn't the underwear. It hasn't been that long since things ended with Neil—"

She quickly cuts me off with a stern voice. "That shit was over long before you found out. Let's be real." Her voice softens a little but still sounds annoyed. "I'm gonna be brutal here. Neil is not the issue. You are. You get in your head and you think you're not good enough. Why?"

"Because …" I trail off. I don't know why. That's the problem. I don't know why I can't accept that a man like Jackson would ever want to have dinner with me, let alone anything more. I've never felt special. I was always second best. But the worst thing isn't that people told me those things—the worst thing is that I believe them. The only place I'm worth a damn is at work. Sometimes when you're told something long enough you eventually believe it.

"Well, that's a great answer!" she screams, loud enough that I have to move the phone from my ear. "Here's the deal. Your dad did a real number on you, and I'm sorry. Your mom has always made you feel like it was your fault. And don't even get me started on Neil." She clears her throat and her tone softens dramatically. "Please listen to me this once." She takes a deep breath. "You're so much more than you give yourself credit for, but Jesus Christ stop for one goddamn minute. Stop being so deep in your head that you're blind to the fact that life is short and if you keep letting others influence your decisions, you're going to be that crazy bitch with a hundred cats. We all know a woman should only have one pussy."

"Ashton!" I laugh.

Her voice softens again. "I love you. You're my best friend. You're worthy and one of the best people in the world. You've always deserved more than the bullshit you always seem to get. So go and be the beautiful girl I know you are and live for the moment."

A tear falls down my face at Ashton's sincerity. If we were face-to-face, I'd hug her and never let go. "Thank you," I say softly, never more grateful for our friendship. "I should get ready."

"I love you, Catherine. Now, open the outside zipper of your suitcase, put what's inside on under your black dress, and get laid already!" She laughs and hangs up before I can say anything more.

Shaking my head, I walk over to my suitcase, open the compartment, and sink into the chair. I pull out a black corset, which I've never seen before. When the hell did she put this in my bag? I need to focus and pull myself together. I'll worry about clothes in a bit and finish getting ready now. I head into the bathroom to dry my hair. I style it with curls at the end and then do my makeup, making sure it's perfect. When I'm done primping, I walk back into the room where my dress and corset are lying on the bed, silently mocking me.

Picking up the corset, I hold it to my chest and look in the mirror. My eyes widen as I take in my reflection. I don't look like the same girl. My hair falls softly down my back. My eyes are rimmed in a chocolate color and my lashes are thick and long, which makes my brown eyes look big and sultry. I put the corset around and hook each eye, pull up the matching panties, and stare at myself in the mirror. My breasts are pushed up and it cuts in at the perfect place to give me an hourglass figure. Satisfied with how I look for a change, I smile as I run my hands down the silky fabric. Yeah, I'm definitely wearing this tonight. Even with no plans of Jackson ever seeing it, I feel sexy. I slip my black sleeveless sweetheart dress over my head. It hugs each curve and tapers down, clinging to my legs, ending right above the knee. I pair it with my open toe, strappy gold heels.

I send a quick text to Ashton, thanking her for earlier and letting her know that I owe her dinner for packing the corset. Needing to keep moving, I clean the room a little and check my makeup at least two more times. I have fifteen minutes before I'm supposed to meet Jackson at the restaurant downstairs. He texted me about an hour ago saying he had to run out and it would be easier to meet there.

Pacing the floor and watching the never-moving clock, I decide to go to the bar and get a drink to kill some time. I keep telling myself this isn't a date, but in the back of my mind I know I'm only fooling myself by saying this is a business meeting. Maybe Ashton is right—I need to see where this goes and stop fighting my desires when it comes to Jackson. If we can talk and come to an agreement, maybe it won't affect my career.

chapter fifteen

here's an open seat at the end of the bar. I sit down, ordering my signature drink—lemon drop martini. As I place a ten-dollar bill on the bar, a hand presses over mine. I look up to a pair of deep brown eyes and a shy smile.

"Hi. Can I help you?" I ask timidly.

"Sorry, but a beautiful woman such as yourself shouldn't have to pay for a drink. Ever." His smile widens and he extends his hand. "I'm Pat. Nice to meet you."

Not wanting to be impolite, I return the handshake. "Hi, I'm Catherine. Thanks for the drink."

"So, are you from Virginia Beach?" He asks and takes a sip of his beer. Really? How original.

"No." I give a short laugh. "I hate to be rude, Pat, but I'm meeting someone."

"He isn't here though, is he?" Pat asks.

Before I have a chance to reply, a deep, sexy voice rasps, "Yes, he is," from behind me.

Chills run down my spine. My body tightens as my breath hitches. A warm hand slowly travels up my back and rests on my bare shoulder. Jackson's presence is so distinct. I know it's him even without turning around. His thumb rests on the back of my neck, rubbing up and down. The entire lower part of my body is warm and tingling from his possessive touch.

Jackson's voice is low and warning, and I can only imagine the look he's giving Pat right now. "Catherine,"—he leans close and presses his lips to my temple—"sorry to keep you waiting. Our table is ready."

Pat's face is stoic as he returns to his beer. I smile at him and place the ten-dollar bill back on the counter. Poor guy. He didn't stand a chance.

I gather my things and hear Jackson inhale loudly as I stand. When I turn to him he's standing there with his jaw slack. I look around to see what has his attention, but he's staring at me.

I try to break his trance. "Jackson?"

"You look breathtaking. I can't take my eyes off you." He looks me up and down, stopping leisurely at my neckline before his eyes make their way back up to my face.

"Ummm, thanks." I don't know how to take his compliment, the way he said it, or the way he seems to be undressing me with his eyes. I'm suddenly very hot—and bothered.

"You don't see it, do you?"

"See what?" I ask.

"Every man in this bar wants you right now." He takes a step forward, never breaking eye contact. "Every man wants to be me right now." Another step. "And none of them see what I see." One more step. We're now toe-to-toe as I lift my head to stare into his eyes. My heart beats so loud in my ears I have to strain to hear his words. He places his hand on my hip, pulling me against him. "I'm going to kiss you now, and I don't know if I'll be able to stop."

He lowers his head and hooks his other hand around my back, slowly sliding it up as the gap between us closes. His full lips are only a breath away when my lids flutter and shut. Then I feel his lips, soft and warm, pressing against mine. He pulls me even closer, tightening his grip and intensifying the kiss. I thread my fingers into his hair as his tongue sweeps across my lips, seeking entrance. I've died and gone to heaven. This is one of those moments I'll remember forever. Every girl dreams about a kiss like this. I sigh and give him access as our tongues brush against each other. All too soon Jackson loosens his hold and ends the kiss. He lets out a soft breath and then presses a brief kiss to my lips once more. His voice is raspy against my ear. "That should've been our first kiss."

I'm afraid to open my eyes and face a repeat rejection like last time. I lower my arms, still holding on to his shoulders, and take a deep breath. Hesitantly, I open my eyes and look up. Intensity like I've never seen dominates his stare, and my doubts about him wanting me, about this crazy attraction between us, disappear. With that one look he's torn down every wall around my heart. All my futile reasons to stay away from him are gone, replaced by this undeniable pull toward Jackson Cole. They simply don't exist anymore, and I realize I never had a chance against him. I open my mouth to speak but can't find my voice. I've never known this kind of feeling. It's heady and intoxicating, filling me with fear and excitement. He gently places his finger under my chin, pushing my jaw shut, and the dimple I love so much reappears with his warm smile.

My smile is shy when I finally speak. "So ... dinner?" *Dinner?* That's my fabulous response? My cheeks flare red—I'm so embarrassed. He makes me so self-conscious. The confidence he exudes is hard to keep up with.

Thankfully, he smiles and nods. "Yes, let's eat and talk."

Jackson places his hand on the small of my back and I grab my drink before making our way over to the hostess. Once we're seated, I basically down my martini and order another one. My palms are sweating and I can't stop fidgeting.

The restaurant is beautiful. It's done in rich blues and greens, which reminds me of Jackson's eyes. There's a large oyster bar on the right wall and the entire back wall is windows overlooking the ocean. Our table is situated with a perfect view of the water. I look around, smiling at the opulence of the scenery and clientele.

Jackson clears his throat as a handsome man walks toward us with a smile on his face. "Carter!" He stands. "How are you? It's been a long time," he says as they hug and clap each other on the back.

Carter glances down at me and back over at Jackson. "Yes, brother, it has been. Didn't mean to interrupt."

Jackson smiles and shifts his weight. "No problem. This is Catherine. She's the new publicist working with me on the cosmetics company."

"Oh, well, I thought maybe you were finally getting back out there." Carter places his hand on his shoulder and Jackson's eyes narrow as he subtly shakes his head.

Hmmm … that's weird. Back out there? And what's with the head shake? My stomach plummets as fear grips my heart. A hundred scenarios race through my mind.

"I should get back to my dinner." Jackson's tone is flat, lacking the buoyancy it held moments before. "It was good seeing you. I'll call next time I'm in town."

"You know Mad—"

"See you, Carter," Jackson cuts in.

"Right. See you, brother. Don't be a stranger." He pats his back and Jackson returns to his seat.

He won't look my way. Gone is the warm and sensual man from a few minutes ago. I can feel the tension coming off him in waves. I want to say something but—well, I don't really know what the hell any of this is. I'm not his girlfriend or even his friend, really. I'm his publicist. He made that crystal clear. I'm such a fool. I knew it was a mistake to get all dressed up and think there could be anything more to this. Taking his cue, I straighten my back and decide to rebuild my wall.

The waitress comes over and takes our orders, and Jackson starts talking about the business. An hour and three martinis later, dinner is done. I want to go to bed. I'm upset and exhausted. I kept myself in check. I didn't get all gooey—I did good. It's not as if he was being charming anyway. We created a plan on where he wants to see things go. He asked a lot of questions regarding the market and buying behaviors, but we steered clear of anything other than the end goal and how he wants to handle the launch. I gave him my best suggestions on how we get there, but the entire dinner Jackson barely spoke other than to ask pointed business questions.

Resting my hand on the table and fiddling with the martini glass, I'm lost in my disappointment. Jackson blows out a deep breath and leans forward then back again. Looking into his eyes, I can see the turmoil churning. After a few seconds, he leans forward again and places his hand over mine.

Glancing at our joined hands, I pull mine out of his grasp and place it on my lap, refusing to look at him. I'm hurt and angry. Two times he's kissed me and two times he's rejected me. The last time was different but the pain is the same.

His deep voice breaks through my ruminating. "Catherine, don't pull away."

"I'm not." I say sharply. I didn't pull away—he did. And so what if I did? He's not anything more than a client and I don't have to get personal with him.

He narrows his eyes and places his hand on the table palm up. "Yes. You are. We need to talk about this. Please give me your hand."

I look down at his hand, open and waiting for me. All I want to do is place my hand in his, to feel his skin against mine. Yet I don't want to. I close my eyes and shake my head.

"Please. I want to explain."

I lift my eyes and see nothing but sincerity. His hand is just lying on the table, waiting, and I'm paralyzed. I remember my rule and promise—I won't allow any man to hurt me again, not that I can prevent it entirely. I place my hand on the table next to his, sending my own message. "Explain, then."

"I'm sorry. I didn't expect to see Carter. He was like a brother to me. There's a lot of history and bad blood between us, to say the least." He inches his hand closer to mine. "I wasn't sure what to say and didn't want you to be in the middle of it." I'm torn. I understand being surprised, but why wait until now to say anything? He places his hand on top of mine and his voice is apologetic. "I want us to figure out whatever this is between us. Can you forgive me for being an asshole?"

In all the years I was with Neil, I don't think he ever apologized. I've been around Jackson for two days and he's not hesitated once. There's something now, though, about how cold he grew that has me on edge. His hand glides up and down the back of mine, but it's his eyes that break through my trepidation. "I forgive you for being an ass. So let's talk." I sigh and he grips my hand.

"I can't and I won't lie to you. I feel something for you. I have since the first day we met." His eyes blaze as he gazes at me. "I think about you all the time. I want to kiss you every time I look at you. Every time I try to focus at work, somehow I'm distracted thinking of you. I can't explain it but I think you feel it too."

I look away, trying to gather my thoughts and express them in a way that doesn't make me feel stupid. How can I explain it to him when I can barely describe it myself? "I don't know how to fully put it into words." I take a deep breath. "I've been hurt. When we met, obviously, I was wearing a ring." His finger rubs across my naked ring finger. I look up and he has a small smile, but his eyes are urging me to keep going. "Anyway, he ... well, he wrecked me. To say things ended badly would be putting it mildly. But honestly, you're my client, Jackson. You could ruin *everything* I've worked for. I'm not willing to throw my career away." I hesitate before saying more. There's no way I'm ready to tell him what's in my heart. I already know where this is going. I'm on a one-way trip to more heartache. Every single man in my life has chosen someone or something else over me. Jackson will be no different.

"I wouldn't ruin anything for you. I'm saying there's something between us. Can you honestly tell me you feel nothing?"

Nothing? No, I definitely can't say that. His blue-green eyes pierce through me. I'm searching, trying to read any emotion telling me I should turn him away. He smiles expectantly and I sigh. "No. But I don't trust myself with you. It's so intense some-times and if I get caught up ... " I trail off, afraid to finish my sentence.

He flips my palm over and traces the inside of my hand, sending tingles through my body. "Look, I'm saying let's take it slow. Have some fun. No mat-ter what, I wouldn't jeopardize your career."

"So, what? We date? I don't know what you're looking for. I don't want another serious relation-ship right now. I can't ..." Emotion chokes me. I'm not sure why all of a sudden I'm struggling. I guess I just don't want another Neil. I'm not strong enough to deal with it.

"Yes, we date. We'll be spending a lot of time together anyway. So either we keep fighting this ... pull or whatever this is ..." he trails off and runs his hand through his hair. "I don't want to pretend anymore. Being around you, seeing you, listening to you laugh, just makes me want you that much more."

I want what he's offering so much, but the other part of me is fighting it. "And what if this ends bad-ly? How do we work together day in and day out?" It's a valid question, and it's really the last flimsy excuse I can voice to him.

He places his palm flat against mine and smiles tentatively. "We're both professionals. I already told you I wouldn't hurt your career." He chuckles.

"Why are you laughing?"

"I've never had to work so hard to get a woman

to date me. I always thought I was a pretty good catch." He lets out a short laugh again.

"I guess it further proves I don't find you charming or endearing." I smile at my line of bullshit. He's absolutely charming, so much so that I'm fighting the urge to crawl across the table and into his lap.

Jackson stands and strides to my side of the table with his hand extended. "Dance with me."

His strong hand engulfs my tiny one as he helps me stand. It's symbolic of how I feel when I'm around him—consumed. We walk to the middle of the small dance floor. Jackson places his hand on my hip and his warmth penetrates my dress. Slowly he lifts my palm and places it on his chest, right over his heart. I can feel its steady beating, the constant thrum as it calms my own. I close my eyes and sink into him as I listen to the singer croon about coming away with her for a while. If only I could get away for a while, ignore all the painful turns my life has taken. He leads us through the song as I replay the last few weeks. Somehow, Jackson has taken my life by storm. He's found a way to make me feel alive, as if a light switch has been turned on, illuminating all my dark corners. He sharpens my senses and fills me with so many different things—excitement, fear, humor, anger. It terrifies me.

The song ends and I look into his kind, warm eyes. He leans in purposefully and gives me a tender kiss.

I smile and a soft giggle comes out.

"What?" Jackson asks.

"Oh, nothing." I shrug. "Just rethinking—maybe you are charming."

"You haven't seen anything yet."

I bet I haven't.

chapter sixteen

We finish dinner and head through the lobby, and over to the elevator. As we wait, I consider my options. Do I invite him in? I mean, we aren't a couple. We're agreeing to stop flirting around the fact that we have some serious sexual tension. I don't know if I'm ready to sleep with him, but if he kisses like that, I can only imagine what he fucks like. I'm not even going to let myself go there. I don't really have time to make a pros and cons list, but I'm pretty sure the pros would win. I'm also quite sure that I could make anything into a pro at this point. Regardless, there are cons and the biggest one is how badly this could end for me. Sure, he doesn't want to ruin my career, but how do I know I can trust him? Look how great my track record has been. No, there's no way I'm going to sleep with him. We decided to take things slow. I need to pace myself with him or I'm going to get burned.

When the elevator door closes, all the feelings I was questioning are amplified by a thousand. I peek at Jackson who appears to have the same thoughts brewing. Our eyes lock and for a moment neither one of us moves. Then, all at once, we reach for each other, colliding in a haze of lust. I couldn't give a shit about being burned—right now, I'd gladly turn to ash. Hands, teeth, lips are everywhere.

Jackson has me pinned against the wall as his mouth greedily devours mine. There's no finesse, no tenderness—this is primal, raw, two people desperate for each other. This kiss is weeks of flirting, toying, and resisting the urge to rip each other's clothes off. His hands roam my body, groping, grasping, squeezing. I'm panting and moaning—I need *more.*

"Catherine ..." He sighs heavily against my neck as I claw at his back.

"Please," I beg. "Don't stop."

I hardly get the words out and his mouth is ravishing mine. Jesus Christ! Who am I? I no longer have the ability to form rational thoughts. All I am is desire, want, lust, and I can't stop. I barely hear the ding of the elevator, but I'm definitely aware of Jackson's absence.

I'm panting, staring incredulously at him as he leans on the wall opposite me. An older gentleman enters the elevator and looks at both of us with a knowing smile, clearly aware of what we were doing. Now I understand why he moved. My lips are swollen, and I can only imagine what my hair looks like after having Jackson's hands tangled in it. I fix my dress and try to regain some semblance of composure. I swear I've completely lost control. The girl who wasn't going to do this? Yeah, she's gone. We're like two teenagers going at it in an elevator— well, interrupted in an elevator, but I enjoyed every second of it.

The door opens with a ding, and Jackson grabs my hand and pulls me out of the elevator. His fingers intertwine with mine as we walk through the hall toward our rooms. He lifts our hands, kissing the back of mine. The feel of his calloused fingers brushing against me increases my need to have them everywhere. When we arrive at my door, the nerves coursing through me smother the yearning I was struggling to control. The fear of being hurt and vulnerable all over again is almost crippling.

Jackson speaks first. "Look at me." He places his hand under my chin and lifts my head. "I want nothing more than to take you to bed, but I'm not going to push you." There's so much honesty in his words.

I nod, unsure of what I want. The woman who wore the corset wants him to come inside. However, my sensible and responsible side says I'm being crazy and I should take things slow. There is an angel and a devil on each shoulder and I'm not sure which one I should listen to. I'm not even sure there's a choice.

He leans down and the instant his full lips press against mine, the sparks ignite into a raging fire that consumes every fiber of my being. I'm burning and I need him to extinguish the flames. His tongue explores my mouth and all I can taste is Jackson. Strong hands roam my body and pull me close, making me feel like I'm being branded. Fuck being sensible!

Somehow we manage to open the door while our mouths are fused together. Jackson's tongue swirls with mine as we stumble through the room. My legs hit the edge of the bed, halting our movement. His deep voice drips with sex. "Turn around."

Breathless, I obey his command. He lifts my hair and brushes it to the side, placing hot kisses against my neck. The anticipation buzzes from my head to my toes and back up to my stomach. *Oh God, I want him so bad.* Shifting my weight as the fire burns in my core, desperate to relieve the aching,

I whimper as he pulls my zipper down agonizingly slow. Other than my erratic breathing and the teeth of my dress coming apart, there's no sound in the room. In a husky whisper I beg, "Jackson, please ..."

"Please what, baby?"

My dress pools on the floor and a long moan escapes my lips as he trails his tongue across my shoulders. The heat of his tongue in contrast to the cool room is wreaking havoc on my body. He turns me around and his breath hitches. With hungry eyes, he devours my body as I stand before him in my corset and heels. He steps forward and groans. "You are so fucking beautiful." His mouth slams against my swollen lips and he pushes me on the bed.

I claw at his clothes, needing to feel his skin against mine. He rips his shirt off and my fingers press against his abs. Jackson hisses as my nails graze his chest, feeling every inch of his perfectly toned body. At the same time, he grabs my ankle and his hands roam up my legs, pushing my need for release to a throbbing ache. "Jackson ..." I moan, trying to control the sensations his touch is educing.

"What do you want, Catherine? You're going to have to tell me."

"You—I want you." I groan as his hands make their way higher.

"Oh baby, you're going to have me." He leans down against my ear and slowly traces the outside shell with his tongue. "I'm going to watch you come. Over and over." I nearly shatter from his promise alone. His voice is low and primal, assuring all of what's to come.

His hands slide down my body and unhook each

tiny eye of my corset. With every pop, my chest tightens instead of finding relief. Finally, the last hook is free and the material falls to the side, leaving me exposed before him. Jackson leans down as I grab for his neck, pulling him toward me and devouring his mouth. He breaks the kiss and moves down my neck and chest, licking and kissing, until he reaches my breasts. The swirl of his tongue across my nipple makes it hard. He pulls it in his mouth, sucking, while his hand pulls and teases my other breast. My eyes roll back and I moan in ecstasy. "Oh God ..."

Jackson groans and moves a hand to my panties. Moving them to the side, his fingers open my pussy. "Mmmm. So fucking wet for me." He moves to my stomach and then pulls the tiny black thong down so that I'm completely naked except for my gold heels. The hunger in his eyes knocks me off center—I've never felt as sexy as I do right now. I need him. I want him so bad it hurts.

I lean in and grab his belt, needing to feel him. I manage to get his pants off, but he grabs my wrists before I can pull his boxers off too. I look up and he smiles softly. "I won't be able to control myself if you do that. Lie down." I comply. "I need to taste you. Right. Fucking. Now."

He leans in and places slow kisses from my knee up to my thigh. As his mouth moves higher, I start to tremble. I close my eyes and fist the sheets as his tongue swipes at my center. It feels so incredible. He continues to lick and suck at the bundle of nerves and then stops. Then he starts again, bringing me closer and closer before suddenly stopping again. I'm almost to the point of tears. I need to release so bad it's becoming physically painful. I moan and beg, "Jackson! Please, I'm so close."

Jackson licks and sucks my clit, bringing me higher, almost to the breaking point. He inserts a finger, slowly curling it around, while he presses harder with his tongue. I detonate and my back bows off the bed as I repeat his name over and over, losing myself to the most intense orgasm I've ever had. Holy fuck!

I open my eyes as he crawls over me. "So fucking sexy. I'm going to enjoy watching you do that again."

I sit up and press him down against the bed, straddling him. He lets out a groan while grabbing the back of my neck. His tongue swirls with mine, allowing me to taste myself mixed with Jackson. I moan, breaking the kiss as my lips travel down his body. I lick and kiss every ridge from his neck to his stomach. I pull his boxers off, setting his impressive erection free. There is nothing small about him—anywhere. I glance up as I lick his cock from root to tip and grip my hand around him, stroking him.

"Fuuuck. You're about to unman me, Catherine."

I'm about to do a whole lot more than that.

I smile and pull my hair to the side so he can see me take him in my mouth. I lick the bead of precum from his tip and circle the top before sheathing my teeth and taking him into my mouth. His fingers tangle in my hair as I hollow out my mouth and take him deeper. He groans as I pump him up and down, applying pressure with my tongue on the underside. I feel him growing larger as I take him in to the back of my throat. Trying to control my gag reflexes, I do it one more time and he pulls tight on my hair as he moans. I want to make him come apart. I want to see if I can make him lose control the way he did to me, to call out my name over and over again. I reach down and roll his balls in my hand.

"Catherine, you better stop." Jackson barely gets the words out and I do it again. "Baby, I'm gonna come."

He erupts in my mouth, pumping in and out as he rides out his orgasm. I swallow every drop as he says my name over and over with reverence. I've never enjoyed giving a blowjob but that was worth watching.

I roll over while both of us try to catch our breath. I'm still coming down from my orgasmic bliss, but as my mind catches up with what just happened, I start to shake. What did I do? I never do this. Ever. I was so absorbed in the moment and now … there's no going back. Until tonight, I'd never taken a man home before at least two months had passed. I've always been the one to put the brakes on—this time I was begging. I freaking begged him. My mind is reeling and the emotions are so intense my chest tightens.

Suddenly, Jackson lifts me and I'm facing him. He brushes the hair off my face as he rests on his arm beside me. He's assessing me, watching each breath, watching how my eyes close as I try to mask my emotions. The way he's reading me makes me tense. My emotions are all over the place and I know he can see it. I look off to the side while I grip his forearm. When he turns my head to look at him, worry is etched on his face. "Hey, what's wrong?"

How do I explain this to him? "I just don't do this—random hook-ups and one night stands." I don't know whether I'm more mortified by the fact that we barely know each other or that I enjoyed it. I close my eyes and focus on how amazing every-thing felt, how during that entire time he made me feel good, beautiful.

Jackson's face softens and he smiles tenderly. "I never said this was random or a one-night thing, did I?"

"No." I shake my head and look away to hide the tears forming. I ruined everything with my dumb insecurities. "I'm sorry."

"You have nothing to be sorry for." Jackson rolls onto his back and I try to get up. He grabs me, pulling me against his chest and wrapping his arms around me. He whispers in my hair, "Can I stay to-night?"

What? He wants to stay even though I've ruined it? "If you want. Of course you can stay." I want him to so badly. I don't know why, but I want nothing more than to lie in his arms and fall asleep.

Jackson doesn't say another word. He just rubs his hand methodically on my back. I curl into him with my arm draped across his chest as I drift off to sleep.

"Mmmm." I moan as I feel strong hands knead my breasts. I arch back and my eyes snap open as I pro-cess that someone is in bed behind me. Someone with his hands on my breasts.

His deep, raspy voice breaks through my fog as he croons in my ear, "Catherine ..." Jackson pulls me against him as his hands roam my naked body. I guess this is a benefit to sleeping nude. He stayed.

He didn't run when I spooked. He held me all night and gave me comfort.

I've never wanted him more than I do right now. He begins kissing my neck and moves to my ear. "Jackson, now. Please." I reach behind me and start stroking his cock.

"Soon enough, baby. I'm not sure you're ready for me yet." Jackson's voice is hoarse as he makes his way down, spreading my sex and inserting two fingers. Slowly he pulls out and uses his thumb against my clit, drawing a long moan from me. I'm desperate for him. The need crushes me, making it difficult to breathe. Jackson continues to bring me higher and higher.

He flips me onto my back and gazes at me with an intensity so fierce my heart skips a beat. He rolls on a condom and I take a deep breath.

"You have no idea what you do to me, how you make me feel," Jackson says as his jaw ticks, trying to control some unnamed emotion. "I'm going to take you now. Make you mine."

My eyes widen and my mouth drops open as he slowly enters me. Bliss—complete and total bliss. I can die a happy woman from this moment on. Nothing has ever felt this good. Every inch of my body is alive as Jackson claims me. I will never re- cover from him no matter how hard I try. "Oh my God," I say in a breathy moan.

"Not God, baby, but pretty damn close. Now open those sexy brown eyes and watch me." His rough voice is strained as he sinks deeper.

"Jackson." I sigh and try to keep my eyes open, but the pleasure coursing through my body is driv- ing me insane. "More. Please," I beg, desperate for all of him.

"Just feel me. I want you to feel this moment every time you close your eyes." He pushes deeper, eliciting a strangled sob from my mouth. "Feel how deep I am inside your pussy. Feel how fucking hard you make me." He rears back and slams into me. "Feel it, baby." There's no way I couldn't feel it if I tried. He's everywhere—every sense, every breath, and every heartbeat right now. He owns me.

Jackson reaches between us and applies pressure to my clit, making me cry out and claw at his back. I grate my nails down and he pounds into me harder and faster. We're both becoming frantic, desperate. Meeting him thrust for thrust, my eyes are locked on his as I cry out and shatter into a thousand pieces. I ride out my orgasm, unintelligibly yelling as Jackson follows with his head buried in my neck.

I rub my hand down his back languidly for a few minutes before he rolls over and heads into the bathroom. I look over at the clock and stretch. What a way to wake up. Jackson walks back over and I take a minute to appreciate the man before me. He oozes sex and confidence and for some reason, he's attracted to me. Out of all the females he could choose, he wants me? I shake my head as he gets closer to the bed.

"What?" he says, smirking.

I smile and bite my lip, embarrassed for being caught staring at this glorious man yet again. There's so much more to him than just looks, though. He makes me laugh and compliments me. He consoled me in the car after I got the news about my father. Unlike most men I've had in my life, he seems to care about others before himself. He climbs into bed and raises a brow. I sigh. "Nothing.

Just thinking."

"About what?"

"You. Me. Us. I don't know. Everything." My heart is pounding as I relay more than I wanted to. It's like he forces the truth out of me without even doing anything.

"Don't overthink this. We'll take things as they come." He pulls me against his chest and tucks my hair behind my ear. "I want us to spend time together and stop fighting what we feel. I want to kiss you and not feel like I'm doing something wrong. I know we have a lot going on, and the fact that I'm your client complicates things. But we keep it professional at work and when I have you alone"—he drops his voice so it's low and seductive—"I make no promises." He rolls us on our sides so we can look at each other.

"I don't want this to affect my work. When we're in the client-publicist role, I need you to let me do my job." I smile and rub my hand across his stubble. "My career matters to me. I need to know you understand that."

"Do you think *my* career doesn't matter to me? I own and run two companies, one of which takes me away for periods of time. Though, I didn't want the cosmetics company. If it weren't for Danielle, I would have sold it by now." His admission takes me back a little. If he didn't want the company, why does he own it? And why does Danielle matter in that equation?

"I'm not sure I understand."

"Danielle is a long-time friend of the family. She's worked extremely hard to make Raven what it is today. She helped run the business when I was tied up with the security company, but her heart is in the lab. She really didn't want to handle the business end." He rolls back and puts his hand behind his head. "I entered the Navy when I was twenty-two. I did eight years, saved every penny I made, and invested it well. When—" He pauses and takes a deep breath. "Anyway, I got out of the Navy and invested in the security company. I didn't know it would do so well." I lie with my head on his chest and trace the tattoo there. I sense there's more he's not telling me about why he got out of the military. I can't put my finger on it, but I felt him tense when he got to that part.

I rest my hand on his chest and put my chin on it. "Why a security company?"

He smiles at me with a glimmer in his eyes. "I figured that was obvious. I mean, I'm pretty badass. I have to keep this persona." Jackson grins and taps my nose.

"So humble." I roll my eyes. I run my hands down his chest and give him a playful smile.

"What?"

"Oh, nothing, Mr. I'm a Navy SEAL who's charming, endearing, oh, and God's gift to women." I smile and remember his bullshit reason to get me to dinner with him. I sit up and pull the sheet around me. "Hey! You made me a bet, Muffin. I want to know my time from that insane course yesterday."

He pulls the sheet down, exposing my breasts, and rips it farther away when I try to grab it. "Muffin, huh?" He leans up and I try to hold my ground and not back away. "Are you sure you want to call me that?" His one brow raises and his eyes darken. Oh shit. I'm in trouble now.

Mustering my courage, I respond, "I'm pretty sure I already did. Now I want my time!"

Jackson crawls toward me and I scamper backward. I'm smiling, but I know I'm going to pay for this. "Where are you going? You started this game, baby." I try to scoot back but I'm going to be off the bed in about two seconds.

"You owe me my time and a spa day."

He smiles and lunges for me. I laugh as he starts to tickle me relentlessly. "Jackson ... stop," I try to say through fits of giggles. "Oh my God ... Stop!" He doesn't let up.

"Will you call me Muffin again?" he asks while I try to catch my breath.

"Yes!"

The mischief is back in his eyes as he begins tickling me again. I squirm and writhe on the bed. He stills suddenly and I realize he's extremely turned on. I'm gasping for air as he brings his mouth down, stopping right before his perfect lips connect with mine. His eyes crinkle in the corners and I try to kiss him, but he backs away. So not fair! "Wanna rethink your answer?"

Two can play at this game. I raise my arms over my head and stretch. His eyes shift to my breasts and I smile. Good, it's working. "What if I called you a different muffin?" He doesn't respond, so I tilt his chin so he's looking in my eyes. "Jackson?"

"Huh?" The confusion is evident as his gaze shifts back to my exposed body before returning to my face.

I raise my eyebrows at his question.

Seeming to recover, he smirks and leans toward me again. "What kind of muffin are you referring to?"

"Oh, I don't know ..." I sigh dramatically. "You know, there are a lot of muffins. Corn, blueberry, chocolate chip, stud muffin—"

Jackson crushes his mouth against mine, effectively ending the conversation.

chapter seventeen

*A*fter one of the best mornings I've had in a long time, I kicked Jackson out so I could get ready. We're heading back to New Jersey late in the evening and I needed to get some work done. I managed to get some emails sorted and check my voicemails. All in all, I've been pretty damn productive. I don't think I've stopped smiling, and my cheeks are starting to hurt.

I hear a ding on my phone.

Jackson: Hey, I need to go to the office. We need to leave in 30 min.

Me: Okay. No problem.

There must me something serious going on. He's been on the phone several times, has gone in to the office, and seems tense when it comes to anything regarding his security firm. I start to pack my bags and close my laptop. Luckily, there isn't too much stuff to pick up. I close my eyes, remembering how Jackson was so reluctant to leave this morning, how he melted another part of my carefully constructed wall. It's so easy to be comfortable around him.

Twenty minutes later, there's a knock at the door. Grabbing my bags and giving the room a once over, my trepidation soars. What do I say or do? I'm not good at this crap, which is why I've always been in a relationship. I don't know what this is, so I don't know how to act. Another bang on the door. I can't hide since he's my ride home. I channel some inner strength and head to the door.

"Hey, gorgeous." He smiles and leans in, pressing his lips to mine.

Maybe this won't be so awkward.

"Hey." I look him over and grin. Now that I know what's underneath those clothes, it's virtually impossible not to stare. His eyes narrow and his dimple reappears.

"Are you mentally undressing me?"

Cocky ass.

"No!" Damn him and his ability to read me. "What time is our flight?"

He smiles and grabs my bag—always the gentleman. "We leave around six, but I may have to push it back depending on what I find out when I get to the office."

Letting my curiosity get the best of me, words tumble out of my mouth as we head to the elevator. "What's going on? Can I help?" He looks over with his head cocked to the side. "I'm not trying to pry." And here I go with my overstepping. I swear one day I'll keep my big mouth shut.

"You're not prying." Jackson's fingers interlace with mine and my heart skips a beat. Just the small physical touch he gives me is reassuring. "I told you we have contracts, but our contracts are very different. Basically, my company trains men and women to go to a war zone. They get paid a lot of money, but it's hazardous. We get funded by the government and we send a team to do various missions or security details."

"Wow, sounds dangerous."

"It can be, but we make sure our people have the best equipment, training, and anything else they could need while they're out there. It's why most of my team are former SEALs or prior military."

It's insane to think people volunteer to go to Iraq and Afghanistan when they aren't in the military. Ice shoots through my veins, freezing me in place. What if Jackson has to go? I'm sure he's been before and it's obvious he's trained, but still. Would he spend long periods of time there?

Jackson stops and cups my face. "What is it?"

Unable to articulate my sudden anxiety, I shake my head and smile. "Nothing. Sorry. I'm trying to understand why anyone would do that voluntarily." I'm not going to bring up that it's him I'm worried about. For all I know this relationship—or whatever it is—could be done next week. I break his hold and head toward the elevator. I need to shake this dread from the pit of my stomach. Otherwise, this thing we have might be over before it actually begins.

"Well, for a lot of us it's that we miss serving. But it's different for everyone."

I guess that makes sense. I'm hoping he doesn't have that same desire. I'm not sure I'd be strong enough to handle it. However, I'd rather not go there right now.

The ride to the office is quiet. About thirty minutes later, we arrive at Cole Security. I'm hoping to see a little more of what Jackson's world is like. We walk in and head straight to his office. A few people raise their hands but they're either immersed in paperwork or on the phone. I head over to the wall of photos and take a closer look. Mark is in a lot of them along with three other men. They look like they're really close.

"Jackson?" He looks up. "Who are these guys?" I ask, pointing to the picture of the five of them all smiling in their uniforms.

He walks over, smiling, and takes the picture down. "This is Mark." He points and then hangs the photo back on the wall. "The other guys were in my unit. Aaron." He points to the one guy in the middle. "He works for me here. But Brian and Fernando died on a mission." He runs his fingers through his hair with his eyes downcast. I want to console him but someone walks in before I have the chance.

"Hey, you're here. Good." A stocky guy with a goatee comes in the door. I recognize him as Aaron from the picture. He heads over to Jackson's desk as he searches through the papers in his hand.

"Aaron, this is Catherine."

I smile and lift my hand. He smiles and looks back to Jackson. Okay. A man of few words.

"I talked to a few people at the base, but so far nothing. I think some of us should head out and oversee the team in place now. The information is sketchy and I don't like it. There's something that doesn't feel right." Aaron speaks so fast that I have a hard time keeping up. He keeps grabbing at his neck, obviously stressed.

Jackson clears his throat and starts to pace. After a few minutes of back and forth, and what appears to be a lot of consideration, he answers, "Talk to Mark. If you both agree, then fine, get a team together. I want you or Mark on point. I don't know what's going on out there, but we need to get it settled and I don't trust anyone else."

"I agree, Muff. I'm going to see who's on stand-by and also work some other angles. I don't want to head out there with Natalie so close to delivering, but I will if it comes to that."

"Fuck, I forgot she's due soon. Let's try to avoid anyone going if we can. See if you can work any more contacts and find out why their shipments are delayed." Jackson glances at me and then looks back to Aaron.

"Okay, I'll keep you in the loop." Aaron heads back out and I smile, nodding as he walks past.

I stand by the wall, unsure of what to do. There's something going on in his company and he's dealing with launching a new campaign with his other company. It's a lot to take on. How do I fit into all this? This question and my own uncertainties are always looming. I make myself a promise to keep this under control. Jackson brings out my strength and I'm going to find a way to let that show more. Looking at his friends and all the things he's done is astounding. He's a leader, a friend, and seems to be loved by many.

"Ready?"

"Ah!" I nearly scream as he scares the shit out of me. Lost in the photos and my own inner thoughts, Jackson's stealth mode catches me off guard yet again.

His deep, throaty chuckle is against my neck as his arms wrap around me from behind.

"Seriously, this is getting old." I mean really, am I that oblivious?

He runs his face against my neck, his stubble scratching against my skin. Leaning back into his embrace, he places chaste kisses on my shoulder and neck as he runs his hands up my arms and squeezes. When he stops, I turn to face him. His eyes are desolate—completely void—as they look at the photos on the wall.

"Jackson? Are you okay?" I ask apprehensively.

When he looks at me, he looks sad. He winces when I place my hand on his arm so I drop it. It's the same look he had the last time he glimpsed at the photos and, like then, I'm unsure how to proceed. I don't want to push him, but I want to know what's causing him pain. I try again by placing my hand on his face, rubbing it on his scruffy cheek. Our gazes lock and I watch his eyes gloss with unshed tears. Leaning up, I place a gentle kiss on his lips.

"I'm fine. I'm just lost in memories," he finally replies, giving me some insight into what's troubling him. I hate seeing anyone hurting, but for some reason Jackson's pain feels like my own, worse even. And that scares me—a lot.

"Wanna tell me about them?"

"Not today." He gives a small smile and places his lips against mine. I feel his tongue across the seam of my lips, asking for entrance. I grant him access and our tongues brush against each other. He kisses me slowly, tenderly, never rushing the kiss. It's sweet, almost timid. My hands roam up his arms and around his neck as his fingers gently tangle in my hair. Our kiss stays soft, as if he's pouring his emotion into me. Tears form as my own emotions are unleashed. My hurt, pain, sadness, and loss from the last few days bubbles up. His hands are sliding down my neck and then my shoulders when we hear a cough and a loud laugh behind us.

"Don't let me interrupt. I don't mind watching." Mark smiles as he enters the room. He plops in a chair and puts his legs on the table.

I laugh as my heavy emotions quickly change to embarrassment, which is surely displayed across my face. As I start to move, Jackson grabs me and pulls me close, glaring at Mark. "By all means, ass-hole, make yourself at home."

Mark looks around, smirking. "I need an office like this. You're never here. I think I'll move in after you leave."

"I think maybe I'll let Papa Smurf stay off the mission. You really could use some time in the sun," Jackson goes back at Mark.

I giggle. Seriously, what is with these guys and their names? I don't even want to ask who Papa Smurf is or how he earned that name.

"Did she just giggle?" Mark asks before snort-ing.

"Did you just snort?" I reply with a smile.

"Well played, Catherine. Well played."

I love when men think they can get one over on me.

"She got you, fucker," Jackson says while laugh-ing and pushing Mark's feet off the table. "What do you need?"

Mark and Jackson start talking about the mis-sion that's in trouble in Afghanistan. One of the trucks never delivered their second shipment of ammunition and they're both worried. The stress of knowing their friends are in harm's way must be insurmountable. No wonder Jackson was pissed the other day.

"Listen, Kitty." Mark leans in since he's finished talking with Jackson.

What the hell did he call me? "Kitty?"

"Yeah, I mean your name is Cat, so I figure Kitty is a good call sign for you. You get all cute and cud-dly, but I bet you could claw someone's eye out if they pissed you off. Right?" Mark laughs and raises his brow.

Jackson stands there with a smug smile on his face.

"Seriously, I don't need a call sign. I'm pretty sure I'm not going on any missions anytime soon."

"Nah, Kitty works. Plus, now that I know it pisses you off, this shit is going to be even more fun. Make sure fat ass stays out of trouble in New York. I don't want to have to come up there and kick his ass."

Jackson laughs, "Keep dreaming, fucker."

Mark walks out of the office, whistling the melody of "The Cat Came Back" as he goes.

I turn to Jackson with my mouth hanging open. This can't be real. He's just smiling away, completely amused. I start to walk over, narrowing my eyes, and he raises his hands in mock surrender.

"Catherine, Mark is a jackass." He starts backing away as I move closer.

"Yes, I've learned as much, but you—" I point my finger as I get closer. "You didn't even try to stop him." I smile and bite my lip as Jackson takes a step forward.

"Don't worry. You don't have to see him too much. Plus, if I intervene, it'll only get worse. Besides, kittens are cute." He reaches out, grabs me around my waist, and pulls me flush against him. My heart races and my breathing accelerates as he leans down and kisses me. He lifts me up and turns me, pushing my back against the wall. I wrap my leg around his waist as our mouths fuse together. Forcefully, passionately, he plunges into my mouth, claiming me. I moan, knowing that with every touch, with every kiss, I'm becoming his. The low flame that burns whenever Jackson is around turns into an inferno. I pull my mouth away, trying to push him back.

"Jackson, we have to stop." My voice is weak and breathless.

He ignores my futile attempt for space and puts his arms against the wall, not allowing me to move anywhere. "I told you, in private I make no promises."

"Yes, but we're not in private. Two of your employees have already made that clear. Plus, we have a plane to catch."

"I own the plane," he whispers seductively against my lips. "It'll wait until I'm ready. Tell me you don't want me," he commands and pulls his mouth back. I'm against the wall, breathless and unable to lie. I want him more than my next breath. "Tell me."

"I want you," I say, closing my eyes to the sound of my shaking voice. I'm so damn turned-on. I've wanted him since day one. Feeling his arousal on my stomach, I open my eyes and look into his. The lust in them spurs me on. I lean in and grip his shirt. He pulls back slightly and his cheek lifts in amusement.

"Good. Now we have a plane to catch." He leans backward, making it impossible for me to kiss him again.

"Jackson, you don't want to play this game, do you?" I say, dripping with desire.

"What game, baby? I'm just following your wishes."

"I don't think so. I want you." I snake my hand around his neck and yank as his eyes crinkle. I'm practically climbing my way to his mouth.

"You want me, huh?"

"I think I've said that already." I inch closer to

his mouth. He pulls back but shifts me up higher on his waist.

"Too bad." He leans in and gives me a brief kiss.

It seems Jackson likes to play games. Good thing I never lose. He may not know it yet, but he has met his match.

I spent the entire flight keyed up from Jackson's teasing and subsequent refusal to quench my desire in Virginia. Then, of course, he found any way he could to continue the torturous game. He'd brush against my leg or just barely touch my arm, fueling the hunger coursing through my veins. In order to avoid begging him, I spent the flight plotting a way to repay the favor. Payback is a bitch and he's about to see how big of one I can be—in a nice way, of course.

We finally settle into the car and enjoy the comfortable silence. It's nice not to feel as though you have to always talk. After ten minutes Jackson shifts over, putting his arm behind my seat and pulling me against his side. I look up and smile.

"It's going to be a few days until I can see you again. I have a lot of shit to get settled at the office and there's still the situation in Virginia." He smiles and rubs my arm.

"I don't expect anything." If he feels like I'm going to be needy because we had sex, I need to squash that quickly. I need space to think about all that's already happened, plus I have work to do too. When I'm around him I lose the ability to say no, so it's a good thing we'll have time apart.

"Never said you did. But I don't want you to use

this as an excuse to push me away again or get any ideas in your head that I'm avoiding you." His brow rises as he somehow reads my mind.

"I understand your job, just as I hope you understand mine."

The car stops once we reach my apartment, but Jackson's strong arm still surrounds me. I haven't addressed his last statement and I don't intend to. Slowly he lifts my chin, placing a tender kiss on my lips. Without a word, he exits the car and I press my hands to my mouth. It's tingling from the brief but warm moment. It's astounding to me how much he affects my mind and body.

Standing there with my bag, he tells the driver he'll be a moment. He grips my hand and pulls me into him, almost like we're dancing. I gasp as I stumble into his solid chest. He stares intensely and my body begins to quiver under his gaze.

"Tonight, when I'm alone, I'm going to think about how good your legs felt wrapped around me, how your voice sounded when you screamed out my name. I'll remember how it felt when my dick sunk into your hot, wet pussy." He leans closely and whispers against my ear, causing the hair on the back of my neck to stand, "And I'll be counting down the minutes until I have you again."

I let out a low moan as he presses his lips to the spot right below my ear. Oh. Fucking. Shit. Without thinking, I grip the back of his neck and crush my lips against his. His chest rumbles as he returns the kiss, giving and taking as his words spur an undeniable passion. His fingers wrap around my arms and he pushes me back with a cocky smile before turning to leave.

What? No way!

I grab his arm before he can escape. "You can't say shit like that and then freaking leave!" My eyes are wide and I'm practically panting.

"What? You don't like my dirty talk?" His eyes are liquid, showing he's affected as well.

"Oh, I like my Muff dirty, but you might want to remember two can play at this game." I smile, trying to quell the desperation I'm feeling for him right now.

Jackson leans in close and his lips whisper across my cheek. "I can't wait to show you how dirty I can get. That's to make sure you don't pull away." His warm breath washes over me, heating every part of me, before his lips reach mine. "Until next time. Don't miss me too much."

He turns, leaving me standing there, stunned and completely turned-on. Bastard. I'm going to make him pay for that shit. I see a serious case of blue balls in his future.

chapter eighteen

J've been home for a week and haven't accomplished a damn thing. The song for the Raven Cosmetics commercial is no longer legal to use. The approval I obtained beforehand expired, and now the music company is dragging their feet. Then Taylor told me the partners met yesterday about who would be given the promotion. It was a fifty-fifty split between Elle and me. So much for me being a shoo-in for the promotion once I landed the Raven account. They plan to wait until we both finish with our current clients to make a decision.

Jackson and I haven't seen each other since he dropped me off after our trip. We've talked a few times on the phone about what he needs to do to get ready for the launch and we made plans for this weekend. But he's not happy about the ad delay. Plus, Neil's been calling again. Worse than all that, though, is how I have to go for the reading of my father's will in three weeks. I keep trying to push it to the depths of my mind, but it keeps creeping up at the most inopportune times. In my life, when it rains it doesn't just pour, no—it's a full-on monsoon.

I grab my journal and decide to write again. It's therapeutic and helps me get my thoughts together. I've been so busy that I haven't really had much time lately. I miss it—I miss watching my heart bleed onto the paper.

I put the pen down when I hear a loud voice. "Biffle, time for a drink." Ashton stalks toward me holding a bottle in her hand.

"Good." I shrug and decide not to fight her this time. "I need one." Or four.

"I'm not sure what to do with this attitude," she says with a cat-ate-the-canary grin. "Usually I have to threaten you. By the way, just-fucked is a better look for you. Maybe you should call him and get that taken care of. We need to make sure frumpy, nasty Cat stays away."

I groan and roll my eyes. She's been pushing me to go to him, to not let him get away. I'm not sure why she's so up my ass about it. "I don't feel like calling him. I feel like having my best friend pour me a shot and get me drunk."

"Well now *that* I can do. I've got bubblegum vodka or whipped. What's your poison?"

"Whipped, baby!"

We grab some shot glasses and get comfy on the couch, laughing about the new doctor in Ashton's lab. He's been hitting on her and my crazy friend is feeding it.

"Well he's ugly as all hell, but if he wants to keep buying me dinner, I'm not an idiot."

"Ashton! That's just so ... so ... wrong." I slap her arm.

"Maybe I'll tell him I'm a lesbian." She shrugs, laughing, and hooks her arms around me. "Wanna make out?"

"Oh good God. Get off me, jackass."

We've been drinking for a few hours. Ashton has analyzed my trip in great detail. I think she's falling in love with Jackson. It's kinda funny. We laugh and swoon, only stopping to refill our shot glasses. I know I'm three sheets to the wind since I can't feel my tongue anymore.

"Ash, I gotta pee." I practically fall off the couch and laugh as I try to stand straight. I'm completely shit-faced. I make my way to the bathroom and back by the grace of God. When I get to the living room, my eyes go wide. Either I'm hallucinating or Jackson is sitting on my couch.

"Catherine, aren't you a sight for sore eyes." He smiles as he gets up and walks over to me. When he leans down to kiss me, I quickly put my hand up to his mouth before he can touch my lips. "You can't kiss me," I whisper and look around. I'm still not sure it's really him. Maybe my mind conjured him up.

"Oh, why not?" He stares at me with one brow raised and that cocky smile I love so much. Awww, fake Jackson even makes the same gestures.

"Well, imaginary Jackson, I'll tell you." I lean in real close and somehow get the words out between giggles. "I like a boy and I don't think I should kiss you." Ashton is laughing hysterically and I join her, although I'm not sure why we're laughing.

"Imaginary, huh? And tell me, baby, what's this boy's name?" He leans close and places his hand on the back of my head, pulling me against his chest. I lean into him and take a deep breath. Imaginary Jackson even smells the same.

"He's not really a boy. He's *all* man, if you know what I mean." I slur the words and giggle.

"How much have you had to drink?"

"Ohhh, you know, six or eight. I can't remember." I close my eyes and rest against his strong, hard chest. My mind is a beautiful place right now.

"How did you know where I was?"

Ashton speaks first. "I think you're cut off. Jackson is really here and you are gonna hate yourself tomorrow."

Imaginary Jackson pulls us to the couch, where I sink into him further.

"Nuh uh," I retort, drifting to sleep.

Next thing I know, strong hands are cupping my cheeks and lifting my face. My lashes flutter open and I'm staring into Jackson's—or imaginary Jackson's—gorgeous turquoise eyes. Damn he's hot. I so want to break off a piece of that again. He continues to gaze with a fierce intensity—it almost sobers me. Fuck! He's here!

And I'm drunk—really drunk.

His deep voice breaks through my alcohol fog. "Hi there."

"Hi," I say breathlessly.

"Hi! I'm going to bed in case anyone was curious," Ashton yells, and we all start laughing. "Jackson, it was a pleasure meeting you. Hopefully I'll see you in the morning." She winks at me and starts to leave, giving me a thumbs up as she heads to her room.

Jackson scoops me into his arms effortlessly and places a quick kiss on my forehead. "Where's your room?"

I point at what I hope is my door. "Ummm that one. I think." He laughs as he opens the door to the bathroom. Oops.

The next door he opens is my bedroom. "Lucky door number two." He walks over and gently places me on my bed. Crap! Jackson is here—in my room—and I'm not even sober to enjoy it. "I'm going to stay tonight. I'll be a gentleman," he whispers in my ear.

"Okay. But feel free not to be." I laugh since I've become a giggly, drunken fool.

I watch as he undresses. At least I'm going to enjoy this! His gaze as he pulls his pants off stops my urge to laugh. Nope. Nothing funny about that.

"I like your room," Jackson says, looking around.

"I like you naked," I say, then slap my hand over my mouth.

"Are you sure? Maybe you like imaginary Jackson better." His brow lifts and his dimple appears.

"I like *all* the Jacksons." I fall against my pillow as the room spins. Ugh! Please don't let me get sick.

"I'm glad. I was starting to wonder." I feel the bed shift as he slides his arm under my head. "Sleep well."

"Good night." I nuzzle into his neck as I pass out, suddenly not feeling so sick after all.

I crack my eye open and slam it shut again—too bright! My head is pounding and my mouth feels like I have a million cotton balls in it. I roll over and my hand slaps on a warm, shirtless, rock-hard chest. What?

"That wasn't very nice," a deep, husky voice croaks.

I slowly open my eye and see Jackson's wide grin. Ummm, why is he in my bed and when the hell did he get here? Well, I'm fully clothed so that's good ... I think. I open my mouth to speak but nothing comes out. Water. I need water. I look over at my nightstand and see two aspirins and a water bottle. I quickly sit up, groaning as I grab the side of my head.

"Not feeling so hot this morning, huh?" Jackson yells, or at least that's what it sounds like in my head.

"Shhh. Too loud," I whisper and reach for the medicine.

He leans over, swipes the pills, and places them in my hand. "I was whispering, babe. Here. Drink."

Hopefully this medicine is fast acting, otherwise I'm going to be worthless all day. I lie back down and try to recall what happened last night. We drank. I remember that much. I remember going to the bathroom and eyes … I remember his eyes. I roll over and face Jackson, hoping he can fill me in. "So …"

"What? You like imaginary Jackson more?"

"I …" The puzzle pieces start to click. Imaginary Jackson! Please someone kill me. That would be a lot easier than the embarrassment I'm dealing with now. "Look, I drank a lot. Nothing I said—or did—can be held against me."

He rolls and faces me, pushing the hair back off my face. "You were adorable and nothing happened last night—well, at least not what I was hoping for." Jackson's grin is wide as his eyes shift toward my breasts.

"Hey!" I quickly cut him off. "I didn't mean that you did anything. I mean I vaguely remember a few things." My hand makes its way to his chest and I trace the tribal sun. It's so beautiful. The tattoo on my hip is more of a celestial sun, but his is huge and takes up his entire pec, completely covering where his heart is. My fingers roam the rays and he sighs, placing his hand over mine. "We both have suns," I observe.

"The sun is constant," Jackson states.

"I got mine on my eighteenth birthday."

"What made you get the sun?" he asks.

I could very easily give him a girly answer like I usually do, but I want to share this with him. The sun has great significance to me, even if it also brings a fair amount of darkness. "When I was a child, my father used to sing 'You are My Sunshine' to me when I was sad. I always remembered that about him. I still sing it when I need to calm myself." I sigh and look up with sad eyes. "It's probably the only good memory I have of him, or at least one I remember. He would either sing it or whistle it if he was upset with my mother. I carried on that tradition, which basically means it's my theme song."

"Tell me about him," Jackson says quietly and holds my hand steady against his chest.

"I don't really have much to say." I take a deep breath. "He left when I was nine, on my birthday, and I never saw him again. He walked away while I cried on the floor. Never looked back."

"I'm sorry. That must've been hard."

"Well, yeah. I was a kid. I begged him, literally hanging onto his leg." I pause, remembering how desperate I was for him not to walk away. Unfortunately, that was only the beginning of my heartache. "I would write letters and beg my mom to take me to him. But she didn't know where he was. He disappeared. It was awful because before he left, he adored me. He told me every day how much he loved me and how special I was. Then he just ..." Tears start to leak as I recall my childhood. "I cried a lot in the beginning. Then I would tell people he died because it was easier than explaining he didn't love me."

He smiles sadly and presses his lips to my forehead, giving me the strength to say more. I haven't even touched the surface of the years of damage his absence caused.

"I never understood it. How do you love someone so much and then walk away?" I take a shaky breath and continue, "I wanted him to *want* me. Or explain why he deserted me. If he didn't love my mother anymore, I could handle that, but to not love me anymore—I still don't fully comprehend it. I don't have kids, so I don't understand a parent's love. But I've seen my friends and there is nothing they wouldn't do for their children. I thought a parent's love was supposed to be unwavering." I hate thinking about this but the floodgates have opened and they don't want to close. Jackson lies here, staring at me with compassion as he holds my hand and gives it a small squeeze. I sigh before going on.

"There was a time I used to hope he would return and we could just go back to the way things were, but I realized it was never going to happen. I blamed myself for a long time. I thought I did something wrong to make him leave. If I was good enough, or if I didn't cry all the time, maybe he wouldn't have left." Jackson's calloused thumb catches one of my tears. I've never told anyone other than Ashton these things.

"I'm so sorry, Catherine. But you didn't do anything wrong. *He* fucking decided how to handle it, not you."

"I know I didn't do anything wrong *now*, but he really fucked me up for a while." And then it hits me out of nowhere. The reality comes crashing down around me, smothering me. "He's really dead.

He's never coming back. I'll never get any answers. Do you know what kind of crushing guilt I'll carry forever because I never tried? I could've tried as an adult. Searched for him. But I didn't. I gave up."

Jackson's arms encase me and he pulls me close as I start to cry in earnest. Tears fall like rain and the last week of emotions pummels me. My dad is gone. I'll never get a chance to reconcile with him. There will never be a chance of him being a part of my life or my future children's lives. He'll never know who I am and I'll never be able to let this go. I'll have to carry around all the hurt and pain of an unloved child because he was too selfish to try. He broke me and I'll never be fixed because he's dead.

Jackson simply rubs my back and lets me unload years' worth of unshed tears. After a few minutes, I lean back with red-rimmed eyes and he places a small kiss on my lips. He hasn't said a word, but there's pain in his eyes as he closes them. "I'm sorry you're hurting, baby. I know more about guilt than you can ever imagine."

I lean on his chest and place my hand on his cheek, gently stroking his face and enjoying the way his stubble feels against my skin. "What do you mean?" I ask timidly.

"I'll talk about it at some point, but not today. You've had a lot to process," he says as he rolls onto his back, taking me with him. I curl up on his chest.

"Will you tell me about your parents, then?"

He lets out a half laugh. "I'm afraid my story isn't very interesting. My parents are pretty boring and still happily married. My dad is former Air Force, so he was gone a lot. Even when I was a kid he always emphasized that hard work is essential to any man and I should get used to it.

"My mom is your typical military wife. She was mother, father, friend, disciplinarian, and everything in between. She cooked, cleaned, made sure my sister, Reagan, and I didn't kill each other, and then she'd replace the alternator in the car when it went out."

"She sounds like an amazing woman," I say, looking at him as his grin spreads across his face. I love watching those eyes crinkle when he's truly happy.

"She really is. She could kick my ass and then turn around and bake cookies for my class. I feared my dad—but Mom, she was a force of nature. You know how mothers always say, 'Just wait till your father comes home?'"

"Yeah. Ashton's mother invented that phrase. We heard it a lot. We were kind of a handful. I'm sure you find that hard to believe." My brow rises, waiting for him to challenge me.

"Not you!" He laughs and tickles my sides. I squirm before he continues on. "Anyway, my mom never said that. It was my dad who probably could've said it. She still scares the shit out of me."

"They sound great." I'm happy that he has such a wonderful family. No child should grow up without love. It's obvious his parents have done an amazing job with him.

"Don't get me wrong, there were times when my dad being away was rough. He missed a lot of birthdays, Christmases, and other holidays. My mom had to make sure Reagan and I didn't notice or at least that it didn't fuck up the whole day if we did. That's the life of a military kid, though. Dad was a pilot, so even when he was home he was usually doing work-ups."

"Wait. Your name is Jackson and your sister's name is Reagan?"

"Yes, why?" He looks confused at where I'm going with this.

"I'm noticing the dead president theme going on with your family, that's all. Am I missing something?"

"Out of everything we just talked about, that's what you want to ask me about?"

"If my name was Thelma and I had a sister Louise, you would think it was funny too!" I laugh and shrink back.

He grabs me and flips me on my back, hovering over me. I love the playfulness dancing in his eyes. "Are you making fun of me?"

Batting my eyelashes and tilting my head to the side, trying to feign innocence, I smile. "Who, me? Never."

With a warm smile playing across his lips, he leans down and gives me a long closed-mouthed kiss as he grips my leg and wraps it around his waist. Enjoying where this seems to be heading, I push up into the kiss. Jackson rolls me so I'm on top of him. The alcohol fog has completely dissipated as the kiss deepens. Our tongues volley back and forth—I couldn't care less about my head throbbing or anything else. Right when things are about to get better, he stops and slaps my ass, hard.

"Owww!" I laugh, rubbing my butt, and he rolls off to the side, matching my laughter. "Jerkface."

"That'll teach you to be such a smartass. Now, what else did you want to know about my nonpolitical parents?"

I crawl back to my former position and nestle

in. "How did your dad feel about you going into the Navy?"

"He didn't care, honestly. He thought I was fucking insane for wanting to be a SEAL. When you know the life and what we really go through, it's different. There is no idolizing." He runs his hand through his hair and pulls me close.

"Did you always want to be a SEAL?" I wonder.

"There was never a doubt. Dad was adamant I finish college first. So I went to school and double majored in finance and criminal justice. Then I enlisted as an officer, but I knew I'd be a SEAL. If you're going to join, might as well be the best. And that's what we are—the best." He smirks and juts out his chin, showing his arrogance a little.

I can see why he's proud. He's accomplished something many have failed at.

"Pretty sure of yourself, aren't ya?"

"Well, what's there not to be sure of?" He laughs and kisses the top of my head.

"Your humility needs some help. Your head gets any bigger, I'll need to get a larger apartment so you can fit." I laugh and he chuckles.

"I speak the truth."

I shake my head and lay down against his chest.

We both grow quiet, comfortable with the silence between us. Nuzzling into him, I close my eyes as my head throbs from the night of drinking I'm still paying for. The onslaught of emotions probably hasn't helped either. My mind drifts, thinking of a young Jackson and how it must have been difficult knowing his dad was away but wanted to be home.

"Hey," he says quietly. I must've fallen asleep. "You awake?"

"Yeah, I'm up. Sorry. Between the hangover and crying I guess I was beat."

"I need to get going but I want to take you out tonight. On a date," Jackson says against my neck.

Before I can respond, my cell phone rings. Jackson reaches over, grabs it, and hands it to me. Neil again. I roll my eyes and huff. I'm pissed he's still calling—there's nothing left to say. I silence the phone and put it down. Jackson gets up and starts getting dressed. He looks over and smiles, then heads out of my room. Maybe he saw the name? He doesn't know who Neil is, though. I hear the voicemail alert and decide to check it real quick.

"Hey, Cat. I need to talk. I know you see me calling." He takes a shaky breath. "I understand why you're not answering, but please—I need you."

I slump on the bed and put my phone on the charger. Simple things I can handle, but Neil? No, not today. My chest is tight and I'm suddenly nauseous. He didn't need me three months ago, hell, seven months ago when he made his choice to sleep with Piper. He didn't *need* me when he told me I wasn't enough. Screw him. He can need *her* for all I care. Yet, somewhere deep in my heart, I know I'll cave and answer my phone or call him back at some point. It's unlike him to sound desperate. Something could be seriously wrong. Whatever. Not going there.

I get up, put my sweatshirt on, and head out to get coffee. Despite my tearfest this morning and the stress of this Neil predicament, the medicine kicked in. I lean against the door and watch as Jackson and Ashton laugh together. It warms my heart to see them getting along. I can't recall if I ever saw her talk to Neil when I wasn't around. Smiling,

I walk over and start my coffee, allowing them to keep talking.

"Good morning, hot tits." Ashton laughs as I roll my eyes. Please don't let her embarrass me again. She turns to Jackson. "So you were about to tell me about your sexy, available friends, right?"

I bust out laughing and grip the edge of the counter for support. Of course she's trolling for men. "For real? You're trying to score a hot friend?"

"Hey, I'd enlist if I knew I could look at guys like him all day. I'm cooped up in a lab with nerds who think they're hot." Her grin is wide as she leans in, tilting her head to the side. "Don't get all stabby." She returns her attention to the sexy man sitting at my table. "Well?"

Jackson smiles and leans back in his seat, patting his leg. Grabbing my coffee, I smother my trepidation and snuggle into him. He looks at me brightly. "Why don't you answer her? Any of my friends hot?" Oh sure, make me say it.

Deciding to play coy and give Jackson a taste of his own medicine, I say, "Well, there is this one guy." I smile, turning my back to him as I lean on the table with both hands holding my head. "He was *so* dreamy. Almost made think twice about Muffin over here."

She plays along. Her eyes widen and she grins devilishly. There's nothing Ashton enjoys more than taunting people. "So he's like super hot, then?"

"Oh yeah, I'm talking off the charts." Jackson leans against my back and his body heat pulses through my sweatshirt. His hand grips my hip before slipping underneath the hem and splaying across my bare stomach. I gasp.

"What's wrong, baby?" he asks as I turn and

look at him over my shoulder incredulously. "Just curious who you think was off the charts?" Slowly his fingertips trail against my stomach. The shirt is baggy, so hopefully Ashton can't see anything that's happening.

I bite my lip and lean back against his chest. "It's hard to say—" My words cut off when his finger slides against the underside of my breast.

Ashton smiles. "What's wrong? Cat got your tongue? Or is it that Jackson's feeling you up?"

Jackson leans back, laughing hysterically. Busted! My face is painted in red as I get up and put my mug in the sink.

Ashton yells at my back as I walk to my room. "Oh c'mon, hot tits. I'd touch them too if I were him. Don't be like that."

"I hate you both!" I yell back, laughing. Out of nowhere I'm airborne and squeaking as Jackson lifts me and throws me over his shoulder. We laugh as we make our way back to my room.

"I'm going to head into the city and get ready. I want us to go out and have fun. Pack a bag. You can stay at my place tonight," he says with a serious look.

"What time?"

"I'll text you details. I need to make some calls." His lips press against mine and I lean into him. I don't think I'll ever tire of kissing him. Even though we've just started whatever this is, it feels like it's been so much longer. It's like every day I'm with him, a little more of the broken me mends, making me whole again.

chapter nineteen

$\mathcal{A}$fter spending the next three hours agonizing over what to wear, I finally settled on my red, one-shoulder, A-line dress. My hair is curled and swept to the side and I'm pretty happy with the overall turnout. I've packed my overnight bag and threw my nude heels in there since I have to take the train into the city—there's no way I'm running around in heels. Ashton is going out later, so she agreed to drop me at the station on her way.

Stepping out into the living room, I ask, "Well, what do you think?" She lets out a whistle.

"You look holy shit hot! Wow. He's gonna be tenting all night long."

"What?" I ask, dumbfounded.

"You know, be pitching a tent in his pants." She giggles and nudges me.

"Grab your keys. I'm nervous enough without your asinine comments." I huff and nudge her back. My nerves are out of control. I don't know why since we've already slept together. We had a rather powerful talk today, but this seems so different— probably because our date is actually planned and I wasn't roped into it.

We exit the house with Ashton's arm around my neck. "No need to be nervous. You need to be you and he'll see how special you are. I'm pretty sure he already does."

"Just ... I don't know. Things got heavy this morning," I say to her as we get in the car. "I don't mean sexual heavy either. I kind of had a huge breakdown about my dad," I admit reluctantly. It's weird telling her this. Ashton and I share everything, but there are parts of my relationship with Jackson I want to keep to myself.

"Wow. You never talk about him. But he still wants to take you out, so it didn't scare him off. Jackson seems like a good guy. He came over last night to see you. You were plastered and he stayed. He's obviously into you." She takes a deep breath while the words sink in. "I know it's hard for you to see, but please don't push him away. Let him see what I see." She places her hand on mine and squeezes, offering me comfort I'm reluctant to receive.

"Thanks, Ash. I guess I'm just waiting for the proverbial shoe to drop."

"Well that's no way to live. Live for the moment." The car stops as we arrive at the train station. Ashton turns to me with her lips pursed. "I know this is hard for you. Here's the thing—nice guys like him don't come around twice. From everything you've told me, he's only been good to you. Yeah, he's intense, but you guys have this insane chemistry. Stop fighting it!"

I lean over and give her a kiss on the cheek. "I'll try. Love you, Ashypoo!"

I run to catch the train. Thankfully I get on just in time. Grabbing the first seat available, I sit and text Jackson.

Me: On my way. Where am I going?

Jackson: A car will be waiting with your name. See

you soon.

I smile at his gesture. He really is a good guy, and I'm going to try to relax and enjoy tonight. The train ride is only about ten minutes, so I don't have time to do anything other than change my shoes and check myself over once. Exiting the train, I find a tall man in a suit holding a sign with my name on it.

"Ms. Pope, I'm Xavier. I'll be your driver for this evening."

"Nice to meet you." I smile and follow him to a sleek black limo.

Wow, he really went all out.

"Do you know where we're going?" he asks curiously.

My eyes widen at his question. "No, do you?"

He lets out a throaty laugh and opens the door for me. "Yes, ma'am." I take a deep breath and scoot into the back. "It'll only be about ten minutes to our destination. There's champagne chilling in the bucket if you'd like a glass."

"Yes!" I say, almost too eagerly.

Get a damn grip.

I take a small sip and the bubbles tickle my nose. Jackson's thoughtfulness warms my heart. Even though we saw each other a few hours ago, I'm excited to see him again. It appears he managed to plan quite a bit in a short amount of time.

We arrive at what I'm assuming is a restaurant. Xavier comes around, opens my door, and sweeps his arm to the side where I see Jackson walking toward me. He looks breathtaking. I know that's not the manliest way to describe him, but there is no other word. He takes my breath away.

My eyes eat him up and I'm pretty sure I lick my lips at the sight of him. He's dressed in a black pinstripe suit with a white shirt, the top button undone, and his eyes burn even in the darkness. I can see the blue shift to green and deepen as he approaches me. That may be a trick of light and shadow, but I like to think it's lust making those eyes change like that. The same lust that has my heart racing a mile a minute right now. His smile is wide when he reaches me, but he doesn't say anything.

Finally, after an eternity—or what feels like it—his low, rough voice breaks the silence. "You look beautiful."

"Thank you for this. The limo, last night, everything. It's too much. I never really thought of you as a limo guy."

"I'm not, but you deserve to feel special. So no, it's not too much. It's only the beginning." He takes a step closer and extends his hand, giving me a single stargazer lily. Does he know they're my favorite?

Between his words and now this gesture, I'm liquefying. "I love lilies. How did you know?"

"Ashton," he says matter-of-factly. Of course she would know, but it surprises me that he thought to ask.

"I think you'll like these plans better than the last." Jackson grins and grips my hand. Hell yeah. I won't be climbing any walls in this dress.

We begin to walk forward when suddenly he stops. He turns and tenderly grabs my face with both hands, pulling me gently until we're an inch apart. "You really are beautiful, baby." Before I can respond, his lips are on mine. My eyes flutter closed and I grip the lapels of his jacket. His strong arms wrap around my lower back, pulling me into him. What may have started as a tender kiss turns into a passionate exchange. Jackson pulls that out of me. He consumes me, making me forget where, sometimes who, I am.

Dropping his hand, he squeezes my ass and I giggle. Well, that's one way to stop it. And very Jackson-like. My hand slaps him playfully across the chest as I shake my head at his antics.

"Come on, Muffin. Let's go eat."

"Keep it up and I'll show you how much you'll pay for using that name."

"I don't take lightly to threats, Muff." I smile and walk forward. He growls and wraps his arms around my waist, pulling me flush against his chest.

"Well, wait until I show you how fucking good it feels when it's no longer a threat," he murmurs seductively, staring straight into my eyes.

My stomach clenches and I tremble from the timbre of his voice before he releases his hold. Could he be any sexier?

I'm grinning ear to ear as we enter the restaurant and are seated. It's beautiful. Candles sit on all the tables and huge chandeliers hang in the center of the room, creating beautiful rainbow prisms everywhere. The walls are deep burgundy and almost look like fabric, which only adds to the ambiance. Everything seems so upscale. It doesn't surprise me Jackson would choose a place like this. He's rugged but sophisticated—a walking contradiction.

"I've ordered for us already. The chef is a good friend. He's making us something special."

Typically, I would be less than excited about someone deciding my meal for me—I've had enough of that shit to last a lifetime—but with Jackson it feels different. He's not trying to take away my choices. He's simply being kind. "Thank you for all of this, Jackson. It's very sweet."

He leans forward. "You're welcome. I'm just lucky you fell into my chair that day."

I laugh and turn my head to the side, hiding my embarrassment. Not one of my finest moments. When I finally recover, I look up to find him smiling warmly. "Thanks for reminding me."

"Hey, look where it got us."

"Where exactly is *this*?" Because of my constant self-doubt, I need him to spell it out for me. I don't want to get too attached to him and have the rug pulled out from under me. Jackson is a man any woman could easily fall in love with, and he seems to have a direct line to my heart.

"I don't know where it is, but I know I want to be around you. I know I've thought about you every day and every night since we've met. There are a lot of things we need to learn about each other. But you fell into my life and I won't let you fall out. So whatever this is … it's ours."

My eyes swim with emotion. It takes everything inside of me not to cry. That was the best answer he could've given me—it's honest and real. I sigh and look at him with a hopeful heart. "I want us to get to know each other. I never thought we'd be here."

"Why?"

"Because I thought you were like all the other guys I've met—cocky and looking for one thing." I shrug and smile. "Not to be a bitch, but you were so intense. I'd never felt anything like that before. Then you turned out to be my client. You keep breaking my rules." It's true. Each time I tell myself I'm not going to do this or that, he finds a loophole and I no longer care about my rules anymore.

We fall into a comfortable silence as we let the words settle around us. There are a lot of truths yet to be told. I don't know how to tell him about what Neil did, or that one of his trusted consultants is a part of my past. There's no way to know for sure if he heard what she said that day in the conference room. I don't even know if Piper's still working with Raven. Regardless, it's going to come to light at some point.

Throughout dinner we talk and laugh. He tells me more about some of the antics he and his sister, Reagan, got into as kids. We talk about my mother a little and how I haven't spoken to her since the phone call in Virginia. Jackson makes me nearly fall out of my chair laughing when he tells me the story about Mark and Aaron when they first became SEALs and some of the prank wars they had.

"Okay. So you seriously glued ketchup packets to the toilet seat?" Insane. They're all insane.

"Fuck yeah, we did. And when Mark sat down, you would've thought a bomb went off in the head. There was ketchup everywhere." His eyes are filled with humor.

"And what did he do back? I can't see him being like, 'Good one,' and letting it go."

"Oh hell no, there's no backing down. Mark has one thing I don't."

"Which is?" I ask.

"Patience. So he waited until my guard was slightly down. My truck is my baby—you don't fuck with my F150. Mark, being the prick he is, decided I needed to really suffer. So he took my license plates and flipped them upside down, but then he somehow got into the cab." I smile and roll my eyes at the talk of his precious truck. As he remembers whatever his friend did to repay him for the bathroom casualty, his smile fades. "It was December and cold as shit. The motherfucker took pepper spray and soaked my floor mats and my air vents. Every time I turned the heat on I couldn't see because my eyes watered so bad."

Laughter erupts from my chest and there's no chance of stopping it. My hands fly over my mouth, trying to contain it as I imagine Jackson crying every time he got into his truck. Tears are running down my cheeks, and the look on his face only makes me laugh harder. "I can't breathe."

"No, baby, I couldn't breathe. I had to ride around in the freezing fucking cold with my windows down so I could see. It was hell. But payback's a bitch and Twilight learned that shit quick." He smiles again, laughing at the memories as I swipe the tears from my face.

"Oh God! What did you do?"

He steeples his fingers and his devilish grin grows. "It was a multilayered attack. Phase one was all about making him think it was coming. So there were small, subtle hints. I had the gate guards search his car every time he arrived on base, which takes about twenty minutes out of your day. Not a big deal, but he was late a few times and he got his ass chewed." I'm starting to see how much he must have enjoyed this. His eyes glimmer and he's lost to the memory. "Phase two was a little more ... difficult."

"Difficult how?"

"I had to make sure it would work perfectly. I needed other people's help, but they didn't want to be the next casualty of our war. After watching some of the shit we did, no one wanted to play. We didn't fight fair. I plotted very carefully and also had to be ready in case I was on the other end of his attack. Plus, if he fucked with my truck again, he'd be on the missing persons list."

"I'm seeing that this truck is worth more than friendship." I laugh and sit back in my chair, wondering how their war finally ended.

"You don't mess with a man's truck."

"Okay, I get it. Please continue."

His eyes are excited as he gets back to his story. "Mark had done a few small things, but nothing really epic. We all had lockers that we kept our gear in, so I had the supply guys open his for me." He lets out a small laugh. "I rigged it so when he opened it, a glitter bomb exploded. It went everywhere! Him, all his gear—everything covered with glitter!"

"Holy shit!" I gasp. Glitter gets everywhere. I can't even imagine the mess that made.

"But wait!" He leans in and smiles ear to ear. "I didn't stop there. Fuck with me and there is no limit to the lengths I'll go for payback."

"Seriously, I'm a little worried."

"We were leaving for a training mission the next day, so Twilight literally had to scrub his shit before he could go. *Hours* it took him and it still didn't come out. But while some would think that was enough retribution, I didn't agree. When we were out on the mission, I put glitter in his shampoo and body wash."

"Oh Jesus." My eyes widen as he sits back, arms crossed over his chest. I make a mental note never to get into a war with him because I'll lose—epically. "I would say you won, huh?"

I'm so engrossed in the story I don't notice the

waitress standing at our table.

"Can I get you anything else? Dessert?" she asks.

"No way, I couldn't eat another thing," I smile and Jackson shakes his head and grabs the check. "Everything was delicious, Jackson. Thank you for tonight."

"Tonight's not over." Standing before me, he extends his hand tentatively. Without any hesitation I place mine in his. Was he afraid I'd say no? There isn't a damn thing that would stop me. The feel of his hand surrounding mine makes my heart skip a beat. Almost like the world has righted itself. I'm in trouble. I'm falling fast.

We exit into the cool night air and I shiver. "Hey." He stops and encircles my waist. "Thank you for letting me break your rules."

"Of course." Leaning in, I place a brief kiss on his lips. Passion erupts the moment our lips meet and the kiss becomes more frantic. His hands grip my sides as his fingers dig into my hips. I welcome the feeling. His need pushes my own. I feel his arousal against my stomach and suddenly couldn't care less about the rest of our evening. Jackson pushes me back against the car as his mouth devours mine. Time is irrelevant. Everything else fades away. Once again, he overtakes me and I'm lost to him. All I hear is the sound of his breathing, his moans. All I feel is him around me—touching me, wanting me, making me fall faster. He pulls away and turns, rubbing his hand roughly down his face.

"Fucking Christ," he mumbles. "I can't control myself when I touch you."

His words stun me. They're exactly how I feel. As soon as his skin meets mine, I lose all self-control. I need to get a freaking grip. The constant battling of emotions when I'm around him is draining. One minute I can't get close enough, and the next I'm fighting to keep my heart safe. Why does this have to be so damn difficult?

Once he's composed himself he walks back up to me and opens the car door. "In." My body obeys him without hesitation.

Jackson takes a minute outside the limo and tells Xavier where to go. I roll the window down and look at him. The air between us is charged, and though he's listening to something Xavier is saying, his unblinking eyes are locked on mine. The depth of his stare is almost too much. My yearning grows and I lick my lips, gripping the bottom one between my teeth as he opens the door. Before it even clicks shut behind him, his mouth is on mine again. I can't get close enough. I've never been this girl. I've never desired a man as much as I do at this moment. It's primal, raw.

Our lips are fused and the need to be closer is unbearable. It's clear Jackson is fighting the same urges. He pushes me flat on the seat, and hovers above me. My heart is pounding, my lips are tingling, and all I want is to ease the aching between my legs.

His eyes shift from lustful to resolute and he pulls me back up. We're both breathing heavy as we recover from the rush of the moment. I would have let him fuck me in this car. With the window open for all to see! What the hell is wrong with me? I turn and look out the window, thankful for the cool air as I try to reel in my libido.

Jackson grasps my hand and I look over. "If you think I don't want you, you're wrong. I promise I'm going to do that and so much more, but we need a lot more time than a ten-minute drive." His brow lifts as his dimple appears.

I bite my lip at the hunger evident on his face and the promise of things to come. The longing to kiss him is too great to fight. I lean in and brush my lips against his.

"Not that I'm complaining, but what was that for?" He smiles.

"For everything." I shrug and return to watching the city pass by.

Not even a minute later, the car stops. We're on the Upper East Side of Manhattan, right by Central Park. I love this area of the city. It's gorgeous—and extremely expensive. Jackson's hand extends as he exits the limo. He pulls me forward as Xavier retrieves my bag. I look at the huge apartment building and it hits me—we aren't going to the park. He lives here. Ashton and I looked at a few apartments on this side of the city, but even with both our incomes it was out of our price range. I shouldn't be surprised. He does own two companies, but he never seems to flaunt his money.

"Catherine?" he says softly, causing me to jump. "Ready?" I swear one day he won't be able to sneak up and scare the crap out of me.

We enter the building and I'm surprised by its contemporary design. Everything is clean lines, reminding me of his office in Virginia.

"How long have you lived here?" I ask.

Jackson rolls his neck and drops my hand before answering. "About a year."

"It's beautiful. I love this part of the city."

We enter the elevator and head to the twentieth floor. Jackson's hand snakes around my back. "I do too."

"I wish our office were closer to the park. I've always wanted to go there for lunch and just people watch." Central Park is spectacular. Sometimes it's a little scary, but for the most part it's wonderful. My father took me to the zoo there a few times. I always thought it was amazing that this little piece of the wild was placed in the perfectly manicured park in the perfectly chaotic city.

"Every morning I go for a five-mile run in the park."

"I'm not surprised you run every day." There will be none of that for me.

"We can wake up tomorrow and go." He smiles, knowing damn well that isn't happening.

"You're funny. The only way I'm running is if someone or something is chasing me. And even then, I might say screw it. I'd much rather eat a bag of Doritos, thanks."

"I bet you'd do it if I made you." His brow lifts as he leans in close.

I scoff and throw my head back. "Never gonna happen, babe. Besides, you owe me my time, Muff. Until I get that, there will be no more obstacle courses or stair climbing happening here."

"Who said anything about stairs?"

Before I can retort the elevator dings. My stomach is in knots. You'd think this was our first time being alone or intimate. This is the last barrier we have. He already knows where I live and work. Now both of us will have stayed at each other's homes. I'm excited to put together another piece of the puzzle that is Jackson Cole.

We reach his unit on the twentieth floor. He smiles and opens the door, allowing me through. "Welcome to my home."

While my apartment is modern, it has nothing on his. Jackson's place is masculine, but a woman could easily fit in.

"This is it," he says with a shrug and places my bag in the middle of the living room.

I take my shoes off and walk into the middle of the room. "It's amazing. I love the architecture and the color choices."

He slowly walks toward me. I stand rooted, unable to move an inch. Once he reaches me, his rough hands graze down my bare arms and I briefly close my eyes. "Let me show you around."

It takes a second to process that he said something. "Sure." As long as the tour ends in the bedroom I'm completely fine with it. My body is still humming with lust from our hot and heavy make out session outside the restaurant and in the limo.

Jackson shows me around the rest of the apartment. Every room has the same feel, like fire and ice—cold blues against warm reds. However, it's all somehow in perfect harmony. We enter his bedroom and the view ... The view is magnificent. The bedroom is warm and romantic, its ambiance completely different from the rest of the house. The massive king size bed faces windows that overlook the park. Jackson turns on the wall-mounted fireplace and the tension from the car returns full force. Desire courses through my body. Fire, heat, and lust are all I feel.

"I had other plans for the night," he says smoothly as he walks toward me.

"What happened?"

"You did." Jackson stops. He stands still, illuminated by the flames. I take a step toward him.

"Me?" I whisper, and he takes the final step so

we're within reach.

"Yes. You, Catherine." His hand cups my face as his thumb rubs across my bottom lip. My head naturally tilts into him palm.

Please don't hurt me, I silently beg.

His eyes are warm and even though I'm fully dressed I feel completely naked. "I told you before, you do something to me. I need you and I haven't allowed myself to need anyone for a long time." He leans down, pressing his lips against my cheek. His voice is low and gruff. "When I'm around you all I can think about is being buried deep inside you." Jackson's lips graze the corner of my mouth as he continues his seduction. "I see you and all I see is every beautiful inch of the skin I know is underneath your clothes. I watch you talk and I think of what your mouth looks like wrapped around my cock."

I moan as his hands slip around my back and unzips my dress. No man's ever talked to me like this. I'm so aroused I could come from his words alone. He's speaking to every part of me—my heart and my core. I try to reach for him but he steps back.

"Stay still." His voice is strained as he makes the demand.

My body is begging for him, needing to touch him, yet I stand still as he circles me. His right hand stays in contact with me as he approaches my back and slowly pulls my hair to the side, opening my unzipped dress and pushing it off my shoulders. I stand facing the fire, so I can't see when he steps away from me, but I know just the same. The loss of his body close to mine is unmistakable, even in the heat. It feels like forever since he's moved or done anything and I can't take it anymore. I have to move. I need to see him, touch him. It's too much to fight.

I turn and he's standing there staring at me with fire in his eyes. My dress was too tight to require a bra and I chose not to wear panties since I didn't want lines. It seems to have worked in my favor. Now it's time to turn the tables on him. I shimmy out of my dress completely and approach him as his eyes drink me in. It's unnerving, yet I'm empowered by his silence.

"You know..." I pause, letting the statement hang out there while I reach for the top button of his shirt. "You aren't the only one who's turned on." My hand drops to the next button. I make sure to take my time with my words and my hands. His eyes are locked on mine as I start to seduce him. "I think about you all the time. I have to fight the urge to beg you to take me." After undoing the final button, I slide my hands back up his chiseled chest and his head drops back. I glide them under his shirt and push it down his toned arms, feeling every muscle tense beneath my touch. His reaction makes me stronger. It's exhilarating to know I elicit the same reaction he pulls from me. "You're impossible to resist." I tug on his belt and pull him closer to me, unbuttoning his pants and sliding them and his boxers down, trailing my fingertips on his legs as they descend. We're both bared completely to each other now, and I stand back up before speaking my last words to him. "But when you touch me, I'm lost to you."

His head snaps up at my admission and I realize we're both fighting the same temptation, both fighting something neither of us can explain—a connection that's powerful and scary. I see the emotions I'm feeling mirrored in his eyes.

His lips inch closer to mine and his words are soft and dripping with honesty. "You're never lost, Catherine. I'll always find you." His mouth crushes down on mine as his words resonate through me, bringing tears to my eyes. And there he is—my hero.

There's no more time for talking as we express what our hearts are feeling with our mouths and tongues and hands and bodies. He hooks his arm under my legs and carries me to the bed. Tenderly, he lays me down and hovers over me. This time is different for me. A part of my heart will be his tonight, and I'm willingly giving it over. I know I'm not in love with him yet, but he's breaking my defenses slowly but surely. I fight him and myself all to no avail. It's only a matter of time.

Our entire night was foreplay and now, I'm aching for him. "Jackson, don't make me beg."

"No need for begging." His head drops to my neck as he kisses and licks the sensitive skin behind my ear.

I start to shift and squirm, desperate for him to fill me and make me whole.

"Stay still," he says as he pins my arms down and restrains me.

"I need you. Now."

Instead of responding to my pleas, he releases my hands and glides his tongue down my side, purposely avoiding my breasts. Making his way farther, I grow anxious as he continues across my stomach and then up my other side. I'm going fucking crazy! His strong arms keep me still and my body is tight, vibrating with need. When he makes his way back up to my ear, I've lost all control. I can't take another second.

I've finally snapped. "I want you to fuck me. Right. Now."

"I have all intentions of it, but first I'm going to drive you absolutely fucking crazy. Just like you do to me. This has just begun. The more you beg, the more I'll make you wait." The combination of his words and the timbre of his voice when he says them is too much. My muscles contract and deep-seated need courses its way through me, calling for him to take me and claim me.

He pushes up and puts the condom on, moving me higher on the bed. Lifting my leg, he pulls it to his mouth and makes his way down to my core. I lie there watching as he gets closer and closer, and my breath hitches as he avoids the one place I need him most. His tongue trails to the other leg and I groan and throw my head back. My breathing is erratic. I'm going out of my mind. We lock eyes as his tongue swipes up my center. My eyes close from the intense pleasure of finally being touched only to have him stop.

"I want you to watch me. If you look away, I'll stop." His low voice is fierce and commanding.

Keeping our eyes locked, he leans back down and licks my pussy again, stirring an involuntary shudder. I watch as he begins sucking and licking over and over again. I'm fighting the urge to close my eyes. If he stops, I might combust, so I keep my eyes trained on him. It's the most erotic thing, watching him. He looks up as he inserts two fingers, pumping, and my body tenses. Every muscle is locking, ready to finally release, and my eyes slam shut. Immediately, I feel his loss. *No!*

"I told you keep your eyes on me." I nod, unable to speak from being so close and then having it taken away.

Jackson wastes no time as he sucks on my clit. When I feel his teeth bite down, I'm gone. I shout his name over and over and writhe in a pleasure only he gives me. I splinter into a million pieces as he pumps his fingers, drawing out my orgasm until I finally settle and become coherent.

When I open my eyes he's above me, waiting for me to come back to reality. I bite my lip as I feel the tip of his dick brush against my sensitive clit. I spread my legs and press the heels of my feet on his ass, pushing him into me. His jaw is tight and he seems to be fighting his own needs. I push again but he's so much stronger than me, so he barely moves.

"Please, fuck me," I beg softly.

"I'm not going to fuck you this time," he says in a hushed tone. "I'm going to go slow." He leans down and kisses me deeply, swirling his tongue with mine as I moan, begging for more. "I'm going to show you how sexy and irresistible you are, how you test my patience." He nips at my ear and then runs his tongue over where he just bit. "Then I'm going to fuck you until you beg me to stop."

I rub my hand against his rough cheek. Once his eyes meet mine I groan and say, "Then do it already."

His eyes blaze as he slowly fills me, stretching me and then pulling out fully. He enters me again and my eyes are heavy-lidded as he stares through to my soul. With each thrust he's tearing me apart and then putting me back together again.

Quickly, he flips our positions so I'm on top. I

push against him, grinding down and enjoying the intense fullness while he holds my hips and sets the pace. I lean back, bringing him impossibly deeper. He rubs his thumb on my clit and I lose my breath as the force of my sudden orgasm rips me apart. My body takes over, riding him harder, and I hear Jackson groan as he orgasms, both of us riding out the bliss together.

chapter
twenty

I'm spent.

Completely and totally useless.

I'm lying against his chest, still unable to catch my breath. He runs his fingers lightly against my back before shifting me to go clean up. I groan and stretch as my muscles loosen from the aftermath of our intense sex session. The tightness reminds me of the obstacle course and how much my body ached afterward. But this is the kind of physical workout I welcome.

Jackson returns and flops on his stomach, giving me a view of his perfect ass. He really is magnificent. I kind of want to pinch myself—surely this can't be real. He turns his head toward me with a smile and I place my hand on his back. I've never gotten a good look at the art on his shoulder. It's really remarkable, so intricate, and has so many different parts to it. In the center are the bones of a frog. Its body wraps around from the front of his shoulder and ends with the head facing down on his back. In the frog's hands is the trident of Poseidon, only the three spears of the trident aren't spears, they're names. Brian, Fernando, and Devon are written in an elegant script and the number four serves as the handle. It's surrounded by black tribal ink. My finger grazes the frog and the labyrinth of tribal markings around it. Below it is the most beautiful quote.

We have this hope as an anchor for our soul, firm and secure. – Hebrews 6:19

It's profound and speaks to my heart. There's meaning behind each word. Hope is something we all have, and it's often the only thing we can grasp when our world is shattering. I hoped for my father to return. I hoped for Neil to be faithful. Neither of those things happened, but that hope is what kept me going every day.

Jackson rolls and faces me with sad eyes, so different from just moments ago. I reach up, placing my hand on his heart, and he pulls me in, close enough so I can see the front of the tattoo. "What does your tattoo mean?" I feel him tense.

"It's the tattoo you get when you lose someone on the team," he says matter-of-factly.

"Is that the loss you've mentioned?"

"Some," he replies and laces his fingers with mine, holding our clasped hands between us.

I want to push him to tell me. I want him to share with me—more like I want him to *want* to tell me. I'm just not sure I should try to force it.

"Why a frog?" My curiosity gets the best of me. I don't understand some of his world.

"SEALs are referred to as Frogmen." He smiles and squeezes my hand gently. His eyes are warm and he continues on, "I got that tattoo to remember my three friends who died on a mission."

My heart swells that he's opening up, but aches for the pain of his loss. "I'm so sorry."

He removes his hand from mine and wraps his arm around my middle. I scoot closer and return his hug, placing a small kiss on his chest. My mind begins to wander as the silence persists. Do I push again?

Jackson takes a deep breath and begins to speak. His voice is low, pain threading through his words. "It's my fault."

Pulling back, I look in his eyes. The agony there is evident. "What's your fault?"

Jackson struggles to hide his emotions, but I watch each one play like a movie—sadness, anger, guilt, hatred—before his expression goes void. "Their deaths—I was in charge of the mission."

"Jackson, I doubt that," I say softly, hoping he'll hear the disbelief in my voice.

He tugs me back against his chest. I'm not sure if he's done talking or if he wants to hide from me. Giving him what he's silently requesting, I wrap my arm around him and stay quiet.

Right as I'm starting to drift to sleep, feeling safe and content in his arms, I hear his deep voice. "When we were in Iraq, we got into some heavy firefight. I was in command of my team." He pauses and runs his fingers up and down my spine methodically.

I look up and his eyes are closed tight as if he's fighting an internal war. Every part of him is rigid and tense. I bring my hand to his face, brushing my thumb across his cheek. "Hey," I whisper.

His eyes are vacant as he speaks. "There were six of us and we had bad intel. Something wasn't sitting right, but I had my orders." He takes a deep breath and his voice is distant. "So we deviated a little, hoping it would give us the element of surprise. I split the team in half. Mark, Aaron, and I took to the left." He pauses again and I watch as pain lances through his features. Every single bone in my body is aching for him, but I stay still and quiet as I wait for him to go on.

"Brian, Fernando, and Devon took to the right of the village. I knew something was wrong. I had that sinking feeling but we didn't have a choice. We had to fucking go and do our job. When we split up, it made it easier to pick us off. I heard the gunfire, but we couldn't get to them quick enough. They were shot and killed. I was in charge—it's on me."

"Oh, Jackson." I gasp and pull myself up.

I want to comfort him. I'm just not sure what to do. The pain in his voice, the torment in his eyes, it's lashing through me. I want to take it from him, carry the burden so he's not hurting, but he keeps going.

"By the time our extraction team got in, it was too late. They were already dead. Mark and I were both shot. Aaron was the only one who got out without getting injured. Mine was on my arm." He points to a faint scar on his bicep. I lean over and kiss him. He smiles weakly at me, but there's nothing but sadness in his eyes. "I carry their deaths on my shoulders."

I can't imagine how much the tattoo hurt, but the agony of reliving that memory while someone permanently etches it into your skin ...

"I'm sure no one blames you. I mean Mark works with you and so does Aaron. Surely, they know what an amazing man you are."

Anger flashes in his eyes at my statement, like it couldn't be true. "They don't need to. *I* blame me." He bangs his fist on his chest. "It was my call. Their wives had to bury them, Catherine. They had to go to their funeral. They had to tell their kids that their dads would never come back again. Had we stuck together, we all would have lived." He shuts his eyes on the memory and me.

"You don't know that. You can't know that if you stuck to the plan, or together, that all of you wouldn't have been killed." My voice is small but strong. I'm trying to give him the other side of things.

He doesn't respond. I know it's futile to try to argue. Ashton tried to tell me hundreds of times that my father probably had a reason to leave, and how Neil might not be the best guy for me. Sometimes it doesn't matter because you can't see past the image in your own heart.

We lie here together, unspeaking. Two broken ships trying to find a way through rough seas. I close my eyes and settle back on his chest, listening to the steady thrum of his heart as he tenderly holds me. And though I feel for his loss, I'm grateful he was spared.

He kisses the top of my head, and I move back so he can see the truth in my eyes. I need him to really hear what I'm saying. "I think you're a wonderful man. From what I've seen you're kind, loyal, trusting, and wouldn't purposely put anyone in danger. You've comforted me and I saw how worried you were over the situation at your company."

I grab hold of his face, forcing him to look at me. He shouldn't carry guilt over something that wasn't his fault. "You, Jackson Cole, are a man worth following. Those men wouldn't want you to carry their deaths on your shoulders."

"Those men should be alive," he says almost inaudibly. Then he tries to move his head out of my grasp, but I'm not having it. I'm not done.

"True, they shouldn't have died. No one should have to die, but would you have taken the bullet for them?" I raise my brow, already knowing his answer.

Without hesitation, he responds forcefully, "In a heartbeat."

"Well, don't you think they would do the same for you? I know loss too, Jackson. I'm living it now."

I know he's upset and hurt, but he's failing to see that he wouldn't want them to suffer if the situation were reversed. If it were Ashton and, God forbid, something happened and I was gone, I wouldn't want her to live with that kind of guilt. I would want her to pick up her life and live on.

"You're not telling me anything I haven't heard before. Bottom line—I was there. I lived it." His eyes narrow in anger. "I watched it happen and I couldn't stop it. I fucked up and no one is going to tell me different. Their blood is on my hands. Did you kill your dad? No. So don't compare." His voice is cold, fused with frustration and defeat.

"You didn't kill them either," I whisper and drop my hands. A tear forms and I try to choke it down and hide my face from him.

I'm hurting for this entire situation and for my own guilt. No, I'm not responsible for my father's death, but I never tried to find him either. I wrote him off. Some may think I was justified. Whether I was or not, I'll never get that chance now. And now I've brought all of Jackson's pain to the forefront. Regret is a shitty thing to live with and it seems both of us have an entire truckload of it.

"I'm sorry." I feel him shift and his strong arms encase me.

"You have nothing to be sorry for."

"You're crying." He releases his hold and turns my head to look at him.

What else is new? I'm emotional. With all the
stress of the last few months and my lack of sleep,
I'm a little frayed. The impending reading of my
father's will is wearing on me too. I want to get past
all of this so I can get back to who I once was.

Swiping the tear from my face, I smile and retort, "No, I'm not."

"I didn't mean to be an asshole and ruin our
night."

"You didn't, Jackson. I'm sorry I pushed." I
smile and place my hand against his cheek. "But
I'm going to keep telling you how incredible you
are, okay?"

His smile is soft, placating. It's clear he doesn't
believe me. I wish he could see what I see. I shrug
and give him a quick kiss. I'm not giving up on him.

"Come on, let's go to bed."

I put my finger up and hop out of the bed. "One
minute. I just need to brush my teeth and all that
good stuff."

Seeing Jackson's shirt on the floor, I grab it and
throw it on, then enter the bathroom. I try to fix my
now disheveled hair and quickly brush my teeth. I
take a few extra minutes to get my head under control. He's seen and been through so much. Are we
both too fucked-up to work? No, if I think like that,
I'm doing exactly what I always do. He's not fucked-
up, nor am I. We just have some healing to do.

Climbing back into bed, Jackson pulls me
against his solid chest. "You look good in my shirt."

I chuckle and smile at him. "You look good in
your shirt too."

His voice is low and oozes sexual promise. "You
look even better out of my shirt."

I laugh and shake my head. He effortlessly lifts

me so we're eye to eye and leans in to kiss me. It's a slow, easy, and careful kind of kiss. It's the kind of moment your heart will never recover from because you're both saying so much. My head is spinning. I try to hold myself back. Between all the details tonight—the dinner, the earth-shattering sex, and then him finally opening up to me—Jackson has obliterated my walls.

He finally releases me, settling me into the crook of his arm. "Good night, baby."

I smile even though he can't see me. "Good night, Muffin."

chapter twenty-one

*O*ur night together put us over some imaginary threshold. We've talked almost every day and we saw each other for lunch a few days ago. It's been two weeks of laughter and falling into a nice rhythm together.

I grab the subway and head to his apartment, where he has another day of surprises in store for me. He's standing outside waiting, and the sight of him causes my pulse to spike. His dark brown hair is in sexy disarray and his white T-shirt is tight, which lets me see his defined muscles perfectly. Butterflies stir in my stomach. It astounds me that we're dating—he's magnificent, commanding, sweet, and so many other things. I can't keep my eyes off him when he's around. The chemistry between us crackles like flames on a log. My body comes to life when he touches me—it's a heady feeling.

As I approach he gives me a lopsided grin. "Hello, gorgeous."

"Hello yourself." I smile and he immediately reaches out, pulling me flush against him. "Do you always have to manhandle me?"

"Well, baby, I'm all man and I sure as hell love to handle you." His eyes glimmer with humor.

Hell yeah he's all man—every single fantastic inch of him.

"You're ridiculous." I shake my head.

"Yet you keep coming back, so I must not be that bad." He smirks and gives me a long, panty-melting kiss.

Right here on 5th Avenue in New York City, he has once again rendered me helpless. Shoppers, families, cabs, and bikers all fade away as his lips move with mine. Jackson pulls back and wraps his arm around my shoulders.

I love how physical he is, almost as if he can't keep his hands off me. It's such a contrast to anything I'm used to. Whether it's holding hands or something as simple as touching legs when we watch television, those small moments say so much. They're unspoken words that show the true depth of what we're both feeling.

"So what's on our agenda today?" I ask with a light heart.

There's happiness dancing in his eyes when he responds, "The park."

My face falls at his answer. Jackson told me to make sure I was comfortable today. No heels, no dresses. He said to be sure I wore sneakers. I made him promise no military training exercises, no entering me for some kind of race or marathon, and no other strenuous physical activity that would have me aching for days after completion. After my ribbing about his love of running and exercise in general, I was a little hesitant, but he swore I would love today. I trusted him—first mistake.

"Why do I think I should've stayed home in bed?" I groan.

He laughs and pulls me tighter. "I wasn't in bed with you, so that's reason enough to get up," Jackson jokes in my ear as we walk. "One day I'll get you to agree to a mud run or something, but you'll be happy to know I kept my end of the bargain today. They don't have an obstacle course in Central Park—yet. And there's no marathon."

"Yet somehow that doesn't comfort me." I smile and nudge him.

We keep walking until we stop in front of the Central Park Zoo. My smile is so wide I can't contain it. I leap into his arms, wrapping my legs around his torso and pressing my lips to his. His eyes are bright and full of happiness.

"Jackson!" I squeal, hugging him tight.

"Happy?" he asks with an irresistibly devilish grin.

I've thought it before and I'm thinking it now—Jackson can read my mind. Or we're just that in sync. The zoo. This is one of the few places that holds any kind of happy memories for me and my dad. I love that he brought me here.

I let him see it all in my eyes, allowing him to see how very much this means to me. My whole heart is open to him as we stand wrapped around each other. After a few seconds or minutes—I don't know which—I give him another kiss and untangle myself.

"Come on, babe. Let's go inside." His husky voice wraps around my heart, warming me from the inside out.

Our fingers lace together as we enter through the brick archway. I pull him around the zoo, looking at all the animals and laughing with him throughout our miniature safari in the city. We walk and catch each other up on the days we were both swamped and couldn't talk. Jackson informs me about his upcoming trip to Virginia in the next few weeks. I tell him about Ashton's newest fling.

When we approach my favorite animals, I'm practically bouncing up and down.

"I love the camels!" I shout, pulling him to the fence. "They're the most underrated animals."

Jackson's laughter peals through my cooing at the camel in the back. "You're kidding. This is your favorite animal?"

"Whatever! I think they're cute. They have the humps and they're strong." I stare through as the one I'm wooing comes closer.

"I like to hump and I'm strong. I'm sensing a pattern." His brow lifts.

My brain blanks out as I envision Jackson doing a variety of things in the bedroom. I need to move off this topic quickly before my thoughts go further in the wrong direction.

"Anyway. They're my favorite." I smile.

"I seriously can't believe this is what you wanted to see. I mean, how 'bout a lion? Monkey? Something cool," he says with humor and a trace of incredulity.

I shake my head at his indifference toward this beautiful creature.

"They're cool. They even have a song about them." I raise my brows.

"What song?" he asks, laughing and clearly confused.

"You know, 'Sally the Camel has Five Humps,'" I say in a singsong way. Back in college I babysat a child whose favorite show played that counting song all the time. It was annoying and repetitious and would inevitably get stuck in your head and drive you crazy. If he thinks I'm going to sing it to him, he's lost his damn mind.

"I have no clue what you're talking about, but

by all means feel free to sing it." Jackson's smile lights up his face.

"No, I don't think that would be enjoyable for either of us." I laugh, returning my gaze to the animals. "If I lived on a farm, I'd own one."

"They're gross and they smell. Plus, I've ridden them plenty during deployments. I promise there is nothing special about a camel. Now, you want to talk about a tiger, I'm all for it." He grins, enjoying his teasing.

The camel walks over to the fence and a young boy lifts his hand up, feeding it from his palm. I giggle, but Jackson looks like he's disgusted.

"See. You couldn't feed a lion from your hand." I tilt my head, toying with him. The machine to get food for the camel is a few feet away. I dig through my purse for the quarter I need as Jackson scoffs.

"No, but—" Before he can finish his sentence, the camel spits and it lands not even an inch in front of him.

I bust out laughing. Tears stream from my eyes as he stands there looking like he wants to climb the fence and teach it a lesson, which only makes me laugh harder. Jackson stares at me before his own grin and chuckle break free. "Oh my ... She showed you!" I barely get out.

"So not funny." He rushes toward me and grips my hand, pulling me away from the animal, which clearly does not like him. "Fucking thing almost got me."

"If only my beautiful Jessica had better aim." I giggle and wrap my arms around his torso, trying to control myself.

"You named the camel that tried to spit on me?" Jackson asks, sounding wounded.

"Jessica the camel. She only spit because you were being an ass and talking shit about her." I wink.

"Glad to see where your loyalties lie."

"Jessica and I have a strong bond. Sorry, babe, Jessica and I are like this." I say and hold my crossed fingers up.

We stop in front of the next animal and he wraps his arms around my waist, pulling me against him. I gaze at him, breathing in this moment in time. I love the way he makes me laugh, smile, and enjoy a normal day. Jackson brings out parts of me that I'd buried after Neil. But I don't have to pretend with him. I can just *be*. Knowing that he doesn't want to change me, that he wants to be with me as I am— it's liberating. I snake my arms up his taut back as my mind drifts to all the ways Jackson's infiltrated my heart and soul. I think of him as soon as I wake up and before I go to bed. He's in my dreams too. He's wrapped up with every aspect of my work life, but even when I'm not looking at the launch, someone will say something that brings me back to him.

Jackson's eyes bore into mine. "I don't know what I did to deserve this chance with you." His fingers tenderly brush a loose strand of hair back behind my ear. "You're beautiful, smart, funny ... I can't get enough of you. What's going on in that gorgeous head of yours?"

I'm taken aback by his intensity and what he's saying. He thinks he's undeserving? It's me who doesn't know how I somehow have him.

I place my hand on his cheek. "I think you have it mixed-up. It's me who's lucky. I keep waiting to wake up and realize you're a dream." I rub my thumb against his stubble. He's real. We're real. No pretending, no dreams—only us.

"Believe it, baby. I'm not going anywhere," he says softly before his lips meet mine.

We continue our day walking through the zoo. He refuses to let me say good-bye to the camels, no matter how hard I try. We walk through the park hand in hand, stopping to grab a dirty water dog and pretzel from the hot dog truck. It's your typical day in New York City. No fanfare or crazy planning. It's perfect. Every single solitary second is all I could ever want.

"How about we head back to my place and watch a movie?" Jackson asks.

"Sure. Only if I can pick it." I smile, happy that he wants to spend the rest of the day together.

I note that he didn't answer, but he's crazy if he thinks I'm going to let him win—again. We head to his apartment and memories of the last time I was here flood back. The way he seduced me, touched me, brought me to the brink, and then opened up about the mission. How in the morning there was no awkwardness. We had breakfast and I headed back to my apartment, floating on cloud nine.

"Pick something good," Jackson warns as we head into the living room.

"You didn't give any contingencies, so you get no say." I smirk and head over to the wall of DVDs. I could be a total pain in the ass and pick something I know he'd hate, but then again his selection doesn't exactly give me many options. Scanning the endless rows, I find one and gasp.

"Oh my God! You have *Empire Records*?" I grab the DVD and rush over to put it in the player.

"You know this movie is cinema gold," Jackson says as he brings over popcorn and settles into the couch.

"This is the best movie ever!" I exclaim and snuggle into his side. "Okay. Before we start watching, if you could be anyone, who would you pick? I'd be Lucas. He's hysterical." I smile and grab the bowl, putting it on my lap.

"I guess Joe. He's the boss."

I laugh at his choice. Of course he'd pick the one who's in charge. Joe is pretty badass, though.

"I think you'd be a great Rex. Oh Rexy, you're so sexy." I smirk and push play as he scoffs.

We spend the next hour laughing and reciting lines. Just as Rex Manning and Gina are getting it on in the copy room, Jackson runs his fingers up and down my arm. Suddenly I'm not so interested in the movie anymore. I shift, trying to stifle the lust bubbling up, but he moves his hand to the back of my neck and starts making small circles on my skin with his fingertips. My breathing becomes heavier as the pad of his finger rubs the spot right below my ear. Every caress increases my yearning. Heat pools as he makes his way back down my neck, lingering there.

I move my hand higher up his leg and hear him swallow loudly. The urge to touch him, to feel him, to make him come apart in my hands grows with each beat of my heart. Slowly I turn to look at him. His eyes drink me in before his mouth crushes against my lips with savage intensity. He shifts us and swings me on top of him. Feeling his erection against my core causes my arousal to rage like a storm.

His lips lower and his tongue traces my neck and shoulders. "Jackson, I want you," I say in a breathy whisper.

"Understatement of the year." He pulls the strap of my tank top and bra down, exposing my breast to his hungry mouth. Jackson pushes me back as his tongue circles my nipple.

My lids close as I absorb the sensations of his warm breath and mouth on me. His hand glides up my back and tangles in my hair as he tugs, exposing my neck and arching me forward to give him easier access. I try to sit up but he grips my hair and pulls harder, bringing my chest closer to him. He sucks and nips as I writhe in his lap. His other hand digs into my ass, gripping, kneading, and pushing me into his cock.

Using his teeth, he pulls the other strap down and pays the same attention to my other breast. The scruff on his cheek grazes my already sensitive skin, sending tingles from my head to my toes.

I push forward and pull his shirt off before fusing my mouth to his. Our tongues tangle as the kiss becomes aggressive and desperate. God, I want him so bad. I'm dripping with need, aching for him to fill me. I rake my nails down his arms, extracting a low rumble from his chest.

Breaking the kiss, my tongue grazes his ear before I say huskily, "I want to fuck you."

He groans before pushing me up and tearing my pants off. I hastily pull his off as he reaches over and puts a condom on. I'm straddling him when he says, "Then fuck me, Catherine."

I slide down on him as he fills me to the brink. So fucking full. He's so deep his cock is hitting every nerve inside me. Jackson's eyes close and his head falls back against the couch. My hands grip his shoulders as I start to move.

"Your pussy feels so good." His voice fills the

room and he groans louder.

Every breath, every moan goes straight to my core.

Gripping my hips, he sets the pace. Raw passion spreads through me at the sweet friction of his bare skin against mine. Watching him lost in my touch, in my body, as I rock back and forth is incredible. Our eyes connect, awakening something deep within me. His fingers dig in so tight it's almost painful, but we don't drop our eyes. The unrestrained emotion behind his gaze mirrors mine. With each thrust, each caress, each kiss, we're both giving each other everything, all the good and bad. I don't know where he ends and I begin. I ride him hard and fast, embracing this intimacy, climbing my way toward ecstasy.

Jackson slips his hand between us, applying pressure to my clit. I lean against his chest, absorbing the heat from his body. "Let go," he groans against my neck. "I want to feel you grip me. Ride me harder."

"Don't stop," I pant as he continues to draw pleasure from me.

He rubs in small circles, keeping pace from below, pushing me harder and faster so every nerve surges with liquid heat. I lose control at the intense pleasure and sink my teeth into his shoulder, biting down as my orgasm tears through me.

"Holy shit!" Jackson calls out as he pounds into me, taking control of my movement.

I lean back with a seductive gleam in my eyes, but it's nothing compared to the fire burning in his. My heart clenches. He's either angry or extremely turned-on. Jackson lifts me off him and places me on the floor, gripping me from behind as he lifts my ass in the air. Definitely turned-on.

"You fucking amaze me," he says, low and raspy as his hand glides up my back. Then he grabs my shoulder, entering me roughly. "This. Us. You. Your body—was made for me. You're mine."

"Oh my God, yes." I moan as the feeling of him deeper than he's ever been overtakes me. He tangles a hand in my hair as he plows into me, hard. My breasts hang heavily and the sound of our bodies connecting over and over fills the room.

"You look so fucking sexy." Jackson's voice is strained as he slams into me. His fingers wrap around my hip, gripping me so tight. He shifts his position, hitting the sweet spot inside me. The sound of him slapping his body against mine only drives me higher. "I want to fuck you all day and all night, so all you see is me. When you walk, I want you to remember where I've been and how good it feels when I'm inside you."

His words go directly to my core, reviving my previous orgasm. My mind is a sponge soaking up every syllable. Jackson reaches his hand around, finds my sensitive clit, and rubs it, bringing my orgasm closer.

"I'll never get enough of you. Mine goddamnit. All fucking mine."

That word: enough. Only this time he's telling me I *am* enough. Telling me he wants more.

I shatter, crying out his name as he continues to hit every sensitive spot in my body. My bones are melting from the sheer force of it.

He pumps a few more times before following. "Catherine … My Catherine."

We both crumple to the floor, exhausted and sated. I look up at him as he rubs his shoulder where I bit him. Oh my God, I bit him. I actually sunk my teeth into him because I was so far gone.

"Sorry about that." I smile as my cheeks flame with embarrassment.

He smiles back at me. "You can bite me." Jackson's lips find purchase on mine. "Any fucking time." He lies on his back and shifts me closer.

He's everything I could have wanted but never knew to ask for. We enjoy and entertain each other. The one thing my grandma always said was to find someone who makes you laugh. We can be serious or playful, and either way it works. As scared as I am, right now I feel content, happy. I close my eyes and listen to the rhythm of his heart.

He kisses my head. "I've got you, baby." The sound of his voice lulls me and I drift off, hoping we can handle whatever comes our way, because the thought of losing moments and days like this scares me.

chapter
twenty-two

It's been the week from hell. Nothing has gone right. My car broke down and I spilled coffee on my shirt first thing this morning. Worse than anything, Jackson and I haven't seen each other much. He's coming with me today to the reading of my father's will, which is also causing me extreme stress. Ashton wanted to be there for me, but she's working on a breakthrough and it's been keeping her in the city for the last week.

I'm working on the final version of Raven's ad campaign today since the approvals finally came through. It's been the only thing Jackson and I have argued about. I scheduled a few press releases, but he's been fighting about getting in front of the camera.

"Cat," Taylor's sweet voice comes through the intercom.

"Yes?"

"I have Neil on the line. He says it's urgent." Taylor sounds as irritated as I am at his calling.

He's been relentless. He calls or texts almost every day, but this is the first time he's resorted to calling the office. He's wearing me down and my patience is already nonexistent.

"Tay, I can't do this today. Tell him I'm out of the office or whatever." I drop my head on the desk, making a loud thump. Fucking Neil. Will this ever end?

Taylor comes in after getting rid of my annoyingly persistent ex. "He said he would try again later." She's wringing her hands as she sits to go over the Raven account.

"I don't want to take his calls, so don't even let me know anymore. Just don't put it through. Okay?"

"Sure, no problem." She smiles and nods her head.

"I have a meeting on Wednesday that I need the video ready for, so let's get to work." I return her smile and open my folder.

We have so much left to do to get things to where I want them. I'm an overachiever by nature, but I'm borderline obsessive on this one. It's different when you know the client, even more so when you know them intimately. My need to please people is always a problem, but with Jackson it's kind of scary. I want him to be blown away by what I've done.

"It's almost time for you to leave," Taylor reminds me. "Do you want to finish up Monday?"

"Oh shit! Yes, let's plan to be in the office late next Monday and Tuesday. I need to have a few meetings with some magazines and meet with the marketing team. Plus, I need the print ads done before the release and the photo shoot." I stand and smooth my black dress. I figured black would be appropriate. Even though I'm not going to a funeral, in a way it's my own personal version of one. I'm saying good-bye to my father today in more ways than one.

"Sounds good." She shifts her weight and looks away.

"What's wrong, Tay?"

She doesn't say a word as she walks over and wraps her slender arms around me. After a moment of her squeezing, she inhales and swipes at her eye, looking forlorn. What the hell is going on?

"Are you quitting? Is that what this is?" I ask, panicking.

"No! I felt like you needed a hug. You've had a lot happen in the last few months, and I can't imagine today is going to be easy for you. I know you've been trying to pretend this isn't happening. I'm just glad you won't be alone."

I didn't want to tell Taylor or anyone in the office about my relationship with Jackson, but I trust her. That, and she saw how happy I was after the trip, so she knew something was going on. She knows what a risk I'm taking, but she's genuinely excited about Jackson and me. This is the kind of person I want in my life. People like her remind me not everyone is awful. I didn't even put two and two together as to what had her bothered, and come to find out it was concern for me.

"Thanks. I'll be okay. Maybe I'll finally get some closure." I muster a small smile.

I hear someone clearing their throat and turn to see Jackson leaning against the door of my office with a huge grin.

"Jackson! What are you doing here? I thought I was meeting you at the lawyer's office." I smile as he walks toward me, taking in his perfectly tailored suit. He brushes my hair off my face and stares at me. All I can do is smile back in wonder. I'm so far gone—I'd be a fool to think otherwise.

"I was close. I figured I'd ride there with you," he says, wrapping his arms around me.

Suddenly aware that we're in my office, I quickly

step back out of his embrace. It's so easy to fall into a pattern with him and forget he's my client. He may not care about my rules, but the bottom line is I can't risk losing my job.

"Jackson, not here please," I whisper, looking over at the wide open door.

Hurt flashes in his eyes before he recovers. "You almost ready to go?"

I step forward but keep a professional distance, allowing my eyes to convey all I can't show him physically. The thin line between being his publicist and girlfriend can hurt both of us if it isn't clear.

"You know how badly I wish I could wrap my arms around you? But you're still my client and you promised. My assistant is outside the door and my boss could walk in at any moment. So I'm not trying to push you away. I'm asking you to think about how it would look."

My heart stutters when I think about how thoughtful he was to come here and make sure I'm not alone on the ride over. Once again he's giving me something I didn't know I needed. He knows me. He gets me. It baffles me that he's wormed his way through all my layers without any resistance. Well, very little resistance.

A slow, sexy smile glides across his features. "It's fine, baby. In about three minutes we won't be in your office. Remember, outside of our business relationship I make no promises."

Returning his smile, I can see he wants to kiss me, but instead he strides out of my office.

Taylor and Jackson spend a few minutes talking and laughing while I clean up my desk. I grab my phone, unsurprised that I have a few missed calls from Neil, a text from Ashton, and another from

Gretchen.

> *Ashton: Be strong and remember you're loved.*

> *Me: Thanks Biffle. I love you. See you tonight.*

I check the next message from Gretchen and smile.

> *Gretchen: Call me if you need anything and text me a picture of the new hottie. Ashton said I'd shit myself.*

> *Me: I will! Can't wait for you to meet him.*

> *Gretchen: Where's my picture?*

> *Me: You'll get one soon.*

I look up as Taylor glances over, eyes wide and mouth agape as she points to Jackson. I resist the urge to laugh—he is ridiculously gorgeous. But more than that, he sees me. He sees everything I am and doesn't run.

I glance at the clock and close up my office. We only have about twenty minutes before we have to be there. "Come on. Stop flirting with the office staff."

Taylor laughs and we say our good-byes. Jackson has a town car waiting downstairs for us—another sign of his thoughtfulness. We climb in and he clasps my hand in his. A sad smile spreads across my face. I'm glad he's here with me. But as far as we've come in the short amount of time we've known each other, I can't shake the feeling that it's only a matter of time until Jackson walks away. It's like there's this barrier around him that only permits me to get so close, and I have a nagging feeling that he's hiding something. I can't put my finger on what exactly, but it's there in the way he breaks off his thoughts sometimes or the forlorn look he occasionally gets when he thinks I'm not paying attention. It keeps me from trusting my emotions. I want to give myself freely, allow him into the deeper parts of me, but I need the same in return.

"Hey, you're quiet. What's going on?" Jackson says, breaking my inner thoughts.

"I'm just thinking. A lot could happen today."

My nerves are all over the place. I don't know what to expect. It's not like I have anything to go off of.

He rubs his thumb across my soft skin and my heart flutters. "Did your father have any other relatives?"

"I honestly don't know," I mutter. "I don't remember much about my father or his family. I know he had a brother, but I don't think they were close."

"These usually aren't long. It's really a formality," he says and looks out the window, taking a moment to himself. As he faces forward again, I notice his eyes, glossy with unshed tears. Releasing my hand, he grips his pants, looking uncomfortable.

"You okay?"

Quickly he glances up, giving me a half-hearted smile. "Yeah. Sorry. I hate lawyers. Will your mother be there?"

I want to call bullshit but something holds me back. I hate a lot of things, but most don't make me emotional. I take a moment to weigh my response. As much as I want to press him, we don't have enough time and my head isn't clear enough for anything too deep. "No. I didn't even tell her about it. I don't really want her to be there. Let's just say our relationship is strained at best."

"Were you always like that?" he asks.

No, sadly we weren't.

"There was a time when we were close. She worked hard throughout my childhood to make sure we had the basics—food, shelter, clothing. Eventually, it wore on her. Being a single mother and having to raise me alone with no financial or emotional support from anyone else was hard. I remember my grandmother being around when my father first left, but she died when I was twelve. That was when everything fell to shit. My mother started trying to replace my father and I became irrelevant.

"There were times we had fun. I remember a family vacation to Florida, and I clung to that memory when I was younger. But the older I got, the more and more bitter she got, until I left for college— which she refused to help me with. She thought I was an idiot and wouldn't make it through year one, let alone get a degree. I really hated her during that time. But I proved her wrong. I busted my ass and got grants and loans to pay for my education. I refuse to fail and school was no different." I look away, embarrassed by my rant. I didn't mean to tell him all that. A simple no would have sufficed.

The car slows and comes to a stop in front of a tall building. This will be the final piece to my father's part in my life. The moisture builds in my eyes as I think of the few good memories I have of him—the times he showered me with adoration, when he sang to me, when we played games, and when he helped with my homework. It surprises me that I remember any of them since they weren't a large part of my life. Still, they were all I had to cling to during my darker times.

Whatever's showing on my face gives Jackson pause. "Catherine, what's wrong?" The concern in his voice chips away at my resolve.

"I'm fine." I turn away, trying to gather myself so I can face this. Suddenly it feels like the car is closing in—I need to get out of here. Practically falling out of the car, I right myself and clench my hands. *I can do this.* I can go in there, find out what I need to be here for, and leave.

Jackson is behind me in a heartbeat, turning me around to face him. "If you're fine, then why do you look like you're about to pass out?"

"I'm just ... nervous." I try to shrug it off so I can get this over with. Am I scared? Yes. Am I ready to lay to rest a piece of the puzzle that's been missing since I was a child? Yes. I close my eyes, shake my head, and gather all the strength I can.

"You don't have to do this. We can come back if you're not feeling well."

"Jackson, I have to do this now."

"No, you don't." His jaw is set and his features appear angry, yet his voice is filled with empathy and understanding. "You need to be sure you're strong and ready to face it. Let's go up and reschedule. When you rush trying to get it over with, it only leaves a mess afterward."

I glance at him curiously, wondering about that last statement. "No, I'm doing this today. If I leave here, I'll never come back." I take a step closer to him, grasping his hand in mine. My eyes soften and my heart swells from his concern. I need him. I need his strength even if it's only him sitting beside me through this. "Please, I can't do this alone."

His body stiffens at my plea, but he doesn't answer. I beg with my eyes as he looks away and releases my hand. He takes a deep breath and grips the back of his neck. Though it's my father whose affairs we're here to settle, by the way he's acting you'd think Jackson was just as upset by this whole thing as I am. I can see how hard this is for him, but I don't understand why. It goes beyond his worry for me. It's personal. What inner struggle is he battling right now?

He takes a step forward. "I'm not going to make you do this alone. I promised I'd be here. If this gets to be too much, you say the word and we're gone."

I manage a half smile as I lift my head. Another piece of my battered heart was claimed by Jackson Cole.

"Thank you," I say. Our fingers interlace as we enter the building.

Jackson lifts my hand, tenderly pressing his lips against my fingers. The whisper of his voice radiates to my heart as he gently says, "Of course."

He lifts me up and keeps me safe. I hope he doesn't let me fall.

chapter twenty-three

*E*ntering the upscale Manhattan law firm of Coogan, Goldstein & Leibowitz, the fear of the unknown is choking the life out of me. I have no idea what to expect or what my father could have left for me. All I keep thinking about are the possibilities—I could get answers today, or more questions. Why was I required to come to the office? Why couldn't they have mailed me the paperwork? Is there something here I need to see? I can't answer any of these questions, but they keep coming. What if he left some kind of video? Will I want to watch it? With each new thought comes a sickening feeling in the pit of my stomach. My fight or flight reflexes are in high gear, and if it weren't for Jackson holding my hand, I'd be fleeing back into the elevator and getting the hell out of here.

Jackson gives my hand a small squeeze and I look at his apprehensive face. "I know you said we should do this today, but you're pale and shaking."

I'm shaking? I didn't even notice.

"I'm just nervous because of all the possibilities. I don't know what to expect. What if he had another kid and they're here?" I somehow manage to choke the words out.

Stopping, he releases my hand and moves to cradle my head. My heart rate slows at his gentle touch. His eyes penetrate my fear and his voice is tender. "I'll be here the whole time. All that's going to happen is the lawyer will read the will, you'll find out what you were left, and then we'll go. No matter who else is here, if you don't want to deal with them, you don't. Okay?"

I give him a nod, trying to keep myself together while drawing strength from him.

We enter the office. It's nondescript and simple—and empty. More than anything I'm grateful for this because if there were a long lost sister sitting here, I might have collapsed. Jackson's strong hand grips mine. He's pretty focused on making sure I'm not having an emotional breakdown. As long as he's here, I'm okay.

Mr. Goldstein enters and shakes our hands. "Catherine, I'm Avi Goldstein. I'm the lawyer in charge of your father's estate."

"Nice to meet you. This is Jackson Cole, my ..."

"Boyfriend," Jackson finishes matter-of-factly.

My head whips around to look at him. Boyfriend? Well that was unexpected. After the last date we had, I guess it's true, but it still shocks me. He didn't hesitate or question, he seemed proud to say it. The smile on his face rocks me. I'm sure it mirrors mine, and I'm also sure my heart grew to twice its size.

Mr. Goldstein clears his throat and begins. "Nice to meet you both. I'm very sorry for your loss, Ms. Pope. I know these proceedings are hard, especially when you lose a loved one suddenly. Whether it's a father, mother, or spouse it's never easy. I hope you can find peace and closure." Jackson's hand releases mine abruptly. When I look at him, he seems anxious, uncomfortable. The loss of his warmth and support leaves me bereft. Jackson shoves his hand in his pocket and looks away.

"Thank you, Mr. Goldstein," I say with a tremble in my voice. There will be no closure because I've gained no answers. I don't even know how you close something that was never opened.

"Please, call me Avi. I assure you this is the least favorite part of my job. I was on your side not too long ago when my wife passed, so I'll try to make this as easy as possible," Avi says with a smile.

Suddenly Jackson gets up and walks over to the window. I can see his chest rising and falling powerfully.

"Jackson?"

He looks over with sadness in his eyes before returning to his seat.

"You were saying, Mr. Goldstein," Jackson says. Any trace of sadness is gone, replaced by the mask of determination I've come to know so well.

Avi nods and begins. "I'll get down to it. Your father's estate is rather simple. You're his next of kin. There are no other living relatives, so everything he possessed when he passed is now yours. There is a house in New Jersey as well as some cash and stocks. You were also named as his beneficiary on his life insurance. However, I asked you here so I could give you a letter from your father. His wishes were simple. You are to read this when you're ready. He mailed it to me in a separate envelope with a letter asking for me to personally ensure you received it." He stands, extending the letter to me.

A letter. From him. I stand and move forward. My hand is unstable when Mr. Goldstein places the letter in it. As I clasp my fingers around the envelope, a single tear escapes. This could contain all the answers to my doubt, or it could break my heart even more. Placing the letter on my lap, I cover it with my hand, holding on to the last piece of my father. Dread, pain, sadness, wonder, and so many more feelings seep through my veins at all the possible things this letter could say. Did he write it to tell me why he left? Why he never looked back? Will it tell me that I just wasn't that important to him? All my insecurities come forward full force as the fear of what it could hold nearly cripples me.

"Ms. Pope, I didn't know your father very well, but I met him a few times. He was a wonderful man. I truly hope he's at peace." Avi smiles kindly. "I'll try to keep this brief. You are due to inherit quite a bit. All your assets total around $300,000 plus whatever the property is worth. His life insurance will need to be dealt with separately, but his policy was around half a million. It's obvious he wanted you well cared for. Were you close?"

I glance at Jackson, completely overwhelmed. He extends his hand and I eagerly accept the warmth and solace he's offering. Lacing my fingers with his, I try to fight back the tears as my heart shatters a little more. "No, Avi, we weren't close. I haven't spoken to my father in about twenty years. This is very overwhelming for me. I don't really understand why he left me anything."

"Well, I can't answer for him, but maybe his letter will give you the answers you're looking for. I just need you to sign the paperwork. I have the key here for the house and if there is anything else, I can call you."

I place the letter and key in my purse and take a moment to collect myself. Walking over to the desk, my hands shake. This is it. The end. The finale to my father's life. I'll have no chance of finding out more. There are no living relatives, no family to ask. Whatever's in the letter is all I'll have.

The pen is shaking so hard I have to stop twice to try to get my hand under control. Tears stain the paper, and my heart plummets as I finally finish my signature. I let out a strangled sob and press my hand to my mouth to stop the pain trying to make its way out. Somehow I manage to smother it. Squaring my shoulders, I wipe away the tears staining my face.

Avi shakes my hand and places his other on top. "Catherine, even though you didn't know your father, I know he loved you. My clients come to me because they want their loved ones to find peace and move on. Even when they're gone they are always a part of us. We never have to truly let them go. They live in our hearts and memories forever."

Closing my eyes, I absorb his words. "Thank you, Avi. I …" I shake my head, unable to speak, but the understanding in his eyes tells me he doesn't need a response. He releases my hand with a sad smile and I gather my belongings.

Jackson stays quiet off to the side. As I approach, I notice his furrowed brow and the way he keeps gripping his neck as if he's uncomfortable.

"You ready?" he asks.

"Yeah, let's go."

Once we're out of the building, I take a deep breath and let the tears roll down my face again. It's over. I have nothing left. I'm empty. All I want to do is rewind the last ten years and change it all. I want to know who my father was, why he made the choices he did, go back in time and rewrite my story—but I can't. I miss a man I didn't even know. How is that possible?

Jackson sees the tears and takes a hesitant step toward me. "I don't want you to be alone. I'm staying with you tonight. No arguments."

I couldn't argue if I wanted to—which I don't. If Jackson's close, maybe I can keep it together long enough to read the letter burning a hole in my purse.

The train station is only a few blocks away, and I could use the walk. All I want to do is curl into Jackson, but since we left the office he hasn't touched me. Even with my scattered mind, I've processed that much. Wherever Jackson is, it's not here. Oh my God. I didn't take into account how hard this might be for him with his history of loss and grief. Of course bringing up death would push him away. He's never felt this distant to me. Now I know why. It was selfish to ask him to be with me today.

The two blocks seem to take forever, and with each step it feels like miles separate Jackson and me. He's stiff and keeps his hands in his pockets while he processes whatever he's feeling. I want to slap him and force him to talk because his silence is shredding me. Not because he's doing anything wrong, but because I need to stop my mind from racing over what just happened. Both of us walk in silence until I can't take it anymore.

"Jackson?" I ask tentatively.

He looks up but doesn't respond. Every indication, from his tight jaw to his rigid posture, is saying he wants to be left alone.

"Forget it." I look away, taken aback by his aloofness.

Neither of us says anything else as we approach the train. Where I was quiet and sad a moment ago, now my frustration is growing. If he didn't want to be with me, then he shouldn't have said he was coming to my place. He could've gone back home and left me alone. I could've processed this on my own instead of having him brooding next to me and adding to my stress. I need his arms, his strength, but right now all I'm getting is nothing.

I can't take another second of this. "Are we going to talk or keep ignoring each other?" My voice is full of the annoyance I'm feeling. Part of it is directed at him, part at this entire day.

"What do you want to talk about?" he says with narrowed eyes.

Apparently he's irritated by my approach. Good. "Oh, I don't know. The weather? Why you're being so quiet and haven't said a word since we left the office? You can choose." I'm being a total bitch, but at this point I really don't care.

"Nice to see you haven't lost your attitude." Jackson huffs with a sarcastic smile as the train approaches.

"*You* said you wanted to come back to my place. I didn't ask you to."

His answer comes fast and angry. "I know that."

"If you didn't want to be around me or whatever, you didn't have to." I throw over my shoulder as I board the train. Fuck him. He wants to be a jerk, he can do it alone. I'm going home, pouring myself an overflowing glass of wine, and finding the courage to read this freaking letter.

Just thinking about it makes me nauseous. There are so many things it could say, some of which I'm not ready to face. But I know myself well enough to know I'll never sleep if I don't get it over with soon. His attitude isn't helping.

I'm facing the window, refusing to look at him,

when the seat next to me moves. He doesn't say a word, but the warmth of his hand on my leg stills me and a tear falls from the corner of my eye. God! I'm a mess! One minute I'm livid, and then he touches me and I cry.

"I want to be with you. That's why I'm here." His voice is low, full of the strength I've come to rely on.

I turn and face him, hopeful that he means that. "This isn't easy for me, you know? Trusting you, letting you be here for me. You don't understand how hard this is."

He wipes the tears from my face and gently cradles me to his chest. "I know more than you think."

"How so?" My voice is barely a whisper, but I know he hears me when he lets out a long breath. I sit up and stare at him through blurry eyes, waiting for his answer.

The pain that lances across his perfect face erases all my anger.

"You know about the fucking hell I've been through, Catherine. Do you think I wanted anyone around me? I hated myself. I hated everyone who talked to me, touched me, or made me feel. I wanted to die with them." His hand touches his chest and then moves to his shoulder. "You can't imagine the man I was during that time. Anger?" He scoffs before going on, "Baby, you can't imagine what angry looked like. So you want to be mad at me, be mad."

The train stops, halting our conversation. I don't fully understand his withdrawal. He's the one who's pushed me repeatedly, and now suddenly he's retreating? And yes, I'm mad. I'm mad at him, at my father, at my mother, and anyone else who made me this way.

As we exit the train, my mind begins to wander, thinking about the pain he must have been in. Losing people you know and love, people who understand you and stand beside you ... I can't think about any of this right now. My brain can't contain any more. I want to change into my comfy clothes, drink a bottle ... errr glass of wine, and forget this day ever happened.

Standing here, facing each other, the silence stretches for miles. Both of us trying to read the other. Both lost in some form of grief. Gripping my hips, he pulls me close. I close my eyes and relish his embrace. Here I feel okay. I'm safe when his arms are around me, protecting me, but is my heart? In this moment I don't care. I mold to him, allowing his strength to surround me.

"I won't let you fall. I'll be here, but sometimes I'm going to be a dick. Sometimes I'm going to say the wrong thing. But if I didn't want to be here with you, I would've walked away."

I look up and the sincerity on his face matches what I heard in his voice, but the last thirty minutes did nothing to allay my fears. If anything, my doubts have intensified. "Then why were you so distant before?" I ask.

He speaks in a low, hushed tone. "Today brought up a lot of memories for me. Memories I've tried extremely hard to forget."

Jackson takes a deep breath and places his hand on the small of my back as we start walking to my apartment. He's silent for a few minutes and I sense he needs the time to collect his thoughts.

"I just want to he—" I stop short when I see someone in front of my apartment complex.

Neil. Why the hell is he here? Today of all days. My stomach drops as the reality of my past and present collide. I've tried to get rid of him. Ignoring him hasn't worked, so now he's apparently going to stalk me. Great. My body begins to tremble, shaking uncontrollably as fear, anger, and hate overtake me.

"Catherine?" Jackson asks, looking for whatever caused me to freeze.

Neil steps forward with his eyes fixed on Jackson. "Well, it seems you didn't miss me all that much, did you?" he sneers.

"What do you want?" I return acidly.

"I've been calling. We have to talk. You have something that's mine," Neil says.

Obviously he's been calling and I've been avoiding him. I swear he wasn't this stupid before. Or maybe he was but I was too blind to see it. Either way, I don't think I can handle this confrontation today.

"I have nothing of yours," I say, trying to step around him.

Jackson moves next to me, angling his body so he's between us. "Who the hell are you?"

Neil steps to the side, blocking me from getting past him. He jerks a thumb toward Jackson. "Who's this guy?"

Jackson takes a step closer to Neil, who huffs and steps back.

"I'm her fiancé," he says with a sardonic smile.

"No, you're not!" I scream. "Are you fucking kidding me?"

He's purposely trying to ruin my life. Why? What the hell did I ever do to him? He broke my heart and I didn't do a damn thing to retaliate. I didn't steal from him, hurt his precious career, cheat on him, or anything else. Now he stands in front of my apartment, trying to take something else from me. Rage pulses through my body with each heartbeat. The first good thing I have he's going to try to ruin. I look to Jackson whose eyes are wide. No! He can't believe this.

Jackson stands there and crosses his arms across his broad chest as he lets out a mocking laugh. "Care to explain?"

I'm struggling not to cry. The emotions I've been swallowing all day are making their way back up. "Jackson, this is my *ex*-fiancé. He's a liar and a piece of shit!"

"Don't let her fool you," Neil sneers from behind me.

I'm unable to control myself anymore. I'm done. I'm lost. There's no stopping me as I unload my anger in Neil's face. "Shut the fuck up! You cheated on me! Why are you here? We haven't been together for months! Go away!" I'm breaking. Every single part of me is falling apart.

I turn back to Jackson. The look on his face makes my stomach clench. He looks like he's wavering between anger and pride. Both of us are dealing with too much right now, but I desperately need him to listen me.

"None of this is true! He's with another woman. He's lying!" I yell, feeling my sanity slip away. "This is Neil Mullins. He works for Boyce. We *were* engaged and then he cheated on me with *Piper*." This is definitely not how I planned to talk about my ex, if I ever decided to talk about him at all. I implore him to believe me with my eyes. "Jackson, please. We've been over for months!"

Neil barks out a laugh. "Your memory is a little off, love. You stole my numbers so I left you. I should've had the Raven account. Now, I want my fucking ring and the money you owe me back."

Jackson steps away from me. He curls his lip while flexing his hands and glaring at Neil. "Wait a fucking minute," he says and then looks at me. "Neil? From Boyce, the other PR firm?"

I nod, trying to choke back the tears that keep spilling down my face. This is the worst day of my life. It feels like my heart is being ripped out of my chest.

"Since you know who I am, I'll ask again. Who the fuck are you?" Neil says, puffing out his chest.

Jackson glares at Neil. "I'm Jackson Cole."

Recognition registers on Neil's face as his angry smile grows. "Well, that explains everything. You fucked the client, Cat. I didn't think you had it in you." He steps toward me, his eyes hard and cold.

Jackson pushes me back behind him as anger rolls off him in waves. You can smell the testosterone in the air. His knuckles are white from clenching his fists so hard, and the vein on the side of his neck is protruding. I need to calm him before this gets out of hand. I place my hand on his shoulder and move around him, but his arm grips my waist, keeping me safely behind him.

From behind Jackson, I yell at Neil, "You need to leave. Now!" My entire body is trembling. I'm not sure if it's anger or hate or any other emotion you can name.

Neil steps forward and Jackson tenses. Neil isn't a small guy, but he's no match for a man Jackson's size. Not only that, but I'm pretty sure Jackson is trained to kill him in one move.

Could this day get any fucking worse?

Jackson clears his throat and pulls me against his side. "She told you to leave. I suggest you go." His voice brokers no argument. He's reached his max.

"Right, well this is between me and Cat. So I think I'll just finish what I came here for." Neil smiles and moves closer.

Jackson's reaction seems involuntary as he steps forward and pushes against Neil's chest, sending him backward. The commanding sound in Jackson's voice scares me. "I don't think so, asshole. You're going to fucking leave right now—either by free will or by force. But I promise—you don't want to fuck with me."

I step between them, trying to get Jackson to calm down. The tears have stopped, but fear has taken over.

My voice is strangled as I plead with them both. "Please! Stop! I can't take any more." I step toward Neil with narrowed eyes. "You need to go! I don't have anything of yours, and I don't have anything left to say to you. Just leave!"

Neil snaps. His nostrils flare and his lip pulls back. He barrels toward me. The noise from his throat is a guttural roar. "You owe me my fucking ring! So you can either get it, or I'm going to do everything in my power to ruin you." He grips my arms, squeezing them painfully.

Before I have a second to process anything, Neil's on the ground and Jackson's on top of him. The sound of their bodies hitting the pavement echoes around me.

He hits Neil in the face and blood splatters on the sidewalk at the impact. "Stop!" I scream, trying to stop the madness in front of me.

Punch after punch he lands on Neil. Neil manages to get a fist to Jackson's face, but it only seems to stoke Jackson's rage. I rush over and pull at his arms, but he shakes me off easily, continuing the onslaught, undeterred.

"Motherfucker! You don't touch her!" he says as he hits him again, his fist finding his mark. With each blow, the sound of his knuckles connecting with Neil's face cuts through the night air.

"Jackson! Stop!" I yell over and over. My voice falls on deaf ears as they continue to assault each other. Tears are pouring again, and my entire body is running on adrenaline.

I lean down, grabbing for Jacksons arm, finally snapping him out of his rage. He towers over Neil lying on the pavement. "I'll fucking kill you if you ever touch her again," he says, his voice venomous.

Jackson turns and looks at me. His expression shifts from anger to pain to worry when he sees the tears streaming down my face.

"Are you hurt?" His hands grasp my face as I pull away from his touch.

It's too much. I can't do this. All I can do is shake my head back and forth as I pray my legs don't give out on me.

"Catherine, talk to me. Please." His voice breaks on the last word and my heart goes with it.

Neil staggers to his feet and Jackson's back stiffens as he readies to protect me again. "You better have a damn good lawyer, Cole. This isn't over." He swipes the blood off his mouth and turns with vengeance in his eyes.

I squeeze my eyes shut and pray for strength because I don't have any left.

chapter twenty-four

Tears are streaming, leaving rivers of black mascara on my cheeks. Jackson's strong arms encase me, holding me tight as I crumble. I breathe in his scent, which usually calms me, but right now it does nothing to help my state. My eyes close and the numbness takes hold. I'm floating, completely weightless—I've finally lost it. I think we're moving but can't be sure. I'm enjoying the peace and serenity my mind has given me, the reprieve from all the hell that broke loose a few moments ago. Images of Neil and Jackson brawling blur before my eyelids, and I fight for the numbness again.

When I open my eyes, I'm shocked to see we're in my apartment. I don't remember walking, but then again I'm almost positive I've snapped. Jackson holds me in his arms and tries to speak to me, but I don't hear him. I barely register his touch. His warmth is absent.

Maybe, like everything else, he's gone cold, the tenderness he once felt for me destroyed by the display on the street. He's been distant all night. Maybe Neil just sealed the deal. The thought sends a wave of panic through my body, but I'm too defeated to fight it. He'll take the last remaining part of my heart and shatter it. I knew it would happen. He'll do what every man in my life does—leave.

His arms wrap tighter around me, but I don't

want his arms. I don't want anyone. I'm better off alone, making a clean break now before I fall further. I need to protect what's left of myself. He's already claimed parts of me that I'll never get back. I wish I could get the numbness back. I want to stop feeling so much all the time. It hurts—everything hurts.

His grip tightens, but I need to get away. I step back, pushing against his chest. His arms reach out as if I'm falling and he needs to catch me. But I'm done falling.

I place my hands in front of me to stop him. Gone is the uncertainty I had hours ago. All my resolve is back with a vengeance. Stifling the tears, I take a deep breath, ready to salvage what's left of myself. I look over to see his unsure face and posture. Ensuring my voice is clear, I answer the questions in his eyes. "You should go."

"What?" He steps back with a shocked expression.

"Leave, please," I croak out and point to the door.

He looks at me cautiously, like I'm a wounded animal. Tilting his head, brow furrowed, he responds, "Why would I leave? I'm not going anywhere. I told you I was staying." He stands defiantly, ready to fight me on this.

"I don't want you to stay here. I need to be alone," I say with as much steel in my voice as I can gather. There's a small part of me that knows pushing him away could be a mistake, but at this point I can't trust myself. He's already taken so much—I'm already in too deep. The last time we made love, he owned me. I knew then I'd never be the same. He's going to destroy me if I don't put an end to this now.

Jackson takes a step closer, shaking his head at my request. "I'm not leaving you."

There's no way he's going to walk away on his own—it's not who he is. This is the man who'd stand in front of a bullet and bear the pain so someone else wouldn't have to. But I don't need a hero. "I'm not asking you, Jackson. I'm telling you to leave. I want to be alone. I can't deal with anything else right now."

He strides toward me with his lips pursed. "Don't push me away. Don't make me the bad guy here." He reaches for me, but I take a step back.

I throw my hands up. "Really? Push you away? You pushed me away back there before the fight. I didn't do that—you did. I needed you! Do you have any idea what this was like for me today? Huh?" I step forward and push against his chest, but he doesn't budge. Instead he stands there and lets me unleash my fury. "Did you think about how this would be for me when you beat the shit out of him? Did you hear me screaming and begging you to stop? My God! Do you get it now? I was engaged to him. He was supposed to love me and cherish me! But instead he pushed me away, cheated on me. He left me for someone else because she was better than me!" I slap my hand against his chest, broken and hurt, but he doesn't move. He takes it. "I need to be more than that, Jackson. I need to be someone's everything. I deserve that! I'm tired ... I'm tired of being hurt. I want to be *enough* already!" I take a few steps back, needing some space.

Jackson takes another step, but I put my hands up to stop him. No. He can't touch me. He's already shown me what all the important men in my life have told me—I'm not enough. Not good enough to open up to. Not enough to share himself with. Will I ever be enough? "Don't touch me." Jackson's face contorts as if I've slapped him.

"Really, Catherine?" He shifts forward and clenches his jaw.

I take a shaky breath before continuing, "In the last two hours, I've had to face every fucking man in my life who's ever meant anything to me—my father, Neil, and now you. I can't do this. Please, just go!" I shake my head over and over, trying to grab on to the anger instead of the crushing pain of pushing him away.

"You think this has been easy for me? I've never made you feel irrelevant. I haven't cheated on you, or hurt you. No, I've been there for you, giving you everything I could. I held you when you cried and listened to you. I didn't make you feel cheap or worthless." His hands are shaking as he pauses to take a deep breath. "I've tried to be the man you say you deserve. Tell me what I did to make you think otherwise! So I pulled away on the train—we got past that. Did I get pissed off and beat the shit out of your fucking asshole ex? Yes! And if he fucking touched you again, I would've killed him. Is this about him? Do you still love him?"

I gasp and press my fingers to my lips, shaking my head back and forth in disbelief. How could he think that? "This has nothing to do with him. But it has everything to do with me."

"So you're going to take this out on me? I deserve this?"

We stand there in the middle of my living room, staring at each other, trying to get the resolution we're each fighting for. I look away and glance at his shirt. The blood there reminds me of everything that's happened.

"I just need time." The faint whisper of a voice I manage to get out sounds so broken—even to me.

His head tilts back as he grips his hair. "Fucking time? Time to what? Push me away and convince yourself that I'm like *him*. Are you sure you want me to leave? You're ready for me to walk away?"

"I need some damn time. I can't think with you around!" I turn away from him.

"You want me to walk out so you can hate me and blame me for leaving you. Well I won't let you play some fucking bullshit game with me."

I let out a breathy laugh and roll my eyes. "A game? You think this is a game for me? What do I win, huh?"

"You tell me. You're the one telling me to leave. I can't fucking believe this." He throws his hands up and then claps them against his legs. "If I walk out this door, I won't come back until I know you want me here."

"I'm used to watching men walk out the door." I say bitterly.

"Maybe you should stop pushing them out, then."

My heart stops as his words rip my chest apart. The pain is dragging me under, but he's standing there, watching the tears fall, watching how deep his words cut. "You don't know a fucking thing."

"I know you're fighting me because you're afraid. You think I'm like every other man. Have I hurt you? Have I lied to you?"

"Not yet!" I cry out.

Jackson takes a step closer. His breathing is heavy but he's trying to keep his tone soft. "You've already sentenced me for someone else's crime."

I weep into my hands because he's right. "You can't expect me to process all of what happened today with you here. My feelings for you ... they scare me. You make me feel too much! Every time you're around or you touch me, I lose something inside," I say earnestly.

"You think it's any different for me? I fought against this! Every time you walked in the room, I fought the urge to take you. If you think you're the only one who loses, you're wrong." His voice grows warm and seductive. "Somehow, at every turn, you've made me feel more than I've wanted to."

He closes the distance and I'm unable to fight him anymore. I allow his arms to hold me one last time. After this, I won't let him back in.

"Please," I cry into his chest as he clutches me to him. "Please, if you care, let me have time to think."

His arms fall from my back and he slowly moves to hold my face, tilting it so we're staring into each other's eyes. Jackson's expression is pained, but his eyes express so much more. "Fine. You win. I'll go." His eyes close as though the words are bitter in his mouth. When they open again he looks fierce and determined. "But hear me. You're it for me, Catherine." His thumb brushes a tear from my cheek. "I'm not walking away from you or us. I wasn't ready to love again when you came crashing into me. But you made me want to try again." Our lips touch briefly. When he looks back up, his eyes are intense. "Leaving you right now goes against every fucking thing I want. I'm going to let you push me away this once. But I mean it, when I walk out it's up to you when I come back. Don't make me wait too long." He leans down and places a long, tender kiss upon my lips. Our eyes meet again and he waits for a second before continuing, "I told you I'll always find you, but you have to want to be found. Let me find you, Catherine."

Without another word, his hands disappear. I want to beg him to stay, but I need him to go. It's as though someone is sawing me in half. I'm fighting against the pull, but I honestly don't know what I want anymore. He opens the door and hesitates, turning back to give me a sad smile before walking out.

When the door closes, I fall to the ground and let out a strangled sob. What have I done? Why does this always have to be so hard?

You're it for me, Catherine. His words repeat in my head.

I crawl to the couch and curl up, letting the tears come, hoping they'll wash away the pain. He asked me not to push and I basically shoved him. I fight the urge to run after him, to beg him to stay and hold me. Hoping I made the right choice, I curl into myself and rock back and forth.

What if I'm the reason they leave?

Maybe you should stop pushing them out, then.

If I truly pushed them all away, what does that say about me?

You've already sentenced me for someone else's crime.

Have I?

I lie here, soaking the cushion as I let out twenty years' worth of devastation. I cry until my tears have dried, but the hollow feeling in my chest has grown. I'm truly alone. There's no one here. What I wouldn't give to go back a few hours and skip ever going to the lawyer's. I would've waited for Ashton to go, or I'd go back even further to when I first met Jackson and not give in to him. Then I could live my life and not have to suffer all over again. If I thought the pain of losing Neil was bad, it's not even a tenth of what I'm feeling right now. Jackson took pieces of my heart with every kiss, every gesture, every smile, and I'll never get them back. Though, as I sit here and replay everything that's happened, I wonder if maybe that's not true. Yes, he claimed those pieces, but not to keep. He used those moments to put my heart back together. And then I made him leave.

I need to find my phone. I need Ashton. As I grab for my purse, it tips over and all the contents fly out. Why not? At this point I'm not surprised the hell won't end. I reach for my phone and see my father's letter on the floor. Every bone in my body freezes and my heart plummets into my stomach. Am I ready to read this? I reach for the letter and hold it in my hands. It's now or never.

Sitting on the floor, my finger slides under the lip and I gently tear the envelope open. I hesitate for a moment. Once I read this I can't unread it. My eyes water again but I stifle the tears. I'm tired of crying. Tired of feeling weak and not in control of my life. My heart is racing and the tightness in my chest is making me dizzy. I say a silent prayer as my fingers gently tug out the letter. Slowly, I open it and begin to read my father's last words to me.

My Dearest Catherine,
I'm sorry you're reading this letter and not hearing the words from me. It means that I was never brave enough to come find you. I'm a coward. I want to try to explain, and I hope that someday

you'll forgive me. You see, I loved your mother very much, but we couldn't make it work. You were never to blame. Ever. Not one single thing that ever happened between us was your fault. I'm sorry for hurting you. I know my absence must've caused you a lot of pain, and for that I'll have died bearing that burden on my shoulders. I thought about you every single day since I walked out that door. I wondered about you, hoping you grew to become a beautiful woman, never doubting you did.

I'll start at the beginning. When I left that day, you broke me. Your tears ripped through my heart. The pain of having to pry you off my leg destroyed me. Having you beg and promise to be good ... I can't describe my emotions because there aren't enough words to do so. You couldn't have been any better—you were already perfect. I didn't know how I was going to walk away. The agony was almost more than I could bear. At first, it was easier to stay away than imagine having to watch you hurt every time I had to leave. You were my world, Catherine. You gave me something I never knew I was missing. When you were born, you stole my heart. Then your mother and I realized it wasn't working, and I had to make a choice. That choice changed the rest of our lives. After I walked out the door that day, I knew I could never do it again. I couldn't walk away from you. Your tears, your hurt—they were caused by me that day and I've never forgiven myself for it. If I close my eyes, I can still see the anguish on your face. I can hear your pleas as if I'm right back there again. That does something to a man. When he sees the face of his daughter breaking, it forever changes him. I'm not excusing my absence because there is no excuse. I stayed away because I couldn't see that again. I didn't want cause you any more pain. I regretted that decision every birthday, every Christmas, every holiday, and every event that you've ever attended that I missed. A father I was not. A man I was not. Because I was too scared.

I want you to know I did follow you. I went to your dance recital when you were thirteen—you were an amazing swan. You were breathtaking in your prom dress—your date was a lucky guy. I attended your high school graduation. You looked beautiful—I was so proud. Standing in the back as they called your name, I realized how wrong I'd been. You, Catherine, deserved more. You should've had a father who was sitting in the front row, clapping for his daughter, not cowering in the back of the room. At that moment my shame and self-loathing was never clearer. I didn't deserve you. Which is why I continued to stay away after that. You were doing so well without me. If I came back into your life again, it would only confuse you. I'd already done enough of that.

When I was diagnosed with cancer, I started to re-evaluate my choices. I spent days in the hospital alone, contemplating how stupid I was. I couldn't call you and ask you to be there for me. I'd never been there for you. I wouldn't expect it and I couldn't ask you to do it—it was my penance. I still don't know if things would have been different, but please know I'm sorry, Catherine. More than I can ever fully express. I am so sorry. I'm sorry I wasn't the man you needed. I can only hope that as you read this you see that I loved you. One day you'll marry and he won't be good enough for you, because you, my daughter, deserve nothing less than perfection. I hope that he will love you with his whole heart and not make the same mistakes I did. I hope he'll show you every day *just how special you are. I hope he'll be the father to your children I was never able to be to you. He should fight every day to show you how worth it you are. There will come a time it will get tough, but if you truly love each other, you'll find your way.*

If you're still reading this, I want you to know that I'm looking down on you and smiling at the woman you've become. I wish I could turn back the hands of time, but I can't. I can't take all the hurt away, but I hope you understand that it was me. It was never you. I'm sorry. I want you to know the last person I'll think about when my time is up, is you. Every time the sun shines down upon you, I hope you'll think of me keeping the gray skies away. I love you, Catherine.

Love,
Your Father

It's too much and yet not enough. I place the letter down, lie on the cold floor, and cry myself to sleep, hoping for blackness to take hold. But there's no darkness, no absolution from the pain.

Even in my sleep I can't escape it. My dreams shift and change, haunting me with what I never had but always wanted. I wake up feeling nauseous, my headache now a throbbing migraine. Crying yourself dry of tears will do that. I glimpse at the clock. It's only nine thirty. Sheer emotional and physical exhaustion is all I register. I hate that I couldn't even sleep past midnight. At least then this horrific day would've been over. It's seriously the day that's never going to end.

Shaking my head, I try to clear the remnants of my bad dream involving Jackson, Neil, and my father. I grab the letter and my phone and head into my bedroom. Grasping my father's farewell, I curl myself around my pillow and text Ashton that I need her before passing out, letter and phone still in hand.

chapter twenty-five

*W*hen I wake up, I roll over and hold back a yelp when I realize someone is in my bed. For a moment I allow myself a sliver of hope that Jackson came back, but when I see the deep crimson hair, I know it's Ash. She must have come home and crawled into bed with me knowing something happened.

"Ash," my voice croaks as I wake her.

She groans and turns over, facing me and opening one eye. "Morning, lover."

It's as if I'm back to how I felt five months ago all over again. My lip quivers as the agony of last night returns full force. "Ash ..."

She pulls me into her arms and rubs my back. "Shhh, Cat. It'll be okay. Tell me what happened."

We sit and talk, going over the previous day's events. She listens and offers support, never saying more than a few words or pulling me back into a hug. I show her the letter and Ashton sobs as she reads the words my father wrote. Her pain is my pain and my pain is hers. We're like sisters—she knows how much this means to me. There are no secrets between us. She's fully aware of how hard my childhood was.

"How do you feel about what he wrote?" she asks, swiping tears away.

His words heal, but hurt a little more. I've longed

to hear them from him, but they've come after so much damage has been done. Growing up, feeling unloved and alone for years, and then having another man I loved abandon me … For the longest time, I truly believed I was unworthy. I still believe that. "I'm not sure. It's all a little late, don't you think?"

"I don't know. It's obvious he thought of you and felt a lot of remorse."

"But why not come and find me? Why not make amends before he died?"

"He was scared, Cat. I can't imagine how he would have just shown up after twenty years. Would you have given him a chance if he did?" she asks.

I sigh and think about whether I would have been able to. A part of me wants to say, "Yes, of course," but I was angry for so long. I was furious to the point that I would have probably slapped him and told him to leave. His absence hurt, which caused my mother to lash out at me in turn. She would always say things about how *we* weren't good enough for him.

"It would have depended, but he never tried." I shrug.

I continue recounting the rest of the night and Ashton grows more and more furious. She stands and then sits several times when I tell her what Neil did. She doesn't hide her anger easily. I start to shake as I recall his rage.

"I'll fucking kill him!" Her eyes narrow into slits as I show her the bruises.

"I think Jackson threatened the same thing."

"Well, good. He's at least trained and could probably get rid of the body. No one would miss that piece of shit." She stands and starts to pace.

"I swear to God, Cat, he's going to pay for this. We need a plan."

I can see the wheels in her head turning. "Ashton," I warn.

"Don't *Ashton* me! He comes here and assaults you over his ring? No! I wish I majored in biochem. Then I'd have access to the good stuff in the lab." She continues to pace, formulating her revenge.

"Seriously, he's not worth it." I try to break through her plotting.

Ashton continues as if I haven't even spoken. "Maybe we can ..."

I stretch, lifting my arms over my head as I arch my back. Ashton's eyes go wide and she gasps.

"What?" I ask.

She rushes over and holds my arm up. "Look."

When I look down, I can't believe what I see. I have huge bruises on my arms where Neil grabbed me.

She sits on the bed, takes out her phone, and starts snapping pictures of my arms. "You need photos in case this gets ugly."

I nod, wishing I'd thought about that. Whatever brought Neil to talk to me in the first place hasn't been addressed. Now there's the fact that he got his ass kicked, knows who Jackson is, and is angry—not good.

"It's already there, Ash."

"I'm sorry I wasn't here. I got tied up at the lab. When I finally got home, I came right in here when you didn't answer my text." She softly rubs my back.

"I understand. You couldn't have known this was going to happen."

Ashton lifts my chin. "Now tell me why Jackson's

not here."

I rehash the entire argument with tears forming, but somehow I manage to keep them at bay. She doesn't comment on my fight with Jackson, she just shakes her head. When I tell her how I threw him out, however, her blue eyes grow darker. She's pissed but is choosing to keep her thoughts to herself, which definitely surprises me. I sit there and wait for it, but she looks off.

"What? You can't tell me you have nothing to say," I say after her silence drives me insane.

She smiles as she places her hand on mine. "I don't know what to say, Cat. I think you were on emotional overload. You'd had one of the worst days of your life. Do I think you made a mistake? Maybe." She shrugs before she goes on. "Jackson may have been a little distant, but I don't think he did anything wrong. I think Neil has some serious issues and Jackson protected you."

"He's going to leave me," I choke out and wrap my arms around my center, trying to hold myself together.

"You made him leave." Her voice is soft and nonjudgmental. She understands, but I can sense her disapproval.

"I had to."

She lets out a sad sigh, shaking her head. "No, honey, you didn't have to. Not every man is going to leave you. You need to take a few days and really think about how you feel about Jackson. Remember what you felt when you were with him. Then think about whether you can let go of the past and find a chance at a future. If it's not Jackson, it'll be the next man. You've always questioned if you were good enough, never considering that they weren't good enough for you. But Jackson? Well, that's for you to decide."

"What if he wrecks me? What I feel for him is so intense. I've fallen for him so fast. It scares me."

Ashton gets up without answering my question. She grabs something off my dresser and places it on my pillow. Before I can grab it, she puts her hand over it and looks at me.

"I don't think you're the only one that's fallen." Her brow rises and she places a kiss on my forehead. "Now, it's up to you. Is he worth the fall and possible heartbreak, or is he strong enough to catch you?"

Without another word she leaves my room. I look over at the small, torn paper, curious as to what's on it. Lifting and turning it over, I see Jackson's handwriting.

I spend the weekend pretending nothing happened, trying to come to grips with my emotions. Ashton leaves me alone most of the time, giving me space to sort it through. There are so many times I almost cave, call Jackson, and beg him to come back, but I know I'm not ready. His shutting me out really hurt, but more than that I'm terrified of how much I care for him. I fear the way he stormed into my life and churned up my emotions.

When I wake from my second nap on Sunday, there are multiple text messages from Neil threating his lawyer, but not one from Jackson. I'm not sure whether I should be relieved or disappointed. His message was clear when he left—I have to choose him, fight for him. Instead I've been fighting against it. Fear grips my soul. It smothers me, and I'm not sure how to get past it. I would rather be alone than go through another devastating loss.

Much to my chagrin, I call out of work on Monday. My eyes are swollen and I want a day to wallow—alone. Ashton rolls her eyes, giving me an earful before leaving for work.

"So you're going to stay home and mope?"

"No, I'm staying home because I have a migraine," I retort.

She huffs and narrows her eyes. "I know you better than that. Funny, you didn't miss work after Neil. In fact, you became almost obsessed with your job. What gives?"

"Well it didn't hurt this bad. And my staying home has nothing to do with Jackson." I grab my coffee and try to leave the kitchen.

Ashton follows behind me. "Then what does it have to do with?"

"Everything! It has to do with everything, dammit. I'm so tired of it all. That letter ... I don't even know what to do with it."

Ashton continues, unfazed by my outburst. "Why don't you sit down and reread it? You've had a few days to digest it now. But I don't think that's really the issue." Her brow rises. "I think it has to do with a certain sexy SEAL who you're in love with."

"Jesus!" I throw my hands up. "This has nothing to do with him. Do I miss Jackson? Yes. Are you happy now?"

"Are you?" she fires back with a calm voice.

"Do I look happy?" Again with the damn tears!

She leans against the wall, casually sipping her coffee. "No, but one phone call would fix it. So what else is making you skip work?"

"I ... ugh!" I grip the sides of my head, irritated with her.

"I think you're making yourself live a lie. You need to look deep down and figure out what you're willing to walk away from. If you can look me in the eye and tell me that you don't have some serious feelings for him and he doesn't make you happy, then fine. Good riddance. But from the look on your face right now, I don't think that's how you feel. Fear is going to drive away the one man who's strong enough to walk through this with you."

Without a word I head to my room, slam the door, and lock it. I'm batting a thousand right now. Is there anyone in my life I'm not pissed at? Why does she always push me so damn much?

I hear my phone ringing, but the number isn't one I know. I hesitate and calm myself before deciding to answer it.

"Hello?"

"Ms. Pope. This is Avi Goldstein."

"Hi, Mr. Goldstein. Is there a problem?"

"No, nothing serious. Sorry to bother you, but I received a call regarding the property in Scotch Plains," he says, seeming distracted.

"Scotch Plains?" I ask, confused.

"Yes, it's the house you inherited. I'm afraid I

didn't give you the address when you were in my office. Anyway, I received a call stating there was a door open in the back of the house. Nothing has been damaged, but you might want to go secure it until you decide what to do with the property."

"Oh. Ummm, okay. Can you give me the address?"

"It's 198 Mueller Court. I'm sorry, I have to go. I'm due in court in ten minutes, but please don't hesitate to contact me if you need anything, Ms. Pope," Avi says before the line disconnects.

I guess my day of wallowing in self-pity just went down the drain. Scotch Plains is about an hour away. Determined to avoid rush hour traffic, I grab my keys and head out the door. All I want is to shut my brain off. I think it's time for some chic rock music. Blaring my radio, I get lost in the sounds of angry, scorned girls singing about how much they don't need a man.

As I get closer to the house, I start to feel a familiar pang of nerves. The last few days I've realized how strong I am. During all the tears and pain, I've held it together for the most part. I ate, I showered—which Ashton was impressed with—and I functioned. Even so, the aching was still there, hovering behind the bravado.

I contemplate why I called out of work and if there's any validity to Ashton's claim that it's because of Jackson. If I'm being completely honest, yes, it has a lot to do with him. I miss him. I haven't spoken to him in three days and every time my phone beeps, I pray his number will show. Even if it makes no sense—since he's doing exactly what I asked—the emotions are still there.

Pulling up to the address, my heart starts beating

faster. The street is adorable. It's filled with cute little Cape Cod style homes with plush green lawns. Exiting the car, I look at number 198 and sigh. It's a muted yellow with white shutters. There's a large oak tree and some overgrown bushes against the house. As I approach the door, I stop myself from dreaming of what it could've been like living here. It could've been worse than what I grew up with.

"Hello? Can I help you?" A quiet old voice stops me before I can put the key in the lock.

"Hi," I respond.

"I'm Mary. I live in the house right over there." She points to the house on the left and then takes an unsteady step toward me. Mary is beautiful even in her old age. She must be around eighty, but you can see the youth in her eyes. She has an aura around her that makes you want to smile.

"Nice to meet you. I'm Catherine. I guess I own the house now. I received a call I needed to check on things."

Mary clasps her hands together as if she's praying. Her smile is bright and warm. "Oh! I'm just … Catherine." She walks a little faster to reach me. "Let me see you."

My eyes widen. Somehow she seems to know who I am. "I'm sorry, do we know each other?"

Her smile doesn't fade when she reaches me. "No, dear. I knew Hunter—your father—for a very long time. I always hoped I'd get to meet you."

"Me?"

"Yes, of course. Come. Let's go inside and you can tell me all about yourself." Her grip is surprisingly firm as she takes my hand and pulls me inside.

When I enter I try to take it all in. It's nothing

like the home I grew up in. The rooms are large, but everything is stark—bare white walls, hardwood floors. It lacks any warmth. Everything is ... cold. There's a small television in the corner with a recliner and a small sofa situated in front of it.

I continue on as Mary walks through the hall into another room. The outdated kitchen has a card table with four chairs around it. On the wall there's a calendar and a phone list. I look through the names, most of which are doctors.

"Would you like some tea, dear?" Mary asks while filling the kettle with water.

"Sure," I say with a smile. I don't drink tea, but she seems so kind and she knew my father, so maybe she can answer my questions. "So how long did you know my father?"

"I've lived in that house since the day I got married. It was my late husband's wedding gift to me." You can hear the smile in her voice as she places the kettle on the stove. "My husband, Ray, was a wonderful man. He served in the Army," she says with pride.

"He sounds wonderful. You're a very lucky woman."

"I was," she says, holding out the chair for me to sit. "We were married for sixty-two years and we were blessed with four boys. They've all grown and now I have beautiful grandchildren that I get to spoil. But enough about me." Mary places her hand on mine. "You want to know about your father, don't you?"

"Yes, ma'am." I look around the room at the house he lived in. If I were to judge how he lived based on what I've seen so far, the one word I can think of is *empty*. There are no photos, nothing adorning the walls, it's merely a house.

"Well, he moved here around fifteen years ago. It took him about a year until he warmed up to us. Ray was good at forcing him to come out of his house by asking him to help fix things." Mary looks away wistfully. "Ray could've done the things he asked for help with, but Hunter couldn't say no to an old man." She chuckles. "Eventually, he opened up little by little."

The kettle whistles and Mary and I get up to make the tea. She already set out the cups and tea bags. Listening to how she knows him breaks my heart. I'm jealous of the woman who knew the man I so desperately needed. However, I'm grateful in a sense for people like her and Ray, who were there for him. He wasn't completely alone. And neither was I—I had Ashton, Gretchen, and my mother.

Once we have our drinks, we sit back down. "Thank you." She takes a sip before beginning again. "I came to learn about you from your father. He was very sad in the beginning. At times he would talk about a girl named Catherine, but didn't tell us you were his daughter. Anyway, one day I asked him to tell me about her. He sat with me for quite some time, telling me all about you."

"He left when I was nine." My voice is tiny and I'm not sure that Mary heard me.

"He told me. He wasn't proud of what he'd done. I think as the years went on he convinced himself that it was for the best. But then he'd show us a photo or tell us about something you did. There was always such pride in his eyes when he spoke about you, dear."

My eyes lift to hers and I read the truth behind them. He said he'd followed me. I guess he'd shared what he learned with Mary. I'm conflicted by the years of hate and anger now turning to sympathy. He said he stayed away because he wanted to protect me, and initially I thought it was a cop-out. Now I'm confused. Maybe everything he wrote in the letter wasn't a lie.

"He wrote me a letter while he was sick. Did you know that?"

"No, he never mentioned a letter." Her gray brow rises. "When he found out he was sick, he changed a lot of things. He didn't suffer for long. It was very late in the disease when he was diagnosed. He talked a lot more about you and what he gave up toward the end, though." Mary pats my hand, giving me a warm smile. "You know, when we know our time is running out, we think more about the choices we made. I'm sure his letter was sincere." She gets up from the table and washes the cups before she returns to sit with me.

"I don't know what to think anymore. It feels like everything I knew was a lie." A tear drops as the sadness returns. "I blamed myself all my life. I always felt like I'd done something as a kid to make him leave. Then I get this letter saying it wasn't me, it was him. My entire life I've believed I wasn't good enough for him to come back for."

Mary places her hand on my arm. "The heart knows the truth. When times are hard, we have to rely on the voice in our hearts. Trust yourself, Catherine. I do know the Hunter I knew would've never left because of you."

"I wish I'd known him." I sigh and look away. That's the bottom line. I know nothing about him. I don't know how he lived, if he was sad or happy, if he wished things were different—although his letter says he did.

"There's an office down the hall on the left. He spent a lot of time in there. There are probably some things that might give you some peace." She wipes the tear from my cheek. "Sometimes the heart and mind don't work together, but a child is never to blame for the errors of the parent. We all make mistakes, but forgiveness sets the soul free." Mary rises from her seat and I stand as well. "I'm going to lie down for a bit and give you some time alone, but promise you'll come back and visit soon."

"I promise," I say as she walks out the door, giving me time to absorb everything.

I walk through the rooms, looking around and trying to figure out who he really was when I come across the office she spoke of. There's a small desk and a bookshelf inside. I gasp and my hands cover my heart when I see the top shelf. It's lined with photos of me. Every picture is in chronological order, from my infant photo at the hospital all the way through third grade. There are even some where I'm older. My high school graduation picture and my newspaper engagement announcement are framed. He has little bits of my life all around the room.

I make my way to his desk and look around. He was so alone. It has papers and bills, but the photo sitting on top causes a sob to break free. It's a photo of us on my birthday. He's standing behind me right as I'm inhaling to blow out the candles on my cake. The love in his eyes shines as bright as the flames.

Overloaded with varying degrees of heartache, I rush out of the room, gasping for air. Nothing makes any sense. The world seems to be shifting, but I'm not shifting with it. I can't wrap my mind around why he chose to keep that door closed. He could have come to me and talked to me, tried to explain. I might have been mad, but we could've had a chance at *some* kind of relationship. So much wasted time, so many tears that didn't need to be shed. He was there for parts of my life even though I never knew.

Is this the life I'm heading toward?

I lock up the house and make sure everything is secure. I need to decide what to do with the house, but not today. I feel a sense of peace settle around me. I've gained some answers or at least some insight. Getting into my car, I allow the silence to surround me as the sun shines upon on my face.

chapter twenty-six

Tuesday morning rolls along, and I know I have to get up and get it together. I have a job to do, one that ultimately will force me to deal with Jackson again. This was what my fear of getting involved with him was all along. He promised it wouldn't affect my career, and now it's time for him to prove it. I stroll into the office in my black slacks and coral top, hoping the bright color will draw attention away from my swollen eyes.

"Good morning," I say with a forced smile.

Taylor stands and follows me into my office. "Morning, Cat. How are you feeling?"

"Fine. We have a lot of work to do. Can you see where we are on the advertising piece getting released to the press next week?" I say quickly.

I don't want to talk. I don't even know what to say. *Hi. I had a mental breakdown. My ex and my current boyfriend got in a fight. Oh, and my dad, who I haven't seen or heard from in over twenty years, wrote me a letter telling me he loved me. But the best part is I threw Jackson out after he told me I was it for him. And I still refuse to call him because I'm a chicken shit.* Yup, that about sums it up.

"Okay," she says slowly while glancing around. "I'll get the graphics people on the phone."

Great. I've made her uncomfortable. With a smile, I try to ease her tension. "No, I think I'll just go there and check it out myself. If you can get the schedule for the next month of potential accounts coming up, that would be great."

Her eyes widen as her head tilts to the side. "For upcoming clients? I thought we had another month or two on the Raven account?"

I know I'm not making sense, but moving forward is all I have. I debated sending Taylor in my place on Wednesday and letting her give over all the finalized plans, but I'd lose my job. I could always hand it over to Elle and simply state the client and I weren't agreeing on how to proceed, but the idea of Elle's breasts and her lack of clothing anywhere near Jackson makes me sick. So, I'm stuck. I need to put my big girl panties on and deal with it.

I'm fighting the real problem, which is how much I miss him. The thought of losing him makes it hard to get through the day. I imagine running into him with another woman on his arm, kissing her, touching her, and telling her he loves her. Pain radiates from my heart out through my body. There's no way I could handle that. Why does he have to be so damn irresistible? And why do I have to be so stubborn?

"Cat?" Taylor breaks me from my thoughts.

I shake my head, drawing air into my lungs before pushing it out loudly. "Sorry, you're right. I wanted to see what was coming up, but it's fine."

"I can grab them, no problem. I just—"

"Seriously, not a big deal." I smile, trying to ease her confusion. "My head is all over the place."

Taylor steps forward and sits in the chair. She doesn't say anything as her eyes assess me. "We're friends, right?"

"Of course," I respond.

"Then, no bullshit. What's wrong?" Her eyes are soft and caring. It's the same look I got from her when I opened up about Neil's affair. Taylor sits with her hands in her lap, patiently waiting.

As much as I want to take this moment and lay it all out there, I'm not sure I want to hear a lecture. Every minute that passes, I'm less convinced I did the right thing by throwing Jackson out. Also, I'm realizing my feelings for him run far deeper than I've allowed myself to admit. He's given me strength but never made me feel weak, and along the way he's embedded himself in my heart.

"Let's just say that my weekend was less than stellar. The night of the reading of the will was horrific. I've got a lot on my mind. I'm sorting it all out."

She smiles sincerely. "I'm sorry. It's not like you to call out of work. You're usually here no matter what."

"It was a good thing I wasn't. I needed to take care of some stuff regarding my father. You know me. I'll be fine."

"If you want to talk, I'm here."

Taylor is one of the few people I know I can talk to without fear of judgment. She listens with an open heart. When she moved to New York, she vowed not to let the big city take away her country roots. She's innocent but not naïve, which allows her to cut through the drama. She has an old soul, one of the purest of anyone I know. And her best asset—even at her young age, she sees and understands things people three and four times her senior wouldn't. It's an exceptional gift, but one I have no desire to take advantage of at the moment.

Before she uncovers it all, I cut her off. "I'll be

downstairs with the design team. Page me if you need anything."

She nods, pressing her lips into a fine line. "Sure thing. I'll just be out here doing my job, pretending you didn't just try to deflect."

"Good. Pretend away." I smile and head out of the office.

I spend an hour downstairs checking in on the marketing and graphic side of things to get the first press release ready to go out. It gives me the small reprieve I needed from my mind. No Jackson, no Neil, no thoughts of anything else but work.

Once I'm content with everything, I decide to head out for lunch. It's a beautiful day and I think an hour to myself will help my mood. I grab the subway and head to Central Park. I walk toward an empty bench and kick my heels off. Taking a deep breath, I close my eyes and embrace the sun and fresh air. The park is tranquil even in its chaos. It's never empty, but you can always find your own section of heaven.

During the first few minutes, I clear my mind and focus on everything around me. I hear the birds making beautiful music, the leaves rustling in the tree above thanks to the gentle wind blowing through them, and the sound of running feet pounding the pavement, moving forward with each stride.

My mind drifts to Jackson. I imagine him here in the mornings jogging, running through life and finding the courage to keep going. He's strong in the face of adversity and has found a way to rise above his grief. Every day he cares for the people in not one but two companies. More than that, he cared for me. Jackson's strength kept me together even when he wasn't there. I pushed him so hard because I couldn't take another man leaving. I thought if I shoved him out the door, I'd be protecting myself. As I sit here thinking of the runners and their path through the park, I consider their options: they can stay on the paved road, on solid ground, or they can take a dirt trail and see where it leads. Sure, the road less traveled is bumpy and may be scary, but it could also be amazing.

It applies to me. I can keep on handling things the way I have with Jackson and protect myself, push him away, and keep building the fortress around my heart, or I can rip down that fortress and see where it goes. If I give him the benefit of the doubt instead of assuming he'll devastate me, we might have a chance.

I glance at my watch. I've been enjoying this serenity for over an hour. With a little lighter heart, I trudge back to my office to finish securing my position in the company. Time to be epic.

"Did I miss anything?" I ask Tay as I walk past her.

She jumps a little, holding her hand against her heart. Taking a second to recover, she responds, "I forwarded a few calls to your voicemail. Also, I grabbed the upcoming accounts in the cue, in case you wanted to look." She smiles and hands me a few papers.

"Perfect. Please hold my calls for the rest of the day. I have a ton of stuff to get done before for tomorrow."

"No problem," she replies.

With the door closed, I gather the latest sales figures and start getting everything together. We have a press release going out this week and need to finalize everything, which means I'll see him again tomorrow. I'm terrified. When he's around it's hard to keep things in perspective or focus on anything but him. And he has a way of seeing through my mask, so I know I'll need to be extremely careful.

Closing my eyes, I remember his touch, the way he says my name, and his smell. I can almost feel his hands moving over my skin, touching every part of my body as I give myself over to him. I remember the feel of him filling me over and over, the sound of his voice calling out my name as he came.

The door bursts open, pulling me from my erotic memories. I look up to see Piper glaring at me as Taylor tries to stop her from entering. Well, this is unexpected and unwelcome.

"Catherine, I'm sorry. I tried to stop her!" Taylor says quickly.

I stand, needing to be on equal ground with her.

"It's fine. She wouldn't have listened anyway. She obviously has no class or tact," I tell Taylor.

"Do you want me to call security?" she asks, glaring at Piper.

While that's probably the smart thing to do, Piper must be desperate to come to my office and barge in like this.

"No, I'd love to hear why she felt the need to show up unannounced." I give Taylor a small nod. "You can go ahead and close the door. I'll yell if I need you."

My gaze returns to Piper as Taylor closes the door. "Why are you here?" I ask coldly.

She walks forward and sits in a chair, seemingly unaffected by my glacial tone. Piper looks around, picking at her fingernails. "You got me fired." Her eyes lift as she purses her lips.

"I have no clue what the hell you're talking about." Clearly I'm thrown by how she figures I have anything to do with her losing a client.

"Right," she scoffs. "You had nothing to do with your boyfriend firing me? I doubt that."

"Piper, I don't have time for your shit. You come to my office—uninvited—and start talking about something I have no knowledge of." I roll my eyes at her ridiculous riddle, but I have a feeling there's more to this. Considering everything that happened on Friday, she could be using this to try to get information. Subtly, I reach for my phone. I press the voice recorder, hoping it works. I don't trust her at all and I won't leave her any chance to spin this meeting.

She steps toward me with her hands on her hips. "You owe me a client. A big one."

I don't try to hide the short laugh that escapes me. Owe her? I don't think so. "I owe you absolutely nothing. And it's not my problem. Maybe you can talk to your boyfriend and he can get you a new client. Plus, I've never spoken to Jackson about you." I give a snide smile. "You're not worth my time."

Taking another step, she leans on my desk. "Here's how I see it. Not only did your boyfriend assault Neil, he then fired me because I refused to sleep with him." Piper leans back and smiles. "I hope he has a fantastic lawyer because I'm going to bury him."

Right. This is absolutely insane. No matter what she says, there's no way I believe Jackson tried to sleep with her. If he fired her for any reason, it's because she's incompetent.

"Gosh, Piper. I'm so sorry you lost your client, but I couldn't give two flying fucks. And you *really* don't want to threaten me or Jackson." I smile, sarcasm oozing out of my mouth. I start to walk toward her. With each step I find more strength to confront her. She's on my turf, in my office, and there's no way she's going to make me cower. "If Jackson—sorry, I mean Mr. Cole. Isn't that what you called him?" I ask petulantly. "Well, if Mr. Cole fired you, I'm sure there was a good reason. Maybe he didn't like the fact that you,"—I wave my hand in a casual way as if searching for the words—"oh, I don't know, are a complete idiot and a liar."

Piper steps back with each step I take in her direction. "He came on to me. How does it feel to have two men you've slept with want me instead of you?"

For a half-second I *almost* believe her. It would be so easy to think it's true. She's trying to use her words like knives, but this time they're not cutting. She's desperate and it shows. I don't think Jackson would purposely hurt me that way. He told me I was it for him.

"If I believed you, that might've actually hurt. But since I don't and I can see you're grasping at straws, I don't feel a damn thing but pity." I give a cynical laugh.

"Fuck you and your pity," she yells back.

"Oh Piper, you poor, poor girl. It must suck to have nothing. Your workload just got a whole lot lighter and you're dating a cheating asshole that can't fight. And here I am with my dream job, an extremely sexy boyfriend,"—I lean in and whisper with a huge grin—"who's a hundred times better than Neil in *every* possible way, if you know what I mean." I wink and move closer to the door.

God, it feels good to say this to her. I'm

completely calm, enjoying Piper's unease. She's got nothing and for once I have it all. She doesn't know Jackson and I aren't speaking, but *he* fired her. No matter what his reason is, it feels good to see karma finally making the rounds to someone other than me.

Piper sneers but recovers quickly. "You don't have to believe me. The truth will show itself in time. But don't say I didn't warn you." She smiles, walking toward the door. "You could've avoided all this." Piper shrugs, patting my arm. "Just remember, all you had to do was get me a client."

I grab the door handle, opening the door as Taylor looks up. "Tay, could you please take out the trash?"

"Sure thing." She smiles and turns to Piper. "Right this way, Ms. Carlson." She extends her arm, showing Piper where to go.

Piper stops, turning back toward me. "It's only a matter of time and you'll be alone. Again."

I step toward her, trying to make sure I don't cause a scene in my office. "I'd rather be alone than be with a man who cheats, steals, and assaults women." I take a step back with a plastic smile. "Have a great day, Piper."

I make it back into my office feeling strong. Jackson fired her. There could be hundreds of reasons, but I want to believe it's because he learned the truth. He saw who she was and was protecting me in some small way. Or it could be because she really screwed up. Whatever the reason, it's one more way she's gone and out of my life. I have too much to get done to sit and ponder over Jackson's decisions. I stop the recording and check to make sure it worked. I hear some of it and shut it off. I didn't want to hear what she had to say the first time and I certainly don't want to hear it again.

I take a few minutes to refocus. There are papers all over, I've got to return about a hundred emails, and I still need to get my notes done. Time to kick a little ass. I immerse myself in my project, putting everything else in the back of my mind.

Time goes by, but I have no idea how long it's been when Taylor buzzes through on the intercom. "Hey, Cat, it's almost seven. Did you still need me to stay?"

Wow. I didn't notice it was so late. I pick up the receiver. "I don't think so. I'm going to head home to finish this. Ashton is staying in the city again this week, so it'll be quiet. I can probably get a lot of this done there," I reply.

"Okay, I'll see you tomorrow," Taylor says sweetly.

"Have a great night." I smile and hang up.

Sighing, I gather all my papers to take home, prepared to get this done.

chapter
twenty-seven

With a large box filled with everything I needed, I made it home before the rain started. My table is now covered in papers and diagrams while the storm rages outside. I've got my music going, comfy clothes on, and copious amounts of coffee in a gigantic cup. I never should've called out on Monday. This meeting will be a disaster because I'm not prepared. Looks like an all-nighter is in my future. My phone keeps ringing. It's the fifth time in the last hour, but I don't have time to deal with it.

Finally, after the tenth missed call, I grab it and see Jackson's name across the screen. My heart starts pounding and my throat goes dry. With shaking fingers, I swipe across the screen.

"Hi," I say softly.

"Hello, Catherine. Sorry to call so late but I just got out of a meeting." His tone is all business.

Hearing him is a shock to my system. I've missed the sound of his voice. The way he says my name—it's like home. However, he doesn't sound like he returns the sentiment.

I straighten my back, hoping to grab on to my professionalism. This is business. He's not calling because he missed me or wants to talk. "Not a problem. What did you need?" My voice sounds weak, even to me.

He takes a deep breath before answering. "I know we planned to finalize everything tomorrow, but I need it tonight."

"Tonight?" I look around at all the incomplete papers. I can't have it ready tonight! I already needed to work well past midnight to get it done.

"I'm in New Jersey. I'm assuming you're home since you didn't answer your office phone."

"Yes, I'm home but I don't have everything with me. Some things are still in the office. But I can get it to you tomorrow. Besides, it's storming," I say, trying to stall him. Shit!

"I'm going out of town tomorrow and I'm not sure when I'll be back. I won't have time. It has to be tonight," he says, clipped and almost angry.

"You're leaving?" I ask, confused. He was going to leave and not tell me. I know we're not in the best place, but it still hurts to hear it.

"I need to go to Virginia. I would've called earlier but, like I said, I've been tied up. I'll be at your house in twenty."

I look at the clock and then at what I have done. While most would be satisfied, I'm not. It's not my best work and the idea of giving it to Jackson unfinished makes me nauseous. There's no way he's going to be impressed. I'm shaking my head and trying to find another excuse when I hear him clear his throat.

"Jackson," I sigh. His name rolls off my tongue while tearing a hole in my chest. "I can meet you tomorrow morning, before your trip. I have some stuff in the office that would complete the press release and the other items for the launch. I don't want to give it to you incomplete." I close my eyes. He feels so close, almost like I could touch him through the phone.

"I won't have time tomorrow. I'll take what you have and you can have the rest sent."

If he wants to treat me like a business associate, then he should know showing up at people's apartments at night isn't exactly professional.

"I'm not happy about this. It's late and I—"

"If I could help it, I would. I have to leave early in the morning, and I need this set in motion before I get back. So you can either have me come get it now, or you can bring it to me in New York tonight." He takes a long pause. "I was trying to make it easier for you since I'm in New Jersey."

"Fine, but just know you don't have everything."

"See you in a few," he says and disconnects the call.

I throw down the phone and blast into action. I quickly put a bra on, pick up some dishes and other things lying around, and try to make some kind of sense of the paperwork. I only have about ten minutes until he's here and I'm starting to panic. I snatch the phone and call Ashton.

She answers on the second ring. "Hey."

"He's coming here," I say quickly.

"You called him? Finally!" Ashton sounds ecstatic.

I huff, pressing the phone to my shoulder so I can keep cleaning. "No, he called me. He needs his project early because he has to leave for Virginia tomorrow. I don't know, Ashton. Why am I freaking out?"

"Because you love him and you know you fucked up? Just a hunch."

"No, I—" I stop unable to complete the sentence. Do I love him? No, it's too soon. Isn't it? We've only begun getting to know each other, but he makes perfect sense. He's everything I want, everything I need.

Ashton breaks through the silence as I stand shell-shocked. "You just had your epiphany, didn't you?"

I hear a knock at the door. "I gotta go," I say and disconnect the phone. I don't have time for a damn epiphany.

After a few deep breaths, I walk to the door. He's right there on the other side. He said he wouldn't come back through this door if I didn't tell him I wanted him here. And I do want him here. All I want is Jackson. But that fear of losing him is always looming, making its way into my head, causing me to second-guess everything. I'm out of time and now Ashton's made me even more nervous.

Another knock.

I press my hand on the door and rest my head against the cool wood grain, trying to settle my pulse. I'm brave enough for this. Maybe.

Enough stalling.

Time to be strong.

I open the door and freeze when our eyes lock. Jackson's even more devastatingly handsome than I remember in his black pants and light blue shirt with the top two buttons undone. His hair is disheveled, but all I see is perfection. The stubble on his jaw is much thicker, making him look darker, more mysterious and dangerous. He looks tired, but I see the underlying emotions as his gaze travels my face. Despite the dark circles forming beneath his eyes, he still looks flawless.

When he gives me a small smile, everything in my world shifts. That grin and the perfectly placed dimple cause an explosion around my guarded heart. It hits me. I love him. It's a different love than what I had with Neil. It doesn't feel forced. It's strong and hopeful. He doesn't want to take from me—he gives. My weaknesses don't scare or bother him and he doesn't want to exploit them. No, he wants to make me stronger. And when I can't be, he'll be strong enough for the both of us.

I take a step forward, but before I can speak, he grabs me and pulls me against him. My eyes widen and a second later his lips crash against mine in an angry, hot kiss. Jackson's arms wrap around me, holding me close. It's almost crushing, but I couldn't care less. My fingers tangle in his hair, pulling him closer even though we couldn't get any more attached than we already are. I breathe in his scent—all male and pure sex. I try to pull him into the apartment, but he won't budge. He breaks the kiss, but hovers over my mouth. I whimper at the loss of his lips.

"Do you want to let me in?" His deep voice goes straight to my core.

I nod yes, but he doesn't move. Every cell in my body is awakened. I need his touch. I want him to fill me up and make me whole again. But I know that's not what he's asking.

"I told you when I walked out of here the last time—"

I cut him off, leaning up and pressing my lips against his. It's pure survival. His lips are breathing life into me. Our time apart has me desperate for him. I want to ingrain this moment in my mind in case things don't go the way I'm hoping.

Jackson grips the side of my face and pulls back. *Bastard.* He has the height advantage. He smiles when my lip juts out in a pout. Looking into his eyes, I know I can't walk away from him. The last few days were hell, but now that the truth of my feelings is clear, I know the pain of really losing him would cripple me. I will fight all my fears for him.

His gaze doesn't break, but his voice does. "You need to make a choice."

The words tumble out of my mouth effortlessly. "Find me."

With his hands cupping my face, his lips press against mine as he crosses the threshold. When the door slams closed, the energy changes—three days of anger, longing, and doubt rip through us. Jackson's hands hold my face tight as he pours himself into the kiss, giving me every emotion through his mouth.

The growl emanating from his chest travels straight to my core. Every part of me is alive and desperate for him. I grab at his shirt, unbuttoning it as we move into the house. I want to feel his skin, need to feel the warmth and heat of his body against mine. But he has other ideas. Jackson twists his fingers in my hair and tugs, causing a loud moan to escape. He doesn't hesitate as his tongue enters my mouth roughly, each stroke edging my need up and out of control. He's pushing me back as I'm pulling him closer. I grab onto his shoulders. I've missed his touch.

Jackson slams me back against the wall. He breaks the kiss, ripping off my shirt and drinking me in as his tongue slides across my lips. My hands reach out to grab him, but he grips my wrists and holds them above my head. Jackson crushes his body against mine. The ache to have him grows with each second.

"Did you miss me like I missed you? Do you know how hard it was every fucking day fighting the urge to see you? How many times I had to stop myself from coming here and breaking down your goddamn door?" he asks against my ear, causing goose bumps to form everywhere.

Before I can respond, his lips are pressed against me, tongue probing for the answers I wasn't able to give. He has me pinned, completely at his mercy, and there's nowhere else I'd rather be. It baffles me how I could've turned this man away.

Jackson moves his knee between my legs, further restricting my movements. Warm lips descend to my neck as he nips and kisses. I hear his phone ring but neither of us stops or cares. All I'm thinking about is him touching me. I rub against his leg, trying to create some friction to relieve the pulsing between my thighs.

He grips my hips. "Not yet, baby."

With my hands now free, I begin to roam his body. His shirt is still half buttoned. I grip the sides, ripping it open and sending buttons flying across the room. My fingers trace the hard, taught planes of his chest, enjoying the feel of it rising and falling heavily. Leaning forward, I use the tip of my tongue, running it from the middle of his chest up to his ear. He braces his hands against the wall as his head drops to the crook of my neck. Jackson's breathing is labored and I'm savoring how much I'm affecting him. It's a heady feeling to have such power over a man like him.

I reach his ear and graze the edge. "Jackson," I softly whisper, "show me how much you missed me." I smile against his ear before he becomes ravenous.

His tears my bra off, then lifts me with his leg and rips my pants and panties down. I quickly remove his pants and start to push him toward the bedroom, but he grips both wrists in his one hand, pressing me back on the wall. His other hand slips between us as he circles my clit.

"I'll fucking show you, baby. You're soaking wet for me." Jackson moans as he slips a finger into my pussy. "Did you miss me, Catherine?"

I try to pull my hands away, but he grips them harder, keeping me at his mercy. "I want to touch you."

Jackson inserts a second finger. My legs buckle, but he holds me up easily. "I'm going to make you remember why you're not allowed to run anymore." His voice is primal and demanding. "You want to be found, baby?" Jackson's thumb presses against my clit, eliciting a long moan as my eyes roll back.

Does he actually want me to answer? I'm incapable of speaking let alone answering any questions right now. With his one hand still restraining me and the other doing incredible things to my pussy, he leans forward and licks his tongue around my nipple. He brings it into his mouth, teasing and sucking. I writhe against him but get no relief.

"Jackson, please!" I'm begging for everything. I feel everything, everywhere, and I need to release. It's too much. My head falls back as the sensations threaten to overwhelm me.

"Are you going to push me away again?" he asks forcefully while he twists his fingers and presses on the bundle of nerves with his thumb. My vision becomes fuzzy as he increases the pressure and bites down on my nipple.

"Oh God." I'm so close. My impending orgasm is right there and I'm desperate. I move my hips, trying to get there. Jackson releases his thumb and withdraws his fingers. My eyes open in protest.

Jackson releases my hands, grasps my legs, and lifts me while rubbing his cock against my sex. "Wrap your legs around me. I want you to come when I'm inside of you." I comply as he thrusts his dick inside me. His eyes roll back and he takes a second before he begins to move. "Fuck. You feel incredible." His voice is thick with pleasure.

Incredible doesn't begin to explain how I feel. I'm in complete ecstasy. All the days of being apart are gone. I've never been more with him than I am right now. We are one. Our bodies are connected and I'm giving myself to him in every way. My heart will never be mine again. Every fiber of my being is screaming *I love you.* The three words are on the tip of my tongue, but I bite them back. It's too soon to tell him how much he owns me. With every push, I fight hard to keep them to myself. But I hope one day he'll feel the same.

Jackson pushes deeper, slamming my back against the wall. It's pleasure and pain combining, taking me higher toward release.

"Are. You. Going. To. Run?" He enunciates every word in between thrusts. "Tell me. Tell me you're mine!" It's anger mixed with hunger and need. When I don't respond, he stops moving and stares into my eyes. "Don't fucking run from me again!"

"Jackson!" I call out as he pounds again, harder. I swear I'm going to black out from the pleasure overload. As soon as I reach the brink, he slows, holding off my orgasm. "Please," I beg.

"Answer me," he demands, holding me against

the wall and refusing to move.

"I'm yours!" I cry in out in frustration. "Now move!" Each nerve in my body is burning. I'm shaking, on the verge of tears.

"Damn fucking right you are." He lifts me slowly, gradually increasing his pace and adjusting his hips to ensure he hits every nerve while his cock rubs the sweet spot inside of me. He grinds his teeth, trying to hold off his own orgasm. "Let go, Catherine."

As my muscles coil, Jackson rears back and plunges hard, causing my orgasm to rip through me. "Yes! Jackson!" I shriek over and over as he fucks me until he finally releases.

I'm pressed against the wall as we both try to slow our breathing. That was the best sex I've ever had. Then I realize why it felt so different—no condom. Jackson slides out and kisses the top of my nose. I love when he does that. It's sweet and tender. Our eyes meet before I go to the bathroom to clean up. When I come back, Jackson's sitting on the couch with his head in his hands.

"Well that was one helluva a hello." I laugh as I sit beside him.

His shoulders are hunched even after I sit. "I didn't plan that."

"I'm not complaining." I raise my brow, giving him a playful smirk.

He pulls me against his chest with a chuckle. "Good to know. Also, I'll make a mental note— you're more agreeable when I fuck it out of you."

"Asshole." I feign anger and slap his chest. "Maybe next time I'll refuse to answer."

"Go ahead. It'll just make it that much more fun to get you to agree." His smirk reaches his eyes, fully erasing the expression he wore when he first arrived.

Jackson gazes at me with reverence. It warms me, offering reassurance in my decision to let him in, find happiness again, and stop running from fear. Some of my newfound peace comes from dealing with my father's death. Another part is because I did push Jackson away and it forced me to see how life without him would be.

His thumb whispers across my lower lip, releasing a flurry of butterflies in my belly. A simple touch says so much. "You felt so fucking amazing. I couldn't think straight." He looks away with regret in his eyes.

My lips part as I kiss his thumb, enjoying how his eyes close at my touch. I look up from beneath my lashes. "We probably should've talked before this, but we're good. I'm on birth control." I smile.

Jackson gives a crisp nod. "Yeah, we probably should've."

"Well neither of us thought about it, so I guess we both fucked up."

Lacing his fingers with mine, his voice drops to a sad whisper. "We need to talk."

"About?" I try to keep my voice steady. My heart begins to race as doubt seeps through me. Please tell me we aren't going to go back now. I told him I was his. He pushed me to answer him. I've allowed myself to admit I love him. This would devastate me.

His phone rings again, but he silences it.

"The last few days were horrible. I know you thought you needed space, but I won't be pushed away again. If you push me, I'll push harder. I'm not your piece of shit ex who's going to run away like a pussy." His eyes pierce through me as he squares his shoulders. "I meant it. You're it for me." The sincerity rings clear in his voice.

I want to tell him. Tell him how I won't run. How I can't run away anymore. I love him. I love how he makes me feel. My heart clenches as I gather my strength and prepare to lay it all out for him.

"Jackson—" His phone rings again, halting me from saying anything more. He groans at the incessant ringing. "Go ahead and grab that. I'm not going anywhere." I give him a reassuring smile.

Jackson stands, walking toward the window as he answers the phone. "What?" he says in a clipped tone.

I get up to gather the clothes we shed by the door when I hear him slam his hand against the wall. Looking over, I see his shoulders are slumped as he listens to whoever's on the other line. "An IED?" He stops talking for a moment. "Casualties?"

I stop moving. I watch Jackson, waiting to hear what happened. It happens so fast. Jackson rears his fist back and punches a hole in the wall. My mouth is agape as I watch him continue to slam his hand against the wall. His face is contorted in pain. He looks ... defeated. Do I comfort him? I don't know what's wrong or why he's so upset.

He yells into the receiver, "How fucking many?"

The pain in his voice breaks me. Something's wrong—very wrong. I walk over to him, but he puts his hand up to stop me.

His entire body is shaking and his voice cracks when he asks, "Aaron?" A short pause. "Fuck! No ..." The sound that comes from his chest tears through me. It's a cry and a scream all mixed into one, and I'm sure it's the worst thing I've ever heard.

Immediately, tears begin to form in his eyes. I want to go to him, but he turns his back to me.

I start putting the pieces together. Aaron is his buddy that works for him. He was also on the mission in Afghanistan, the one where they lost friends. He was going to maybe handle something overseas? My hand covers my mouth as I start to draw conclusions.

His hands fist into his hair as he leans forward with his head against the wall. I pray this isn't what I think it is. He can't lose another friend.

Please, God, don't do this to him.

"I can't—" he says but stops as a tear falls from his eye. "No! I'll call her. Get the fucking plans in motion. We leave tonight! I don't give a shit what you have to do. Wake everyone—we're wheels up in three hours." His phone tumbles to the floor as he stands there with a vacant look.

Jackson's chest is heaving with exaggerated breaths. Hesitantly, I take a step toward him.

"Jackson, what happened?" I ask quietly. He turns, eyes glistening with tears, but he doesn't respond.

I watch as he crumples to the floor. Every part of his body is quivering. I rush over, wrapping my arms around him as he sobs. He's breaking. My chest is cracking open watching the man I love fall apart. Tears fall with every strangled, broken sound that Jackson releases. All I can do is hold him close while he unloads his grief.

chapter twenty-eight

"Talk to me. What happened?" I croon softly, not releasing my hold. "Hey." I lift his face, trying to get him to look at me.

He shifts, pulling away from my embrace. I feel the loss everywhere and see the change as soon as he stands. He's shutting down. Two steps forward, one step back. The mask of indifference has secured itself.

With eyes closed, he takes two deep breaths before speaking. "What happened?" Jackson asks sarcastically. He pushes the air from his lungs in frustration. "I'll tell you what happened—I did it again!"

"Did what again?" I ask quietly.

He throws his hands in the air and begins to pace the room. "I fucking knew it."

I start to approach him, trying to keep my tone calm. "I don't understand. What did you know?"

Jackson stops moving. His eyes widen as if he forgot I was here. The harshness in his voice slices through me. "I'm no good for you."

"Why would you say that?" His statement stuns me, especially since he just said he'd fight for me. What the hell happened on the phone to make him think this?

"Don't you get it? Everyone I love dies!" Jackson approaches but stops. "I can't let you be the next one. I'll die before I let that happen."

I'm lost. "Jackson, talk to me." I place my hand on his arm, but he shoves it away. The rejection burns through my veins. "Don't push me away. I'm trying to understand," I urge him.

"I'm not pushing you away. I'm saving you!" he yells and walks over to grab his phone. "I won't let it happen to you too!"

"Let what happen? You're not making any sense!" I say to him as he heads toward the door. "Stop! Talk to me!" I beg him. He made me promise not to run but that's exactly what he's doing.

It's like we've gone back to three days ago, only now I'm on the other side. He's breaking and I can't stop it. Desperate to get him to listen, I run in front of him, placing myself between him and the door and hoping it will stop him. His eyes are unfocused and void as the storm rages within him. He's going to break my heart right here. The irony is not lost on me—I gave it to him only to have it shattered. My stomach churns as I see the truth of that reflected in his eyes. Whether I'm standing here or not, he's walking out this door. I've already lost him.

His face is ashen as he chokes out the words. He's speaking but not to me. "How many more tattoos do I have to get? Huh? How many ways do I have to mark my mistakes?" Jackson looks at me, desperation flashing across his face. "I'm protecting you, Catherine. I won't let you love me."

A tear cascades as the words fall out. "Too late."

His eyes snap up at my admission and his nostrils flare. He quickly pushes forward. "Don't! Don't say that!" The muscles in his neck are pulsing with rage and frustration.

"I will say it because it's true. What did you think was going to happen? I knew I was falling for you. Then you told me ... you told me I was it for you! Don't walk away. Don't give up on us."

Leaning close to my face, his warm breath washes over my cheek while my tears fall freely. Ever so slowly, his hand lifts. He gently removes a droplet of pain from my cheek only to have more follow in its path. His lips tenderly find purchase on my temple. "I'm not giving up. I'm giving you a chance."

I refuse to move from the door. If he leaves, I'll never get him back. I can't lose him. My pulse is racing, but I stand strong. I have to do something to make him see me.

"Jackson, I love you! Give *us* a chance," I beg him, praying he'll listen to me.

His arms wrap around me, dispelling my fears and the breath I was holding. With my eyes closed, I take this moment, finding the tiniest bit of relief in it. He didn't leave. I told him I loved him and he's here, enveloping me in his warmth. I could stay in his arms forever. I feel his lips press against my forehead. When I look up into his eyes, hoping to see him recovered, the color drains from my face. There's no love or recovery there, just determination. It rolls off him like thunder.

"No ..." The strangled sound of my voice doesn't register.

Jackson's hold disappears along with my hope. With each step he takes, the floor falls a little further down, and my heart follows. He doesn't stop or look back.

No.

His hand touches the handle and my breath hitches.

Please don't do this.

I want to tell him, but the words won't come

out!

Dammit, Jackson, stop!

"Jackson." I say his name like a prayer.

He stops but doesn't turn as his hands clench the door jam. "You said I shouldn't run." The pain lances through me, fueling my anger to flames. "You lied to me! You're doing what you promised you wouldn't—leave." Still he says nothing, so I step toward him. "Fine. Be a coward! Go! Walk away just like they all do."

His hands drop but he doesn't turn. Shoulders slumped, defeated, broken—he's not the man I know. Jackson is strong, a fighter, loyal, and I'm desperate to get him back.

"Coward? I'm fucking saving you. The only thing I'm afraid of is losing you."

"I can't do this again, Jackson. Please don't walk out that door after I've told you how I feel."

I watch his head shake from side to side and everything inside me rattles. Jackson remains in the door with his back to me, his voice quiet and strained. "I can't lose you like that. I'd rather walk away."

Anger that was simmering beneath the hurt is starting to boil. How dare he do this? He comes here, fucks me, tells me not to run, and then he's going to do exactly that? I'm pissed. I'm talking volcano erupting, fire burning, hulk smashing kind of pissed the fuck off.

"You're going to listen to me, goddamnit. Four days ago, when we went into that lawyer's office, I was falling apart. Everything in my life felt out of control. It was *you* who held me together. I drew on your strength to get through that fucking day from hell." I close my eyes, remembering what came after that. "But after everything else, I was terrified. You could hurt me so much. I was falling in love with you weeks ago, but that day I saw it all vanish. I ran because I was so afraid you'd let me go. I thought if I pushed you away before you got rid of me, it would be better. But it wasn't!"

Jackson turns and looks at me, the battle still raging inside him. "I'm not running, Catherine. Aaron is dead. I'm going to collect his fucking body and deliver it to his pregnant wife. Guess whose fault it is again? I give up trying to fight a war I'll never win."

"It's not your fault."

He goes stone-cold, every muscle rigid and tense. The blue-green eyes I love are black and glossy. "Try telling Natalie that. I leave tonight for Afghanistan to get his body and bring it home. I'm done arguing with you. I'm just ... done."

If I don't get this out now, I'll find a reason to hold back. I'm trembling from adrenaline as well as the fear of him walking out this door.

"I'm ready to fight for you. For so long I thought it wasn't my choice if things worked or not with any man. But with you—it's different. You told me I was it for you. Well, same here. I love you." I look into his eyes, completely vulnerable. No walls, nothing to hide my emotions. I'm giving him the truth with everything I am. "So you choose, Jackson. You tell me now if you want me to walk away. You walked through my door today. It's up to you to keep it open. I'm not talking about going to do what you have to do. Please, don't close the door on us."

The silence surrounds us, giving me the answer I was dreading. I drop my head while I struggle to keep the tears in check. When I feel his hand on my chin, my heart sputters. Once I look up, I'll have to face the truth. My gaze drifts as my chin glides toward his eyes. His face gives nothing away. My emotions are like a dam about to break.

"Say something, dammit!" I yell with tears in my eyes.

Jackson's hand drops from my face, leaving me bereft. "I've said it all already. You're not listening."

"That's your answer?" I ask, defeated.

He looks up, shaking his head, then exhales. "Everyone I love or care about dies. I'm protecting you."

"No. You're protecting yourself. People die, Jackson. It's tragic, but it happens."

His fingers sweep the hair off my face, lingering in my hair. "You know that night we met in the restaurant? It was so intense. I'd never felt so connected to someone so quickly. You walked away. Then, by some miracle ..." Jackson's hands cup my face. He takes a moment with his eyes closed. "You found your way back. I won't allow anything to hurt you. Including me." Releasing a heavy sigh, he drops his hands.

"The only thing hurting me is you leaving."

"I don't have a choice." He grips the back of his neck and looks at the ceiling.

There has to be a way. If I can keep him talking, maybe he won't go. "Of course you have a choice! Please. I'm begging you. Stay tonight, fly out tomorrow—please stay with me. We can figure this out. You're too upset to drive or be alone. I want to be here for you, but you're pushing me away."

Jackson stares at the window, unwilling to look at me. "The plane leaves tonight."

If he has to leave because he needs to deal with

whatever is going on, fine. But he's leaving and planning to end things. If he walks out the door, I fear it's truly the end.

"I won't give up on us. I know you're hurting and I understand you have to handle this situation, but you can lean on me. Let me carry some of your burden. *Talk* to me, Jackson. Let me in."

Our eyes meet for a moment before his lips crush against mine. I'd give everything up right now if he'd keep me in his embrace. His tongue demands entrance and my lips part, allowing him access. Every organ clenches as he pours himself into the kiss. I give him everything right back. All the love in my heart, my body, I offer him at this moment.

Needing an answer, I break the kiss. My heart is pounding so loud I'd swear he could hear it. I take a deep breath. "Don't kiss me if you're going to break my heart."

He looks at me with a mix of fear and regret. Then he closes his eyes and whispers, "Good-bye, Catherine." Jackson walks out the door without a backward glance.

I stand there, waiting to wake up from this nightmare. Surely that didn't happen. I'm asleep—that has to be it. I'm at my kitchen table with the papers strewn everywhere because *that* did not happen. Only it did. I look around my apartment, at the hole in the wall where Jackson punched it in anger. The door he walked through is still open, waiting for him to walk back through. I stare at the space he walked away from. It seems to be growing smaller, shrinking into itself as time does the same. He doesn't return. The thunder booms outside, snapping me from my haze. The tempest within becomes a hurricane.

He's gone.

He walked out on me after he promised he wouldn't. My heart splinters like glass on the ground—jagged and raw and ready to cut with all its sharp edges. I knew this was going to happen eventually—I'd hoped not to fall, but I guess it's too late for that now. I've crested the mountain only to fall down the other side, and no one is going to catch me.

CHAPTER TWENTY-NINE

JACKSON

Seven days later-Afghanistan

"Fuck. I didn't miss this shithole!" I glance over at Mark, who's looking out at the village on the left, checking for anything out of the norm.

"Need to clean the sand out of your vag, Muff? Does Kitty know you're this big of a pussy?" Mark taunts like the douchebag he is.

I scoff at his sorry attempt at a jab. "Kiss my ass. Try not to sparkle too much while we're here. You might draw some hijab attention." I give him the finger and he starts laughing. "Also, don't talk about Catherine."

"Touchy. Have you told her yet?"

"No," I say with no room for further discussion. He's already told me I need to tell her about my past, but I wasn't going to drop that shit on her lap and rush off to deal with the mess here.

Mark and I didn't speak for the first leg of the trip, both of us dealing with the loss of yet another member of our team. This shit is fucking with both of us. We started with six—and then there were two. When you're active duty, you know your time is numbered. Once you're out, though, that's not how you think anymore.

I look to the left, take a deep breath, and regret

doing that immediately. The Humvee smells like shit, but we've been traveling for five long ass days, so we aren't any better. We flew into Spain and waited there for two days. Rota reminded me of the trouble we got in during the last deployment here. It was a fucking joke. We drank, ate, drank some more, and worked out. Made bank and went home.

Then we flew into Dubai for another two days. At least in Dubai there's a ton of shit to do. Of course, it was only supposed to be a five-hour layover, but when you're flying on Navy equipment, you expect the unexpected. Which is a nice way of saying prepare for that shit to break.

Since we've hit the sandbox, it's been nothing but constant bullshit. Our convoy never met us at the base we flew into. I had to call a bunch of old friends to get someone to come get us, then take us to Camp Victory so we could claim Aaron's body. Normally that's not how it works, but I don't give a fuck. He's our brother and we weren't leaving him to fly alone. Mark had to pull a few strings to get it done, but he felt the same way. We owed Natalie that much.

Now we're heading to the IED site. Another favor I cashed in. Whatever. At this rate, I just want to get some damn answers on how they fucked this up.

"By the way, asshat, this doesn't count as my vacation," Mark lets me know through the mics on our helmets.

I adjust my Kevlar so I can breathe. This shit didn't get any lighter. We're fully loaded and tacked out. "You said you wanted the sun and the sand. I delivered."

"Funny." He laughs.

We approach the site and my guard instantly goes up. I slip right back into battle mode.

I get out first.

"Hey, Muff, watch your six," Mark says seriously. We've done enough missions together to know when the tone changes, it means something's not right. "I have a bad feeling about the mountains up on the left," Mark says, pointing to the rocky terrain.

"Yeah, I have a bad feeling about this whole fucking place. Cover me."

I hear the door close behind me. The debris is cleared for the most part. Considering we're a week behind, a lot of the intel I could've gotten is pretty much gone, but you never know. I've seen insurgents sing like canaries for a soda. Everyone has a price and today, I'm the banker.

I scan the area. So far there's a few kids playing soccer and a woman standing by the fence, talking to another child. Ahead of me I see what looks like some pieces of the explosion. I lean down right as a ball comes flying in front of my face. The kids are laughing at the almost collision. I grab the ball and smile—I've just found my bargaining chip.

I crouch low to the ground and sling my gun onto my back. Probably not the smartest move, but I need the kids to come close. Plus, Mark's behind me along with the other two guys we grabbed when we rolled out. "Want the ball?" I ask, holding it out.

The two kids nod and walk over.

This might be too easy.

I hold the ball out and the little girl gives me a huge smile. She's cute as hell. I place the ball between us and pull it back. She giggles and reaches out. We do this four times before I hand it over. "Do you speak English?"

We didn't bring a translator with us, so I'm on my own. We may have to draw pictures in the dirt.

She nods but doesn't speak.

"I'm Ja—Muff. What's your name?" I almost told her my real name like a fucking idiot. It's bad enough we're in uniforms with our names on them. I get to walk around bumfuck Afghanistan with my last name on me. Perfect.

She stares at me and finally responds, "Cat."

My eyes go wide. What the fuck? Cat? I don't know if it's her name or if it's the only English word she knows.

I shake my head and go back to the little girl. "Your name is Cat?"

She holds her ball and nods her head yes.

I smile and think about Catherine, going back to the day I left. The way she looked. How I was so blind with rage I couldn't even talk to her. She has no clue what it was like for me to walk away from her. It was bad enough when she pushed me away, but to know it's me this time—it's fucking killing me. She captivates me, makes me want to try again, to feel things I swore I'd never allow myself to feel. Those brown eyes get me every time. It's only been a week, but I miss her. I wish I could hear her voice and beg her to take me back. Something's kept me from calling her, though. It's better this way. I don't care if someone thinks it makes me a pussy. I'm far from it.

Suddenly the little girl turns and runs back to her brother, who's screaming her name.

Fuck.

I turn back to Twilight, who's staring off at the perimeter. I kick myself for thinking the little girl would give us any answers. Mark was right when he said this was stupid. There's no court of law and no one gives a damn here, but I couldn't let it go. Again, because of me and my choices someone else's blood is on my hands. It was my fucking mission—I sent him. I made *him* go, even though his wife was seven months pregnant, because I was dealing with the stupid cosmetics shit—which I never wanted in the first place. It was never supposed to be my job. It was for her. Now it's my goddamn mess. Running one company was responsibility enough, but two?

As I walk to the detonation point, the air shifts.

My entire body goes still. Not a muscle moves.

The hairs on my arms rise. I take a breath as everything around me becomes crystal clear and moves in slow motion. The tree on my left is moving. A bird flies to the north. A sense of calm washes over me as the sound barrels toward me.

I can count the seconds. I know it's coming.

The heartbeats of time pass.

Until it hits.

The bullet rips through my skin and muscle before exiting the other side. I jerk back from the impact of the gunshot. Everything stops as my body registers what my mind was prepared for. I've been shot.

Pain. Numb. Pain. It crushes together.

I hunch over as another bullet shreds through my body. I buckle and crumple to the ground as the agony becomes too much. Holy fucking shit! I curse and yell as the sound of bullets rains down.

"Shots fired! Shots fired!" I hear from a distance.

Yeah, no shit shots fired.

"He's down!" I hear Mark call out from behind the Humvee.

The bullets hit the ground around me. The sound of each one bouncing on the dirt just inches away from me vibrates in my head.

I start to crawl toward the truck for cover.

Another bullet hits.

"Fuuuuuuuuuuuuuck!" I scream out as it tears through me.

"Don't move!" Mark yells franticly as I try to roll and grab my gun.

"On the roof! Sniper on the roof," I cry out.

Pop. Pop. Pop. I hear them over and over. Heavy gunfire fills my ears as Mark continues to yell at me. All I see is red. My vision fades in and out.

Black.

Red.

White.

"Kill them and let's go!" Mark's loud voice says over the sound of bullets. "Up on the ridge. There's another one!"

I return fire, trying to shoot my way to safety. The sounds of screaming and gunfire are all I register.

"Muff!" Mark calls out as my vision starts to fade. The pain is unlike anything I've ever felt before.

Everything becomes foggy. My eyes. I'm so tired. But then I see her. She's beautiful. Her dark blue eyes pierce through the pain, giving me numbness. Her long blond hair is exactly as I remember. She walks toward me with her hand outstretched. "Madelyn." Her name rolls off my tongue effortlessly. She steps closer as I extend my arm. Closer and closer, her eyes stay locked on mine.

"Jackson, no! Stay with me," I hear. Catherine's voice. The sound of it jolts me and I drop my hand.

"Catherine," I call out to her.

Opening my eyes, I see Mark's face contort as he continues to shoot. "Motherfucker! Move!" Using my arms, I try to crawl closer.

I see him throw his gun down and rush toward me.

"Mark," I croak. My vision is hazy.

I'm weak. I can't hold on.

The pain is taking over and I can't fight the black.

I close my eyes. There's no fight. I'm too tired. She's here, waiting for me with her long brown hair and chocolate brown eyes—she's perfect. It's too much. In the dark, I see her. In the dark, there's no pain, no guilt—just her.

I focus on the warmth in her eyes and succumb to the numbness.

TO BE CONTINUED ...

bonus

scene

"Hey, beautiful. You're coming with me," Ashton proclaims at the door of my office with her hands on her hips. Her auburn hair is pulled to the side and her eyes narrow as she takes in my office, which is currently a disaster.

"I'm really busy. I have to get this press release out today for Jack—" I stop myself from saying his name. The hurt surges through me as I stifle the anguish of living another day without him. "I mean, Raven. The product launches in a few days so I need to take a rain check."

He left me a week ago today—walked out the door with no hope of him coming back to me. The almost slip of his name reminds me of the feeling of watching him leave. The way my heart felt like it was tearing out of my chest in complete agony. Then there was the voicemail I left which went unreturned by him. I pleaded for Jackson to come back—to fight for us. There was nothing I wouldn't have done for him. I know he was hurt, but in return, he destroyed me.

Ashton steps further into the room and her voice softens, "The press release can wait. You've barely been home before nine since he left. I asked Taylor and she said you haven't been eating either. So I'm putting my foot down and we're going to lunch. You have to eat." She steps around my desk and grabs my purse then looks at me with a no-non-sense gleam in her eye.

I look down at my paper, not in the mood to deal with her right now. "Can we do this tomorrow? I really want to get this done." I stumble for an excuse.

Of course she won't be put off. "Look, I know you're busy and all, but I came across town for your sorry ass, so we're going to lunch whether you come willingly or I carry you out on my back ... your choice."

The choice is clear and either I go to lunch now with what little dignity I have left or my crazy best friend drags me out of here kicking and screaming. All Ashton really knows is that something happened with Aaron, and Jackson had to leave. She has no idea what happened leading up or the fight we had. There's a part of me that knows once I say it out loud it'll be real. I glance up at her again and huff with resignation.

"Fine. You're paying and you have thirty minutes. I really do have to work." I grab my bag from her and start walking toward the door. There is no strength left to fight her or anyone else.

"I knew you'd see things my way," she crows victoriously behind me.

The last seven days I've thrown myself into the Raven account, busting my ass to make everything perfect. It's a blessing I have my job as a reprieve. Being swamped in all things Jackson at least lets me feel close to him through his company. Nobody has heard a word from him since he left and it's been torture. I just want to know he's okay. I want to hear his voice and convince him to come back to me. Why doesn't he see it? We're worth the fight.

Ashton and I arrive at the deli down the street and order. I've barely said more than a few words and she allows me the peace for once. I swirl my spoon around in the soup she forced me to order.

"Are you going to eat that or stare at it?" she questions.

"I'm eating."

"Right. How about you tell me what the hell is really going on."

Slowly my eyes lift, but I'm empty. I have no witty remark to give back to her. There is a part of me so broken and alone it's starting to smother the living pieces. Like a black haze, it seeps through me, taking the untouched parts and tarnishing them.

"He's gone."

"Yeah, he had to go handle Aaron. You told me that. I don't understand why you're acting like *this*!" she exclaims and points her finger at me.

"No, he's *gone*."

Her eyes squint as she tries to understand. "Gone where?"

"Jackson left me before he went to Afghanistan. He decided we shouldn't be together. I begged him. I begged with tears streaming not to push me away. I fought!" I choke on the sob threatening to spill out. "I gave myself on a silver platter and he walked out."

"You two give me a fucking headache. He just lost his friend, Cat. He was grief stricken. I know he left, but that doesn't mean you need to shut down."

"What do you want from me, Ash? I'm going to work. I'm doing what I have to do. I'm not shutting down."

Ashton puts her hand on mine to stop me. "Do you want the truth or do you want me to tell you what you want to hear? I'll do either because I'm your best friend, but I need to know."

"I can't do this anymore. I can't keep coming in second place. I fight and fight and I get pushed to the side. I give all I have to give. I begged and he didn't care." Ashton's hand grips mine and I look up at her. I want to cry so badly but I can't. There are no more tears to shed. "He's gone..."

"So go get him." Her voice is full of determination.

If only it was that simple.

"I can't go anywhere, Ashton," I say with no emotion. My voice is flat and resigned. "He's in Afghanistan dealing with the death of a friend. I can't exactly go there. Why should I go anyway? To be rejected again?"

Ashton takes a deep breath and my phone vibrates on the table. It's Jackson's number. I don't know why he'd be calling but all I want is to hear the deep sounds of his voice. Should I answer?

He's calling me...

I grab the phone and quickly swipe the screen, the nerves swirling like butterflies in my stomach.

"Jackson?" I say, unsure.

"Catherine. It's Mark."

My stomach plummets. I was desperate to hear his voice. "Mark? Where's Jackson?"

In my heart, I feel it. Something is wrong. Tears begin to form as unwarranted panic starts to swell.

"Catherine, you need to listen to me." He takes a deep breath. The pregnant pause causes my anxiety to spike. My heart begins to race, my mouth is dry as I clutch my chest. "Something happened."

"What do you mean something happened?"

"He was shot."

Seven days since I've seen his face.

Please don't do this to me!

I can't speak. My lungs struggle to get air.

"Are you there?" Mark's voice breaks through the silence.

Seven days since he walked out the door.

"Catherine?" Ashton says concerned.

I stare at Ashton through the tears blurring my vision as the fear takes over. She grabs my hand and squeezes.

"Yes," I whisper to both of them.

"You need to go to the airport. The plane is waiting for you. I need you to pack a bag and get here to Germany. Can you do that?"

"Germany? I thought you were in …" I pause as pieces of the puzzle start to join.

"We had to fly here. You need to come to Germany—it's where he's being treated."

Seven days since I've heard his voice.

"Is he alive?" I barely choke out the words.

"It's not good. You should get here—fast."

And I may never again.

My chair begins to shake and I realize it's coming from my body. No. No! He's okay. He has to be. He's Jackson Cole. He's a fucking SEAL. I can't lose him.

"Catherine? Focus!" Mark yells through the line.

That's my undoing.

I lose it, tears falling like acid rain, burning my cheeks as they fall one by one.

I hear a deep sigh before he starts again. "You'll come?"

Closing my eyes I envision Jackson's face. I see his cocky grin, his blue-green eyes, his dark brown hair that I love to run my fingers through, and that

perfect dimple. I hear his voice, the way he says my
name and how his laugh goes through me bringing
me to life. I love him and I can't lose him. Not this
way.

"Tell him he better not die before I get there."

The phone falls to the floor and Ashton rushes
over to grab me as I clutch my chest unable to draw
a breath.

Everything moves at a snail's pace when you're in
a hurry. It feels like planes fly slower, cars don't
move as fast, but yet it's not the case. Time passes
with the same tick of the clock as always, yet I feel
like time has stopped. As much as I want to get to
him, to see him and know what's happening—I'm
terrified. The longer it takes for things to happen,
the longer I can try to pretend he's alive. When we
land, I'll have to find out if that's still the truth.
Hours pass while every scenario passes through my
mind. Has he lost his fight while I was trying to get
to him? How bad were his injuries? Is he awake?
Does he want to see me? I need to know, but then a
part of me is afraid to.

Ashton sits next to me, unwilling to release my
hand the entire flight.

"We're almost there," she says softly, as I lie
there looking out the window, preparing for reality
to hit me like a fist to the face.

I know I need to garner whatever strength I
still have. I have to be tough, because he will come
through this. He has to. I can't lose him forever. I
was so angry and upset with him, but now all I want
is to see him and hold him. Mark said he's pretty

bad and we should be prepared, so I'm giving my-self until the plane touches down to be a wreck ... after that no more.

The plane descends and I start to collect my courage. I straighten in my seat and wipe under my eyes. "Ash?" I say tentatively.

"Yeah?"

"Thank you."

She puts her head on my shoulder and sighs. "Catherine, you never have to thank me. You would do this for me."

We don't say anything else on the way to the hospital. When we arrive, Mark meets us and pulls me into an embrace. He looks so broken. I push down the fear and hold on to my resolve to stay strong.

"Cat, I'm so sorry ... I tried—" Mark's shoulders tighten with tension as the moment crashes around us. My chest heaves against his and he pulls me close to him. I hear Ashton's breath catch as we both break down.

"Is he ...?" I can't finish. I can't go there, but the way he's falling apart, the fear begins to take a hold of me.

"No, he's alive. Barely." Mark let's go of me and turns his back to compose himself with a deep breath.

"Can I see him?"

"Come on," he says as he puts his arm around me and pulls me to his side.

With each step, I fight the urge to run to him. Every fiber of my being knows he's here and I need to touch him. Mark slows me down and he pauses when we reach a room at the end of the hall.

"I need to warn you again ... it's bad. And he

just got out of surgery." Mark's blue eyes show the apprehension behind his words.

"I'll be okay."

He nods and opens the door slowly. I take a step toward the man I love and jolt to a stop when I see him.

Nothing could've prepared me for this.

acknowledgements

If I fail to mention someone I'm eternally sorry. Some of you kept me afloat when I felt like I was sinking. Some were my cheerleaders, some were a little more forceful making me write when I wanted to sleep, but all of you have made my life complete.

Cara, what do I even say to you? Because really ... there aren't enough words to express my gratitude. No amount of thank you's can suffice. From day one you stood behind me and pushed—hard. You made me laugh and then bawl my eyes out but it was expected and needed. The jokes and laughter regarding my incessant rewrites and "wait don't read that version" kept me desperate to keep you on your toes. The backroom deals, the quest to find Jackson, letting me talk to myself with you on the phone. #NMCNMM

Mandi, you "got" their story. Your support and honesty was invaluable. Thank you for not letting me try out for American Idol when I couldn't sing and for loving Jackson. Most of all thank you for keeping me grounded. You gave me your time, love, and wisdom when I needed it. You are my Muffin and no one loves him more than you and Cara! #IlovemyMuffDirty

Betas, I have no words to fully express the appreciation I have for you. Livia, Roxana, Stacia, Jennifer, and Lisa ... you pushed me to do better and made me laugh, cry, and shake my head in awe of your genuine love and support. Thank you for dropping things to read and not backing down. For the refusal to let me put out anything less than my best and not allowing me to get away with anything. Beta reading is hard and I appreciate how honest you all were. but I know you all came from a place of love and for that I thank you so much. A huge thank you to my test readers: Alison, Letty, Donna, Jessica, Keisha and Tara. You gave me so much feedback on the finished product and blew me away. It meant the world to me.

Angie, thank you for all of you support, love, and friendship. For taking your time to make sure I had a successful release. You held my hand when I was afraid and gave me words of wisdom when I needed it. I love your face!

Lisa, it's not everyday you meet someone and just "click". Our friendship was never forced, it just happened. Your snark, sarcasm, and love of Jackie has brought us closer than ever. I love ya!

Rose, you are my inspiration. You pushed me to see the courage I had when I didn't think it was there. You forced me to do better day after day. The tears you virtually wiped and then literally wiped I will never forget. Thank you for being my wifey and never letting me down. There are certain people who enter our lives for one reason or another and I'm thankful everyday you are one of them. Our friendship is beyond all of this and I'll cherish it always.

Emmy, Kristy, and Laurelin, if it weren't for you three I wouldn't have had the guts to write in the first place. When I told you this is what I was going to do you all stood behind me and made me go forward. You read my first drafts and said, "keep going". I love you all as writers and friends.

Faith, you made me a better writer and challenged me to listen to my characters! I can't tell you how much your friendship means to me. Every single day I'm grateful I met you. While it may have been a complete fluke that we met you've become one of my closest friends that I rely on more than you may know.

FYW: I can't even say enough about you ladies. During times of doubt, struggle, joy, and happiness we've come together. It has been so special to me and I love every one of you.

To my editor, Megan Ward, you are so much more than an editor. You took a hold of my story and cared for it. Your attention to every detail, every word, and every emotion was astounding. This process was exciting and remarkable because of you. You achieved your goal of making this fun. I can only hope every writer at some time or another gets to work with you. Thank you for empowering me to push harder and see what was there. I will forever laugh when I see anyone wink.

My cover designer, Najla Qamber, thank you for making it perfect. I love every single thing about it. You are truly an amazing artist.

Christine from Perfectly Publishable, you stepped in and saved the day. I appreciate your professionalism, attention to detail, and making this a painless and wonderful experience.

Bloggers – I have so many to thank because without you none of this would be possible. Some of you may not realize what you give to authors … a chance. You take time away from your loved ones to read and then even more time to tell your fans how you felt. It's appreciated and truly respected. I know the dedication, sacrifice, and time you spend. From the bottom of my heart thank you for taking the time to read and review!

Heather Maven, thank you for your friendship, love, and always making me laugh. Everyday I am grateful for you in my life.

To my friends and family, some of you didn't know I was writing *Beloved* so if you're reading this … surprise! Thank you to my mother who won't ever read this but stood beside me every step of the way. You gave me life, then made sure I lived it to my fullest. I never felt unloved or unwanted because of you. My Aunt Donna, you took me to the zoo and made sure I had these memories. You taught me that just because I was hurting didn't mean I had to be alone. I pray that every person in this world has someone like you, because you are one in a million.

The SPQ, There are few people who mean more to me in this world than you. There are so many things you probably picked up on just for you. You stood beside me when I wasn't sure. You pushed when I wanted to quit. You joked when I needed to laugh.

To my beautiful children…Thank you for your daily dinner talks asking how much I wrote. You both are the reason I kept going when I wanted to cry some nights. I know it wasn't easy when mommy was crazy glued to the computer and I love you both so much! To my son who tells everyone his mommy wrote a book even though I pray he'll never read it. To my daughter who told me she was so proud of me for following my dream and would take the laptop and sit next to me and write her own story. You both are my beloved.

I want to thank my husband for his undying love and support. You love the broken in me and have never given up. Our love has never been easy but it's ours. We've gone through so much and still come out on top. Deployments, moves, kids, more deployments but you've always been my constant. Most of all, thank you for being my anchor in the storm. You're it for me, babe.

To my readers ... Wow! The fact that I'm even sitting here writing to you is overwhelming. I had a dream as a little girl to write books, and because of you reading this right now it's no longer a dream, but a reality. I don't even know how to thank you because it's surreal. For some reason you choose to pick this up and read. For that I'm eternally grateful. I know you have kindles filled with books to choose, and a never ending supply of books coming—so thank you.

beholden

CORINNE MICHAELS

dedication

To the men and women who serve their countries and the families they leave behind.

Especially my husband for his years of sacrifice and dedication.

prologue

Catherine

I stand before the mirror in my knee-length, black dress. My hair is pin straight and I've opted against eye makeup. Not even waterproof mascara can withstand the torrent of tears I've shed lately.

I'll see him today.

I'll somehow handle looking at the man who's no longer mine. The one who forced me to love again, give my heart to him—then forced me to be alone. He's gone and I won't get him back.

I'll need a miracle to get through this.

Giving myself another once-over, I'm as content as I'll ever be. What does it matter anyway? Who gives a shit what I look like in the grand scheme of things? I'll be wrecked by the end of today—again. There will be no coming back. I'm in hell—no, purgatory. I walk around living, but feeling dead inside.

"You ready?" Ashton whispers behind me, placing her cool hand on my shoulder.

"Yeah, sure. It's not getting any better than this," I reply without any emotion.

I feel hollow.

He took everything from me.

"Okay ..." she trails off and leaves the room to

let me finish up.

Once I'm done, I head out to the living room. We gather our belongings in silence and head to the car. Ashton drives without the music on, giving me time to do nothing but sit and think of Jackson. I see his face, hear his voice, feel his hands on me, but it's not real anymore. Phantom feelings for a man that isn't real. None of it was real. I sometimes wonder if I just made it all up in my head. Made it into something it wasn't.

As we pull into the metal gates of the cemetery, I stare out the window wishing I were anywhere but here. I don't know how I'll make it through this.

The car stops and Ashton places her hand on mine. "Cat, we don't have to do this. If you can't be here …" She stops and bites her lip. "No one would judge you." The empathy swimming in her eyes rips through my heart, tearing me apart.

I glance at the tent set up at the gravesite. The people starting to filter around to bid their final goodbye to a man they loved. I sit here—frozen. Trying to piece together the parts of my heart that are no longer beating. I hear the remnants thumping erratically in my chest, but I feel nothing.

"I promised I'd be here, Ashton," I say with an air of finality.

I may not want to, but the bottom line is, I love him. I gave my heart to him and I made promises—no matter what, I won't break them.

We exit the car and start to make our way to the sea of black. The dark hearts in pain and sorrow surround the area. My heels puncture the soft grass while the gaps in my heart grow larger with each step. The smell of fresh grass fills the air. I can feel his presence. Every part of my body is tingling in awareness. The tears pool in my eyes blurring my sight and I stumble, but Ashton keeps me from falling.

"Ash ..." My voice quivers as I will myself to keep from falling apart.

"I won't leave your side." Her deep, blue eyes are filled with her vow.

I nod and draw my strength from her.

She's here and won't let me fall.

Keeping my head lowered, I continue moving while she holds on to my arm. I don't want to see faces. I focus on the beads of dew hanging on the blades of grass. I take in each one as if they're tears from God. Tears because none of this is okay. If I can keep my eyes down, I won't have to see the urn that sits on top of the tombstone. I won't see the friends and family with tear-filled eyes. I can pretend this is an awful dream and none of this is happening. I don't want to hear the words telling us we should be thankful for the time we had, because there's never *enough* time.

"I'm right here with you," Ashton whispers and wraps her arms around me.

I nod, not trusting my ability to speak. I'm bare- ly hanging on.

Silence falls upon the crowd as the preacher speaks, talking about heroism and sacrifice. Open- ing my eyes, I take in the scene before me. The four sailors stand off to the side dressed in their dark blue uniforms. Ribbons and medals hang from their chests. I glance at the American flag folded next to the urn, the gift for his ultimate sacrifice. I listen to the words and the quiet sobs of people in pain.

When the reverend stops speaking, the sailor moves and the bugle blares playing "Taps." Each note shreds through my body, penetrates my bones, and shatters my heart. Tears stream down my face unabashed. The uniformed sailor walks over to the front row placing the folded flag in delicate hands. He kneels before her speaking as she nods and trembles. The sounds of her loud cries break through my fragile façade.

"Shhh, Cat," Ashton murmurs in my ear. "You're shaking." She rubs her hands up and down my arm trying to warm me.

If only I was shaking because I'm cold.

I turn into her when a hand ghosts up my shoulder, "Catherine." His deep voice echoes in the eerie quiet.

The sound of his voice is my undoing. A sob breaks through my chest as Ashton catches me while I fall apart.

CHAPTER ONE

JACKSON

"Kill 'em and let's go!" Mark's loud voice bellows over the zinging of bullets raining around us. "Up on the ridge there's another one!"

I return fire trying to shoot my way to safety. Screams and gunfire are all I register through the chaos. The dust flies with each bullet hitting the dirt.

"Muff!" Mark calls out as my vision starts to fade.

The metallic taste of blood floods my mouth.

"Motherfucker! Move!" he yells, trying to get me out of harm's way. Opening my eyes, I see Mark's face contort as he continues to shoot.

Using my arms, I try to crawl closer. It fucking hurts. The pain is everywhere as a bullet rips through my abdomen, stopping me from moving. I lie here out in the open ready for my fate.

I look over at Mark as he returns fire and rushes towards me.

"Mark," I croak out, my vision hazy as he approaches me.

I close my eyes and succumb to the black. I don't want to wake up. The pain is too much. Besides, Catherine is here in the dark. Hearing her voice makes me want to try, but I'm losing my will.

"Jackson, you have to fight!" Her voice is thick with emotion.

"I'm too tired, baby. I want to stay with you. It doesn't hurt so much here. You make me feel better," I tell her, content to see her face and hear her voice. I know she's not real—but I want to stay here.

Her eyes close as a tear falls down her beautiful face. "You'll hurt me more if you stay. You have to go back. *Please.* For me," she begs.

I'll do anything not to hurt her again. I'd give her everything just to stop the look of suffering on her face. I open my eyes and the piercing torture jolts me back to life while the bullets slice through the air around me.

Mark hoists me over his shoulder as I hold back a scream from the impact against my injured shoulder. The pain radiates from my head to my toes, reminding me I'm still alive. If I can still feel, I can fight.

"We have to go. Now!" The tone of command conveys the urgency of the situation.

I'm thrown in the back of the Humvee and the jolt causes me to cry out. "Holy shit! It fucking hurts!" I can't hold back. My vision fades again and I'm not sure if it's from the pain or if I'm coming to the end.

"Muff, can you hear me?" The doors slam closed as we take cover in the Humvee and start to move.

Mark hovers over me. We continue to take fire but the protection of the vehicle allows us to get the hell out of here. Each bump in the road is pure agony. They drive frantically trying to get back to the base as one soldier radios in my injuries.

"He's been shot three times. Get the HELO on standby!" Mark yells out to him as we take a sharp turn, causing me to shift.

"My fucking leg," I cry out.

"Put your hand over your shoulder." He presses my hand over the bullet wound, trying to force me to put pressure on it. "I have to deal with your leg, so you have to hold it."

I try to hold on but I can't feel my arms, every limb is heavy. My hand starts to slip. "I can't—" I start to say.

"You don't have a choice, you son of a bitch!" Mark yells in my face. "Shut the fuck up and hold on to your shoulder!"

Mark grabs a needle from the medic bag and injects something in my arm. Everything becomes foggy and numb. I'm so tired. The smell of sweat, blood, and fear filters through the Humvee.

Something slaps my face forcing me to open my eyes. "Eyes open, you fuckbag! Don't close them!" Mark's eyes are wide and focused. I feel my pants rip. "Muff, this is going to hurt," he says calmly before he clamps his hand around the bullet hole in my leg, pushing down.

"Fuuuuuuuuuck!" I scream out as a hot fire spreads through my veins burning everything in its path.

The pain is taking over and I can't fight the black.

He pushes again as my eyes fly open. "I told you. Keep. Your. Eyes. Open!" He turns to the driver. "Faster!" Mark ties something around my leg creating a tourniquet. His voice is harsh but I hear the undertone of fear. We both know this isn't good. The blood loss, the multiple bullet wounds, and the fact that we're not close enough to the base is the reality we face.

Mark rips open my shirt and sees the blood around my abdomen as his hands tremor in terror.

My hand falls again and he positions himself to put pressure on my stomach and my shoulder.

"Be there in three," the driver calls back to us.

"You have three minutes to tell me all the reasons I should keep you from bleeding out. You close your eyes, I'll fucking push harder. Try me, motherfucker." He grips my face making me focus on him.

"Tell her—"

"Not a chance. Tell me."

"I love ..." I pass out from the agony.

I awake to the constant stream of beeping behind me. Where am I? I feel something warm in my hand but I can't open my eyes. The weights holding my eyelids closed are too heavy to lift. I hear mumbling and I swear it's Catherine and Mark, but that wouldn't make sense.

Attempting to get my limbs to cooperate, I try to lift my arms but they won't move.

"Jackson ..." I hear her call to me. "Please wake up. I don't know if you can hear me, but God, I hope you can."

Catherine.

She's here.

She takes a deep breath and lets it out, clearly upset. "Mark called and I ... I just ... come back to me." I hear her sob and the need to comfort her overwhelms me. I want to wake up and tell her it's okay, but everything is locked. Every part of me is heavy and unwilling to cooperate.

"God, there's so much to say. You have to be okay, because I c-can't. I can't live with knowing this w-was all we h-had." Catherine's voice tears through me. "I'd give anything to go back and never let you leave my house that night. I'd barricade you in my damn room. I-I'm so s-sorry, baby. Please be okay."

She has nothing to be sorry for. I did this to her. I was a chickenshit. I created this doubt of how I feel about her because I chose to walk away. I didn't want to destroy her, yet that's all I've done.

"I wish I would've called you. Or come to you that night. Shit. But as soon as Mark called I came. I ran ... to you, Jackson." She lets out a shaky breath. "I love you and I'm here now. I just want to see you open your eyes, baby. It's been too long since I've seen your eyes. I miss your smile, and your voice. I miss you being an ass, and being charming. I miss it all. Please, Jackson. Wake up, dammit!" she begs and sobs.

The sounds of her cries echo in the room. Each hiccup guts me. I can't speak. Hell, I don't know how long I've been out for. I'm obviously alive, but am I really? If this is death—I'm being robbed. There's no white light or anyone calling me to another side. I'm lying here. Trapped in my own body, listening to people around me.

"Cat, come on. You need to sleep. It's been two days and you haven't moved." I hear Mark's voice. "He'll wake up. He's too much of a dickhead to die." He laughs and her half laugh makes my heartbeat accelerate. The monitor beeps louder and they both stop talking.

This is complete bullshit.

"It's been a while, Mark. Plus, I don't know if

I ..." She trails off sounding hurt. *Fucking eyes—
open!* "The doctors said his leg is in bad shape.
What if he has to have another surgery? He barely
made it out of the last one."

"He'll be fine. Remember who we're talking
about. Trust me, he's been through worse than this.
He's just going to make us all suffer for a while,"
Mark says, trying to reassure her.

"What if he doesn't want me here?"

I shouldn't have left, but I couldn't stop. Rage
consumed every part of me. My failure was all I
could see. Catherine would be next and I will *not*
allow it. I'll break myself apart before I let anything
happen to anyone else.

"Listen, Kitty, he wants you here. I know you
guys haven't been together that long, but he cares. I
wouldn't have called you and gone through the red
tape if I wasn't sure what you mean to him."

"You weren't there that night." Her voice cracks
and so does my heart.

"You have to understand him—he's an idiot. A
big, giant, fucking moron."

Catherine's soft laugh stops her sniffles.

"I'd bet on him, Cat. He'll wake up." Mark is
comforting her and I'm here helpless. I hear her
muffled sobs and each part of me tears open—I
hate hurting her.

I feel something against my bedside. It's torture
to hear and know what's going on but not be able
to talk or move.

Mark begins to speak in the distance. "I think
you should get some rest at the hotel. Ashton leaves
today, you could go with her—"

"No! Not even an option." I feel her hands touch
my hair and guide it to the side. "I'll go to the airport

to drop her off, but I'm not leaving until he wakes. And if he wants me to leave … I'll … well, I don't know, but I'm not leaving until he throws me out." She sounds strong and sure.

I try again to open my eyes, give her a sign that I'm alive. But they won't budge. Fuck this. I'm going back to sleep. Then I can stop feeling so weak.

I listen to the beeping, counting each one as my mind replays the shooting. Remembering the feeling of metal shredding my skin, the smell of death in the HELO, the blood staining my clothes and skin. I have no idea how bad my injuries are.

"Of course he wants you here. Why do you keep saying shit like this?" he asks.

He doesn't know I walked away from her like I did. He doesn't know the pussy I was and the dick move I made when I got the call. I went there and things happened so fast. I was ready to tell her everything. We were going to talk and figure our shit out. Then I got the call from Mark and I lost it. The failure of not being able to save someone else weighs on me.

"You don't understand. When he left—"

"Knock, knock," an unfamiliar voice says.

"Is everything okay? The last nurse was just here." Catherine's voice is strained.

"We're going to give him a little more meds to keep him comfortable," an older woman's voice comes through. "He's been having some irregularity in his heart rate."

"Is he okay?" Catherine asks, sounding scared.

I'm fine. Just pissed off.

"Yes, we're going to make sure he's not in any pain," the nurse explains.

"Jackson." Catherine's small hands caress my

face. "I'll be right back. I have to take Ashton to the airport." Her lips press against my cheek and she leans in close to my ear whispering so only I can hear her. "I love you. You're it for me, so don't go anywhere." I feel her lips press against my face again as the meds drag me into the black.

"He's crashing!" The helicopter noise drowns out most sounds but I hear them frantically screaming. "Stay with us, Cole. Only two more minutes."

Two minutes. I can hold on for two minutes.

My eyes fly open as they work on my chest and inject something into my IV. Jesus Christ, I can't take much more. The fighting and trying to hang on is exhausting. I want to be done. I want the fucking black and numbness because there's no pain there.

"Give him another round of epi," the medic calls out while he stabs something into my chest.

The sound of my gasps and gurgling is horrifying. I'm going to die. I feel it in every bone in my body. The blood loss from the three gunshot wounds I sustained is too much. Even in this state I feel pain. It runs from head to toe and amplifies with each second that passes.

"Hang on, buddy, we're almost there," he yells in my face trying to make me focus.

The helicopter touches down and I'm moving before we stop. The colors of light flash quickly as I'm being pulled out and thrown on a gurney. The sun is blinding and each part of me feels heavy as they run toward the hospital. I want to scream out—yell at the top of my lungs to let me die. I don't want to feel any more. I close my eyes and I see her again. I see her dark brown eyes glaring at me. I hear her quiet cries and it tears at my soul. Her face is contorted in pain. The tears are filling in her eyes as she refuses to break contact.

"Don't leave me," I hear Catherine call out but her voice is fading.

"Prep him for surgery. Now. Trauma one." There are voices all around yelling different orders. Trying to get control. People barking numbers but I can't focus. I open my eyes and only see the bright light above. Either God is calling or it's one of those bright ass lights they use in the hospital.

I moan and try to move my arm but someone clamps it.

A man in a blue mask comes into view trying to get me to focus. "Stay still, Cole. We're going to take you into surgery. You need to calm down. Knock him out. Now!"

Calm? He's fucking joking, right? I can't calm down.

"Catherine!" I scream out.

CHAPTER TWO

Another fucking flashback. I can't determine what's reality anymore.

I'm tired of being tired. When I'm in this awake but paralyzed state, I'm battling my mind and my body. I want to tell Catherine what I think and feel. But my goddamn body won't get with the fucking program.

Then the fucking nightmares exhaust my mind. Haunting me with the shooting—forcing me to recall everything over and over. Either I see the bullets ripping through me or I see the aftermath. I'd rather go through Hell Week again—at least there we had fun crawling through dirt and mud.

"It's been four days and he still hasn't woken up, Mark." Catherine sounds weary and worn.

"I know, Kitty."

"You know I hate that," she replies and I imagine her eyes rolling.

"Yeah, well, since I don't have Muff here to give shit to … you're the next best thing." His laughter is short and forced.

I've known him long enough to hear the fear. It's the voice we used when we were on a mission and things were going south. Full of lies but the words we needed to hear to get through it. Sometimes you need reassurance things are going to be fine even though you know they're not. He's doing his best to hold out for her. I must be in worse shape than I imagined.

The small hairs on the back of my hand move when she breathes. The ability to feel it gives me hope I'm coming around. Maybe soon I can open my damn eyes.

"I'm happy I amuse you, Twilight." That's my girl. Give it back to the fucknugget. "When do you have to head back to the States?"

"Soon. I have to make sure the rest of the contracts run smoothly and are under control, but ..." A chair scrapes across the floor. "I can't leave yet, Cat. I know I need to, especially with Aaron gone, but ..." He trails off and takes a deep breath. "We only have two other guys who know this shit like we do. I've been with him since day one. This company may have his name, but it has all our blood, sweat, and tears."

Another chair grates making a loud sound. "Is the company in trouble? I can try to do some press stuff from here. Manage the story as much as possible. You know this is what I'm good at. Plus it's my job. I can't fail him." Catherine seems anxious to help. She speaks quickly trying to get him on board.

She must be going out of her mind. Everything in her life stopped so she could be here. I have to wake up. But when I do, will any of it matter? I'll be injured at the very least, and we're broken.

"No, we're okay for now. We have the contract in Afghanistan that's still not in a good place, but I have a liaison in place. What about Raven?"

That stupid company. It's tied to me and bringing me down. If I get rid of it, there's a part of *her* that goes. If I don't, there's a part of *me* that will lose everything. Of course, there's the fact that Catherine knows nothing of my past and what it all means. Who the fuck even knows if she'll understand once everything comes to light? She may bolt and I don't know if I'd blame her.

I remember how I felt when that prick, Neil, showed up at her house saying he was her fiancé. The idea of her being tied to anyone that closely ripped me apart and made me see red. I'm aware other men have had a place, but I still hate it.

"Raven is good. Danielle's handling things well. I've released a few updates about his condition, and the shareholders seem to be staying put for now. There hasn't been a dip in the stock either. I have a few people with ears to the ground if anything comes up. I cancelled my meetings with the press for next week. And pushed the launch off." I feel her fingers brush my hair back. "I guess it's a good thing he's my job." Catherine's short laugh is followed by a sob. "God! I just sit here and look at him and ask the same question over and over. Why? Why is this happening? I'm so scared he's not going to wake up. That we won't have a chance to make things right and I c-can't!"

"Shhh, it's okay," Mark murmurs, and her sobs destroy me.

Even though I can't move, every piece of me is in pain.

I fucked up.

"It's not okay. None of this is *okay*," she sniffles. "I thought we were going to find our way, Mark. I was ready to fight everything for him. Then he ripped me apart and he *left* me! He fucking left and didn't look back. I know he had to leave to handle the situation with Aaron. I wasn't against him leaving for that … just him leaving *me*! There's something else. I know it." Catherine's voice shakes in anger.

My mind is slipping as I try to keep up with their conversation. I struggle to focus but the sounds are blurring together. I'm fucking drained.

"He has his reasons, Cat. You may not like them. Fuck, I don't like them."

"What reasons?" She sounds small and scared.

The exhaustion is overtaking as I fall back asleep unable to know what Mark will tell her.

Pain. The pain is back. It travels through me as I try to process what is going on.

"Okay, motherfucker, I've been patient. I've let you lie here and not said shit. I've held her while she cried. I've called your family. Done everything waiting for you to man up. But I'm done now, Muff. Wake the fuck up!" Mark's voice interrupts my foggy sleep.

Oh, I'm awake now, dickhead.

"I'm so mad at you! You go and get shot in front of me. You always have to be the fucking martyr. You couldn't take cover like I said to? I told you to watch your six. Now look, you're fucking half dead." Mark's voice cracks on the last word.

"I'm not going to be the only one left here, asshole. You think you're the only one here who lost them? I fucking lost them too. So, what? You're going to quit and make me carry all of it? No, you wake up and you deal with this shit too. I was on the same mission! I watched them get carried out. I heard the same fucking sounds and lived the same hell. You weren't the sole person responsible for them going into that village. I was there too," he stops and exhales.

"I could've said we should stay together, but it was risky either way. Selfish fucking asshole you are. I've let you be this self-sacrificing prick for long enough. You don't get to be the only one allowed to hurt. There were six of us! Six of us who walked into that fucking village and only three came out. There's not a day I don't think about them. I remember walking into that fucking funeral watching Melissa grieve. Watching Crystal hold on to that flag. Now there are only two. So who carries the fucking guilt if you die? Huh, you selfish son of a bitch? That's what I thought. Just lie there and let me deal with this alone. God, you're such a pussy." Mark breaks off, drawing a few deep breaths.

I want to scream, choke, and claw my way out of my own skin. Selfish? Fuck him. He didn't send them to their deaths. He wasn't the one who had to make the call. I did. When I get out of this coma, I'm gonna kill him myself.

"And then what? You're going to walk away from her too? Why? You need to get your fucking head straight. I was there for that too, you know. I watched her almost ruin you. But Catherine isn't Maddie. And if you're going to do this to her then you don't deserve her. She loves you for some stupid ass reason. She didn't hesitate for a second to come running when I told her you were hurt. She jumped on a plane. Maddie wouldn't have. But you don't see that because your head is shoved so far up your ass. You forget the bad and focus on how this was somehow your fault. You're not responsible for all the bad shit that happens in life. I swear to God, Jackson, you die and I'll fucking find you in the afterlife and kill you myself." His own emotions become too much as I hear his breath catch.

I hate him in this moment because he says all this when I can't defend myself. There's no chance for me to tell him to shut the fuck up. I don't want to hear what he's saying about Madelyn or Catherine. They aren't the same, but he wasn't there. He didn't see it. He didn't know that once again my decisions had consequences. No, instead he wants to tell me how I'm wrong? Mark better pray I don't come around right now.

After some silence, Mark's breathing returns to normal.

"Hey," Catherine's voice is close and soft. "You okay?"

"No. I'm not." Mark sounds empty.

"Yeah," she pauses and lets out a deep exhale. "Me either."

How long have I been out? It's like I'm in some alternate universe. Some Tim Burton movie where you think you're being drugged. I'm waiting for dancing ponies or a talking pumpkin to appear.

"How long have you been standing there?" Mark questions.

"Just long enough to hear you threatening to kill him yourself. Which I'm sure if he can hear us, he's ready to choke you for." She gives a small half-hearted laugh.

"I'm sure, but at this point I don't give a shit. Hopefully I pissed him off enough to wake up. I thought by now ..."

"Mark, it'll—" Catherine's voice is low.

"Sorry, Kitty. Come here."

She sighs and I imagine he has her wrapped in his arms. Holding her close while I lie here and get to picture it. Why the fuck am I not waking up? The idea of Catherine in any other man's arms is enough to make me want to tear my heart out. I know Mark would never cross that line, but I'm going out of my mind. I need to touch her, hold her, and let her know it's all going to be okay.

"You know, I keep hoping I'll wake up and be back in my apartment and all this will be a bad dream," Catherine says with a shaky voice.

"He's always been that guy in the group who wanted to prove everyone wrong. I hoped I could get him angry enough that his eyes would snap out and he'd be swinging at me." He gives a short laugh, "Well, at least he could try."

He's not that far off. If I could've gotten my body to work I would've. Dickhead.

"But hope is for the weak—I have faith," Mark tacks on.

"Each time you and I talk, I realize I don't know him. We happened so fast, but everything was intense and felt right."

She's wrong. She knows me more than anyone. Catherine sees the things I don't show anyone else. I let her in where it matters. Yet she thinks she knows nothing?

Shimmering lights all around, twinkling and growing brighter as the music plays. The sound of the bass reverberates through me as the drum solo plays in. My entire body vibrates with it.

Bam ... bam ... boom.

Standing at the beach with the sun shining upon my face. No one is here, just me as I wait for her. I close my eyes and breathe in the salt air. Allowing it to calm me, reminding me how I feel at home with the sea.

Slowly my eyes lift and I start to take her in as she walks toward me.

No shoes.

White dress.

As my eyes travel up to her face, I stand rooted in shock. Again she's here.

"Jackson," she whispers. "Come back to me."

My heart stops beating as I gape at her. Six years she was my life and then she was gone. Taking all my hope, my love, and part of my heart when she left. I was empty and dead inside, but now she's here again. Why? Why does she have to take from me over and over? Can't she let me be?

I open my mouth to tell her … fuck, I don't know what I want to say. Each part of me wants to say something different. To yell, beg, scream, and punch my way through this fucking nightmare. Tell her how she destroyed me, made me give up everything for her, only to have her take more.

"Why?" is the only word I'm capable of saying.

She stands unmoving letting my question hang in the air while my heart beats erratically.

"Why?" I ask again more forcefully. She needs to answer me. I step toward her and a smile crosses her perfect lips. "Goddammit, why?"

Her features soften, and as I get closer she finally says, "It wasn't supposed to be."

I stop moving and my eyes close in pain. Ice shoots through my veins leaving me frozen and void.

When I open them she's gone.
All over again.

"Fox, what's your view look like?" I ask trying to get the other half of the guys to give me a status update.

Nothing.

I try a different one. "Razor, do you copy?"

Silence.

"Bronzer, come in. What's your status?" I look around trying to remain still since it's daylight and I have no idea what the fuck is going on.

I turn to Mark and signal him to try. "Fox, Razor, Bronzer, do you copy?"

"We copy. We need to move. Out."

Their location must be compromised. There's no other reason they'd move in daylight. I signal to Aaron and Mark that we need to move.

"If they're on the move, something's wrong. Let's take to the other side and we'll meet them when it's safe," I say as we prepare to head out.

Everything feels rushed. Every moment feels like it's on fast forward. We make it to the edge of the village and try to find a place to wait it out. We're out of range to talk to the other three now, but Razor's in charge. We've done enough missions together to know each other's moves. If I were him, I would wait until the time we selected. We have our extract in three hours. It gives us about two hours to get what we need and get the fuck out of here.

I turn to Aaron, and before I can get a word out,

the percussion of gunfire explodes in the air. We drop to the ground, ready to shoot back.

Pop. Pop. Pop.

Fast and steady, but it's not close to us. We hear screaming and the continuous shooting on the other side of the village. Mark starts calling on the radio to the other half of our team, but we're still out of range.

"Fuck this. We're going in." I grab my gun, and Mark and Aaron are on my heel.

"Muff, the left." I take the guy out before he gets a shot off.

We fall out to the side of the building and start to creep in. I see them. They're shooting, but they're outnumbered. Everything happens in slow motion. I watch the bullet perforate Brian's neck when he stands to take a shot. The stream of blood and the strangled scream he makes echo as he falls. Either Mark or Aaron shoots and kills another three men. We're moving as fast as we can, but it's too late. I eliminate another four by the time I reach Brian.

"Fuck. Hold on." I squeeze his neck trying to stop the bleeding, but his eyes are fading. "Fuck. Call and get the extract in here *now*!" I scream as Aaron's already radioing in our location. "Where is the rest of the team?"

"Jackson! Can you hear me?" Catherine is frantic. Why is she here? What is she doing here? *No!*

She has to get the fuck out of here. She'll die. *Please God don't take her too! I can't.*

"I have to leave soon, I need you to wake up before I go," she whispers and I snap out of it.

Leave? What? No!

"Fight for me, baby."

I'm trying. If only I knew how …

chapter three

Catherine

*D*ays pass by and nothing changes. He doesn't move or speak. I sit here wondering when or if he'll wake. Will he be the same man he was?

Jackson's mother arrived early this morning and she's everything he described her as. Her warmth is evident even in the situation we're currently facing. After she and Mark embraced, she took me into her arms and held me close. I hadn't been sure what to expect, but it certainly wasn't that.

"Mrs. Cole, do you need anything?" I ask timidly.

She smiles and places her hand on mine. "No, sweetheart. I'm okay, and please, call me Nina. I'm just waiting for him to stop being a stubborn ass and wake up." Her sweet voice reassures me that she has all the faith we need.

I smile at her as she sits in the chair next to Jackson. I take the seat on the other side of his bed with the man we love in between us. I grab his hand and hold it, feeling the heat that reminds me he's alive. The constant beeping of the machine gives me something steady to hold on to.

Beep.

Two seconds pass.

Beep.

One. Two.

Beep.

Nina clears her throat drawing my attention. "So tell me, how did you two meet? I wish I knew these things, but Jackson has been distant. His father and I are lucky to hear from him once every six months lately."

She smiles, but even I can hear the undercurrent of disapproval at his lack of contact.

"I didn't know he was being so ..." I struggle to find the right word, because really, I wouldn't know. We never had a meet-the-parents discussion. Not that my family would even require that.

"Oh, honey, it's not your fault. I raised him better than this. Once he wakes up, I'll give him hell, don't you worry. Now, tell me about you and Jackson." Her eyes are alight at the prospect of learning about us. Not that our story has a very happy ending at this point.

"Well, it's kind of embarrassing ... but I fell on him." I giggle remembering that night at the restaurant. "I was out to dinner with my friends, and I tripped and literally fell into his lap. He asked me to have a drink, but I turned him down."

"You did?" Nina smirks, and I blush.

"Yes, I wasn't really ready to ... I don't know, date or contemplate dating anyone. I was hurt pretty badly by my ex. So the last thing I was looking for was a relationship," I try to explain. Too bad I didn't stick to that—it would've saved me some heartache.

Nina shakes her head in understanding. "Ahh, we all have one of those men, don't we? Mine was right before Brendan. I swear I thought we had it all. There was always something keeping me back from going forward. However, as fools in love, we usually push forward against our better judgment. But then Brendan came along and showed me what true love was. So how did you and Jackson end up together?"

My voice softens as I tell our story. "Well, I'm a publicist and my company was bidding for Raven. I won the account and Jackson was thrown back in my life."

"Sounds like fate intervened," Nina says with the voice of wisdom.

Fate or Jackson Cole.

"Yes, it did. We both tried to fight our feelings but I fell all over again. He's patient and understanding. He's everything I need. It was like no matter how hard I tried, I somehow found myself unable to resist him." I bite my lip and sniffle thinking about how much he owns me. "Sorry, I get a little emotional."

"You love him," Nina says as a statement.

"I do." I don't hesitate because it's true. "But I don't know how he feels anymore. He pushed me away when Aaron died. He told me we were done. I just … I couldn't."

"You don't have to explain to me, Catherine. I understand these stupid, stubborn Cole men better than anyone. Jackson has a lot of issues from losing a lot of people he's loved. You have to give him time. He's one of those who feels the weight of the world on their shoulders. He's always been that way. Even as a child. You'll work it out—I have faith."

That word again. Everyone is always saying to have faith. To trust in each other and our faith that things will work out. I've learned on more than one occasion it's not always reality. Life has a way of slapping you in the face and then kicking you a few times just for good measure.

"Our relationship happened extremely fast," I pause trying to figure out how to explain what's in my heart. "It's been a whirlwind, but I thought we were finally on the same page."

Fate intervened again by rearing her ugly face. Reminding me what a cruel bitch she is and that I shouldn't get too comfortable.

"When it's meant to be, things have a way of working themselves out. Brendan and I separated once," Nina says holding my gaze.

"Jackson never mentioned."

"Jackson and Reagan were still young and they probably don't know or don't remember," she explains. "I couldn't take the deployments anymore. The nights of being alone, waiting and wondering. Then there was the fact that he was following his passions while I was stuck at home. I felt trapped."

I'm stunned.

"Wow. What made you guys work it out?"

"I loved him. He was gone, but it wasn't because he didn't love me and the kids. It was quite the opposite. He hated being away. Loathed the times he missed, but he was willing to walk away from his dream for me. But I never wanted to be the reason he gave up the Air Force. I knew he would resent me at some point, if I forced his hand. Imagine knowing you were the reason he gave up his dreams. Give him time, honey. He'll come around."

"God, I hope so."

I have to leave tomorrow. Despite my intention to stay, there's talk about Raven and problems within the company that need to be dealt with. I got an email from my boss asking when I'd return, and I'm running out of excuses as to why I need to be here. Yes, he's my client, but I don't need to sit vigil by his bedside to manage the story. Nina and Mark are out talking to the nurses trying to get answers on the recent spikes in heart rate.

"Jackson," I whisper, softly brushing his hair back. "Baby, I can't do this. I don't know what to think anymore. I need you. Please. Please, I'm so alone." My heart is aching as I beg him. "I l-love you, Jackson. I love you. D-Do you remember the zoo? Remember how you held my hand and we walked through the park?" I pause as the memories of our time together start flooding back. "I remember every moment. I remember how it was when you left me too, and I can't have it end like this. I can't have the last memory I have of you being you walking away from me. I need you to love me. To choose me." The steel in my voice hardens as I become more resolved. This has to work out. "I need you to wake up and be the man who watches movies with me, who holds me when I cry. I need more of that, Jackson. But I'm so scared. I'm so scared you're going to wake up and push me away again—or not wake up at all. I'm terrified that this is it for us. I'm begging you—I …"

"Catherine, honey," Nina says softly behind me.

I swipe my hand across my cheeks and take a calming breath. "Sorry. I'm just …"

There's really nothing I can say at this point. It's unclear when he'll wake, and each day that passes, my hope dwindles.

"He'll come through. You have to be strong."

"I'm trying. It's been so long. And I d-don't want t-to …"

"Do you still have to leave?" his mother asks.

"Tomorrow morning. I have to go back." The words taste bitter as they roll off my tongue. "There are things I can't do from here. God, it's ripping my heart out to leave him when he's still …"

"I know. But you have to keep fighting."

"I hoped he'd be awake by now. I don't want him to think I wasn't here."

"Oh, Catherine, we would never let him think that," Nina pauses. "Why don't I come back later?" She gently pats my hand and grabs her bag.

"Are you sure?"

"Yes, I have some things I need to get done, and I think you need to talk to him. Now, don't you leave without saying goodbye, okay?"

"Of course, thank you so much," I say as she strolls out of the room.

I curl up on his bed careful not to touch any of the wires. I need to touch him, feel his body and warmth. Even if he's not really here with me, it comforts me. All of the anger I held on to is gone. The fact that I could potentially lose him again erases the previous fight. He was so lost in the shock of that phone call and all I wanted to do was be there for him. Yet, he pushed me away.

My hand rests on his chest as I feel his heart beneath me. "I never got to tell you what happened while we were apart." I use this time to tell him about the things we missed during our separation after the fight we had at my apartment. "I read the letter my father wrote me. The night I pushed you away after the fight with Neil, I figured, why not? And I opened it. I sat there on the floor and read everything I always needed to hear from him. He basically apologized for everything. After I got through the entire letter, do you know what I hated most?" I pause, letting the question remain unanswered by him. "That I was more upset about pushing you away. I hated myself for being so weak. For being so scared." Jackson consumed me. He took a part of me I wasn't sure I could give and it made me push against him. "How is that? This man who I've longed for since I was a kid gave me answers, yet all I wanted was you."

And then he left me.

"I never believed in fate, but then I met you. Who falls on someone's lap? I mean, that's just crazy. But it happened." I grab his hand and pull it to my chest, weaving our fingers together.

"Life has managed to slap us around a bit though. We keep fighting this current pushing us the wrong way. Yet here I sit, waiting, hoping, praying you'll wake up and we'll get back on course." Leaning over gently, I press my lips against his cheek and then his lips. I wait, hoping in some ridiculous way I can break the spell. "I hope you know how much you own my heart. And I hate you for it. I hate that you've stripped me of my defenses and made me feel, when all I want to do is be numb. Then this wouldn't hurt so damn much. I would be able to grab my bag and walk away. Let you fight your demons on your own." I take a deep breath. "But instead I'd rather watch you breathe."

Lying here with him, I relish in his touch. I focus

on the man who showed me I was enough, who gave me the strength to love again. With Jackson, I can be me without fear. We both have a lot to overcome, but our love can endure it. He would never cheat or deceive me. Closing my eyes, I let the sound of his monitor lull me to sleep against his shoulder.

I hear the door open and someone moving around. My eyes open and I realize I fell asleep in his bed. Glancing at the sliding door I see the charge nurse enter smiling. Carefully, I climb out of his bed and instantly feel his loss. Being close to him gave me a small amount of solace.

"Sorry, honey, we need to take him for testing."

"Is he okay?"

"They want to run some precautionary tests to make sure there isn't something we're missing," she explains as she moves around the side of his bed.

"Should I be concerned?" I ask as my voice breaks.

She gives me a small smile. "The doctor will be in to talk to you and the rest of his family soon."

I look back at Jackson and bite my fingernail hoping nothing's wrong. It's been eight long days that we've been waiting. The doctors thought he would've woken by now and had been worried about some irregularity in his heart. Suddenly, I see Jackson's hand move.

"Did you see that?" I ask excitedly. "He moved," I say to her, but she smiles and looks away.

"It was probably just a muscle spasm."

The nurse moves his IV, dismissing what I swear I saw. As she moves over to check the paper on his heart monitor, I stare, waiting for something to happen again.

Suddenly, a noise jolts through the room.

Beeeeeeeeeeep.

The sound echoes and time stops. Then everyone is in motion.

"He's crashing!"

"Jackson!" I cry out.

Nurses are running.

"Code blue!"

"What's going on?" I push against the nurse who's lowering his bed.

I can't breathe. Doctors are barking orders, running into the room, but no one will answer me.

"What's happening?" I cry again, trying to get to him. He can't die. "Do something!" I scream and the nurse holds me back.

I fight against her. This can't be happening. "Calm down, Catherine."

"Get the paddles," the doctor orders the people around him.

My stomach falls and I want to die with him.

Please God ... I'll do anything. Please don't take him from me. I can't lose him too.

I sob and clutch my stomach as she pulls me back further. "Jackson, please! Fight!" I call out to him. Begging. Pleading.

"Get her out of here!"

"No!" I try to reach him. "Jackson!"

They push me out of the room and my hands find the cold, glass door. The curtain closes, blocking my view, and my world fades to black.

CHAPTER FOUR

JACKSON

White light.

All I see is the bright glow above me.

The haze of death. This is it.

I inhale and exhale. Fresh air. It's clean and pristine like the radiant light above me. It calls to me, begging me to come.

The luminosity is beautiful and calming.

Am I ready to go?

I know what it feels like to be left behind. The pain of agonizing over the loss of a loved one. Watching them cry and fall apart because they wish it wasn't happening. What will this do to everyone? To Catherine?

I draw a deep breath and wait for something. Hell, anything. Death is pretty anticlimactic. Where's God? Where are the angels and shit? I figured I'd hear some horns or trumpets. "Taps" maybe? I've been gypped.

There are no sounds in heaven.

It's eerie and tranquil.

"Fight, Cole!" I hear someone call out.

Fight for what? For the pain I feel?

No, thanks.

My heart stops and I feel the tension in my body. I try to draw in air but it lodges and I begin to gasp and choke.

Here comes the end.

"Charge to seventy," another voice speaks, and my mind tries to grasp what's happening.

"Clear!" he yells, and a current tears through me.

There are no sounds. No one says anything as the beep registers on the monitor before I let go. I have no fight left.

"Push another round of epi!"

It hurts to breathe, so I stop trying.

The darkness returns and then the light takes over, my vision blurs. I keep my eyes closed.

I'm not ready to go ... to lose everything and everyone. As much as I'd like to live with no guilt and no remorse anymore, I can't leave them all.

So once again, I find the fight I have inside of me. The part of me I rely on when I have to find a way. I'm about to use everything I have left—if I can't get through this black there'll be no going back.

"Charge to eighty."

"Clear."

The electric voltage travels through my body shocking each nerve alive.

"Pulse is eighty," a female voice says.

My chest heaves as I struggle to gain control of my body.

The bright ray returns and it's blinding. Taking all of the warmth I felt before. Now, I'm cold. There's pain everywhere, each bone feels like it's shattering. The fucking agony is unbearable. Maybe death is the better choice if this is the shit I'm going to go through. Although, if this is death shouldn't there not be any goddamn pain?

I'm going to miss her. Maybe I can still hear her, touch her, and see her from heaven. She's my heaven on Earth. She gave me the will to love again, even if it nearly broke us both. She's my downfall too, but it was worth the pain to have the time we had. I never told her though. I never really explained how much she gave me. I'll never have that chance now.

No.

Fuck this.

Regret is a motherfucker.

"Pulse is rising," another voice says.

My eyes open and I see someone in my face. "Cole. Can you hear me? Get the family in here." I struggle to figure out what's going on as my eyes close. "He's waking up."

Time passes and I hear a lot of movement, but I can't focus on anything.

"Jackson, if you can hear us, open your eyes." I feel something press against my arm and tighten.

Drawing a deep breath I smell vanilla. She's here. I will my eyes to open as I feel the pain again. The muscles lock in my body as I will them to obey. The light grows brighter and brighter. Fucking hell, this shit hurts.

"Jackson?" I hear Catherine's voice crack.

I try to move my hand and I feel her soft hand grasp mine. I felt that. All of it. I can feel her skin.

Closing my eyes again, I try to adjust to the light. I'm awake—alive. Tilting my head to the side, I open my eyes and look at her for the first time.

Breathtaking.

That's the only word I can think of. She's beautiful. Even with her puffy eyes and quivering lips—she takes my breath away.

chapter five

Catherine

"Hi," I say softly with tears blurring my vision. He's awake. He's alive. A week of wonder and fear, somehow he fought through it all.

Jackson looks around confused as his heart rate starts to accelerate on the monitor. I wipe the happy tears and try to reassure him by placing my hand against his cheek.

My throat croaks as I try to get my emotions under control. "Shhh ... don't try to talk." His brow furrows as I speak. "You're okay, baby. You're in Germany at the hospital." I reach out and smooth his brow, the desire to touch him is too great. His eyes close as my fingers float across his skin.

When his blue-green eyes open again, they latch on to mine and the emotion shines through. Fear, love, and regret all mashed up. I've missed those eyes.

"Catherine ..." Jackson tries to speak but it's strained.

I lean close and press my lips against his rough cheek. The feel of his skin against mine causes my heart to race. He's really awake and he said my name. "I'm here. Just relax," I try to reassure him. "It's going to be—"

Before I can finish, the doctor draws our attention to him. "Mr. Cole, I'm Dr. Allison. Welcome back. You gave us quite a scare. I'm going to look you over real quick, okay?"

Jackson nods but doesn't try to speak again.

Dr. Allison starts assessing him. "Okay, Jackson. Your heart rate is steady and stable. Blood pressure is a little low, but it's expected. How do you feel?" he asks.

Jackson's strong hand wraps around mine and he gives me a small squeeze. He swallows and winces. "Water?"

"Sure, you can have a little water. I need you to tell me what you last remember," Dr. Allison states in a no-nonsense way.

After he takes a sip, he finally speaks. "I d-don't." He looks around and lets out a huff. "How l-long?"

"You've been unconscious for eight days. Do you have any recollection of how you arrived here?"

Jackson closes his eyes and shakes his head. "I remember the HELO and the sniper." His eyes open as he grips the blanket looking around. "Mark?"

I grasp his hand and he relaxes a little. "He's fine. He'll be here soon. I can call him now," I say looking for my phone.

"No." Jackson tightens his grip. "Am I o-okay?" He asks the doctor apprehensively.

"Your injuries were quite severe and you had a few complications during surgery. And extreme blood loss. Your body has endured an intense trauma and I want to keep a close eye on your heart."

Jackson's eyes close and his grip loosens a bit.

"Is he going to be okay?" I ask

"He's young, strong, and he's out of the coma now. He's not out of the woods, but we'll watch him closely," Dr. Allison explains and looks over the monitors.

I glance at Jackson and his eyes open again. "What about my leg?" he asks with fear in his voice.

Dr. Allison turns and pats his shoulder before speaking. "The injury to your leg was a through and through, which should heal in a few weeks. The bullet that entered your abdomen caused some damage to your spleen. We were able to repair the injury and stop the bleeding. As for your shoulder, there's some muscle damage, but we can address all that later." He takes a break and allows Jackson a few seconds to gather his thoughts.

"Jackson, do you remember anything else?" I ask softly.

His eyes are pensive as he shakes his head. "Not much." He clears his throat and grabs the cup to drink again.

"That's normal," Dr. Allison states.

Jackson's eyes dart to me and he squints. It seems like he's trying to remember. His fingers release mine as he rubs his face. "You shouldn't be …" he trails off.

My heart sinks. Maybe I should've left a few days ago. We're not together, things didn't end well, and then I'm here when he wakes up. I look at the clock and realize my flight leaves in three hours. I can still make it if I leave now.

"My flight is in a few hours, I need to call the airlines." I reach for my phone. "I'll call everyone and give you a few minutes with the doctor." He grabs my arm before I can turn completely.

"Don't." He coughs and winces. "Please," he says, still holding my arm.

I nod while returning to his bedside. "Okay." I'll

stay for now. It feels like it's been so long since the fight happened. In reality it has been, but Jackson wasn't really here and we have a lot to talk about. I don't know where I stand, what he's feeling, so many questions, and I'm not sure I want the answers.

Jackson returns his gaze to the doctor but doesn't relinquish his hold on me.

Dr. Allison checks his shoulder wound and then his leg. "You need to take things easy. Rest as much as you can. You still have a long road ahead of you. I'll be back in a little while to check on you again. Do you have any questions?"

"How long … here?" Jackson says while grimacing.

"You'll be here at least another week. I'll give you something for the pain. For now, we need to make sure there aren't any further complications. If you need anything just buzz me," Dr. Allison explains and leaves the room.

Jackson closes his eyes as the nurse inserts medicine into his IV. I try to extract my hand, but he tightens his fingers and looks at me.

Our eyes lock. "It's going to be okay," I say softly, trying to absorb the fact that he's alive and okay. We gaze at each other, neither of us saying a word, yet it's as if we're having an entire conversation. I give him everything through this moment. Opening myself wide open so he can see all the feelings I've held the last two weeks. The tears stream like raging rivers down my face, but I don't care enough to stop them. It's grief, anger, elation, and so much more. My emotions stack up like bricks around me one by one until I feel buried. I want to breathe again. I want him to be my air.

Jackson lifts his hand and presses it against my cheek. "S-sorry," he stutters and I lean into him. Needing to have the closeness of skin on skin. His eight-day-old beard scratches against my face, but I want to feel—remember how eight days ago his life hung in the balance and today we almost lost him.

How is it possible to love someone this much but hurt so much more? He's taken my heart and I don't know that I'll ever get it back. "Do you want me to call everyone?" I ask, trying to break the silence.

"No," he says with an air of finality. "Just you." His eyes close and he fights to open them again.

My throat goes dry as I try to breathe. "Okay, but—"

"Don't leave me," he says as his lids fall.

I need to be close to him—this could be my last chance. I climb and sit on the bed facing him. My hands brush his hair back as my heart races. He steals my breath, and all the strength I have is gone. I allow the tears to fall as I'm overcome with emotion. I continue to touch his face, his hair, and he settles as his hand rests on my leg.

"Sleep. I'm not going anywhere," I say as he tries to relax, but I can sense his unease.

"Promise?" he asks hesitantly.

"Yes, I'll be here when you wake up." I smile and press my lips against his cheek.

His eyes close as he drifts off to sleep.

Watching him stirs all of my fears. What if he doesn't wake up again? What if he wakes up different than this time? The trepidation gnaws at me and embeds deep inside. I grab my phone and call Mark and his mother to let them know they should head here. Neither one answers, so I send them both messages.

"Hey," I hear Mark come in the room behind me.

"Hi, I sent you a text message." I place Jackson's hand down and he stirs.

"He moved!" Mark's loud voice booms through the room.

"Yes, shhh … he just woke up for about five minutes," I say and push him out the door so we can talk in the hall. "It was really brief but he woke up. I tried to call you earlier. God, Mark. He crashed. I almost died. *He* almost died. Then they came back and brought me in there and I thought he was dead." I take a deep breath and shake while Mark wraps his arms around me.

"But he's okay, right?" Mark asks, trying to sound strong, but I hear the undercurrent of fear.

"I think so. I mean, he fucking died! I was there and they pushed me out of the room. Where were you? I called. I-I was so scared!" I start to sob as Mark rubs my back.

"I'm sorry. It's okay though. He'll be fine?" he asks again.

"The doctors checked him over. He said a few things and then fell back asleep."

"He'll wake back up, right?" Mark asks both excited and a little nervous.

"Yes, the doctors said he'll be tired and needs to rest," I reassure him.

I start to pace a little, trying to work through my thoughts. My heart is so full it could beat right out of my chest, but at the same time I'm terrified. There's a long road ahead for Jackson. He will most likely need physical therapy, his company is going through a lot of changes, and he's yet to deal with Aaron's death. The status of our relationship isn't my first priority, but I can't pretend that it doesn't lie heavily on my mind.

Mark grabs my shoulders, stopping me from walking past him again. "Hey, Kitty, calm down and stand still. What happened when he woke up?"

We stand in the hallway as I replay the few minutes he was awake. Mark looks a hundred years younger just from knowing he was able to talk and move. I bite my lip when I think about how intense his eyes were asking me to stay. I'm so damn confused.

"All of this is good—hell, it's fucking great! Did you cancel your flight?" Mark asks as he pulls me into a hug. His deep voice sounds lighter and more carefree.

I push back and start creating a plan. He's awake now but I need to handle the things I've neglected. "I need to reschedule it. I'm not sure what I should do now." I run my hands through my hair and try to think.

His arms cross his chest as he puffs his chest out making himself seem scary. "Well, you better not fucking leave now. You know he'll flip his shit. All the business crap can wait. He needs you. Whether you two can get your heads out of your asses long enough to see it or not … you both need each other," Mark says with one brow raised, clearly not budging.

"Let me make some calls to the office and see if we can release a statement on his condition tomorrow. It should help both Raven and Cole Security. In regards to the rest of our shit, we'll work it out. But today is definitely not the day, so give me a chance to think."

"I'm letting you know now … I won't watch you

two fuck this up," Mark states standing there as the anger rolls off of him.

Great.

Now I have a big brother—or the male version of Ashton. This should make things fun.

"You can't fix this," I reply with my arms crossed.

"I didn't say I could. I'm just saying you two are going to fix this before I leave. I don't know what the hell happened, but when he got on that plane, his head wasn't right. Then you've been spouting off shit about how you shouldn't be here since day one. So, here's my thinking, which I'm usually right—you two got in a fight before he got on the plane. Now, my first inclination would say Jackson was his normal jackass self. But then again I know what a jackass you were a few days before that." He states and pauses.

"He left me," I say as I ball my fists. He's got me so angry. I don't want to talk about any of this. I was stupid when I pushed him away and then Jackson did the same thing.

"I'm not going to lecture you on the reasonings of Jackson Cole. He acts like he was the only one in Iraq. You'll never meet someone more loyal than him. At the same time, you'll never meet someone who thinks he's more at fault for the bad shit in the world. Like I said: fucking jackass." Mark smiles trying to lighten the mood a little and pulls me into his side. "I've seen him up and I've seen him in the lowest place you can ever imagine. But when he was with you, he was different. Happy."

I look at him with my mouth gaping open at his statement. He squeezes my shoulders and lets that sink in around me.

"Enough of this shit. Tell me, have you talked

to Ashton?"

I laugh and slap his chest. "She'd chew you up and spit you out."

His booming laugh reverberates through the halls and we get a few looks from the nurses. "You tell her any time she wants to chew me up, she's more than welcome." He smirks and walks away.

I stand there thinking about all he said and decide to call Ashton to fill her in.

"Hey, Biffle," her cute voice comes through.

"Hi." I let out a sigh wishing she was here.

"You at the airport?" she asks probably thinking that's what has me sounding forlorn.

"No. I missed my flight. Jackson woke up." The smile spreads across my face as I think about how many days we waited on bated breath for this to happen.

"Cat!" Ashton screams into the phone. "That's fantastic! I'm so happy. Is he okay?" she asks excitedly.

"He died, Ash. Literally. They brought him back and he's okay now, but he died. I thought I lost him."

"Wow, are you okay? Is he okay?" she asks with concern prevalent in her voice.

"I'm okay. I think. Yes, he seems okay," I sigh and shake my head. "It was a short amount of time he was up, but he has a long road ahead of him. The doctor told him to rest as much as he can. But I can't leave now."

She snorts at the last statement. "Like I thought you would. Gimme a break, you weren't going to make the flight regardless. You've stood by his bedside waiting, and I get it. He's your guy, babe."

"He is, but am I his girl?" The words slip out like

poison in my blood. I don't know the answer to that question and it eats at me.

Ash let's me stew before she finally speaks again. "He'll let you know that in one way or another. You both push against each other, for whatever reason. I've said my peace to you more times than I care to think about. Don't fuck this up, Catherine. Do you hear me?" She's stern bordering on hostile.

"Yes, Mom."

We both start laughing at my acquiescence. I miss her so much. Being around her and having her to lean on makes things easier. Mark's been great, but he's no Ashton. Although my friendship with him has grown stronger, she's the rock in my life. I fill her in on the entire few minutes I had with him along with the worries I have.

"They're all normal feelings," Ashton reassures me.

"I'm ready for some damn happy times."

"I think you both need a come-to-Jesus moment and it'll all work out. Until then, be patient and remember guys like it when you push them around a little bit. So be the bitch for once."

I wish I could. It's never been that way for me other than in business. When I'm dealing with a client or the press, I don't back down.

I exhale loudly. "I need to get back in there. I should make sure Mark isn't poking him in the face," I explain.

"How is that dipshit?" Ashton asks at the mention of Mark.

During the few days Ash stayed in Germany, they flirted a bit. I don't think anything actually happened, but they seemed to get along well. Mark needed her strength when I wasn't able to keep it together. After his surgery, Jackson was touch and go for a while. There was no holding each other up because we were both crumbling. I've never seen someone so desolate. But Ashton was there, propping us both up, holding his hand and making sure he remained strong, while also keeping me from falling apart. She's really a remarkable woman.

"He's fine. Have you two spoken at all since you left?" I wonder.

She lets out a deep breath and I picture her sinking in a chair. "No, it wasn't like that for me. He lives in Virginia, number one, and number two, I think we'd kill each other. It's like who can be the biggest smart ass."

I laugh because it's completely true. They would either fuck constantly or beat the shit out of each other. Between her strength and his sarcasm, it's like setting a match to a piece of wood soaked in gasoline.

"It would be so much fun to watch though. I don't know when I'll be back. Is everything going okay?" I ask.

"Yeah, everything is fine. Look, you need to be there. He's going to need you, Cat. In so many ways, that man needs you," Ashton says as her strength resonates through the phone.

"I need him too. I just need him to not dick me around. I want him to want me, not push me away again," I explain with my heart breaking all over again.

"If I remember correctly, you did quite a bit of pushing as well."

I huff at her not-so-gentle reminder. "Yes, I know. I got this lecture from Mark already."

"Good. Maybe you'll realize that you have to

fight for what you want. Nothing in this life is guaranteed. So fight for him! Fight with every ounce of your being."

"I plan to. He's worth it. I can't make him love me though," I say effectively shutting her up.

"No, you can't. Nor do you want to. But I don't think that's a fight you'll have."

I peek my head in to see him still sleeping. "Okay, I need coffee, so I'm going to run. I love you and I'll try to call you in a few days. Miss you, Biffle."

"Miss you more. Kiss Jackson for me and maybe Mark too."

"I will," I reply with a smile.

I put my phone in my pocket and walk to the family waiting area and grab a cup of coffee. I should've been getting on a plane in a few minutes, instead I'm here, because he asked me to stay. So many questions float in my head. Sinking into the chair, I rest my head back and try to get a grip. I've never had a moment as scary as watching him flat line. My heart starts to race when I replay them pushing me away as he was dying. Needing a few minutes of peace, I close my eyes.

This trip I've only slept in bits and pieces, never more than two hours at a time. And never in a bed, most of it was in a chair at his bedside. I think over the conversations with Jackson's mother, Ashton, and Mark through the past week. Some of their words really strike a chord in me. I'm not the same girl I was a few months ago and I'm definitely not the same one who pined over Neil. The girl who thought she wasn't good enough for any man and deserved to be treated like shit. I won't be neglected or cheated on again because I deserve more. I won't stand for someone who will sleep with my friend, or walk away and not look back. Jackson gave me more. He allowed me to open my heart again, but at the same time I'm not sure if he's ready to give me the same ...

I sit there and let it all sink in. I look at the clock and realize two hours have passed. I must've fallen asleep. Scrambling up, I grab my now-cold coffee and head back.

Entering the room, my breath hitches as I look up and I catch a glimpse of his smile as he sees me. He's awake again. Looking at him, I know what I have to do. I'll stay for as long as he wants me to be here, but at some point we're going to talk about everything, because I can't go through him walking out like that again. Neither of us deserves to go through any more pain, and I won't be the one to inflict it upon him.

chapter
six

"I thought you left." Jackson's voice cracks at the end.

I step forward to his bed and give a tiny shake of my head. "No. I was on the phone and then I fell asleep in the chair. I told you I wasn't going to leave."

"Oh," is all he says before looking over at Mark.

Mark scoffs, "Dude, I fucking told you she'd be back. Pussy."

Jackson gives him the finger and smiles. It's nice to see them together. I can still feel the weight of our worry about how this would play out.

I stand there awkwardly in the room, unsure of what to do. We survey each other with the questions and uncertainty stifling in the room. Each tick of the clock my anxiety builds.

Mark clears his throat, "Well, I can see I'm not needed here. And you two need to talk. I'm going to make some calls—including your mother again. She hasn't answered and I'm afraid she might kill someone. That woman scares the shit out of me." He gently clasps Jackson's shoulder. "Glad to see you decided to stop being an asshole and finally woke up. Maybe next time you won't be so dramatic about coming back to life." Mark smiles at me and looks back at Jackson. "We'll catch up later."

Jackson smirks and Mark walks by and kisses my cheek. "Be good and call me if you need anything. Talk to him."

"Catherine, please come here." Jackson puts his hand out and waits.

Stepping forward until my leg hits the bed, I shudder from his proximity. He draws this from me. His presence and power elicits these reactions from my body without permission. Jackson grabs my hand and rubs slow circles against my skin. I close my eyes and savor his touch.

"Are you okay?" he asks.

My eyes open and I stand there shocked. "Shouldn't I be asking you that?"

"Mark told me. He said you were alone in the room," he explains.

"Yes ... no ... I don't know. I've never been more scared in my life. I wasn't sure if you were alive or dead. I just ..." I can't say anything else without losing it. I don't want to think about what happened. My heart pounds and my chest heaves.

"I'm sorry, baby."

"Jackson," I say softly.

"Forgive me. I was a complete tool." His eyes tell me it isn't about what happened hours ago.

"Please, I don't want to talk about this now." I struggle as I say the words. As much as I want answers, his health is far more important.

"I can't wait to make this right. I need to fix—"

"No." I put my hand up and soften my voice. "You can't fix everything any more than you can save everyone."

He pulls my hand and I sink on to the bed. "I can fix *this*. I was wrong." Jackson's eyes swim with unease.

I love this man. That's the bottom line. I don't want to spend any more time apart. We've already lost two weeks because of our insecurities and fears and misguided heroics. At what cost? We're both miserable and fighting for the same thing, but both scared.

"Yes, you were. But please, let's talk about all this later." He looks exhausted and he needs to rest. The last thing I want is to be the cause of any complications.

Jackson looks away uncomfortably. "All I can think about is that you won't be here if I go to sleep. When I opened my eyes and saw you I thought I'd died."

"What? Why would you think that?" I ask confused.

He turns to me with love and conviction as he grips my hand. "Catherine, you're my heaven. So I thought I was dead, because that's when I thought I'd see you again."

I'm speechless. Which never happens, but seriously? That's his answer? I lean forward and kiss him. With my lips pressed against him, everything feels right. It's like the world has righted itself in this single instant. Gently, my fingers touch his face as I memorize this moment. I hold all I need between my hands.

I lean back and meet his eyes still holding his face. "Every time you manage to do this to me."

"Do what?" His brow furrows.

"Disarm me. Make me forget everything. The thing is ..." I draw in a deep breath and let it out, staying locked in his eyes as I do. "You left me. You walked out the door. After you promised you wouldn't do that." Tears form in my eyes as I remember the heartache I felt at that moment.

Jackson reaches toward my face and winces. "I know. I fucked up. I wasn't able to think of anything other than I had to get away from you."

His words are like a knife through my heart. "You had to get away from me?"

"I needed to save you in that moment. Do you understand I killed a man?" Jackson asks.

"No, you didn't." He breaks my heart when he says these things. The turmoil and guilt he carries is unnecessary. The man who would do anything for anyone somehow has this warped view of himself. He's noble, kind, forgiving, and yet he thinks somehow he intentionally or even unintentionally causes these things.

Jackson grabs my chin forcing me to look at him. "I'm not asking you to understand it. Fuck. I don't understand it. But I want us. I want this to work. Stay with me."

"I almost lost you. Not once but twice," I say, enunciating my words, trying to make him understand. "I don't know what I would've done if you had died. I couldn't breathe, I couldn't think. I had to stand there waiting for them to tell me I'd lost you forever."

He grabs on to his shoulder, grimacing in pain.

"I'm here now," he retorts.

The urge to touch him is so great I can't fight it. My hand tenderly tangles in his hair as his eyes close. "Yes, by a miracle. There are a lot of things we need to agree upon before we can just go back."

Settling a little, he opens one eye before saying, "You're still not answering me."

My smile spreads from his playfulness. "We can talk later," I assure him.

His breathing regulates as the muscles in his body relax. I'm hopeful his pain is subsiding. "Promise me," I hear him whisper.

"Promise you what?"

"You won't leave me. I'd be lost." Jackson's eyes lock on mine. I watch the fear roll through them like a storm.

"I'll always find you, Jackson," I say, reciting the words he spoke to me when I told him how I feel around him. Leaning down, I place my lips against his and a low hum comes from his chest. Pulling back, I see the satisfaction shining in his eyes.

Jackson sighs and cups my face with his good hand. "I love you, Catherine Pope. I'm a complete and total fucking idiot for leaving you that night. Please, forgive me. Be mine. Let me fix us."

My lips part at his admission. He's never said those three little words. Each nerve in my body tingles and my throat grows thick.

I lean forward and grip his face in my hands. "You just did."

"I mean it. I love you. I should've told you that before I left. I don't want to lose you." His eyes bore into mine, showing the honesty of his words.

My heart is so full. Jackson looks at me waiting for me to say something. The words fall from my lips effortlessly, "I love you. But there are some things I need from you."

"Anything and it's yours."

"You might want to hear them first," I laugh.

"Name it."

I sigh not wanting to have this conversation so soon, but he's insistent. "Okay, you know I have ..." I pause struggling to find the right word. "Fears ... I've been hurt by a lot of men."

Jackson grips my hand. "I know and I'm sorry I'm one of them."

"Let me try to get this out." Jackson nods and I continue. "When you left me that night, I didn't think I would ever talk to you again. You hurt me much more than Neil ever did. I can't ever go through a breakup like that again. Cheating, lying, manipulating me ... these are non-negotiable—complete deal-breakers. I won't stand for it. I need honesty, respect, loyalty."

"I don't have a problem with loyalty, Catherine."

"You need to really understand. I've seen it all happen. I watched my worst nightmare unfold. My dad left, Neil broke me, and then you turned around and walked away—immediately after I'd faced my own fears. I know what I did was wrong. I know that I shut you out and let my fears push you aside. For that, I'm so sorry."

"I understand fear, baby."

"But you saved me. You gave me hope that I could be enough for you. Losing you would devastate me. If you want someone else, then please end it with me first. I'll promise you the same."

His hand grips the back of my neck and he pulls me to his mouth. His kiss is rough and strong. It penetrates every inch of my body. It seals everything in that moment. We're going to be okay. We'll fight together and find a way. I break the kiss and the smile that forms across his face obliterates any remaining anger. "You'll never have to worry about me straying from you. I've got everything I need right here," he vows.

I sit there and watch him drift to sleep with hope soaring in my heart.

The next few days pass without any issues. Jackson's shoulder and leg are healed enough that they want him to start physical therapy. His abdomen is still where the primary concern is. Most of our days are spent talking and going over business issues. He's not happy with pushing back the launch of the new product. The press release was bumped back a few weeks, and I've now decided there needs to be a party after. I know he's against it, but in the long run it's better for him and for Raven.

"Your father is probably starving to death at this point. Plus Reagan is driving him insane," Jackson's mother says with a smile. Her flight is in a few hours. She was reluctant to leave but said he's in good hands. Plus she has to get back to the States with his sister getting married in a month.

"Probably, she's always been high maintenance."

"Oh, and you're not?"

"I'm a saint."

Nina and I burst out laughing as Jackson looks around as if he's serious.

Jackson clears his throat, "Whatever, I'm sure Dad is living on chips and beer."

"I'll never understand you men. You claim you're all big and bad, fought in wars and all, yet you can't manage to make anything more than a sandwich," Nina scoffs.

"I can also make pasta, so I'm better than Dad."

His mom rolls her eyes and then points her finger at him. "Now, you call me when you get back to New York. No more of this once-every-blue-moon phone calls. Do you understand me?" She straightens her back and grabs the handle of her bag.

"Yes, ma'am," Jackson says with a grin.

It's great watching them interact. He obviously loves her very much and she adores him. She leans in and kisses his cheek and then pats it.

Nina turns to me and smiles, "I want you to call me as well."

"Me?" I ask confused.

"Yes, you. If you ever need to talk, you have my number. Don't be a stranger and take good care of him, but don't baby him too much. He'll become even more of a pain in the ass than he is now." She laughs and kisses my cheek. "Okay, I expect to hear from you both soon and be good to each other."

"Bye, Mom," Jackson says as she throws her hand up but keeps moving out the door.

I watch as Nina heads into the elevator trying to subtly wipe her cheeks. The fear she must've felt having her son nearly die has to be overwhelming. I look back at the man I almost lost and my chest tightens. It was so close to that. Not wanting to be away from him, I climb on the bed and nestle into his chest.

"Hi," he says with a chuckle.

"Hi," I say back softly. I need to feel his warmth.

"You okay?" he asks clearly concerned with my sudden need to be with him.

I snuggle in closer and his hand gently grazes my arm as I relax into his embrace. "I'm fine. I just wanted to touch you," I explain.

His laugh is close to a bark. "I'll never deny you touching me." I feel his lips touch the top of my head and my eyes close of their own accord. "I can't wait until we can do much *more* touching."

My giggle escapes as I slap his chest. "Ass."

"I'm in a hospital bed. You shouldn't ask to see my ass."

I scoot closer so I can look at him. The smile spreads across my face at his teasing. "I don't recall asking to see anything. In fact, I have no desire to see anything at all." I quirk my brow challenging him.

"Really? Is that so?" he asks as his hand slides down my side.

"Yup, no desire." I try to control my breathing as his hand glides back up and gently rubs against the side of my breast.

"Interesting …" He trails off as his hand makes its way around the front, outlining my bra.

My acting abilities are far from perfect and I'm sure he can tell the change in my breathing. I feel my nipples harden as he dips his finger inside my shirt. The warmth of his breath against my ear causes me to shiver. Damn him.

"Still no desires?" His voice is husky and low.

Turning my head toward him, I nod. The fire is coursing through my veins. I try to hold still, but his hand grips the back of my neck and he pulls me down, stopping right before I touch his lips. Somehow, I hold back a groan, but I don't want to always be so predictable. I need to hold my own with him or he'll swallow me up. Plus, I know it turns him on when I give it back to him.

His eyes practically glow as he's waiting for me to make the next move. It's only been a few seconds, but it feels like years as we keep our eyes locked. I grip his face and tenderly press my lips against his. We don't rush the kiss. Jackson's hand tangles in my hair as he holds me against him. I revel in his embrace. His love blankets me and in this moment it hits me like a bolt from the sky.

He loves me.

Warmth radiates through my body and I could cry with joy. This beautiful man who I love with my whole heart loves me back. A tear falls and slides between us.

Jackson breaks the kiss. "Hey," he says with concern. "You're crying. What's wrong? Did I do something?"

"No, no. I think it just hit me," I say earnestly.

"What hit you?"

"It's been a crazy few weeks. I've lived in a constant state of worry, but you're okay, I'm okay, we're okay. I feel like I can breathe again."

"I'm here, baby. I'm not going anywhere. I love you," he says as he cradles my head.

"I love you too, Jackson."

"Good, now feel free to kiss me again." He smiles and pulls me closer.

"You've got a lot of making up to do, Muffin." I bring my lips to his before he can say anything else.

chapter seven

"I'm ready to get home," Mark says leaning back in the chair while propping his leg up. "You fuckers are boring and I miss my bed."

Jackson sighs, "I need you to get back and make sure things are still running. Catherine won't give me any details." He's so focused on everyone else it's driving me nuts.

"You need to worry about yourself, not the companies or any other crap. I have Raven covered. Danielle is doing an excellent job. Mark has everything with Cole Security under control. Stop being a baby," I chastise him playfully.

There's a knock on the door as Dr. Allison enters. "Good afternoon." He approaches Jackson and shakes his hand. "How are you feeling?"

"Good. Ready to get out of here," Jackson replies.

"I bet you are," he says, examining the wound on his shoulder, and I see Jackson's hand clench. "Everything is really healing well. There are no infections and your leg looks a lot better. You need to start your therapy and we want you to start getting mobile. I could see you going home as soon as next week."

"Thank God. I need to get the hell out of this bed." Jackson's entire demeanor changes. He's animated and starts to throw the blankets off himself.

"Don't we want to take this slow?" I ask hesitantly. Taming him is going to be impossible.

Dr. Allison smiles. "Yes, this won't be an easy road, Jackson. You have injuries on both sides of your body. Your left shoulder will be the biggest issue. It has to remain immobile for another week or two. Our goal is for it to heal without further injury. Also, you can't bear any weight on your leg yet, and without use of your arm, you won't be able to use crutches. There will be a lot of things that will require someone to help you." The doctor looks at me.

He scoffs and says, "I'm sure I'll manage just fine." Jackson turns his head, clearly frustrated.

"I'm sure you could, but you'd also be right back in the hospital with another surgery," the doctor states matter-of-factly.

I lean in and grasp his hand before he looks up at me. "What did you think, babe? You were shot. Three times," I remind him gently. "You're going to have to take it easy so you don't end up back in here because you screwed up your leg again."

"I'll be fine, Catherine."

"Yes, you will, because you're not going to fight me on this." I smile and tilt my head letting him know I'm not playing around. He can be defiant all he wants, but he's not going to hurt himself because he has to be all macho. We see where that got him.

Mark laughs, "I see who wears the pants in this relationship."

Dr. Allison steps in before Jackson can reply to Mark. "Jackson, there are some things that will either be too painful or flat out impossible with your injuries. We can arrange a live-in nurse or you can stay with friends or family."

"No," is his only reply.

"Then we can arrange for you to be transported to a rehabilitation center," the doctor answers smoothly while writing something on his chart.

Jackson looks at me and his eyes say it all. He's extremely unhappy. This is a man who fights through pain. He has no desire to be laid up and babied. "Well?"

I laugh at his one-word question. "Well, what?"

"Well, am I going to stay with my parents or do you want to stay with me?" he asks and lifts his brow.

"Are you going to be an asshole?"

"Aren't I always, according to you?" Jackson says with a half-hearted laugh.

I giggle and kiss his cheek. "I guess I'll stay with you, but you're going to owe me."

"Like I don't already," he chuckles and squeezes my hand before turning toward the doctor. "Okay, when can we get back to the States?"

"Let's get you up a few times and then we'll start talking about release and ways you can move around safely." Dr. Allison closes his chart and heads out the door.

Mark walks over and puts his hand on my shoulder. "I'm going to book my flight back home. There are still issues we need to go over and things we need to take care of. Natalie needs some help too."

Jackson's face falls and his entire body tenses. "I need to call her. We need to do something."

Mark nods. "I already had them send his body Stateside. I transferred money over, but knowing you, you'll do more. She's probably ready to have the baby any day, so I'd like to at least be there. I know her family is there, I just feel like he'd want ..."

"Go," is all Jackson says and Mark once again nods.

"The private plane is here so you can get back home that way." Mark squeezes me to his side and kisses the side of my head. "Take care of him. Slap him if he's a dick, which I'm sure he will be."

"Hands off her if you want to keep them," Jackson warns.

Mark laughs at his threat. "Funny, dickface. You're so scary lying in bed wearing a pretty dress. I could haul her over my shoulder and you couldn't stop me."

"Try me."

Trying to diffuse the excess testosterone pulsing through the room I put myself between the two of them. "Okay, okay. Both of you are badasses and *ohhh* so scary."

They both burst out laughing and Jackson pulls me on the bed.

"Oh, Kitty. You're so cute," Mark says and ruffles my hair. "He isn't scary at all. Neither are you. But seriously slap him, and if he's really being a fucker you can poke his shoulder." Mark laughs and Jackson glares at him.

"Don't you have a plane to catch?" Jackson's question is harsher than I've heard him with Mark.

"Relax, he was a perfect gentleman when you were unconscious." I stand and give Mark a hug.

Mark pulls me close to which I can hear Jackson grumble behind me, but Mark was a great friend through this time. He was strong when I felt weak, and he gave me faith that when Jackson woke, we'd find our way. Sure, he gives me hell too, but that's par for the course.

"Don't fuck this up," Mark says as he pulls away.

I'm going to miss him. He's like the brother I never had. The one who picks on you, but if anyone else did he'd kill them. Which he's more than capable of doing.

"When I'm back to normal we're going to roll."

"I think you could use a good ass kicking," Mark says as he laces his fingers and cracks them.

"Dude, you've never beaten me when we wrestle. Ever," Jackson smirks.

Mark puts his arms up and flexes as I roll my eyes. These two are worse than a couple of kids. "I'm ready for you, Muffin. Now be good to her."

"I'm always good. Well ... that depends on your definition."

Mark laughs as he walks over to Jackson.

"Maybe, but I'm better."

"Be careful getting home, glitter boy."

Mark leans close and whispers something and Jackson's eyes dart to me before closing and shutting me out.

My gut tightens as I try to calm the fears that that one single moment brought out of me. His eyes showed pure fear at whatever Mark said.

"Catherine?" Mark says snapping me out of my trance.

"Sorry," I say shaking my head to rid myself of the panic traveling through my body. What could've made him look so scared?

"I said I'll call in a few days. Check in on how we need to handle the press statement for both companies. Is that how you still want to proceed?" Mark asks studying my face.

I smile and nod. "Yeah, that sounds fine. The release is next month so I'd like to maybe push it all to happen at once. If I can control the story we can keep the shareholders happy and show that we're business as usual."

Jackson clears his throat drawing my attention back to him. "Are there any issues I should be concerned about?" he asks.

"Nope," I say turning to Mark so I don't betray my false statement.

There aren't huge issues per se, but there was a dip yesterday. The fact that Jackson hasn't personally addressed his company has spooked a few people. During the last few years, there has been a lot of change and this appears to be another moment of instability. While I've been able to handle a few small things, the bottom line is I need to make a formal statement and I need to be in New York City to stay on top of it. Being here is delaying the news. I'm putting out fires instead of preventing them.

"Okay." Mark looks over my shoulder to Jackson and then back to me. "I'll see you guys soon." Mark walks to Jackson and places his hand on his shoulder. "Glad you didn't die. I would've had to kill you."

Jackson laughs and playfully smacks him in the stomach. "Thanks for being here."

"No thanks needed. Just don't do it again." He winks and kisses my cheek before heading out the door. I'm going to miss him even though he gives me hell.

"Then there were two," I hear Jackson say, his voice heavy with emotion.

Not wanting to be away from him for even a second, I smile softly and snuggle into his side, careful not to touch his leg. We don't speak, we enjoy the solace of being in each other's arms. Together—in every sense of the word—we found our way back through the storm. Despite the rough seas, we discovered our calm waters.

I don't know how I'm going to handle pretty much living with him. Even when I was engaged to Neil, we never lived together. I'm determined to be more open with my feelings, give him everything, including my trust. While there is a large part of me unsure how I'll fight against every defense mechanism I've built, I know it's our only chance of survival.

chapter eight

His breathing grows deeper and steadier after a few moments of lying silently. I hear the vibrating of my phone and extract myself carefully so as to not wake Jackson. Grabbing my phone, I see it's a New York number.

"Hello?" I say quietly as I exit the room.

"Hey, babe, it's Gretchen."

Immediately I smile hearing the sound of one of my best friend's voices. I miss them both so much. "Hey, stranger."

"How's Jackson doing?" she asks with concern.

I smile looking back into the room where he sleeps peacefully. "Really well. I'm hoping we'll be out of here soon. How are you?"

"Good. You know me, always busy. Anyway, I'm calling because I heard some rumors floating around about Neil from a few of my lawyer friends."

My good mood fades instantly at the sound of his name.

"Why would you hear that?"

"When the fight between Jackson and Neil happened I asked a few to listen for your name or Neil's."

My gut sinks. "What rumors?" I ask her, already knowing where this is going.

She sighs and I hear her shuffling some papers.

"Right now he's looking for a lawyer to go after you pro bono for losses he's sustained. The engagement ring and the ring you purchased. I heard a few things about assault but no one is grabbing his case at this point. Ashton told me about the fight before Jackson left. I know why you didn't want to tell me, but she knew I could help. I called in a few favors and had everyone keep an ear out. One of my friends called and I explained I have possession of evidence to show that Neil assaulted you."

"How?" I ask quickly. What evidence does she have?

"You had some pretty nasty bruises. Ashton took photos and sent them to me. Do you want to retain me as your legal counsel?" Gretchen asks.

"Of course. I wanted to tell you, but everything happened so fast and I-I just ..." I trail off not really knowing what else to say at this point.

"I know. I'm going to handle this. You don't need to worry yet. But you may want to forewarn Jackson. Also I think we have a good shot at getting Neil to back down if we can show him our proof. And it's civil at this point, but I'm concerned he'll go towards criminal for the assault if we can't get him to withdraw. Seriously, though," she pauses, "I'm very good at being scary." I can almost hear her smile at the last sentence.

I laugh, "I know all too well."

"I think you need a refresher."

"Have mercy on me. It's been a rough couple weeks."

"Fine, I'll give you this one. Go be with that sexy man of yours. I love you."

"Love you too, Gretch. We'll talk soon," I reply.

"You bet. Don't worry about a thing. I'll handle

the garbage." She giggles and disconnects the call.

All of this over what? Money? A ring? When did he really become so shallow? Sure, the ring is not small, but he makes a good salary. We both do, which is why things were never difficult. It wasn't like one of us was coming into the marriage making a lot more than the other. I made a little more since my last promotion, but his company started him off higher than I did.

I shake my head and head back into the room.

"How's Gretchen?" Jackson asks, rubbing his eyes.

"Good. Sorry I woke you."

He smiles and holds his arm out, inviting me back to where I was before. "You didn't, I just noticed you weren't here," he says earnestly.

"Awww, you missed me, huh?" I tease him.

"I miss you even when you're here."

I smile and climb into his embrace again. "You really need to stop being so damn perfect."

Jackson chuckles as I turn to look at him. "I'm far from perfect." He leans down and presses a tender kiss on my lips.

The feel of his lips on mine causes my heart to flutter. I never want this to end. I could kiss him all day. His lips turn up in a smile, effectively breaking my small moment of happiness as the kiss breaks.

Looking into his turquoise eyes, the joy I see stops my breath. Unable to control my reactions, I grin.

"So what did Gretchen say?" Jackson asks.

The smile fades as I think about what she said and the thought of Neil does nothing to halt my mood change. My immediate thought is to keep this from him, to protect him while he's healing, or protect myself. However, I'm not going to do that again. He asked me to trust him, to give him my heart, and I have. I love him and need to have faith in our relationship.

I groan, "Neil is apparently trying to file a lawsuit. Gretchen is obviously well-known and her friends alerted her that he's calling around."

His entire body clenches and he lets out a snarl through gritted teeth. I shoot up looking at where he's in pain but his hand is in a fist and his eyes are closed.

"Jackson." My voice is small, but I know he hears me.

"I fucking hate him, Catherine." Jackson's eyes latch on to mine and you can see the anger rolling through him. "I'll call my legal team. I'm going to bury that piece of shit one way or another." His voice is cold as ice.

"He's not worth it. Gretchen has photos and doesn't think it'll come to that. She's pretty sure with the proof she has, it'll be dropped."

"What fucking proof do you have?" Jackson asks clearly still angry.

He doesn't know about the bruises. I threw him out that night, and well, we didn't really talk much about anything that happened in the few days we spent apart. Which reminds me about the conversation I had with Piper as well.

"I had bruises on my arms." I see his hand once again ball into a fist. "Before you hurt yourself getting worked up, let me get through this, okay?"

I pause staring at him waiting for some sign he's going to allow me to tell him the story without ripping his stitches or trying to get out of bed. We both glare at each other until he finally lets out the breath he's been holding and nods.

"Like I said, I had bruises on both my arms from where he grabbed me. I'm not completely surprised since I bruise fairly easy, but Ashton took pictures on her phone. Apparently, she sent them to Gretchen to hold on to. I explained Neil's threat to Ash as well."

Jackson goes from anger to hurt. "I should've been there. I shouldn't have left you when you asked me to."

"I needed you to go. You leaving me showed me everything I was trying to ignore. I shut you out because I was so afraid. So you don't get to play the martyr. We both fucked up," I say, sounding much stronger than I feel at the moment.

I'm not afraid he's going to leave since he can't move, but the last time we began this talk a lot of things happened. None of which I'd like to relive any time soon.

I look up at him before he can say anything else. "But that's not all."

"Go on," he says sharply.

I hate every single second of this conversation. Climbing out of the bed, I walk to the window. "Piper came by my office as well. What happened between you two?" I sigh already regretting asking.

Not one bone in my body thinks he's done any of the bullshit she spewed, but I want to hear what happened from him.

Jackson looks confused for a second before he composes himself. "I fired her."

"I'm aware of that, but why?"

"Because she was no longer needed. I hired you and I don't need to keep her on my payroll when I have you there to help me make the same choices she would be advising," Jackson says without any hesitation. "Also, I was preparing for when you came back to me. I wanted to keep her the hell away from you."

Somehow I manage to mask my emotions. It was his way of protecting me, or at least showing me he cared. "Well, Piper tried to tell me it was because she wouldn't sleep with you."

"That's a fucking lie!" Jackson yells and tries to move too fast. He groans while gripping his leg, clearly in pain.

I rush over and place my hand on his cheek. "Babe," I say softly, "I never thought you did. I told her she was full of shit. I recorded the conversation, which I don't know why I thought I should, but it was good I did. I'll send it to Gretchen too in case she needs it. But I need to handle this and make sure this doesn't get out of control. With you in the hospital, we need your image to appear commanding."

"Catherine." His voice is warm and washes over me. He grasps my hand that's holding his face before speaking. "I never touched her. We never even had a moment where it could've happened. I was so mad at you. You infuriated me that night. But never, not once, did I even think of going near anyone else. She walked in my office and I fired her before I even knew I wanted to. Just the sight of her, knowing she hurt you in any way ..." He takes a deep breath. "I never wanted to see her, so I fired her. I told her I no longer needed her advice and to leave immediately. I don't want you anywhere near either of them."

"I never thought you did. None of this is relevant to what's going on now. I'm telling you

Neil is apparently after something. Gretchen has this under control and so do I." I'm not conceding to him. I ultimately don't care about Piper or Neil. They're non-issues. My focus is Jackson and getting home. The launch is coming soon and he refuses to push it back again, so we need to get him ready.

"You need to stay away from him. I'm not kidding."

"I'm not arguing," I say back quickly.

"Stay away from him." Jackson's voice is cold as ice.

I can keep going back and forth with him or I can end this how he wants it. I'm going to handle Neil once and for all. He's pushed me to the point of no return. When I get back to New York, he'll be dealt with. However, I'm not going to keep fighting with Jackson about it either.

Time passes slowly while we wait for the charge nurse to release Jackson. The last week he's improved and of course also overdid it. He's going to drive me up the wall with his defiance. No matter how many times he's been told to slow down and take it easy, that seemed to only spur him to go at it harder. The poor look on the physical therapist's face when he tried to put pressure on his leg.

"What are they doing? It's a simple damn form, not an act of Congress," Jackson says, aggravated and impatient.

Which is his new normal attitude.

"Relax, she said it would be a few minutes."

Jackson sighs heavily while rubbing his hand down his face, "I want to get home."

I smile and try to diffuse his irritation. "I know, baby. I'm sure they want you out of here just as much as you want to be gone." My last words slip out a little harsher than I mean, but he's been less than easygoing. I know men are babies when they're sick but I'm really ready to slap him.

"What does that mean?" he says clearly surprised at my little dig.

"You've been an ass, and that's me being nice. Yesterday, I think you made the nurse cry. I know it sucks being reliant on people, but I swear, if you talk to me like that I will poke you in your bad leg." I grin trying to soften my tone and sound playful while ensuring the message is delivered.

He looks taken aback as though he has no clue what I mean. "She wasn't listening to me."

"Jackson, you've snapped at every single person. You yelled at Mark on the phone yesterday because he did exactly what you asked for. Poor Danielle called me asking why she got an email with a list of things she already did." I pause and sink down to look him in the eyes. "I know this is hard for you. God, I get it."

His eyes harden and he purses his lips. "No. None of you get it. I can't fucking walk. I can't use a wheelchair, or crutches. I need you to help me take a piss." He throws his hands up before rubbing the back of his neck. "I fucking hate this. I can't sleep, I have one leg and one arm that work, but they don't work together."

I reach out and gently rub his cheek. "Hey," I wait for him to look at me. "I have two arms and two legs, and I'm here. Don't push me away. I love you."

Jackson draws a breath and leans his head

against mine. "I love you and I'll try not to make you stab me in the leg."

I laugh and kiss him, "I hope you try hard because I've refrained a few times already and I can't promise I have much willpower left."

Before he can respond the nurse appears.

"Okay, Mr. Cole. You're all clear. You have all the medication for the ride home. Dr. Allison already spoke with the doctor in New York who's going to follow up. All I need is your signature on this form and you can head home." She smiles brightly.

Jackson signs the form and we exit the hospital that's kept him alive. The ride to the airport is quiet as we both enjoy the freedom of the outside world. It's been a rough few weeks and it's not over yet. Luckily, it's not a long ride and we get on the plane easily, thanks to two sailors who rode with us to help. I knew I couldn't lift him, so the SEAL team in Germany sent help.

We head to the bedroom in the back of the plane and Jackson sleeps holding my hand. They gave him a mixture of painkillers for the long journey, and thankfully, he didn't argue about taking them because he knew it would be rough. I lie here looking at him and allow myself this time to let out the emotions of the past few weeks. I let the tears fall and watch each one stain the pillow. They're not tears of weakness, they're tears of strength. There is no shame because this has been hell. I've never been more scared yet determined in my life.

I run my fingers through his hair as he dreams. I listen to his breathing and marvel at him. This strong but damaged man who loves me. Jackson came into my life like a force of nature. Pushing me to feel and refusing to give me a chance to run away anymore. I'm sure I'll run again, only this time I'll run to him.

chapter
nine

"Jackson!" I shake him as he's gasping and clutching his chest.

This is the fifth night in a row he's had a thrashing nightmare. Even with the sleeping pills the new doctor prescribed, he still wakes in a pool of sweat and doesn't remember what happened—or at least that's what he says.

"I'm fine. Go back to sleep." He pushes the hair out of my eyes and cups my cheek.

"What's wrong? Are you in pain?" I ask as I start to shuffle out of bed.

He reaches for the pills on the side of the bed but grabs his leg. "Fuck," Jackson groans as his hand wraps around his thigh.

"I'll get you some medicine." I scramble by the bed trying to find the pills. "I think we should call the doctor. It's getting worse." The nightmares and the pain seem to be getting more consistent. Partly because he refuses to listen to a damn word that anyone says. I catch him without the walker trying to maneuver to the bathroom.

"No doctor. I'm fine!" he lashes out through his clenched jaw.

The first week he was home everything was fine. He seemed to understand his limitations and accepted my help freely. Now though, because he feels better, the aggravation overrides any under-standing he previously had.

"Right ... sorry, I forget you don't need anyone," I say with sarcasm. I'm over his crap. I grab the medication and put the pills in his hand.

Such a jackass.

He grabs my arm before I can walk away. I don't look at him. I'm so pissed and tired of his attitude. It hasn't quite been two weeks yet and I'm ready to call for a live-in nurse and go home. He gently rubs his thumb against my arm.

"Please look at me," he pleads.

I look up but I'm pissed off. This isn't easy for either of us, but there's only one of us being con-siderate—and it's not him.

"You don't get it. My head is all fucked up."

"I don't get it because you won't talk to me," I say quietly, trying not to let this escalate into an-other fight. "Tell me then, what are the dreams of?" I ask, already knowing the answer.

Jackson shakes his head.

He keeps telling me they're nothing or he can't explain. I hear him though. I hear his screams for Mark and Aaron. When he yells about the shoot-er or cries out in pain, it doesn't take a genius to figure out what they're about. I've kept that infor-mation to myself knowing he doesn't want to talk about it. He grows more and more frustrated with each dream. More sullen and pushes himself hard-er to get past this.

"You don't get to treat me like shit because you're hurting. I'm tired too. I'm busting my ass working, getting everything in line for the launch. Then I come here and you're moody and crabby. I *know* this isn't easy for you. I know you're tired and in pain. So don't tell me I don't get it. But you're taking it out on me, babe, and I'm on your side." I let it all out as I fight back the urge to cry.

"All I remember is the end with extreme pain in my leg or arm. So I'm going to assume it's the shooting," he says, surprising me that he even said that much.

"Jackson, you went through a lot in the last month. You lost a friend, and you were shot ... It's a lot."

"I have you though." He looks away and swallows the pills.

Standing before him, I take a deep breath and focus on him weighing each word before I say them. "Yes, you do—but I'm getting close to calling Mark—or your mom. You've gone through two nurses in a week. That's not normal and it's not you," I say the last part softly.

"When you go to work, I'm stuck here with that annoying nurse hovering over me. Maybe you should stay home all day. Or quit your job and come work for me," Jackson says smirking.

I laugh while shaking my head at his ridiculousness. "That's not happening. The launch is in a week. I've been inundated with getting things ready."

Jackson sighs and runs his hand down his face. "This isn't the way I wanted it to be when we spent more than a night or two together. I didn't want it to be because you had to help me fucking get a glass of water. I sure as shit never saw you coming home to me because you had to."

"Jackson," I say softly. "That's not fair. I *want* to be here. I could've let the nurse live here, or had you go stay with your family. I need you just as much—"

"Let me finish. This isn't how I saw this going, Catherine. I'm the guy who takes care of you. Not the other way. Being at the mercy of someone else isn't something I enjoy. All I can do are conference calls, video chats, and email, but even that's hard with my one arm still not back to normal. I wanted to shower together for other reasons." He raises a brow and smirks.

Smiling at him and wishing for the same thing doesn't change the fact that it's not how it is. "First, I wouldn't be here if I didn't want to be. I love you, so get that through your thick head. I know you're going through stuff. I get it. I need you to let me in. I'm trying. You have to lean on me. I want to be here for you, but I don't know what else to do."

"It's on me, baby. All on me." He pulls me close so I'm standing between his legs.

"Do you need something else?"

"No, I just need you." He wraps his arm around my waist and places his head on my stomach. My hands tangle in his hair and I tenderly massage his scalp. I take in this moment and try to remember no matter how much of a jackass he can be, he's alive.

"I'm here, Jackson. I'm not going anywhere." My voice is soft and yet firm.

Jackson leans back looking into my eyes. "Lie with me." There's no request in his words.

I don't miss the meaning in his words. It's been weeks since we've been intimate, other than a few kisses here and there. "But your leg."

"I'm not made of glass."

"No, but you're in pain ..."

He slips his hand slowly up my shirt—well, his

shirt. He insists on me wearing his t-shirts and button-downs since I've been staying here. I swear he's marking his territory. I'm not complaining though. Every time I walk around in his shirt, watching his pupils dilate or his breath catch is enough for me.

Jackson's hand caresses my breast and he rubs his thumb across my nipple. The small touch causes me to tremble.

"It's been too long," he groans as he lifts my shirt and presses his lips on my stomach.

He squeezes my nipple and my head falls back as I moan. It feels so good. His hands, his touch. "Jackson, we can't." My voice is weak and quivers with need.

"You let me worry about that, baby," Jackson says as he kisses lower.

The feeling of his breath against my skin causes goose bumps to form everywhere he touches. It's been so long. Far too long since I've had him and even this feels so good I could weep. "Please ..." I trail off, unsure of what I'm pleading for.

Suddenly, I'm pulled forward as his hands grip my hips. My fingers instantly thread into his hair as he travels lower and slides my panties down agonizingly slowly. I should stop this, but it feels so good.

"I've missed this. I've missed you. I need you, Catherine." Jackson's voice breaks at the end.

"You have me," I say as his finger suddenly enters me. The groan that escapes my throat is freeing. His thumb grazes my clit and I begin to shudder, his touch awakening every part of me.

"Always," he says and I look into his eyes.

That one word causes my heart to accelerate. My need for him to take me, claim me, show me that I'm his bubbles up and grabs hold. "Prove it," I say, surprising myself with my brazenness.

Jackson's eyes harden as he presses his thumb against my clit, provoking a moan. "Oh, I'll fucking prove it. Lie down. Now," he commands.

I remember he's still injured and I hesitate. "Your leg and ar—"

"Get on the bed," he cuts me off with his firm demand, leaving no room for discussion.

Trying to move carefully, I climb on the bed as apprehension fills me. I don't want him to get hurt and I don't want to tell him no. Jackson shifts on the bed so he's lying on his back. He grips my leg pulling me closer to him. I gasp at the movement while his eyes fill with determination and mirth. "Climb on top of me," he says gruffly.

I start to move slowly as worry fills me. This isn't a good idea. He could hurt himself and the work he's put in to get to this point would all be for naught. "I don't think we should do this." The words seep out as I sit on my knees debating this.

"I'm not going to break, baby," Jackson says as he cups my cheek. "But I'm going to have you to-night. I need this just as much as you do. We'll be careful," he reassures, pulling my neck close to his. "If it gets to be too much we'll stop. But I'm done talking now," he says, and draws my lips to his.

We kiss slowly and tenderly. His tongue en-twines with mine in a sensual dance. I give and take from him, allowing my heart to fill with love. His hands drift against my body, gripping the hem of my shirt tugging it up and off as the kiss breaks.

"Now, straddle my face." Jackson's voice drops even lower as he hooks my leg over him. Heat sears my veins, warming me everywhere.

I look at him, as he adjusts my leg over his shoulder, setting me in a straddle over his head. "Jackson?" I ask confused.

Before I can say or even think, his mouth is against me. I feel his tongue move up and down. I grip the headboard as his hand makes it's way up my leg slowly and then back down while his eyes lock on mine. Watching him spurs me higher. It's the most erotic thing I've ever seen. Jackson licks and sucks, pushing my hips to give him better access. The pleasure builds with each swipe of his tongue and my head falls back in pure ecstasy. "Jackson," his name is a whisper but I know he hears it when his thumb rubs against my clit in small circles.

My hips start to move and I ride his face as the heat blazes through me as I climb.

He uses his arm to pull me back, and I whimper from the loss. "Get comfortable, baby. We're just getting started," Jackson says as he inserts two fingers and sucks on and around the nerves that are throbbing.

I need to release, but he brings me to the edge and then backs off. Torturing me in the best way. He stops and again I struggle to remain upright. "I've been patient. I've watched you get undressed unable to touch you. I've had to lie next to you, feel your heat. Feel you brush against me. I'm going to consume you tonight just like you do to me. You're mine."

Tears form as the pleasure builds. I need to come, but Jackson removes his fingers and waits. "Yours. Please. I need—" I beg him.

"What do you need?" he asks as he places kisses on my knee, then the inside of my thigh. Going slow and taking his time before climbing higher up my leg.

"You." His eyes lock on mine as his mouth returns to my pussy. He licks and sucks while watching me. I moan and my head falls forward while I hold on to the bed frame.

"Like that?" He stops and my eyes snap open. "Or do you want me to stop?" Jackson asks while he inserts a finger and I cry out.

I'm so close.

"Don't stop. Please, don't stop," I beg him as the heat of his mouth returns and I fall apart.

It takes a great effort to remember to hold myself up and not crush him. I pulse around him as he pulls every last ounce of pleasure from my body. Once my mind becomes coherent I ease myself to his side again.

"I love you," he says and I press my lips to his.

"I love you, too," I say leaning over him. Raining tender kisses on his chest. I look at the red circle marring his body from the bullet and gently kiss it. "I love every part of you. The bruises, the scars ..." I say as I place another kiss on the other bullet wound from his past. "The pain." My lips press against the tattoo to remember his fallen friends. "The hurt." Our eyes stay connected as I move lower and kiss the second scar on his stomach from where they had to operate. "The fear." I hover over him as I move to his leg and kiss the final injury he sustained. Hoping to take the pain away. "There isn't one part of you I don't love," I say and he shuts his eyes. Refusing to allow him to shut me out, I take this moment and shift a little higher, sucking his dick into my mouth.

"Fucking hell, Catherine." His hand threads in my hair as I surprise him by paying him back.

I glide up and down his hard length using only my mouth. Using my tongue, I lick around the tip and Jackson's grip in my hair tightens. It spurs me on and I take him deeper. When he hits the back of my throat, he groans and pulls me off him.

"Not like this. Not the first time since ..." He lets that statement hang out there, both of us knowing what he means.

I nod understanding. We need to connect and become one again. I reach over him carefully to his nightstand. This will be the first time I feel him since he walked out the door. I want to feel all of him again.

"Catherine? Do we need them?" he asks tentatively.

I look at him and smile. "No, I'm on the pill."

"I want to feel you, baby. All of you. No barriers. Nothing between us," Jackson says, nipping at my ear.

I moan and sit up, aligning myself to take him and not touch any of his injuries. I need him to fill me. Give me back that part of myself only he can give. I lock eyes with him as I slide myself down his length. Jackson's eyes shut as we savor this moment. I stay still being mindful of his leg and abdomen wishing I could lie across his chest. Feel him against my skin, but even this is pushing it. I take him further into my body and adjust to him filling me to the brink.

"Feels so good, baby," Jackson says through gritted teeth. He laces his fingers with mine and I grind down.

I rotate my hips as I ride him slowly and carefully. "Jackson," his name a sigh as I feel him everywhere. I surrender myself to him. His body fits mine perfectly. I glide up and down as we hold on to each other's hands. I start to build again as my clit rubs against him. "I'm gonna come again."

"Come with me," he says as I rock back and forth creating the friction I need. "Tell me. I'm close," Jackson demands.

I allow my mind to focus on the feeling of Jackson. How he makes me feel. The way his body feels inside mine and I start to tremble. "Now!" I moan as I bear down and fall apart. My head falls back as he erupts.

"Catherine ..." he grunts and comes apart.

chapter ten

"Let's go, you big baby," I call out to Jackson who's groaning in pain.

"I think we should call you 'Nurse Ratchett.' You're becoming sadistic."

I try to suppress a smile and stow my attitude. "We're already late, babe. To get across town we needed to leave ten minutes ago. You're supposed to be at physical therapy in fifteen and your orthopedic surgeon appointment is right after."

Jackson's been able to put small amounts of pressure on his leg with the use of his walker and his arm is out of the sling now. However, since he's found his sexual appetite again—not that he ever really lost it—I worry he's doing too much. I took off work today to go with him and make sure he's not causing more damage.

"If you weren't so damn sexy I would've been ready earlier," he smirks and rolls the walker over. "I get distracted."

Laughing and rolling my eyes, I grab my bag. "Let's go, no more distractions for you."

We arrive at the appointment late. They get him started on a few exercises while I stand there and watch him. He pushes himself hard and they're constantly telling him to take it easy. At least I'm not the only one he gives a hard time about what he's capable of. Typical man.

"Jackson, you did well, but I really need you to dial it down a notch," the physical therapist, Christy, chides him.

"I am so dialed down."

"Look, I know this is difficult and you're doing exceptionally well considering you're only a few weeks in, but you will set yourself back," she explains.

"Nah, I'm good."

"You're exasperating."

"Welcome to my world," I say walking up behind him and he huffs.

Jackson wipes the sweat from his forehead. "Another woman to boss me around."

Christy stands there and fixes her ponytail. She's kind but very firm. When I first met her, I wasn't sure if she'd be able to handle him. She's only about four-foot-eleven but she's been doing this for at least twenty years. Her height is an illusion because her attitude is about six-foot-five. Jackson towers over her but I'm pretty sure she could make him cower.

"I won't put up with your crap. I'll call the doctor and let him know you're pushing too hard. Then he'll put you back in that sling and we'll say no weight bearing at all." She crosses her arms as I watch the impending duel unfold.

"You wouldn't." He pushes himself so he's taller.

Christy doesn't miss a beat, taking a step forward and glaring at him playfully. "Try me, soldier."

"Sailor."

"Semantics."

I laugh at the two of them fighting for the alpha

dog position. "My money's on Christy."

She smiles and nods in solidarity. "I like this one."

"She's all right," Jackson jokes.

"Don't let him kid you, he loves me."

Jackson grabs me and kisses the side of my head. "I do."

"Enough mushy stuff." Christy turns to Jackson and sighs. "You're doing more than most of my patients are able to, but that's because of your physical condition prior to the injury. You were in top form and you're much stronger on your worst day than others on their best day."

His smile and eyes brighten. "See?"

"Before you bask in your brilliance, it doesn't mean that you can push too hard. You're not allowed to put pressure on your arm. You need to keep your weight supported, so no walking. The muscles have to heal."

I turn and smirk. "See? I'll be sure to mention this to the surgeon."

"I'll see you next week." She raises a brow and gives him a pointed look.

He gives her a salute. "Don't worry, Christy." Jackson wraps his arm around my waist. "I always behave."

She walks away shaking her head.

We arrive at the surgeon's office and once we get settled in the examination room to wait, Jackson and I talk about the launch plans.

"So, do we have to have this stupid party after?"

I huff and put my hands over my face, "I can't make you, but I think it's a good thing for the shareholders to see you. Alive."

"I'm still going to be in this fucking walker. I

really don't think that's showing such a clear picture," he complains.

We've been over this at least five times. He argues his side. I argue mine. In the end I usually win, but he keeps at it.

"I think this is the best thing for Raven. I feel it will show strength, that even though you were knocked down you were able to rise up."

Jackson grumbles but before he can really put up a big fight, Dr. Flores enters.

"Mr. Cole." He shakes Jackson's hand. "Ms. Pope, great to see you both."

"Doctor, can you please write me a note that it's against the best interests of my health to go to any work parties."

"Ass," I reply before the doctor can give him a chance.

"I don't know that it's against the best interests of your healing as much as it's against the best interests of aggravating her." They smile and look over at me.

I take a measured breath before releasing it. "I think you should tread careful there, darling," I say sarcastically.

"Let's take a look at your stitches and how everything's healing, shall we?" The doctor quickly intervenes and Jackson gives me a coy look.

Dr. Flores is happy with how his incisions are healing.

"Any questions?"

Jackson speaks first, "I want to know when I can start working out again?"

"Jackson, it's been a few weeks since the shooting. I know you're anxious, but it'll be up to your physical therapist."

"So that's never. What about *other* activity?" Jackson's smirk is evident and so is his meaning.

Dr. Flores chuckles, "You should be cleared for other activity as long as you don't get crazy."

I blush and look at Jackson as the grin spreads across his face. "Wasn't waiting for that all clear, Doc."

"Most patients never listen to that one." He grins and I want to die.

This is the most embarrassing conversation I've ever had. The rest of the appointment goes on without any further blushing. We'll return in another few weeks and at that point he should only have to go to physical therapy.

"Are you going in to work?" Jackson asks on our way back to the apartment.

"I should. I have a lot to take care of."

My phone rings and it's Ashton.

"Hey," I say answering the phone.

"Hey, I'm in the area of your office. Wanna grab lunch?" she asks.

I look at Jackson and he smiles apparently hearing her through the line.

"Maybe I can swing it. I was heading in to work anyway."

"Oh, did you actually take a day off?" her voice rises in surprise.

Why does everyone think all I do is work?

"No, Jackson had a few appointments and I wanted to talk to his physical therapist. According to Captain America over here, he was able to start walking without his cane." I look at Jackson with narrowed eyes. "It appears someone wasn't very forthcoming."

"You only heard what you wanted to hear,"

Jackson speaks up.

"Ahhh, well, just tell him you'll make him watch the awful dance movies you've forced me to watch."

"You liked them," I scoff.

"Uh huh, sure I did. Okay, so lunch?"

"I wish I could but I have to make up all the work I've missed."

I hate this. I miss my friends, but right now my life has taken a different turn and I need to focus on Jackson and my job.

"Taylor, do you have the files for the Raven account?" I call out while looking for the paperwork I had ten minutes ago.

"No, it was on your desk last I saw," she says as she approaches my desk. "Did you bring it downstairs when you saw the design team?"

I groan and my head thumps on my desk. "I swear I can't even think anymore. I'm losing my mind."

"Are you sleeping at all? You know I say this with all the love in the world, but the bags under your eyes are ready for vacation." Taylor smiles and plops in the chair while I glare at her.

Sleep. Well, there's a concept. Between Jackson's night terrors and the amount of work I'm trying to get done, I barely get three hours a night.

"Being out of the country has put me behind a little. I'm trying to catch up."

The sad part is as much as I get done at night when he's sleeping, I usually spend another three hours during the day fixing it because none of it makes sense. I feel awful because I don't see or spend any time with Jackson. I've been staying in the office till after seven and then I get home, eat, and he usually passes out early because of the medication.

"Well, you have to take care of yourself too," Taylor chides and stands. "Why don't you head home early? Maybe you can take some time with your sexy sailor man." She gives me a sideways glance and winks.

I lean back in my chair looking at the stacks of papers and orders. I have most of the big stuff done. It's little tasks, which I can give to Taylor to get done easily. The excitement builds at the idea of going and surprising Jackson. We could lay on the couch, watch a movie, I could grab lunch from Little Italy, or take a nap. I grab my bag without allowing myself to back out.

"I'm leaving. Don't call me unless the building is on fire—even then just grab the important stuff. There's a stack on my desk of orders I need you to check on. I'm taking a mental health day. We have a week until the launch, so ... bye!" I smile as she gives me a knowing look.

"Go. I'll get it all taken care of," Taylor responds as I'm practically running to the elevator. I feel free and weightless. Giddy with excitement to have some time to not worry about anything. When I exit the office doors onto the streets of New York I feel the wind whip my hair, and I smile. It's like one of those cheesy commercials where you want to stretch out your arms and spin around. I can breathe and allow the sun to warm my face instead of fighting over why he shouldn't be trying to hop around and use the damn walker.

I grab a cab and head home. Home? I'm now

calling Jackson's apartment "home"? It stops me for a minute. My phone beeps with a text, breaking me from overthinking my mental blunder.

Gretchen: I've sent the files to Neil's lawyers.

Me: So he's going forward?

Gretchen: I've got this. I think he'll cower. This seems to be completely financial.

"Hey, take me to the train station instead, please?" I make a split-second decision and ask the cabbie to change directions.

I'm taking care of this. I won't allow him to put any more turmoil in my life. This ends today, once and for all.

The train into Hoboken gives me some time to plot about how to handle him. This is out of the norm, even for him. Taylor mentioned in an email that Neil's name was floating around the office because he applied for a position there. Apparently, he lost a few clients in his firm and is now floundering. If he's after money, he knows Jackson is wealthy. The bottom line is I will not allow him to use me or Jackson for financial gain.

Not going to happen.

Knowing the ring seemed to be his big concern, I head to my apartment to grab it. I don't know what else he's after but I want this done. There's nothing of his I want or need. Everything he's touched or even came close to is toxic, so good fucking riddance.

Walking through my door, I'm taken back to the call that changed the course of the last few weeks. The wall Jackson held me against, screwed me relentlessly, then everything fell apart. The couch where I promised I wouldn't run anymore, told him how I felt, and the door where I stood watching him walk away. I still don't know how I endured the week after he left. I was a shell of a human. Terrified for him, of him, and knowing I would still have to be around him when he returned. The one thing I feared most in our relationship was always that if things went south, how I'd continue to be his publicist.

My room is still a disaster from the trip to Germany where I literally threw anything I could grab into a bag and Ashton and I ran out of the house. Then coming back since and grabbing more clothes to stay with Jackson. This is going to be loads of fun to clean up.

The jewelry box holding the ring sits in the closet where I placed it months ago. I open it and remove the diamond engagement ring. I hate him and everything this represents. While my feelings toward my father may have shifted slightly, my feelings of disgust toward Neil have only amplified.

Time to end it.

Time to be done.

Time to handle Neil and ensure that my relationship with Jackson doesn't have issues because of him. I grab my "Fuck You" ring as well. I want no part of Neil. I want him gone and every memory to fade away with him. The princess cut diamond shimmers against the wall and one day I know I'll wear a ring again. I'll marry someone who loves me with his whole heart. He'll respect me and be honest, instead of filled with secrets and lies. I don't know if Jackson will be that man, but I can hope.

For a moment I allow myself to dream. I'm filled with a vision of Jackson on his knee, giving me his heart, his love, and promises of forever. I see in his eyes the love that I dream of. The ring he'll place on my left ring finger that I'll never take off because our love will be true.

I can see my long brown, hair in a low knot. I'm adorned in a gorgeous, white dress on the beach by our lighthouse, the place where our magic happened. I smile and walk to him as he waits for me. A single tear forms when I see the smile across his face with Mark beside him. Ashton is on the other side with tears streaming, but I can't turn my eyes away from him. I place my hand in his and we say our vows that speak of the promise to love one another, respect each other, and forsake all others. Before our friends and family, we promise to hold our love sacred. Jackson kisses me, sealing everything spoken through the day, and of course in true Jackson style he somehow manages to do something inappropriate.

The smile spreads across my face as I allow myself to go further into my fantasy. I see my stomach round with child. He's putting together a crib, cursing at the directions and the fact that he can put a gun together in under thirty seconds but it's been four hours and the crib is still strewn around the room. I laugh holding my belly. It's all so beautiful and perfect, but I stop myself before I get too far.

chapter eleven

I rush out of my apartment before Ashton gets home or someone calls. I don't want anyone to know where I'm going. No one will think this is a great idea—maybe it's not—however it's what I truly think will stop this. It's time to be done with Neil and I know him better than most. He's a chickenshit. He'll give up because he's driven by money and I have the upper hand. Gretchen is a fantastic lawyer, but this can't go to court. People can't know that not only did the CEO of Raven Cosmetics beat up a man, but that man is also my ex. It'll destroy us both.

The drive over takes no time. His car is outside his house, which surprises me—I thought I'd have to wait for him. I take a deep breath and ready myself for whatever might happen. Hopefully, we'll both come out of this unscathed.

Ringing the doorbell, I suddenly start to consider this is a mistake. Shit.

The door opens and Neil holds on to the door with his eyes narrowed. "Catherine, this is a surprise."

I place my hands in my pockets and hold on to the rings. "We have some things to settle and discuss," I say sternly. Luckily my voice doesn't give any of my fear away.

"Do we?" he asks, curling his upper lip.

"Why are you doing this? Why would you want to continue this? You've moved on, why am I not allowed the same luxury?" I say emotionless. I'm trying to keep myself in check and to not let my own anger take over.

He pushes the door open and leans against the frame. "I don't care if you move on. You have my things and I need them back. All of this could've been handled easily. I told you I needed to talk but you were being a bitch."

Shoving down the anger threatening to spill over, I remember I'm trying to get him to go away and getting into a fight with him will only make matters worse. "Listen, I'm here to talk and handle all of it, but if you'd rather act like an asshole then I'll go."

I start to turn but he speaks up. "Wait, how do you think we can settle this?"

"I have no idea. That's why I'm here. I want you to leave me alone. So what caused you to come to my apartment and assault me?" I raise my brow and step forward. I need him to see I'm not afraid. He left bruises and I can easily prove it, but I won't play that card until I have to.

He gives a short bark of a laugh. "You're confused, love. Your boyfriend broke my nose. I didn't assault anyone."

"Don't call me 'love.'" I say acidly. "Jackson only kicked your ass after you grabbed me," I remind him and smile. "I'm not here to debate with you. I want to know what I have to do to get rid of you completely. Why are you doing this shit? We broke up. You made it abundantly clear you didn't want me, so why all the theatrics?"

This is the part that keeps confusing me. Things ended, I moved on, I didn't continue to make his life miserable even though I wanted to. Did I destroy some of his things? Yes, and I'd do it again. But something doesn't add up.

Neil shifts forward with his hand in his pocket. "I need my ring back and I need the money you took from me."

"Money? This is what made you come after me?" I ask looking at him wondering how all of this is over money.

He sighs and runs his hands through his hair and grasps his neck. "I need the ring and the money. If you give me that, I promise you'll never see me again."

"Don't make promises you can't keep," I clip, infuriated. "If you need money why didn't you ask your new girlfriend?" I ask and then cut him off before he can answer. "You know what? I don't care. I don't want your rings. I don't want your money or anything to do with you. I'll give you the rings back and you can sell them, wear them, or hell— give them to Piper. I don't give a shit. I want you gone. I never want you to call me, text me, show up at my job, or anything. You'll never have existed except in some horrific memory that I'll do my best to forget." I grab the rings in my hand. "Do we have a deal?"

Neil steps forward and drops his hands at his side. I can't read him but he seems calm. "You have them?"

"I asked if you'll go away if I give them to you. That means you drop this bullshit about coming after me or Jackson. It means you take them and you cease to exist in my life. No more calls, no lawyers, no more money … nothing. I loved you once. You owe me this." I step toward him daring him to push me. I'll take the rings and walk the hell out of here.

"I just need the money, Cat. I don't care about anything else," he says and looks at his feet.

"What kind of trouble are you in?" I don't know why I care but my curiosity wins out.

He looks up at me and shakes his head. "Trust me, you don't want to know."

There's a small part of me that feels for him—an extremely small part.

"Fine, here." I hand him the rings and he grips them in his hand. "I mean it. We're done in every sense of the word." I turn without looking at him and get in my car.

I start the car and when I pull out, I give one last glance at the man who was my world for five years. The first person to ask me to be his wife. Of course he turned out to be the worst mistake, but for a while, I loved him. He's still standing on his stoop staring at me. I fight the urge to wave, so I drive away leaving my past behind me.

I look at my phone and see I have two missed calls from Jackson.

Great.

I grab my phone and quickly call him back.

"Hey, babe," I say trying to act nonchalant as a car honks past me while I try to silence my music.

"Hi," Jackson replies with a hint of confusion. "Are you driving?"

"Yeah, I'll tell you about it when I get back to your place. I'm stopping off at my apartment to grab a few things and I should be there in about an hour," I explain hoping it mollifies him for the time being.

"I can't wait to hear it. I called the office and Taylor said you left early and I should see you soon. I was getting worried since it's been two hours and not a word," Jackson's gruff voice radiates concern.

"I promise I'll explain everything when I get there. I love you," I say as sweetly as I can.

"I'll see you then. I love you, too," Jackson says and then disconnects the call.

No matter what I tell him, the fallout is going to be bad, so I might as well get it over with. He wanted me to stay away from Neil, but I simply needed to handle this. Part of my job is to protect him and Raven, and if he were to get pulled into some assault drama with his publicist's ex-boyfriend, it would get ugly real quick. I have to look at this like I was doing my job.

Now I need to convince Jackson of the same thing.

I get back to my apartment to drop off the car, and of course with my luck I turn and see Ashton is walking in the building at the same time. Seriously, my timing sucks.

"Cat?" Ashton asks with narrowed eyes.

"Hey," I say and walk over to her, wrapping my arms around her. I've missed her, no matter what tongue-lashing's about to come. I'm happy to see her.

She returns the hug and pulls back to look at me. "What are you doing here? I didn't expect to see you. Is Jackson okay?"

"Yeah, he's fine. I had something I needed to take care of," I explain with the hope that she'll let it drop.

Ashton cocks her head to the side weighing my words and somehow knowing I'm leaving something out. She's always been able to read through my bull-shit. I don't know why I thought this time would be any different.

"Just ask me," I say, exasperated by her staring.

"Right, spill it." She crosses her arms and looks as if she has all the time in the world for me to explain.

"There's nothing to spill," I say and try to walk past her.

She grabs my wrist and stops me. "Cat, I'm not stupid. You have that look on your face. The one that says 'Ashton is going to have my ass so I'll pretend nothing's going on.' Plus, you wouldn't leave work early just because you missed me."

One day I'll be unreadable. "I went to see Neil," I say, waiting for the tirade. I know she's going to blow any second.

"Are you dumb?" she asks deadpanned.

"I don't think so, but I'm sure you and everyone else will disagree." I stand there ready to defend myself.

Ashton releases a deep breath and starts to walk toward the elevator. "Well, I can't wait to hear this argument then. Why did you go see the dickface?"

"I gave him the rings back and he agreed to leave us alone."

She laughs and enters the doors. "Cat, do you really believe a word he says? He's a fucking liar. I mean, come on! You can't possibly trust a word that comes out of his mouth. I'm waiting for you to sell me on how you're not stupid because what you just said sure as shit didn't do it."

Do I believe him? No, but then I do. There was gratitude in his eyes when he had the rings, and then there was the way he seemed almost ... apologetic.

"I think he's in trouble. He was home, on a random Thursday in the middle of the afternoon. Either he lost his job or something else. The sense of relief on his face when I handed him the rings, even he can't fake. Maybe I'm dumb. Maybe I fucked up, but I can't have him starting shit up with Jackson right before the launch. Do you get that?" I say frustrated that I need to explain my decisions to her. She doesn't always make the best choices, but I don't berate her.

"I do get that, but do you think going there was the best idea?"

"I think it was the only option I had."

We make our way to the apartment without saying anything else. I think of how the hell I'm going to explain the same thing to Jackson without him blowing a gasket. If Jackson did it his way, who knows what would've happened. Neil was already looking at pressing charges if he couldn't get me civilly. If I didn't handle it, there would've been a press shitstorm. So I did what I thought would keep everything quiet and make it go away. Whether it was right or wrong ... only time will tell.

We enter the apartment and finally her silence breaks. "What do Gretchen and Jackson think?" she asks and that's where this brilliant plan of mine has the snag.

"I didn't tell them yet."

She stands there staring at me, opening and closing her mouth. Which I guess is better than hearing it. Although, the fact that I've rendered her speechless doesn't really make me feel any better.

"Okay, I don't really know what to say to that. Just ... wow. For someone so fucking smart, and, Cat, you are *so* smart ... you're also the dumbest person I know." She shakes her head in disbelief. "But, well, it's done. Gretchen is going to be way worse than I am right now. So if I were you, I would prepare yourself for her. She's going to kick your ass and I'm going to sit back and enjoy the show." Ashton spills her feelings, ranging from frustration to excitement talking about how she's going to enjoy my Gretchen-whipping.

"Well, I'm glad you'll get some amusement from all of this."

"The bigger question I have is do you think he'll actually leave you alone?" Ashton asks in a soft tone.

I shake my head unsure of what to think. "I don't know, but at this point I have nothing left of his. Plus, I didn't want the rings—or need them. I don't want anything he touched or that came from him. He's completely out of my life."

"I get that," Ashton finally says as she puts her keys down and heads into the living room. "Sit, let's talk. I feel like I haven't seen you in weeks. Well, I guess I haven't."

"Wait. That's all you're going to say?" My voice is high and I'm shocked. This is very un-Ashton like.

She laughs and tucks her feet under her butt. "I get it. I would want to be rid of anything that was my ex's. Was spending his money on the ring fun? Sure. But at the same rate, your job is to protect Jackson. You don't come into my lab and tell me how to do my job. I'm not going to tell you how to do yours. I wish you would've let me go with you. Or *told* someone what you were up to."

I smile and snuggle into her. "You're such a good friend. If I brought you, it would've made him feel threatened. Plus, I really don't think he's violent. I think he's in deep shit and is trying to find his way out. If he needs money, those two rings should effectively shut him up. Enough about Neil, what do you want to talk about? Mark?"

She slaps my leg and hops up, refusing to answer my question. After a minute, she returns with wine and two glasses. I open the bottle and Ashton launches into a long rant about her job. It's great sitting and talking like we did when I was still staying here. I tell her about what my days are like, trying to catch up on the missed work and how Elle and I are still front-runners for the new position at CJJ.

"How's Mark?" Ashton asks after a few minutes of silence.

The smile slowly forms across my face as Ashton pretends to pick lint off her pants. "Mark? Do you mean the adorable ex-SEAL who lives in Virginia?" I question, deciding to play coy.

"Oh, don't be so stupid! And adorable isn't the adjective I'd use for that piece of meat."

I laugh so hard I'm clutching my stomach. "Meat? Oh my God, Ash. You're a hot mess."

"Bite me, twunt. Have you talked to him since you've been back?" Ashton's entire demeanor shifts to being interested.

"You and that stupid word." I giggle and take a sip of wine. "Jackson talks to him daily. Have you called him?"

She shifts around looking uncomfortable and grabs her glass. She wipes her finger around the rim while I wait for her to answer. "He's called me a few times but I haven't answered. He's really hot, and I don't know, like I said, he lives in Virginia and I'm not about to start chasing a long distance

relationship." Ashton looks up. Her eyes are probing me to give her answers.

I grab her glass and put it on the table. "Ash,
you don't know what the future holds any more
than I do. Neither one of us is twenty-one anymore.
Mark's a good guy. He was there for me in Germany
and we became good friends. I think he is about the
only man in this world that could handle you. Plus,
he really is hot." I slap her arm and get up. It's been
over a half hour and I told Jackson I'd be back in an
hour. Which already isn't going to happen. "I gotta
run."

Ashton stands and pulls me in for a bone crushing hug, "I miss you. Tell your boyfriend to get his
ass better so I can have my Biffle. Although, I wonder if he'll return you."

I laugh and hug her back. "I'll be back. I don't
think we're at that stage yet."

"You tend to be a little behind on these things,
my friend," she says, throwing up a pillow so I can't
hit her.

"Why would anyone want to come back to this
abuse?" I chide.

She scoffs. "You love it!" she yells as I start to
walk away. "Don't forget about me."

"Like you'd ever let me," I say as I close the door
laughing.

Now time to deal with another headache. Hopefully he won't be in too bad of a mood by the time
I tell him this story.

"Jackson," I call as I open the door into the apartment already bracing myself for what I'm sure is

going to be one hell of a fight. Good thing he can't really move around too much. At least I can run easily.

"In here!" he responds from the kitchen. *Great.* He's around sharp objects.

I smile as I see the mess before me. He has noodles all over the stove, parts of what look like red peppers on the floor, and every ingredient you can name strewn around the counters. "Well, this looks interesting," I say trying not to laugh.

"You try doing this with one arm and one leg. I have no idea if anything is edible, but it has to be better than the dog food that nurse you hired made for lunch."

My smile doesn't falter as I walk over and grip his cheeks and give him a kiss. He drops the item in his hand and grabs my neck refusing to let me end the kiss. Fine by me. I'll kiss him all night if it delays the inevitable battle coming. Jackson releases me and looks at me skeptically.

"So, where were you?" he wastes no time in asking as he picks up the knife to continue whatever cooking mission he's attempting.

I sigh and steel myself for his reaction. "I went to Neil's to return the rings."

The knife clangs against the counter and he lets out a deep menacing sound from his chest. "You're fucking kidding me, right? Because you wouldn't possibly go see the man who cheated on you, grabbed you, and basically stalked you for weeks."

This is going well already.

I stand toe-to-toe with Jackson. I did what I needed to do. Whether he agrees with it or not, I don't give a shit. I protect him the same way he protects me.

"Yes, I did. I gave him back the only thing left. It's done. He's out of our lives, and I expect we'll hear from Gretchen soon that Neil's backing off from his bullshit lawsuit."

"I guess you're not kidding! Goddammit, Catherine, I told you to stay away."

"As your publicist, I needed to get rid of the threat to your company prior to your launch. If you think about all of this, he was playing a game he could win. He knows me, and my number one priority is Raven and you. So you can be an asshole or you can say thank you. Which by the way ... you're welcome," I say, refusing to let him get a word in.

He gives a sarcastic laugh. "That's not going to happen, babe. You shouldn't have gone there."

"Well, I did!" I throw my hands up in the air and they make a loud slap when they hit my leg. "You know you're not the only one who gets to make decisions around here. I'm an equal in this relationship. I could've lied to you but I'm here listening to the shit I knew I was going to have to hear. I promised not to keep secrets from you." My eyes narrow as I let him know how I'm not going to stand here idly and listen. "I'll take my lumps because I believe you're just an idiot who thinks he needs to keep me safe. But guess what, buddy?" I raise my brow. "I've been taking care of myself for twenty-nine years. I think I've done a damn good job so far. Have I screwed up? Sure." I throw my hands up again. "God, you infuriate me."

For a second he looks stunned and unsure of how to respond to my mini rant. He recovers quickly and wraps his arm around my waist pulling me close to him. I inhale his scent and gently place my hand on his chest. Looking up into his eyes I see him battling himself.

"I'm not happy," he finally states while glaring at me.

"I don't doubt that."

"You shouldn't have gone there."

"I don't agree," I retort.

Jackson takes a deep breath and breaks from our staring contest. "You drive me insane."

I shrug and kiss his chest. "You're not the first person to feel that way. I did what I felt was right. It needed to be done." I turn my head and listen to his heartbeat waiting for him respond.

"And what if something happened to you? What if he hurt you? I would've been here, not knowing where you were or what stupid plan you had. When you were hurt or God knows what, how would I deal with that?" he says as I hear his heart accelerate either in anger or fear.

Leaning out of his embrace, I look at him, willing him to look at me. I'm not weak, and while a part of me understands his apprehension, he can't deem me incapable of taking care of myself. When he finally looks over, I smile softly and try to explain more calmly. "You're in the middle of a rather large product launch. You were shot. You lost your best friend on top of a slew of other things. I understand your need to protect me ... most of the time it turns me on." I wink and try to ease the tension. Jackson smiles and I continue. "But ... and this is a big but ... you can't. I'm going to handle things the way I think is best. It might be wrong and I'm going to make mistakes, but I'm allowed to make them. Now, cook me dinner while I go shower."

"This is ridiculous. I asked you to stay away from him. You won't make me out to be the bad guy here."

He's pissed and to a point I understand that, but this isn't about him. "I won't let you make demands, and I'm also not the kind of girl who's going to be obedient. You should know this by now."

"I'm not asking you to obey me, Catherine. I'm asking you to fucking stay away from a piece of shit who bruised you. An asshole who I got in a fistfight with because he put his hands on you. The same bastard who then wanted to come after us." Jackson runs his hand down his face and his chest is heaving.

"I understand you're not happy. I'm not asking you to understand. I'm telling you it's done. He's out of our lives."

He gives a cynical laugh. "I'm assuming *he* told you that? Because he's a real trustworthy guy, right? When he files charges now and we have no rings as a bargaining chip ... then what?"

I draw whatever strength I have left, between Ashton earlier and now Jackson. Besides the fact that I also dealt with Neil, I haven't slept in what feels like a year, and the launch is in a few days—I'm running on a limited supply of patience.

"I love you, but I'm done talking. I need a shower, a nap, and for you to trust me. Do you trust me, Jackson?"

"Of course I do." The exasperation in his voice is clear.

"Do you trust me as your publicist? Do you trust me to do my job?" I ask because I need him to see the two correlate.

"I wouldn't have hired you if I didn't think you were good at your job." Jackson hesitates, as he seems to see where I'm leading him.

"Good, then let me handle it. Now, I'm going to get naked." I smile and saunter out of the kitchen.

I glance over my shoulder and drop my shirt and bra on the floor while he stares at me.

"Not fair."

"You could always join me." I turn standing before him in a skirt, half naked as he drinks me in.

Jackson groans and slowly maneuvers his way to me. "You're going to be the death of me, woman."

My lips turn up. "I think you're stronger than that. Come on and show me just how far I can push you before you break."

chapter twelve

Jackson follows me into the bathroom and I pretend I don't notice. Standing practically naked I turn the water on and then I feel him against my back. He stands there unmoving as I face the glass enclosure.

I wait for him to say something, or touch me, but he doesn't. My breathing grows shallow as the anticipation builds. He's toying with me and I'm a moth to his flame.

Unsure of what to do, I slowly slide my underwear down and I feel his warm breath against my ear. I can feel the heat emanating from his body. His chest barely grazes against my back when he breathes. I close my eyes and inhale the mix of steam and Jackson's cologne. Every part of me aches for him. I want to move or speak, but I don't want to break the spell.

We stand like that for what feels like an eternity. The large glass door is fogging up and I lift my hand to open it, but Jackson's grabs my wrist.

"I'm still angry." His deep voice causes the hairs on the back of my neck to rise.

I slowly turn and my hand gingerly skates across his chest. Somewhere between the kitchen and the bathroom he lost his shirt. My hand falls to his waistband and our eyes remain glued to each other.

"Let me make it better," I rasp as I unhook his belt. "I think your anger is misplaced." I unzip his shorts and they fall.

Jackson grabs my breast and squeezes, his thumb rubs back and forth across my nipple. "Did he touch you?"

My breath catches at his question. "No," I say softly as I touch his face. "He didn't touch me."

His other hand rests on my hip since he can't move it higher but his fingers crush the skin as he tightens his grip. "I can't," Jackson drops his forehead to mine.

"Can't what?"

Jackson releases a measured breath, "I can't think of his hands touching you."

He rolls my nipple in his fingers and I moan. "I wouldn't let him," I croak as he repeats his movement.

His hand drops as he slides the glass door open and nudges me in.

Carefully, we enter the large marble two-person shower. The jets shoot out of the sides and the rainfall showerhead cascades down on us. Jackson seats himself on the bench that takes the back wall. His eyes beckon me forward.

I push my wet hair back and settle between his legs. His hands tug at the back of my thighs pulling me forward.

"No other man should touch you." His lips press against my stomach as his fingers indent my skin and dig in, thrusting me forward even more.

The hint of pain only heightens my senses.

"No other man's hands should feel what I feel beneath my palms right now." Jackson's hand slips between my legs as he pushes them apart. My hands slap the cold marble tiles as I try to stay upright. "You're my everything," his voice is laced with pain as he inserts a finger inside me. "I won't let anyone take you from me."

My head falls back as my legs shake while he plunges his fingers over and over. He twists his hand so his thumb presses against my clit. "Jackson," I whisper as my eyes roll back.

"Only me," he groans with a possessive tinge.

Everything about this time I can feel as if it's his mission to claim me. Each movement is him proving to either himself or me that I'm his. I belong to him. He belongs to me. In this moment we belong to each other.

I look at him and his eyes pierce my soul. "Only you," I reply.

"I'm still pissed."

"Good. I like pissed off." I smirk and his eyes narrow as he weighs my words.

He continues to finger me as I climb toward my orgasm. Every part of me is alive. His hands awaken me and cherish me. Even though I know he's angry that I went against his wishes, right now he adores me. Protecting me even when he's being rough.

My legs begin to quake as I get closer to release, but the desire to be filled by him is too great. I drop my arms and grip his neck. Leaning in I kiss him with everything I have. Our tongues push against each other, swirling and volleying for power. I need him to take it all away. Take the doubt, the pain, and the weeks of dread I've held on to. And he does. Jackson takes it away with each twist of his tongue. Each thrust of his hand ... he takes it away.

"I need you inside me," I say breathlessly as his lips press against my neck.

Jackson groans before I feel his teeth graze the sensitive skin. "Do you now?" His hands don't relent as he grinds his thumb harder against my clit. My knees are weak and I have to hold on to his shoulders for support.

"Yes, now," I beg.

Shifting my leg over his I try to align myself, desperate for him. I close my eyes and try to fight off my release a little longer. I want him inside of me when I let go. I want to feel him fill me to the brink, where I can focus on nothing more than how we fit together.

He grabs my hips, halting me from being able to take what I want. "Not yet," his throaty voice breaks through the fog. "Stand on the ledge," he instructs while I step on the bench. Jackson runs his hands on my leg and lifts my leg up over his shoulder. "I'm going you make you come in my mouth first."

And I know he means it. Jackson licks and sucks while using his finger to torture me. I get closer and closer, but he stops right before I'm ready to burst. Each time is stronger than the last. Each build goes higher than the one before. I'm going to die from the onslaught of pleasure. But what a way to go.

"I need you," I groan as he continues. "To let me ..." I stop unable to say more. When he pushes his tongue inside of me, I lose it. I writhe and scream as he draws out the most powerful orgasm I've ever had. Stars paint the walls and my hearing is gone as I float in complete bliss. There's no strength left in my body as I sink to his lap. The water rains down, keeping me from being cold.

Opening my eyes, I see the desire burning in his eyes. I refuse to wait another second. I gently push him against the back wall allowing myself enough space to move.

"Don't ever let him near you again." Jackson's eyes flash with a hint of anger.

"Don't ever doubt me," I say as I sink onto his cock.

His eyes close as I allow myself a second to adjust. He smirks and it pisses me off. I lift myself up and slam against him. Jackson's head snaps up and he glares at me, but the love is evident beneath the anger we're both fighting through.

Anger at his doubt. Anger at his demands. Anger that he's angry at how I chose to handle it. I'm furious.

I ride him harder than I intend. I hear his grunts and groans, but when I start to let up, his fingers dig into my hips forcing me to keep my pace.

"Fuck me harder," Jackson demands.

I groan and hear the slapping skin as we force ourselves together with reckless abandon. We fight the war between our wills through our bodies. Each grunt reminds me we're still fighting for each other. The sweat that trickles down my back is evidence of the struggle we're ready to endure. The heat that surges through my cells proves how I'll give myself to him.

"I'm gonna come," Jackson says with his jaw clenched.

"I love you," I cry out as I fall back into the abyss again.

The tears form in my eyes as I'm overcome with emotion. I love him with all that I am.

Jackson seems to sense the shift as he brings his hands up to my neck. He cradles my head as I look into his eyes. Gently, he swipes under my eyes. "I love you."

I smile tenderly, "I know."

"I didn't mean to be a dick before. I fucking hate the idea that you could've been hurt." Jackson's hands push the hair out of my face as he waits for me to respond.

"You can't save me all the time."

"I can damn sure try."

We kiss briefly and take a shower after our non-shower.

Jackson washes my hair and body, and I in turn do the same for him. The intimacy established between us takes my breath away.

"Almost done?" Jackson asks.

"I'm going to take a few minutes to myself."

"Okay," Jackson says as he heads out of the shower.

I stand there alone and enjoy the solace. Replaying the last few hours in my head, I realize why he was so angry. Things could've gone differently, but they didn't, and I'm grateful for that. I finish up and decide next time I'll let someone in on my brilliant plans.

Once I'm dressed and comfortable I head out to the kitchen. He stands there assessing the damage. I hold back a laugh because it's going to take hours to clean this up.

"Okay, Chef Boyardee, how about you order take-out?" I smile and come around the counter.

"No, this is perfectly edible," Jackson scoffs and starts to stir the pot.

I cross my arms across my chest and at first I think he's kidding but he continues stirring. "Jackson, I'm not eating that." I look in the pot and it's turning colors. "What the hell is *that*?" I ask incredulously.

He laughs and turns the burner off. "Fine, we don't have to eat it."

"Can you even name what it is?"

"It's a surprise." He smiles and pulls me against him.

I look up biting my lip to stop myself from busting out laughing. "Was the surprise whatever we taste at the first bite?"

"Smart ass," he retorts.

"You like my ass."

"That I do."

"Perv. I'll order Chinese. Maybe we can watch a movie?" I suggest as I call the restaurant.

Luckily they deliver quickly and before I know it, Jackson is in the doorway, leaning against his walker with one of his shit-eating grins.

After a minute of no reply I look up. "What?"

"Food's here."

"Good, I'm starving."

"How about we play a game?"

I don't like the looks of this. I can see the wheels turning in his head. This can't be good.

My eyes narrow as I try to figure out what game he could possibly want to play. "Why do I think this is a bad idea?"

Jackson pretends he's affronted and throws his hand over his heart. "Don't you trust me?"

I smile and shake my head.

"Come on, we can play a board game," he cajoles, clearly already having thought this through.

I hate board games. I always lose, but knowing my competitive boyfriend, he's clamoring for something to win at.

"Anything but Monopoly." I smile and grab the plates.

Jackson's lips turn up in a grin and we make our way to the table. Once we've dished the food and gotten settled, he pulls a box out from the chair beside him. When I see the game he's chosen, I burst out laughing.

"Battleship? For real? Are you twelve?" I say in between my giggles.

"Don't insult this game. It's a classic. Besides there's no way in hell you'll be able to win," Jackson says as he starts to pull the game pieces out.

"You know every time you say these things it makes me even more determined to kick your ass?"

"I know, and it turns me on when I see you get feisty." His eyes darken as his voice drops.

The blush spreads across my cheeks and I try to take a bite to stop my mind from going there.

Once I've gotten myself under better control, I start to set up my game board, placing the ships and wondering about the best positions to confuse him. "Okay, it's been a long time and I don't trust you not to cheat so where are the directions?"

Before I can grab the box, he swipes it and tosses it back behind him.

"What the hell?"

"The rules are simple. You put the pieces in and guess. But for every wrong answer you have to take off an item of clothing." He wiggles his brows and I roll my eyes.

"Right, I'm not sure we played this Battleship when I was ten."

"My Navy. My rules. I'm the admiral." Jackson crosses his arms and leans back in the chair.

"I don't think so."

"Fine, then for every correct answer, you take off an item of clothing."

"And for every wrong one you have to answer a question," I say and smirk.

He seems to consider my counteroffer. After a few seconds of mulling it over, he leans forward. "I'm fine with that. But if you don't want to answer, you can remove an item of clothing."

Now it's my turn to think it over. "You can only pass twice. I don't see you having issues getting naked."

"I also have no issues with you getting naked," his voice is full of humor.

After a few turns I'm left only in my tank top, underwear, socks, and bra. Jackson is almost fully dressed. I swear he's losing on purpose. *This* is why I hate board games. However, we're laughing and enjoying the time together.

"Okay, A-12."

"Miss," I hoot, smiling and batting my eyelashes. "Hmmm, first kiss?"

Jackson sighs before answering. "Reagan's best friend, Sharon, in a game of Truth or Dare. Fifth grade. You?"

"I didn't lose that turn. C-3," I say and he smiles.

"Miss. First kiss?" Jackson asks.

"Andy, under the stars in seventh grade. Honestly, my first kiss was what every girl dreams of."

"How so?" he asks.

"I liked him a lot. We went to the fireworks in town and he kissed me during the grand finale. It was perfect and memorable." I laugh remembering how sweet it was and how as soon as we finished kissing we both ran off to tell our friends.

"Kissing Sharon wasn't memorable in a good way. We had no idea what we were doing and when I shoved my tongue in her mouth she almost started crying," Jackson laughs and then his eyes begin to smolder. "Not like when I kiss you."

I fight off the lust that starts to churn. "I would hope you don't kiss me like an eleven-year-old boy. But, I do like it when you shove your tongue in my mouth."

"And other places."

"You're so gross," I laugh at his crassness.

"Deny it!" he challenges me.

"Nope," I wink and point at his game board. "Make your pick, Muffin."

"F-9."

It takes everything for me to not start dancing when he gets one right. "Hit." I smile and he has to remove another item of clothing. "Take the shirt off." I say for selfish reasons. If I have to sit here, I might as well get to ogle.

"Fine. Your turn."

"B-8." I smile knowing I had to have hit and possibly sunk a ship.

"Miss. You can't outsmart me, baby. I'm not sure I want to ask or get you naked."

"You don't get to decide. Ask," I state. No way, he doesn't get to choose—I do.

"Fine, where did you go to college?"

"Fairleigh Dickenson University for undergrad and then for my master's I went to Seton Hall. You?" I can't help but ask, even though I know it's not in the rules.

"I went to Oklahoma since my dad was stationed there at the time. Then, I enlisted."

Looking at my game, I realize I suck at this game since I haven't gotten one right in a while. Jackson smiles as if he's thinking the same thing. "Okay, A-1."

If I didn't know his competitive streak, I would think he's trying to get them wrong so I have a better chance of being naked. "Miss," I narrow my eyes and he leans back under my scrutiny. Staring at his glorious chest I look at the tattoos. I know what his frog means, but he has the tribal and the sun. "What does the sun tattoo mean?"

He looks confused for a second and looks down where my gaze is. "It was a cover up. Nothing really special."

"What was there before?" I ask curiously.

"That's two questions. You can save that for your next round. Now, pick your next move so I can get your shirt off and stare at something for a while."

I smile and of course guess correctly. Which means I'm now in my bra and underwear—and socks.

"C-1," Jackson guesses.

"Miss! Ha! Okay, now you answer about that tattoo," I challenge him.

"Nothing big, stupid things we get when we're young."

"A name?" I ask. Ashton and Gary went and got each other's names together in college. I thought they were ridiculous. Ashton had hers covered up with a butterfly. Luckily her tattoo was on her shoulder and they had room to play with.

"Yes, a name. Now, let's get back to getting you naked," Jackson wiggles his brow like a villain.

I laugh at the expression on his face and I make my next move.

We laugh and play the remainder of the game. By the end I'm completely topless and Jackson is completely naked. He of course won the game.

Which infuriates me. However, I love the fact that he answered the questions so easily. We've gotten so many funny answers and I've learned a lot about him. What his first car was, why he'll never have an animal, what his favorite color is, and how old he was when he lost his virginity. But I wonder who was important enough for him to get a tattoo of their name across his heart.

I wake up early to another one of Jackson's nightmares. Unable to fall back asleep, I do some work from home. The press release for the upcoming product line is five days from now and then the launch party is that night. I have a few things to do to confirm everything is in order. Taylor has taken care of most things, but I need to make sure it's perfect.

"You're up early and on a weekend," Jackson's deep voice breaks the quiet.

I jump at the sound of his voice and clutch my chest trying to settle my heart. Even without being able to walk around he's still able to scare the crap out of me. "I swear … I'm going to put a cow bell on that damn walker."

Jackson settles on the couch and pulls the papers out of my hand. "We need some fun. What do you say we do something today—just us?"

I link my fingers with his and grin. "I could do with a little us. Plus, I'm actually ahead of the game for once. I like fun and I happen to like you." The blush paints my face as I remember our shower three days ago and how much fun we had with each other.

His throaty laugh echoes in the room. "That kind of fun will be later. How about we go to the park and watch the boats, or we can head to a museum?"

I love the Met, which is only a block from his apartment, but I don't know how fun a museum would be for Jackson considering he can't walk. The boat pond would be relaxing and we could always lie out on the grass at the park. "I think the park would be a great way to spend our day."

Jackson leans in and presses his lips to mine. The look in his eyes when he pulls back stuns me. All I see is love and desire. "You know how I feel about you?"

"I do."

Jackson hesitates and then he cups my cheeks while his eyes pierce through me. "You're it for me. I love you."

My pulse spikes and I lose myself in this moment. "I love you, too."

Needing to feel him, I kiss him again. I feel his tongue against the seam of my lips and I open to him. Our tongues glide against each other's as the kiss deepens. Jackson's hand slowly drifts up my arm and around my back. He presses me flush against his chest as he holds me against him. Kissing me feverishly as if his life depended on it. It's a desperate kiss. One that I feel in every fiber of my being.

Lust spikes and I can't fight it. I need him. My hand cups his head as I push back into the kiss, giving myself over and taking everything. I'm ravenous for him. I devour his mouth, breathing him in. The kiss goes on and on. I lose myself completely and it could be minutes, hours, who knows—I couldn't care less.

Jackson breaks the kiss and presses his forehead against mine as I whimper from the loss. "If we keep this up, we'll never leave." His voice is husky and breathless, clearly affected by our intense make-out session.

"And that would be bad why?" I ask trying to catch my breath.

He laughs and kisses my forehead as I try to pull him back to my lips. "Let's go out first. Then I promise I'll be very bad."

I grin. "Oh, Muffin ... you couldn't be bad if you tried."

"Baby, you're going to pay for that."

"Maybe you can pay me in fun."

Jackson groans and I giggle, running into the bedroom.

"You can run, but you can't hide," I hear him yell from the other room.

I take a little extra time trying to delay coming out but know it won't help. He will take full retribution when I least expect it. I can only hope it's the naughty kind, since our last few times have been really ... interesting. Trying to maneuver without getting hurt has made it adventurous and Jackson's made sure I haven't suffered—at all. I grab my black shorts, a cute tank-top, and throw my hair into a messy bun.

When I get back into the living room, I don't see Jackson there. I start looking around, waiting for him to pop out and scare the crap out of me. "Jackson ... this isn't funny," I say trying to keep an eye out for him.

If anyone had a camera right now I'd kill them. I must look ridiculous walking around the apartment checking each corner waiting for him to suddenly appear. "Okay, babe. I'm going to the park for our date. Looks like you're stuck here." My voice gives away the slightest hint of fear. I turn around and he's standing right there.

"Ha!" he screams and I can't help the squeal that comes from my throat.

Damn him.

"Jerk," I say and start to stomp away, furious that once again he got me.

I hear him behind me as he wheels faster. "Oh, don't be like that. You had to know I always win. I've told you this numerous times. I never lose." His arrogance is shining through.

Spinning on my heels, I turn to face him. "I wouldn't say never, darling."

"When have I ever lost?" He cocks his eyebrow and it takes everything inside of me not to jump him.

For some inexplicable reason I find him sexiest when he's like this. Who am I kidding? I find him sexy all the time. Damn dimple and abs—I didn't stand a chance. I smile since this is the perfect time to finally get my time from that godforsaken obstacle course he made me run. "Show me yours and I'll show you mine." I give him my best seductive grin.

Jackson clears his throat as I slither up to him. "Show my what?"

"Time. I want to see your time."

His head tilts and he looks off to the side. "I'm going out on a limb here, but are you talking about the O-course?" A slow smile creeps across his face as he figures out what I'm talking about.

"Yup," I smirk and start to slide my finger down his chest. "You know, that photo you have of my time." My brow rises as his breath hitches while my hand goes lower. "The one where you owe me a whole lot of shopping and a massage."

Jackson grips my wrist before my hands reach his pants. "What about when you see how much I schooled you?" He leans forward dropping his voice into a low seductive whisper. "What do I get then, baby?"

The heat against my ear causes me to shiver and I hear him chuckle at my reaction. "What do you want?" I try to play it cool and not give away the way he's making my body react, even though it's blatantly obvious.

"What do you want to give me?" His deep voice travels from my head to my toes, igniting the low flame of lust into a raging inferno.

My breaths are shallow and my pulse is beating so loud I'm positive he can hear it. "Well, why don't you show me and find out."

"Nah, this is more fun," Jackson says and stands up opening the door.

"You're not going to think this is so fun in a few hours." With my arms crossed I lean against the door so he can't get through.

Jackson smiles and waits for me to move. He's in no rush and it makes me want to stomp and scream at him. It seems he's back to his playful, jackass self. The walker he uses to get around has a seat and he perches himself on it while I stand there. The smug smile on his face causes my irritation to claw its way up.

"I've got all day," he sighs dramatically and starts to look around.

"I'll make another deal with you," I say. "Even though I don't know why I bother since you don't keep up your end anyway," I tack on just for good measure.

"I'm all ears."

He infuriates me when he's like this. I don't know whether to slap him or kiss him—maybe both. "We'll go to the park and settle in for our beautiful date. Since you're feeling better, you'll tell me my time and I'll tell you yours."

"I'm waiting for the concession here," Jackson cuts me off and taps his fingers on the chair.

I huff, "I'm getting there, Muffin. But you so rudely interrupted." I smile and cock my head to the side. "As I was saying, you give up the goods and if I won then you take me to a Broadway play. Then, you'll treat me to a spa day. If you win, then I won't call you Muffin for at least two weeks, and I'll run that stupid obstacle course again."

"One month," he says quickly, counteroffering my two weeks.

"Two weeks."

"Not good enough, and you'll do a lot more than the obstacle course. As soon as my leg is back to normal and I get the green light from the doc, you'll start running with me every day."

I laugh and roll my eyes. "I think you have a better chance of me becoming a nun before that ever happens."

"Take it or leave it, Kitty," Jackson says, cocky and so sure he has it made.

"My final offer is three weeks." I smile and place both hands on the walker, backing him into the wall. He's completely trapped and his eyes narrow as he looks at the position he's in. "And unless you want to become celibate, you'll retract the running clause."

His lips quirk up into a lazy smile. "You see, baby, I win. I have the time. I have the upper hand. I already know I smoked your beautiful ass. There's no way in hell you beat me, so really this deal has to work in my favor. So you ..." Jackson's fingers wrap around my neck as he pulls me down, "... Are really the one who has to suffer." His lips graze mine and I feel the heat of his breath against my mouth. "Take it. Or leave it."

I can almost feel his smile against my lips. Unable to resist him and hoping this diversion tactic works, I press my mouth to his. My hands thread in his hair and my tongue plunges into his mouth. Controlling every aspect of the kiss, I push further. When he finally let's go and starts to give back, I give him a moment. I need him to get lost in it so I can hopefully have him distracted. Plus, I know he's already excited from our previous kiss. As soon as I hear the moan escape him, I push back and take an extra step out of his grasp. My lips tingle from the kiss and Jackson's eyes are wide as he admires me. The bulge in his pants makes it obvious he was wanting much more.

With his defenses lowered, I move back another step letting him see who really has the power. "You better slow me down before I head out the door." I pause for dramatic effect.

"What game are you playing?"

I start to lift my shirt but stop as I see his pupils dilate, "Jackson?"

He doesn't answer, just watches as I hike it a little higher.

"Do we have a deal?" I ask softly.

"Whatever the fuck you want," Jackson doesn't hesitate in answering.

"I thought you'd say that." I smile and take a step in his direction. He licks his lips and uses his index finger to try to call me over. "Now, come here and finish what you started and then somehow managed to bully me into giving you your way."

Another small step in his direction, but I stop, grab the basket and blanket, and turn on my heels. "Nah, I'm in the mood for the park."

"You're killing me, Catherine. Absolutely fucking killing me," Jackson groans but I hear him moving behind me.

When we're out the door, I turn to him feeling victorious and a little devious. "Guess you don't always win, now do you?"

We quickly reach the boat pond area of Central Park, which is only about a block from his high rise. To say he lives in the most desired area of New York City would be an understatement. It's perfect. I'm glad he pulled me away from work and the launch. We both need this time together.

"I think we should steer clear of any more competitions for today. My balls can't handle it," Jackson says while laughing.

"Awww, my little sore loser."

"When I show you the photo of your time, we'll see who's sore."

I wave my hand dismissively. Even though I added a good four minutes on to his time, the reality is—I have no idea what my damage was. I didn't really fall or struggle too much, but Super SEAL over there didn't even break a sweat. "Want to sit at the end of the hill?" I point to the grassy section that has a small incline. That way he can sit easily and use the height to get up without too much effort. I know how much he hates the limitations his leg injury is causing. At least this is a way to minimize it. Also, he's heavy and difficult for me to maneuver on my own.

"Sounds great. What do you have in that basket?" he asks curiously trying to peek the lid open.

"Just snacks, a few books, and some drinks." I smile as we slowly make our way to the tiny piece of tranquility we'll have in the middle of this metropolis.

"You thought of all that in an hour?" Jackson asks with disbelief in his voice.

"I didn't make a gourmet meal. Also I didn't make a disaster of the kitchen while grabbing things."

He smirks. "I think that night worked out for the both of us."

The blush spreads across my face as I hear the double meaning. Yes, it most definitely did work out for both of us.

Laying out the blanket, I help Jackson get comfortable and I settle in.

"Hey, get over here," he calls and pats his good leg. "Do you want to read for a little while?"

"We have all day, babe. We can do whatever."

It's beautiful out. There's a small breeze and the sun is overhead but we have some shade thanks to the trees. I lie on his leg and look up at him. His strong jaw, beautiful eyes, and short stubble take my breath away. I start to remember the first time we met, how much he affected me. Then, when I realized he was my new client, the electrical charge I fought so hard against was undeniable. But nothing like the first time I saw him without a shirt on—which reminds me of the course.

He leans back on his side and smiles. "You

wanna know, don't you?"

I sit up practically bouncing up and down. "Yes!" I'm so excited. Here comes a play, no running daily crap, and a whole lot of taunting. Well, I hope at least. As quickly as I can, I grab my phone and scroll to the photo with his time and clutch it to my chest. "Okay, you ready, Muffin?" I smirk and ready myself for the moment of truth.

"Oh, baby, I'm more than ready. I hope you get yourself a new pair of running shoes."

"I hope you're ready to lose to a girl."

"If you beat me, I might cry," Jackson jokes.

"Now that I want to see."

Jackson's loud laugh cuts through the quiet as he grabs his phone.

"Ready?" he asks.

"As I'll ever be. Time to pay up, Muff."

"Better get it all out of your system, sweetheart, because that's the last time you'll be saying my call sign for a while."

I shake my head and try to get my excitement in check. "Okay, let's both put the phones face down and then on the count of three we'll flip them over."

Jackson rolls his eyes and hands his phone over. "I'm not worried."

"Neither am I." Tentatively, I hand mine over, controlling my shaking.

We count it down, and then slowly flip the phones over and look at our times.

Game.

Set.

Match.

CHAPTER THIRTEEN

JACKSON

She's fucking kidding me.

There's no way in hell.

I look up at her and her smile says it all. "What's the matter, Muffin?" Her brown eyes are big and she knows she's got me.

"No! No fucking way. No way. How?" I ask, knowing somehow she fixed these times. She did something because I've run that course over a thousand times. I swear I could do it in my sleep. Hell, I could do it now in this stupid walker and still beat her.

She looks up, playing coy, "I have no idea what you mean. I started the timer when you told me to and then you ran it. You must've had an off day."

Off day my ass.

"Catherine, if you don't 'fess up, I promise you'll be running daily and it won't be because of a bet." My brow rises as I try to imply what she'll be running from.

I gotta hand it to her though. She got me—and good.

"A lady never reveals her secrets."

"I'll figure out what you did."

"You can try, Muffin."

"Okay, that's fine. You know you never specified what play, when I had to take you, or what kind of spa treatments." I tap her nose knowing it drives her nuts. Let that sink in ...

Her eyes light up when she realizes the hole in her plan. Like I was ever going to let that happen. "Oh, no. You're not going to loophole your way out of this. I won! I beat your ass. I mean, you are at over twelve minutes. I'm under. I win. You lose." She's talking so fast I have to try to keep up. I love getting her riled up. It's so easy.

I shrug and grab the book, not knowing what the hell it even is but anything to keep pissing her off. "I didn't make the bet. I'm just adhering to the rules."

Catherine scoffs and looks away, "I swear."

"A lady never swears."

She grabs her phone and starts fumbling through it.

"What are you doing?" I ask.

"Looking up what plays have tickets for tomorrow." She gives me a snarky smile.

I cough and grab her phone out of her hand. "Not happening since you cheated."

"We're going to see a play tomorrow."

"The hell we are."

I'll take her anywhere she wants to go, but this is almost too much fun. Her eyes glow as she gets more and more frustrated.

"I hate you."

I laugh because she's so cute when she's petulant. "There's a very fine line between love and hate. I'm pretty sure you love me. I'm pretty loveable."

"You're also a giant pain in my ass. But ..." Her eyes light up and I see it all right there. "I do love you. Even though you feel the need to drive me insane. However, tomorrow there are seats available for *The Lion King* or we can see *The Vagina*

Monologues."

My mouth drops slightly and I wait for the punch line.

"Are there vaginas in the show?"

"None that you'll see." Catherine smirks and slides up to my side. Her voice drops into a seductive whisper, "It's all about menopause. So are we going to see that or are you going to pay up and take me to see *The Lion King*?"

Leaning up, I grab her hand and hold it in mine. I love the way she feels against me. She links her fingers with mine and I pull her forward. "I love you, and I love driving you crazy ... in every way. There's no way in hell we're going to see a play about pussies."

Her grip tightens and she leans forward and kisses me.

I get lost in her. She makes it a little easier to breathe. Shit doesn't suck so bad and my head gets a break when she's in my arms.

"I can't lose you," I say out of nowhere.

She pulls back and her forehead wrinkles as she looks at me. "Why do you think you'd lose me?"

There's so much of my life that she doesn't understand. The constant fear that when she walks out the door in the morning she won't return.

It keeps me up at night.

Haunts me in my dreams. I see her walking away. Asking me for things I'm not capable of giving her and deciding she's had enough. Each night they're the same dreams only different ways of losing her.

chapter fourteen

Catherine

"Jackson?" I ask him again. He's staring off and seems lost. Leaning up I touch his face. "You okay?" The concern is evident in my tone.

"Just remembering something that bothered me. I'm fine," he says, trying to dismiss my worry.

"You know you can talk to me, right?"

Jackson nods and closes his eyes, "Natalie called yesterday."

And there it is.

"She said you guys talked the other day too, right?"

Since Aaron's passing I've grown close to his wife, Natalie. We spoke once while Jackson was in the hospital and since then I speak to her every few days. At first, she didn't want to speak to Jackson or Mark. I understood, considering they were his closest friends, but she said they used the same phrases and it hurt too much. So we talk about life, her pregnancy, and how she wants to go back to work. My heart breaks the most when she tells me about what life is like as a widow and how much she prays this baby will be a boy.

Jackson pulls me onto his leg and attempts to get comfortable. "I sent a large check and arranged the plane to pick up her parents to bring them in. I don't want her to have to worry about anything. She's due this week. Mark has been keeping in touch, but he said she doesn't want to see any of us."

I can't even begin to imagine the pain she's in. Plus, I remember when Neil's sister was pregnant, she was a mess. Crying over toilet paper commercials and then the next minute she was screaming over the way you buttered toast. I wish there was more that we could do for Natalie, but she refused to do a memorial or anything until after the baby is born. I sit and listen to him as he finally starts to open up about Aaron and his death.

"It should've never happened. I want to do more for her. She shouldn't have to go through this alone. I know some of the military wives down there have brought food and things over. But he should be there with her."

"I know. It was senseless and tragic, but you can't make Natalie want your help." It's unfortunate but true. She needs to be ready, and if being near Mark or talking to Jackson is too hard on her then they need to respect that. "She really does seem to be doing better. At least she's talking to you guys now."

Jackson rubs the side of my face and closes his eyes. "I just know if Aaron were here, he'd want his brothers to step up. He'd want us to take care of them. She asked us to arrange everything for him, do a memorial and then a burial. He has a plot in Pennsylvania. Will you be there?"

Without hesitation I respond, "Jackson, you don't even have to ask. I promise I'll be there. No matter what."

"Thank you."

"You don't have to ask if I'll stand by you. If you need me, I'm here."

He lies on the blanket and I scoot up so I can curl into his arm. Jackson grabs our books and hands them to me, letting me know he's done and needs to stop talking. The struggle is evident and I don't want to push him too far.

We both get lost in other worlds, mine of course is about love, while he reads some suspense novel. But we enjoy the solace and the fact that we're here—together.

After about an hour, Jackson starts to get restless and starts shifting and grunting.

"You ready?" I ask, knowing either his pain meds are wearing off or he's asleep.

Jackson lifts his head and looks around. "I'm awake," he says, clearly caught napping.

I giggle and start to get up and put our things in the basket.

"Since you somehow cheated and won the other bet, how about we just let you take what's left of my balls and go to the boats?" Jackson half-laughs and half-snorts.

"There's a lot of truth in that statement, but I'll let you decide which part I mean."

I'm enjoying this winning thing.

"When I first moved to this part of the city I used to come here with Garrett and race him."

"Garrett?" I don't remember anyone by that name.

"You met him. He was at dinner the night we met. Not that you stuck around long enough to really meet anyone, but he's Mark's older brother," Jackson explains while he tries to get up, but he winces and stops.

I put all the stuff down and get behind him. "Let me help you," I say gently, knowing how quickly his mood can shift when he needs help.

"You just want to touch my body."

"You know it," I reply, hoping he'll play along.

We get up pretty easily and he grips the walker and puts his leg on the seat. Only one more week and he will be able to start walking with crutches. His arm is almost fully mobile, and he's growing stronger and moving much more easily.

Jackson and I play for about an hour at the boat pond. I can't for the life of me understand how the man has the drive to make anything a competition. The pond is filled with other boats but there he is trying to maneuver a tiny battery operated boat that doesn't go more than two miles per hour. I let him win since I had no idea what in the world the rules were.

"At least I win this round," Jackson boasts and pulls me against him, kissing the top of my head.

"Yeah," I say without any enthusiasm. "You sure showed me. I'm buying the tickets to the play for tomorrow."

"We're going to pretend this isn't happening. Since you cheated." Jackson places a kiss against my temple and then grabs my hand. "Let's go home. I have some plans for you."

Home. Even he's calling it home when we talk about it. As much as it thrills me that he's so comfortable with me in his home, there's a small part of me terrified we're moving too fast. So much has happened and yet we've skipped the whole getting to know each other stage and fell into the living together stage. I don't doubt my feelings or his, I only want to make sure we don't screw this up.

We walk the block to his apartment with my arm draped around his waist. "I hope those plans include food and maybe ice cream," I say as my stomach growls.

Jackson's eyes dance with mischief. "I fully intend on eating."

It takes me a second to understand the look on his face. "Oh my God! Jackson!" I laugh and he joins me.

"What? I ordered take-out."

"Sure, that's what you were insinuating."

"I'm a gentleman," he says as we enter the lobby of his building.

"Right, and I'm an angel," I say and board the elevator.

He maneuvers us into the corner and spins his walker so I'm in between his arms, making it impossible for me to move. "Did you have something else in mind?"

My tongue swipes across my lips and Jackson's eyes track the movement. "I could be open for suggestions."

His arm slides a little lower and it amazes me that even injured he can find a way to seduce me. "Hmmm," he says as the distance between us closes.

It takes every ounce of restraint to let him lead and not maul him. The rise and fall of my chest has his attention as my nipples pebble. His scent of crisp linen and cologne overwhelms me and I want nothing more than to be surrounded by him. I've never been more happy about the lack of that arm sling than in this moment when he snakes his other arm around my neck and one around my back and carefully pulls me flush against him. "I'm going to love you, and then I'm going to make you pay for toying with me all day." The sound of promise in his voice causes heat to pool in my core.

And he's back.

The doors open and he turns, leaving me in a puddle on the floor. I don't know what I look forward to … the punishment or the love.

"You coming?" Jackson calls over his shoulder.

Oh, I hope so.

I smile and when I turn to close the door, I feel his heat against my back. "Games are over," Jackson says against my neck as his mouth finds purchase against my shoulder. His mouth moves slowly as he rains kisses against my exposed back.

Sensually, he moves the straps from one side down, giving him the access he wants, and my hands press against the door. "Stay like this," Jackson commands when I try to turn.

"I want to feel you," I reply in a whisper. It feels so good being cocooned by his warmth. His arms give me safety like they always do. With him, I'm stronger—we're stronger.

Jackson grips my wrist holding it above my head and his other hand wraps my arm around his neck giving him control. I could easily break from his hold. The hand that holds me is his bad arm and I know he doesn't have much strength, but I know he needs this. The feeling of some kind of power when his life has been anything but in control. "I'm not asking. Stay put." His voice is steel wrapped in velvet.

His hands lower to my hips and his hand snakes up my shirt as he pulls it up over my head.

"God, you're beautiful."

"You're not so bad yourself," I reply over my shoulder.

He kisses his way from my shoulder to my neck. Moving slowly until he reaches my mouth. Jackson's hand grips my head and he pulls me into him. I turn as much as possible into the kiss. My brain ceases to exist as I spin and clutch myself to him and he winces.

"I'm sorry," I say as he grips his leg that's resting on the chair. "I just—"

"Shut up and kiss me," he says as he grabs me and slams his mouth on mine.

And I do. I kiss him relentlessly. Pouring myself into him and taking all he gives me. When our mouths collide, everything else fades away.

I feel his hands twine up my back as he unhooks my bra and my breasts fall free. His hands cup me and gently massage them while rolling my nipples in his fingers before pulling on them. I gasp as pleasure fills my body and I struggle to keep upright.

Jackson grips my hand and pulls me along while maneuvering himself through the apartment into his bedroom. "As much as I'd love to fuck you against the wall again," he smiles while tugging me to him, "I don't think I'm strong enough for it yet. So get on the bed."

I grin while unbuttoning my shorts and let them fall to the ground exposing myself to him. "I'm sure you'll find a way to make it up to me," I say as I hook my fingers in my purple thong and slowly slide it down. "Won't you?" I watch his pupils dilate and his eyes rake my body.

"Fuck yeah I will. Now, stop talking."

When he's like this I feel incredible. Every part of me lights up and I come to life. He elicits this power and raw sensuality from me. I feel bold, beautiful, and more than anything—enough. There's never a time I feel as though I'm lacking with him.

"Tonight, nothing else exists but us," Jackson says as he takes his shirt off.

Now it's my time to stare. Even with his scars, he's perfect. If anything, they make me want him more. Jackson wears his wounds and lives. It reminds me of all that he is and how I wouldn't change a thing. Does it scare me that he could return overseas? Of course. To know the man I love could go and possibly not return scares me more than I care to admit. But when I spoke to Natalie last week, she said something that spoke to my soul. She said, "Even if I could go back and tell Aaron not to go, I wouldn't. This is who he was. He was a soldier, a fighter, a hero, and he needed this. It fed his world. The fact that someone else didn't die and he had to bear that cross—it's what he would've wanted."

Jackson's deep voice breaks my thoughts, "Catherine, stay with me. Only me." He links our fingers and pulls me to the bed.

I climb up and settle on my side while he gets situated so he's facing me. His fingers glide up and down my ribs as we gaze at each other.

"What are you thinking?" I ask.

"About us, about how I wasn't sure I'd ever have you back again." Jackson's voice grows shaky at the end and I close my eyes.

"I think somehow we'd have found a way. But promise me you'll never walk away like that again."

"You don't ever have to worry about that. I'm not going anywhere," he says as our lips touch. Our tongues meet and my hands roam his glorious body.

My fingers trace the ridges on his arms then around to his back as we explore each other slowly and completely. There's no rushing. We savor each other as if this is our last time—or first.

The feel of his hands on my stomach causes the moisture to pool as I envision him going lower. "Jackson," I moan as his hand sinks lower and he rubs small circles on my clit.

I grip his cock in my hand and begin to stroke him, feeling him grow against my touch. "I want to feel your mouth wrapped around my dick," Jackson says against my neck as he thrusts a finger into my pussy.

The sound of my groan reverberates through the room as I imagine taking him. Giving him pleasure while he's merciless to my touch. Knowing I have the physical ability to do just that, I move and feel his loss inside, but I grow even wetter preparing for what I'm about to do. "You asked for it." I smile when he quirks his eyebrow and leans on his back.

Holding the base of his cock, I lick him from root to tip, enjoying the way the muscles tighten in his legs as I run my tongue around the top. His hands grip the sheet as I continue to torment him, refusing to take him into my mouth. I palm his balls and roll them in my hand and he thrusts upward. Once again I rim my tongue before taking him deep in my mouth.

"Yes …" Jackson hisses when I hollow out my mouth. His hand threads in my hair as I sink back down taking him into my throat. "Fuck, you feel good."

I take my time and tease him, enjoying every sound or word that escapes him. It spurs me on, wanting to give him the pleasure he always makes me feel. I bob my head and his grip tightens letting me know he's starting to lose control. I pull up and release him from my mouth, needing to finish what we started together. "I want to feel you," I say breathlessly.

"Lie down."

"That's not a good—"

"Lie down, Catherine. I'm going to love you this time," Jackson says as he cradles my head in his hands. "Now, let me."

Against my better judgment, I lie on my back. He slowly and carefully measures each movement, climbing on top of me. This is the most weight he will have put on his arm since the shooting. The fear is evident in my eyes and he smiles letting me know he's okay.

"If it becomes too much, do you promise you'll tell me?" I ask him, trying to quell my nerves. I don't want to see him back in the hospital because he needed to prove something to himself.

"It's always too much with you, baby." He lowers his lips to mine. "You make me lose control because I can't think of anything else but you." Jackson's tongue traces the shell of my ear as he continues to seduce me with his words. "When I'm inside you, all I feel is your heat, I feel your breaths, and I fucking love every second. Now," Jackson pauses as I feel him start to enter me, "I'm going to make you come so hard you see stars. Hang on, baby." He thrusts forward before I have a second to consider what he said and all I feel is him. I'm filled by him and it's heaven.

"God, I've missed you," I say. Even though we've been together a few times, there's been a part of him holding back. Not now, though. He's everywhere, the energy around us, not allowing me to see or feel anything but him.

Jackson moves slowly as he hovers and pushes deeper. "Look at me."

My eyes shift to his and it's suddenly hard to breathe. He rocks back and forth while staring into my eyes as we become one in every sense of the word. Our souls touch, and moisture builds in my eyes from the pure beauty of the moment. Before the tears can descend he kisses them away and I fight the urge to sob. I'm so overcome with emotion I feel as if my heart is going to beat right out of my chest.

His mouth lowers and he kisses me. I close my eyes and feel everything. The love, the anger, the hurt, and I give myself permission to feel it all. I know he has me and won't let me fall. Jackson will keep me safe even if it's from myself.

"You're fucking made for me. You feel so good, I can't think."

He moves sinuously, driving me higher and I fight the emotional high as well. The pleasure becomes overwhelming, but I don't want it to end. Every second with him feels incredible. Each thrust of his hips fills me with love.

After a few minutes, I can't fight the need to release any longer. I start to set the pace for him from the bottom. I grind my hips as he starts to moan and shake subtly. We're both so close to the edge.

"So close. I'm so c-close," I stutter as I rotate my hips cautiously.

"I'm not going to last much longer," Jackson says through clenched teeth as the sweat builds on his forehead.

Gliding my own hand lower, I start to circle my clit and Jackson groans when he realizes what I'm doing.

"Fuck, Catherine."

"I'm coming. Now," I cry out and fall over the edge as Jackson grunts and finishes with me. He lies on top of me panting and we're both covered in sweat, but I couldn't care less in this minute. I could stay like this forever with him.

"You ready, babe?" I call out to Jackson who is purposely taking his sweet ass time.

"No, I think we'll have to just skip it."

"Jackson Cole! You lost the bet. You agreed to the terms, now it's time to take me to see *The Lion King*." I saunter into his bedroom and he's lying on the bed.

I'm gonna beat him.

"Are you serious right now?" I ask staring at him fully dressed, incredibly sexy, and almost good enough to pass up on the musical. But not quite.

Jackson groans and rolls to his side, "I'm injured. I can't go."

"You're going to be injured. The doorman said the cab is waiting."

His lip juts out and it's so cute, I lean forward and kiss him. He makes me smile even when I want to slap him.

"What was that for?" he asks with a grin. "Are you telling me you're going to admit you fixed this stupid game and now you're coercing me into this awful play with grown men dressed like animals?"

I laugh and shake my head. "We're going."

Jackson grunts and I suppress a laugh. He's so cute when he's not driving me insane. "You know, I was shot. Three times. I think this should score me some sympathy points."

I tap my forefinger on my chin. "Let's see. Since you're so injured, I think you're right."

His face beams but then he narrows his eyes. "I don't believe you."

"And here I thought you were dumb. Let's go." I grab my purse and straighten my dress.

Finally, he gets up and looks at me, smiling. There are times where just one look can melt me to my core—this is one. "What?"

"You're beautiful. Come kiss me, woman."

With a smile on my lips, I walk over and press them to his. Gingerly, Jackson's calloused thumb grazes my cheek and I shiver. His touch elicits so many emotions and I pray we never lose this. I want to get lost in him.

"Enough stalling. Come on, Muffin."

Jackson says something under his breath but I expect it. We exit the apartment and when we get to the street, there's a black town car waiting.

"I figured the cab wouldn't want to wait in case I was able to talk you out of this," Jackson explains with an easy tone.

I shrug and get in the car, "Too bad it didn't work."

We settle in the car and Jackson and I talk about the musical a little. Apparently he has no clue what to expect. He's never been to Broadway before.

"I don't understand how you can live in Manhattan and never go to the theater."

"I work. A lot," he retorts and pulls me against his side. I mold to him and close my eyes feeling the way his rough hand rubs tiny circles on my arm. "Just think, we could be home. Possibly naked. But you wanted to see men in tights."

The giggle escapes my mouth before I can hold it back. "This isn't the ballet, although, if you're interested in seeing it, I'm sure I can get tickets."

"Not on your best day, sweetheart."

We pull up to the theater and Jackson grumbles playfully. I've never considered myself a sadistic person, but I'm thoroughly enjoying his discomfort. It could be that if I lost he wouldn't have hesitated at all. I would have had to pay for it, and knowing Jackson, he would've found other ways than just no name calling.

"Muffin?" He looks up and his lip curls but then he smiles. "Time to find out about the circle of life."

"How long are these things?"

"A few hours."

"*Hours*?" Jackson asks disbelievingly. "As in more than one?"

I laugh and he pushes the walker forward. "Yes, babe. Like two or three."

Jackson and I find our seats and get comfortable. As much as I'm happy to be here, there's so much stuff I need to get done for the launch in a few days. I don't have much time and I've spent a lot dealing with personal things.

"Hey," Jackson pauses and tilts my chin toward him. "What's wrong?"

I smile and softly shake my head. "Nothing."

"If I have to be here, you're going to be happy." His lip curls and one eye closes.

Leaning into my seat, I give myself a mental break. Everything will be fine. Right now, I have the man I love sitting at my side and he took me on a date.

"I'm happy. How could I not be? I won."

He groans and takes my hand in his lap. "Do I get dinner after this?" I ask.

"No, but I did sign us up for the next 5k in town."

I gasp with my jaw hanging. "I'm not running."

"Oh, but you are. While I was paying for these lovely tickets, it popped up as an ad. I knew you'd want to support me the way I'm suffering—I mean, enjoying—what we're doing now." He rubs his hand on the stubble on his chin.

"I didn't lose a bet."

"Neither did I, yet here I am." Jackson smiles and sits back in his chair.

As the first act begins, Jackson's arm slides around my back and he pulls me close. I nestle into his side and kiss his neck. "Thank you," I whisper.

"Don't thank me yet," Jackson jokes quietly.

The show carries on and I look over at Jackson who laughs at Rafiki's antics and I would swear I saw a tear in his eyes when Mufasa dies. Of course I'll never be able to get him to admit it, but I will sure as hell taunt him with it.

The second act is being called and Jackson spent all of intermission explaining why it would be so much fun if we left early.

"That three-mile run is going to be so much fun."

"You can't make me run."

Jackson leans forward and his warm breath blows across my neck. "I can make you want to run."

"You'd have to do something pretty bad to make me run. Like lie or cheat," I smile waiting for a witty response.

Jackson's eyes flash with fear but he recovers quickly enough that I'm not sure that I saw it. Goosebumps form and my stomach tightens. I don't know what to call the sudden wash of emotion. But I can't help but worry there's something lurking.

The lights go out and the stage lights up. I shake off the ominous feeling and I'm lost in the beauty of the colors, the way they brought the African grasslands to life in New York. Jackson and I hold hands through the show and I feel peace. Everything in my life feels right. I have a man I love desperately and he loves me back. I have a job I love more and more each day. And I have amazing friends and Neil is out of my life.

Things are good, and I'm truly and blissfully happy. There's a small part nagging at me telling me not to get too comfortable, but I've been guilty of overreacting before. I suppress it and focus on the good.

chapter fifteen

*S*hit.

Of all the days to be running late it had to be today. The press launch is in two hours and Taylor is making sure everything is in order before we have to leave. I'm running around the office like a madwoman and she's running out the door to get to Raven to set up.

I continue to check through emails and the seating charts so I know who's who and which companies will give Raven the boost they need.

"Knock, knock." I look up and see one of my bosses standing in the door.

"Mr. Cartright, please come in." This is the absolute last distraction I need this morning.

He smiles and enters, looking around at the controlled chaos that is my office. "The press release for Raven is today, correct?"

I nod and grab the file I had opened and place it in my briefcase. At least today he's seeing me at my best. I have a deep crimson, knee-length dress, my hair has large curls cascading down my back, and my makeup is camera ready. "Yes, sir. We're happy to get this off the ground, and then of course we have the party tonight. Will you be attending?" I ask already knowing he won't be. The partners go away for a sales meeting in Bermuda every year at this time. It's really a huge golf retreat that they write off as a business meeting. I made the mistake of going once and was subjected to driving their drunk asses around in a golf cart for three days. To guarantee that doesn't happen again, I try to book this month with anything I can.

"My flight is tomorrow, but when we return on Friday, the partners would like to meet with you. We've been highly impressed at how you've handled the Raven account. You were able to change the tone of the company in a short amount of time, even with Mr. Cole's near death experience," Mr. Cartright says.

"Thank you, I'm glad everyone is happy." I'm beaming at his praise, and also wondering what this means for the promotion that has been on the table for what seems like forever. Taylor mentioned that Elle's last account didn't renew their three-month contract and the rumors are she is out of the running.

"If all goes well today, Catherine, I think you'll find yourself sitting in a very lucrative new position." He winks and strides out of the office.

As fantastic as his pep talk might be, I needed that distraction about as much as I need Jackson's ten phone calls reminding me of what he wants done. We agreed it is best that in front of the camera, he is commanding and doesn't appear injured. Tonight at the party, he'll be able to blend and it will be much easier for him to remain sitting without anyone noticing.

My phone dings again.

Jackson: Are you avoiding me?

Me: No, I'm working. I will call you in the cab so

you can micromanage a little more.

Jackson: I'm not micromanaging. I'm supervising. From home.

Me: Whatever you need to tell yourself to help you sleep at night.

He's driving me nuts.

Jackson: I'd rather help you at night.

I laugh and throw my purse in my bag. Grabbing the files and my speech, I head to Raven for part one of my very long day. Once in the cab, I give him that promised call and allow him to say what he needs so he can relax.

"Hey, baby." Jackson's voice sounds strained.

"What are you doing? You sound out of breath."

Jackson grunts, "I was just moving something."

"Seriously?" I ask incredulously. Does he think he has some kind of magical healing powers? "You're supposed to be resting, and you have the event tonight."

"Look, I'm sitting here watching this on the damn computer. Cut me some slack."

I lean my head back trying to understand, yet wanting to crawl through the phone and smack some sense into him. "Please, I'm begging you. Relax, rest, and no moving furniture, cooking, or anything else that can risk any injury."

"I'll do my best."

"I'm almost there. If you have any questions, call Taylor. She will have her phone on her, but once I get on stage, you won't be able to change the outcome of anything. Trust me to do my job."

He gives a long sigh. "I will. I'll see you later. You're coming home to change, right?"

I smile thinking of the dress sitting in the guest room. It's a deep purple, one-shoulder, satin dress. It's tight in the body and then flows out but pulls up every so many inches, accentuating my curves. It took my breath away when I saw it. Paired with my silver, jeweled shoes, I can't wait to put it on. "Yes, I have to get my dress and pick up my hot date. Even though you can't really be my date."

The cab stops and I hear Jackson mumbling about firing me so he can have his girlfriend.

"I love you," I say, throwing some money and trying to exit the car.

"I love you too," he says and I smile at the petulant tone he has when he doesn't get his way.

I disconnect the call, and before I can step out of the cab, Taylor and Danielle are at my side firing off information.

"Everyone's ready. Everything's in order. You have the intro, then Danielle will present part of the slides. After she wraps up, you can do a Q&A and we're done." Taylor speaks so fast I have to really focus to hear everything.

"Breathe. It's all going to be great. Everyone is aware of what needs to be done. Start gathering the press into the large vestibule and we'll start in about ten." I smile, putting on my best everything-is-just-fine face.

Most of us call this our camera persona. I'm polite, witty, and always smiling. My cheeks usually hurt for a full day after any press or photo junkets. I'm ready to make Jackson and my bosses proud. This promotion is so close I can taste it, and my contract with Raven will be over soon, and then I won't have to worry about the morality of dating a client. Luckily, we've managed to keep things low

profile and the people who do know have been extremely supportive.

"Ready?" Danielle says at my side as we both
plaster on our smiles and open the door into the
launch.

There's a small stage and a podium, with bright
photos of the new products with a sheet over them
for the actual unveil. My adrenaline spikes as the
excitement grows. This is the part of the job I love. I
command the press and all of my hard work shows
in this moment.

"Good morning, thank you all for being here," I
begin with my speech.

After a few minutes of introductions and going
over the booklet they were given, I hand it over to
Danielle for her portion of the presentation. I'm impressed with her. We spent hours going over camera posture and when to pause to allow maximum
attention. Taylor and I prepped her for anything we
could think of, ensuring she was comfortable.

She hands the microphone back over to me and
I brace myself for any questions. This is the one
part of the press conferences I despise. You can
prepare all you want, but you can't predict the way
the questions will go.

The first hand rises and I call on her.

"Ms. Pope, can you tell us a little about when
the product will be available in stores?"

"We expect the rollout to begin in the next three
months. The product has been tested and has been
sent to mass production." I smile and call on the
next hand that's raised.

A short woman with red hair asks, "How do you
feel this product differs from the others in the market?"

"This product line is made with all natural ingredients. There are no fillers and Raven is able to keep the prices competitive with what some call over-the-counter makeup lines. You're getting high quality for a bargain price."

I field a few more questions regarding the price point.

Taylor signals it's time to close, since we want to keep this brief and exciting.

There's time for one more question. "Yes, Miss?" She's blond with beautiful features, her eyes are wide as she realizes I'm calling on her.

"Thank you for taking my question." I nod and she reads off an index card. "Can you tell us how Mr. Cole is handling the company considering his injuries?" I'm surprised it took so long for someone to ask.

"He's doing well. Mr. Cole has stayed in contact with his staff and ensured there has been very little disruption to the company during his recovery," I say as confidently as possible and begin to wrap up but she cuts me off.

"That's great, but the company has had a vast amount of change in the past year. What about the fact that the company's dealt with two new CEO's in eighteen months, with Mr. Cole's wife no longer controlling the company, and the last CEO resigning so suddenly? How is Raven coping with this revolving door of leadership?"

And the floor falls out from under me.

Did she just say "*wife*?"

"I'm sorry, can you repeat the question?" I say trying to catch my breath while appearing completely in control.

"With the company undergoing so many

changes, with different CEOs, understandably first when Mrs. Elliott-Cole departed, but then another quick change of hands … How are the staff handling yet another catastrophe?"

My heart falls to the pit of my stomach. I feel dizzy. Everything around me becomes hazy and I grip the podium, trying to stay upright. He wouldn't do this to me, would he? Would he hide a marriage? How? A wife? Is he still married? The questions bombard me one after another as I try to focus on the people in front of me.

I hear a throat clear from behind me and I realize I haven't answered the question. "This question would probably be best answered by Ms. Masters. She's been an employee through these transitions." I manage a half-mangled smile and the pity in Danielle's eyes says it all.

It's true and she knows I didn't know, which means he deliberately kept it from me.

Married.

I rush off the stage before Danielle finishes her answer. I'm going to be sick. Taylor rushes over with a glass of water and ushers me out the back. I slump in a chair, trying to get a grip on my thoughts.

What the fuck just happened?

"Cat? Are you okay?" Taylor asks, probably knowing I'm so far from all right.

"Married?" I ask no one.

She rubs my back as I try to hold back the bile building in my throat.

"There's no way he's still married, Catherine. You've been with him for how long now?" Taylor says as I push to my feet.

"No? I know nothing. No one ever mentioned a *wife*, Taylor!"

"Maybe because there isn't one. We researched and nothing ever mentioned a wife," she tries to rationalize.

My hand flies over my mouth as I try to stifle the scream threatening to escape. "The name. Elliott. Do you remember? All we found was the single name. There was nothing about a first name or a hyphenated name."

"The press would have different sources, but I don't know. No one ever mentioned a wife? Wouldn't Jackson have told you?" Taylor asks as she suddenly goes still.

She tries to reassure me but I can't be here. I can't think. I can't breathe. The walls are closing in and I look down the hall at his office. The place I sat with the purple furniture, it all starts to click. The vague answers, the photos in Virginia. So much information that he must have buried about his wife. How convenient. I'm a fool. A fucking idiot, who trusted him—and he's a liar. I warned him that I'd never take this road again. I guess he really didn't care or believe me.

After everything, how? I grip my hair and try to calm myself.

"Catherine?" I hear Danielle behind me. "I didn't know—" She stops when I look up at her with tears swimming in my eyes. "You should talk to him."

"No one thought I should know this? As his publicist? As his fucking girlfriend? How could everyone let me go into this blind? You know what … I don't want to know. It wasn't your job to tell me."

Between my phone and Taylor's the ringing has been nonstop.

I've seen her silence it twice but as the screen lights up again, she puts the phone to her ear. I

know it's him. He was watching the press conference on his computer. He got the show of his life—I
hope he enjoyed it.

She responds in short answers and I hear him
grow more frustrated through the line. Taylor
hunches down in front of me. "Cat, it's him," she
puts her phone out for me to take.

He must not know how to take a hint.

I grab the phone. Press the end button and hand
it back.

"I'm already gone," I say and grab my bag heading out the door.

chapter sixteen

I arrive back at my office refusing the fifteen phone calls and unknown number of text messages from Jackson before finally shutting my phone off.

Fuck him.

There's nothing to say at this point. I'm way too angry, hurt, and disappointed to hear his voice. This isn't a conversation we should have over the phone anyway. This is a conversation we should've had months ago.

Taylor comes in and shuts the door. "I've lost count of how many times the line has rung, Catherine. You should at least—"

"No," I say with no room for discussion. "I'll deal with him when I'm ready. And I'm not ready. I have a party to go to tonight for a client. I need to make sure the caterers are on track." My voice begins to tremble as the emotions begin to surface. No. I won't do this. Not today. I need to be in my show mode dammit. "There's a lot I need to do."

Damn him.

Taylor nods and I look away as she exits my office. I will not break down until I've handled my job. It's all I have anymore.

Two hours fly by and I can't put off going to get my dress any longer. There's no way I can skip the party I've planned. I always knew this was a possibility. That's the part that kills me—I knew better. My mind is filled with a thousand questions and none of them I want the answers to. I hoped the time at the office would help me think straight. All it's done is make me more angry and upset.

I was honest. I told him everything. I explained how I couldn't live through this again, couldn't - wouldn't - put up with dishonesty. All this time he had, and not one word. We played that stupid game with all the questions, we spent hours in the park, the hospital ... all chances he had ... besides the obvious "Oh hey, I have a wife" gambit.

My nausea churns as I start to think over all the times we made love and he could still be married. There are so many questions about where she is. Are they separated? Divorced? I can't get my head to stop spinning. I hate the amount of self-doubt he's managed to cause with one question.

I can't delay this anymore. I have to get my dress. Maybe I'll pick up a date along the way and let him see how it feels—maybe Ashton knows someone. This shouldn't be like this. I shouldn't be sitting here thinking this. The plan for tonight was not *this*.

"I'll see you later?" I ask Taylor knowing she and her boyfriend are both attending tonight.

She looks up with wide eyes. "Cat, I-I think," she begins but looks away. "I think you should wear your hair down," Taylor says and I give the best smile I'm able to fake at this point. I know she wanted to say something about the Jackson situation, but being the friend she is, she stayed loyal—unlike some people.

"I'm going to get my dress and then I'll be at the hotel," I say as I stride toward the elevator.

Time to deal with my client.

All the strength and preparation on the subway has completely left me as I stand outside his apartment building shaking. Lies, a relationship built on lies.

I look at my phone and it flashes his face as he calls again. He'll talk to me soon enough.

Again it rings.

This time it's Ashton.

"Hi." I answer the phone but my voice sounds lifeless.

"What the fuck is going on? Jackson called me twice and then Mark called. Are you okay? They said they didn't know where you were." She sounds frantic. Bet they didn't tell her why.

"I'm not going to get into it now but expect me home tonight. So please don't taze me or hit me with a bat at two a.m. After the launch party is done I'll probably crash."

"What? I don't understand. All Jackson said was he needed to talk to you, but you wouldn't answer his calls. Why would you come home?"

I huff and shove away my disgust. "I need to handle this fucking party and tomorrow when I wake up, we'll talk. I love you, Ash. But I have to go to work."

She lets out a long breath. I know she needs more information, but right now, I don't have it. "This doesn't sound like you, but answer me this: On a scale of one to ring the alarm, what are we at?"

"Let's say the alarm is ringing and I'll need someone to break the fucking bell."

"Okay, great, so we're talking nuclear. And you're sure you don't want to talk to me now?" she asks carefully.

"If you want a preview of what our conversation will be, watch the press conference for Raven. Be sure to get some popcorn, because it's quite a show."

"Okay, but that doesn't explain where Jackson comes in."

"Oh, but it does. Ashton, I need to pretend my life didn't go from amazing to shit. Let's just say its broken and there isn't a way it can ever go back together. I have to go to this fucking party and smile, so please don't make me cry right now," I say, trying to control my emotions, but my voice slips when I explain how broken we are. There's no fixing this.

"So we're talking about calling in Gretchen and removing all knives from the apartment. Got it. I love you, Cat. I'm always on your side. I know you don't want to hear it, but nothing is ever broken beyond repair." Ashton's voice is the only thing keeping me from falling to the ground right now.

I take a step into the building and hold on to the knowledge that this won't kill me. I'll survive this.

"I love you and I'll see you tomorrow."

Entering the elevator, I find a way to get myself under control. I slip into another role. The one where I'm on stage and need to perform. I can do this. I just need to breathe and remember I can fall apart later. This entire night will need to be an Oscar-worthy performance, only I won't be accepting any awards. Because in the end no one wins anything here.

I hesitate at the door as the turmoil rages like a war within. I've been living here for almost a month and this makes me question everything. Do I knock? Do I use my key? I'm not sure of anything since I no longer feel like I belong here.

Fuck it. He didn't really give a shit about boundaries, so why should I?

"Catherine?" Jackson calls out when the door closes behind me as he comes around the corner. "Catherine, please."

I put my hand up letting him know I can't listen to him. The sound of his voice is making me feel ill. "If you want me to remain civil at all, you'll shut up. You'll find a way to respect me in this moment and allow me to get through this. I'm getting my things and I have to work tonight, Mr. Cole."

He stops and I can see how much my words affect him. "You're not even going to let me talk, are you?"

"No. The time for talking was months ago. Today, I'm going to fucking work!" I skirt past him into the guest room and slam the door. My back rests against it and I slide down with tears streaming silently. Dammit, I wasn't going to cry.

He's hurt me so much more than I can ever explain. Seeing him standing there with the pain in his eyes just shattered anything left inside of me. He lied to me. Even if he's not married anymore, he never told me. All this time. The months, the countless nights I've been at his side, never once did he mention it. Not only that, his friends and family never said a word. I gave him my non-negotiables and he broke one anyway. I feel like a damn fool.

I hear his walker moving back and forth on the other side of the door. It stops and then moves again. He knocks twice but I don't answer. I need to get ready. Removing the dress from the bag, I wipe the tears from my face. No more crying. Show mode time. I put the beautiful dress on and pin my hair up allowing the low back to be seen. Trying to fix my makeup is more of a challenge. Each time I apply eyeliner, another tear falls without permission. After a few minutes and a lot of counting to ten, I manage to make myself look decent. It took a shit-ton of concealer and waterproof mascara.

Once my shoes are on, I open the door and he's leaning against the wall staring at me. His blue-green eyes are hollow as he takes me in. "You should get ready, Mr. Cole. You have an event in an hour."

"Stop it," Jackson says, taking a step toward me, but I retreat. His eyes go wide when he sees my reaction. "I tried to tell you a hundred times."

"Apparently, you didn't understand what I asked from you. I don't want to fucking hear it!" I scream and close my eyes releasing a breath through my nose. "I won't have this conversation with you tonight. I have a job to do and you've had plenty of chances to talk before. You need to let me go to this party and smile, telling everyone how wonderful you are. Even though right now I want to punch you in the face."

"Punch me, hit me, I don't care, but we need to work this out. You walk away tonight I know you're not coming back. I can't—" Jackson pleads but I cut him off as if he didn't speak.

"I have to look charming, happy, and not like my boyfriend just destroyed my entire world. Not like the man I spent weeks by his bedside praying he would live just single handedly killed me. Or like the hero I thought I had turned out to be a traitor. Does that sum up the emotions I'm feeling right now? Do I need to go on? No? Good. Go put your tuxedo on. If you could do it in this room so I can pack my things, I would appreciate it."

Jackson stands there staring at me while I shake

with anger. My jaw trembles as I try to regain an ounce of control. I turn so he can't see my further breakdown. Just being close to him makes my heart break.

"So this is it then?" He pauses and I nod. "Fine. Once again you're shutting me out. I can explain it all, but you won't listen."

I turn with wide eyes and gawk at him disbelievingly. "I'm going to pretend you didn't just say that. I won't let you blame me for this! Fuck you! You will *not* make me the bad guy here. It was on me last time. This one, Jackson, is all you! Lies of omission are lies. I don't even know what the fuck is the truth. Was any of it real? Did you mean *any* of it? Or was I just a game?" My voice rises with each word. I'm seething. How dare he try to put this on *me*.

"Did it feel like a game, Catherine? Do you really believe any of the bullshit you're saying? You know me!" His voice drops into a gruff whisper. "You're the only one who knows me, dammit. Don't shut me out."

My eyes narrow into slits as the anger boils through my veins. "I don't know you at all! I thought I did. Guess the joke is on me. I warned you. I told you that day in the hospital what I needed from you. I guess your loyalty lies with your *wife*." I step forward wanting to slap him, hurt him like he's hurt me. "Go get ready before we say things we're going to regret." I turn and grab my bag to start filling it. Fuck it, at this point I couldn't give a shit if I have to buy everything new.

"Wow, okay, I see how it is. You've already made up your mind without hearing my side."

"What were the only things I asked from you?" I raise my hand and tick them off one at a time.

"Fidelity, well, that's shot to shit. Honesty, hmmm, we can cross that one off. Loyalty, yup, another winner. So not only did you break one, no, you got all three down in one fell swoop. Good job, Jackson, you sure came out on top." I'm seething. The anger rolls off of me in waves.

"I never—you know what, you're going to make your assumptions regardless of what I say. You'll never know how much I wish I could go back and change things. One day when you learn everything, then you'll feel different." He shakes his head and enters the spare room.

"Doubtful."

When the door shuts, I rush to the bedroom and start grabbing anything I see that's mine. I need out of here, his scent is everywhere. Everything is a memory. I can't look at anything without seeing us. The bed where we made love last night, the couch where we watched movies and read books, the shower, the kitchen, the memories are everywhere and I can't take it. My breathing is heavy and I feel dizzy. Everything is happening so fast. How much more can one heart break before it's past the point of repair?

As I approach the front door with my bag, I hear his voice. "You're going to leave after everything, without even talking?" His voice cracks at the last word.

"Did you miss the press conference?" I refuse to turn and look at him.

"No, I saw it all."

"I figured, since you called a few hundred times. I guess you missed the part where I didn't want to talk to you. You want to talk now, but the months we've been together you failed to mention it. Instead you lied to me."

"I never lied. I didn't know how to tell you," he admits and I still have no idea what part he means.

Is he married? Is he divorced? Is she going to show up one day and he'll run off with her? I spin and look at him with tears threatening, "Well, here is an idea ... hey, Catherine, I know we're getting serious, but I'm married, or I was married, or whatever the truth is. You didn't do that though." I step forward and my voice is laced with venom. I'm seething and my world is crumbling around me. "Instead you let me fall in love with you, care for you, and find out like that!" I hold on to my stomach as the pain slices through me. "I trusted you. I loved you with everything inside of me. I put my career on the line for you—for us. But you kept a marriage from me. Are you still married? Don't answer that. It's not my business anymore because we aren't anything." Jackson's eyes close as he stands there listening to me go on.

"I should've told you. I know this! Don't you think I wish I could go back and tell you about Madelyn?" he says with anger radiating off him.

I gasp and my hand flies over my mouth. God, she has a name.

"Why are you doing this? I don't want to know her fucking name! I don't want to know anything. I can't do this tonight. As your publicist, I advise that with your next PR company, you should be upfront so they don't stand before the press and look like a fucking idiot. Not only did your girlfriend—well, ex-girlfriend—have to find out in the most embarrassing and humiliating way possible, but your publicist was thrown for a loop on camera. Now I have to go to work. My client needs me. That's what you are. You lost me in any other capacity. I'll see you at the party, Mr. Cole."

I turn on my heels and walk out the door. My heart may have just been left in his apartment, but I'm going to work and I don't need it. He can have it, since it's dead anyway.

chapter
seventeen

The hotel in midtown Manhattan is arranged perfectly while everything else in my life is a mess. I look around and want to leave already. This is the worst possible place for me, being in this room, all dressed up but feeling naked and exposed. I was on camera when I found it all out, everyone saw. But more than that, he ripped me wide open when we spoke.

I hear people moving around me but I don't see faces. "Cat, there's a small problem in the bar area." Taylor's hand touches my shoulder and I jump.

"Sorry, Tay. What did you say?" I close my eyes and dispel all my issues for the moment, willing myself to focus.

When I finally look up, Taylor smiles and repeats her previous statement. "The rooftop bar is claiming we didn't reserve it exclusively. I handled it, but I figured you'd want to know," she says and looks at me, waiting.

Everything is in slow motion.

"Catherine? Can you handle this?" she questions me.

"I don't know," I say, looking up into her eyes, begging her to help me in some way. I feel lost. "I'm going to need you to stay by my side."

"Is he coming?"

"I couldn't tell you. I assume he is, but please,"

I grip her wrists and plead, "Keep him away from me. I can't."

She twists to hold my hands in hers. "I think one day you'll see the strength you actually have. You're going to get through this, but I'll be by your side the entire night."

I attempt to smile but fail. "Thank you."

"You look beautiful, by the way." She releases my hands and grabs her phone and answers. "Yes, I'm aware but the contract states differently." She pauses letting the other person speak. "Oh, that's fine, but then I want a full refund." Another pause. "You seem to have me confused with someone who cares what your problem is. I'll either be getting a full refund or you'll secure the roof. Figure it out." Taylor disconnects the phone and I'm impressed.

"Well, looks like my sweet, timid assistant has found her New York attitude."

"After spending enough time around you, it was bound to happen. Besides, when you get this new job, I'm hoping I'll be moved up as well." She smiles and I make a mental note to make sure that happens.

"*If* I get the promotion."

"You'll get it. I believe in you."

A few guests start to filter in and when I glance around the room, making sure everything is running smoothly—I see him. He's sitting at a table watching me. I want to look anywhere else, but my eyes don't move. We assess each other unsmiling and unwilling to break the only connection we have right now. His eyes don't waver even as someone approaches him. The hurt radiates through me remembering why we're like this. This morning, the sight of him made my heart race, but right now it makes me sick. Refusing to give him any more of my attention, I turn my head and walk to the bar.

"What can I get you?" the bartender asks, wiping the granite counter.

"A lemon drop."

"Martini or drink?"

"Shot."

He looks at me with a brow raised. *Yes, I said shot.* If I'm going to spend the next however many hours in the same room as my *client*, I need a little liquid courage.

"One lemon drop shot coming right up."

"You know what, fuck it. Just give me a shot of vodka." No need to pretty it up.

The bartender turns and places the shot in front of me, and before he can say anything, I throw the shot back and savor the burn. At least I can feel it. The alcohol flows through me and warms me.

"Another," I demand, and instead of any commentary, he refills my shot glass. "Thanks."

Without wasting any time I take that shot and place the glass down.

This is going to be a long night.

"So you're going to get drunk?" I turn and see Taylor looking at me with wide eyes.

"That was so I'd be able to be in the same room as him. Is it hot in here?"

Taylor shakes her head, "I think that's the shots. You need to introduce everyone in five."

I nod and head back into the staging area behind the curtain. The party is meant to be a fun way for everyone to see everything and get to meet the members of the company. We wanted to show that as much as Raven is a corporation, they're more of a family. *Ironic.* It seems that statement is true in more than one way.

The room quiets and I take my place back on stage. I wonder what fun information I'll learn this time.

"Good evening and welcome," I smile somehow and hope it's sincere enough. *This is your job, Catherine. Keep it together.* "On behalf of Raven Cosmetics, we want to thank you for all being here to celebrate the launch of the new line. I'd like to introduce the CEO, so please put your hands together for Jackson Cole." I clap and wait for him to stand as Taylor hands him a microphone.

I close my eyes and try to block out the sound of his voice. "Thank you, thank you." He pauses and waits for the applause to end. "I wanted to personally thank you all for being here, and I'm grateful to be able to spend this evening with you as well. This product line has been something that we've worked on for a few years and are extremely pleased it's ready to be launched. Sometimes the timing isn't right," Jackson pauses and looks directly at me. "I wanted to be sure everything was in order before going forward and ensuring success." His eyes don't move from mine. This is not the speech I wrote for him.

Son of a bitch.

"There are many things I planned to say tonight, but I'm having trouble remembering them all." He chuckles and the crowd joins him. "This was never a company I thought I'd have a hand in. As life happens, things change. We have to make choices and they aren't always the right ones, but we have to live with that." He pauses and looks around the room. "Today was a great day for Raven and I appreciate you all being here. Please enjoy yourselves and we look forward to many more celebrations together." He raises his glass and everyone claps.

I stand there dumbfounded at his words spoken directly to me. He's mingling with the guests but manages to look over and cement me to the ground.

Hate.

Love.

Anger.

Pain.

Lies.

Swirling around like a funnel cloud in my heart. Each twist tears another piece of me to shreds. He continues to hold my gaze until I hear someone behind me.

"Come on, Cat." She grasps my elbow and pulls me over to the side.

I draw a deep breath and when I let it out, a sob breaks free. Standing where no one can see me, I lose it. I fall apart. The tears stream down my face and Taylor pulls me against her.

"Oh my God." My breathing is short and I begin to hyperventilate. "I can't be here," I say aloud while I struggle to catch my breath.

"Go. I can handle anything that might come up here. Everything's basically done."

"I'm so sorry, Taylor." I hold my torso hoping to keep myself together long enough to get out of here without falling apart again. "Just being in the same room as him right now ..." I trail off when I see him standing in front of me.

"You're leaving?" he asks calmly but the hurt is lingering under his question.

I look at him up close for the first time since the apartment. His eyes are bloodshot and he's barely holding it together. "Why do you care?" I ask acerbically.

"Really?" Jackson scoffs.

"I apologize, Mr. Cole, that was unprofessional. I've done my job. My staff is more than capable of handling any issues."

Jackson pushes forward and I step back. Seeing me retreat, he stops and looks down. "Taylor, can you give me a moment with my publicist please?" Jackson says softly and I look at her, pleading with my eyes not to leave me. Instead she places a hand on my shoulder and exits the room.

He turns to me, "I know you want space, but I'm asking you to give me five minutes. I don't deserve it. I know that. But please, I need to explain."

A tear falls and I straighten myself to stand tall. "If you would've trusted me, none of this would be happening. I'd be sitting at that table, holding your hand, whispering about what we could do when we leave. Instead, I have mascara down my face, a dress I want to burn, and a broken heart. I don't have five minutes to give you tonight."

I grab my clutch from the chair and start to leave, but he clasps my arm, stopping me. "Don't you get it?" I ask.

"I deserve a chance to explain."

"You're right. You did. A month ago. Instead, you kept something from me. You did what every other man in my life has done. In one second, you managed to prove you're no different. My father, Neil, hell, throw in my mother if you want … none of them hurt me as much as you managed to. But instead I was *humiliated.* I was thrown in front of cameras and left to find out something like *that*— publicly. So while I'd love to let you explain, Mr.

Cole," I sneer while wriggling my arm from his grip, "You had your chance." I turn on my heel without another word.

Each step I take I feel pain—physical pain. How does it hurt so bad?

"I never lied about how I feel," he calls out and I pause. "I love you, Catherine. I would walk through fire for you," Jackson says and my heart stops.

I turn and look at him. "You wouldn't have had to. I would've put out the flames before they reached you. Instead you managed to burn me yourself."

Seeing the agony spread across his face at my words nearly kills me. I wanted to love him, protect him, not destroy him—too bad he didn't want the same things.

"Okay, I know it's only six a.m., but I need you to wake up," Ashton says, rubbing my back.

"Are you for real?" I ask groggily as I look over at my clock, hoping she was lying about the time. "Ashton! It's six in the morning." I roll back over trying to hide my face.

"Yeah, well. I saw the press conference and I need you to talk to me."

I open one eye exasperated at my best friend. "I don't need to talk. I'm done."

"Is he married?"

"I don't know," I say and start to sit up.

"What do you mean you don't know? How the hell don't you know? What did he say?" She fires off questions so fast I can't answer. She stands and puts her hands on her hips. "Answer me!"

"Don't yell at me!" I say as I get out of bed and

head into the bathroom. What is with all the people in my life and their damn demands?

When I come out of my bathroom, she's sitting on the bed with an apologetic look. "I didn't mean to yell, Biffle. I'm worried about you."

I sigh and sit on the bed next to her. Funny how I feel the need to comfort her. "I'll be fine—at some point. He lied to me, Ash. I don't know if he's married because honestly I was afraid of the answer. We were together for months, I was basically living with him, and he never told me. To find out like that—in a press conference—was horrific. I felt like an idiot."

"He's the idiot, Catherine." Ashton places her hand on mine.

"I'm done. Those are the only words I can say. There's no fixing us, because there is no us. I can't go through another relationship where lies and cheating are even an option. If he is married, then I was his mistress. If he's not married and is divorced, how could he keep that from me—or why did he think it wouldn't matter?"

She sighs and gives me a few moments. "I'm in no way defending him, because honestly I hate him right now and I never thought that would happen. I've always been on your side. But I really thought Jackson was the one for you. Knowing all your issues with abandonment and trust, maybe he was afraid if he told you, you'd run. Instead he pretty much guaranteed that you'd be pushed to run."

"Right, and by keeping his marriage a secret he obliterated any trust I had in him." I clutch my pillow to my chest. It hurts so much talking about this. I can't believe we're back here again. "Unless there's something more behind all of this like he's still in love with her. It makes no sense."

Ashton shrugs. "I can tell you he was frantic. He was hysterical on the phone trying to find you. Mark called me too. He said Jackson is a fucking moron and fucked it up."

The half laugh escapes me at Mark's assessment. "Yeah, I'd agree with him on both. But, Ash, he didn't tell me either. You know that's the other part I feel sick over. I was in that hospital for how long with his mom and Mark and no one ever mentioned it. Which leads me to believe they knew he didn't want me to know."

She sighs and squeezes my hand. "I don't know. I really don't. He had to know at some point you'd find out. You going to work?"

"I'm up. I might as well. I gave Taylor the day off, but I'm going to have to figure out how the hell to handle this fucking account. We have less than a month left in this contract, but I'm not sure I can work side-by-side with him." I stand up and pull the dress from last night up off the floor.

"Don't you dare let him win. You go into work and you handle him. Are you going to be okay?"

I wish it were that simple. I wish I had the courage to go in there and pretend seeing him doesn't hurt. That hearing his voice doesn't make me ache … but it does. He's a part of me—far more than Neil ever was. Jackson was everything to me. I wanted to stand beside him, love him, give myself to him, and in a way I did.

"I'll do what I always do—survive."

A small smile paints Ashton's face and she scoots closer. "I'm really sorry. I think we should buy an island and stick these fuckers on it and pick them off one by one."

"*Survivor* for men," I chuckle. "There are so many things I'm upset over, but the biggest is he knew. He knew, Ash. I told him what I could handle." I run my hands through my hair. "I was crystal fucking clear and we spent countless nights together."

"He never even brought anything up?"

"All I can think is there were these tiny moments I felt like he was keeping something. Small things that didn't really add up, but I have a tendency to overthink things, so I was giving him the benefit of the doubt."

She sighs and wraps her arm around my shoulder. "Are you going to hear him out?"

"He owes me answers, that's for sure, but right now I don't want to see his face."

"I get that. I think you're justified in a few punches to the junk."

We both snicker. "I have to get ready." I kiss her cheek and head into the bathroom.

"You'll always have me!" she calls out.

"Oh, how lucky I am."

"Damn right you are," I hear her say as the door closes to my bedroom.

I take my time getting ready and put on a pink shift dress and white sandals. When I head out to the living room, Ashton's keys are gone and there's a note letting me know she wasn't planning to come home, but if I need her, to call and she'll be here. I love that girl.

Once in my office, I sit in my chair and look out the window, thinking about the mess my life has become once again. It's a constant battle. And it's exhausting and I'm tired of treading water—I want to float for a while. I ponder if this is what I need.

Time alone—again. I look out and my mind drifts to Jackson. My heart clenches as my mind allows me to see him again right before I left him. I see the way his eyes held sorrow and he was desperate for me to listen to him. The pain we both were suffering in that moment. I replay it all as a tear drifts down my cheek.

chapter eighteen

"Catherine."

I spin in my chair as I turn to see my boss standing there. "Mr. Cartright. I thought you were away." I quickly swipe the tear and stand up as he enters the office.

"One day you'll remember to stop with the 'Mr.' bullshit." He slaps his hand on the doorframe and his face falls. "Meet us in the conference room in five."

"Yes, sir."

Without another word he strides out of the office.

Fuck my life.

Did he see me stumble on camera? Does he know I left the party early? Did Jackson call and complain? He sure as hell didn't look happy to call me into the conference room. I grab my compact and fix my face as best as I can and head down the hall.

"Good luck, Cat," I hear Elle's shrill voice say as I pass her desk.

"Thanks." I smile and keep walking. I don't have enough patience for a verbal chess match with her today.

The conference room hosts the three partners of CJJ, the head of human resources, and the director of client relations. Well, this doesn't feel promising. My stomach rolls as the fear starts to travel through my body. *Keep calm,* I try to tell myself, but no one is smiling. I clear my throat and enter as they look up.

"Good morning, Cat. Please have a seat," Mr. Jennings says and motions to the chair.

Mr. Jennings is the oldest of the three partners. He's barely in the office anymore and when he is, everyone walks around not speaking. I've only dealt with him a handful of times, but he's always been cordial.

"Thank you."

I smile looking around the room and everyone's emotions are well hidden. I can't get a feel on what exactly is going on.

"Let's get to it, Catherine," Mr. Cartright begins. "The board has been talking and we're very impressed with how you were able to secure the Raven account. More than that, when we reached out to Mr. Cole, he had a lot to say regarding your work with the company." Mr. Cartright pauses and my heart stops beating.

He wouldn't.

Would he? Would he really hurt me this way? Ruin my reputation regarding work?

"Anyway," he continues breaking me from my inner meltdown, "He told us how you nailed down every aspect of the campaign and made sure everything was taken care of. You were on top of the press and the stock regarding his company during his life threatening shooting. He was impressed, and so are we." When he stops speaking, the partners smile at each other.

"Thank you. I'm happy the client was pleased," I

say softly wishing he was still more than my client.

"The company is taking a new direction, and we're opening several satellite offices in the coming year."

"Wow. That's wonderful for the company."

"We think so too," Mr. Jeffries speaks for the first time. "Catherine, we want you to head up one of the offices. You've been instrumental to our growth and we think you'd be the perfect candidate for the new office in California."

"Oh!" I say, completely thrown off guard. Run an office? In California? "I don't know what to say." I let out a nervous laugh and look around. Talk about a curve ball.

"Well, there's a first," Mr. Cartright jokes and it helps ease the tension.

We spend the next thirty minutes going over the details of the new position and the generous pay increase. Ultimately, I would run the entire office and be able to take any of the staff I want from New York for support personnel or I can start fresh out there. The perks are great, and they're willing to supply me with a furnished apartment for six months until I find somewhere else or take over the lease.

I start to think of all the reasons I should go and all the reasons not to. They look at me expectantly and I begin to panic. My heart and my head are at war and the reality is I don't know why. "Do you need an answer today or can I have a day or two?"

Mr. Cartright nods with a smile. "We'd like an answer by the beginning of next week. There are a lot of things that need to happen and we would like to get the ball rolling quickly. Do you think that'll be a problem?"

"No, not at all." They stand and I follow suit. "I want to thank you all for this opportunity. I'm honored and will have an answer to you by Tuesday."

Mr. Jeffries is the first to shake my hand. "Think about it, Cat."

"I will."

Mr. Jennings smiles and exits the room, followed by the rest of the team. I lean against the table and let out a long breath. Wow. My mind is spinning. Everything I've worked for just came through. All my dreams of being an executive and now here it is.

"I fought hard for you," Mr. Cartright says behind me, startling me a little.

When I started at CJJ, I was his intern. He guided me through the first few years and has always been my biggest supporter. "You've always had favorites." I smile the first genuine smile in days.

"No, but I know quality. You were made for this position. You're not married, no kids, I thought I was going to have to look for flights leaving today, not hold off. What gives?" he questions.

I sigh and look away from him. "It's a big move."

He smiles letting me know he doesn't quite believe me, but he doesn't probe further. "Sure it is." He clears his throat and raises his brow. "You haven't been the same for a few months."

"Life has been crazy," I reply.

"What's his name?" he asks suddenly.

"Mr.— " I start but he cuts me off with a wave of the hand.

"I swear if you call me 'Mr. Cartright' I'm going to throw something at you," he jokes.

"Sorry. Sean, it's a fantastic opportunity. But it's clear across the country. I need a day or two to digest it," I explain.

"Liar. I know you better than that, Catherine. I saw you a few weeks ago. You were floating around the office. Not even Elle could get you upset. Now, some might think you were just in a good mood but I know better. I remember what that look in your eyes was like a few years ago. So I ask again ... what's his name?"

Sean has been more of a friend than a boss most of the time, but again I broke company rules by dating Jackson. If I tell him, I could lose this promotion, but if I don't and they find out, I run the risk of the same fate.

"It's over now, so it doesn't matter."

"I've known you for a long time. I've mentored you, watched you grow and become a remarkable publicist. You're able to predict and plan for things that are unexpected, which is a rarity. I, however, am able to see through bullshit. You, my friend, are full of it right now."

I gape at him. I've been trying to keep myself in control. My tears are only in private and I've been doing a damn good job at pretending. "I'm surviving."

"There's a saying I know you've heard about when things are over, but the bottom line is: it's never over until you decide it is. The question I guess I should be asking is is he worth giving up on this job?" Sean gives me a pointed look and turns, leaving the room.

I have three days to make a choice and right now the sun and the sand are looking really good. This is the job of a lifetime and here I stand conflicted. He would've been worth it, but he's a liar.

I head to my office and close my eyes but the nausea rolls through. This stress is going to kill me.

My phone rings and I ignore it. There's too much going on in my head to talk to anyone. A few seconds later the text alert beeps.

> *Gretchen: I'm going to beat you. I hope you understand me. You went and saw Neil? Against my advice. Lucky for you I was informed the suit has been dropped.*

> *Me: I love you.*

> *Gretchen: Yeah, yeah ... you're an idiot but I love you too. Let Jackson know we're all clear.*

Seeing his name causes my heart to squeeze and stutter. How can I be so upset with him and yet miss him?

> *Me: Sure thing.*

The office phone rings and I grab it on the first ring.

"Catherine Pope."

"I thought I'd get Taylor again." I hear his deep voice vibrate through the line and I gasp. "Don't hang up, please. You don't have to say anything, just listen to me."

My eyes prick at the sound of his plea. "I can't. Please, let me go."

"I'm not ready to lose you. There's no one else in my heart but you."

"It's not that simple."

"It *is* that simple, Catherine. I love you. I'm not married anymore. I wouldn't do that to you," Jackson says and my heart beats for a second and then it falters.

A brief sense of relief washes over me as I realize I'm not the other woman, but it doesn't erase the fact that he never told me. There were more chances than I can even name, and somehow it slipped his mind? No, he purposely kept this from me.

"I'm not angry anymore—I'm resigned. You broke my heart. You should've trusted me. I loved you with my whole being and should've heard this from you before anyone else. You had friends and family keep your secrets. What else have you kept from me?"

"Let's talk. Come home and we'll talk."

"It's not my home. There are some things going on here. I need to go," I say and hang up the line.

"Ashton," I call out as I enter the apartment. I sent her a text after the call with Jackson that I needed her to come home. If I do take this new position, it will affect her. She's a huge deciding factor for me. Honestly, she's the only thing holding me here at this point.

"In here!" she calls out from the kitchen. "I have pizza."

My stomach growls and I realize I haven't eaten all day. I've been sick to my stomach over everything. The new job, him, and now the idea of moving. It's a lot to process.

"Yes! My favorite." I smile and grab a slice. "I could eat pizza every day. This is the best pizza in Jersey." I groan and take another bite.

"Okay, so I knew pizza would butter you up, keep eating and remember how much you love me," she says and I immediately stop eating. This can't be good.

"What did you do?"

"Nothing. Mark called me," she says apprehensively.

I look at her wondering where she's going with this. "Okay? Point?"

"He said Jackson is a mess."

"His company is doing well. That was my focus."

"Catherine, we know that's not what he's a mess over," she admonishes.

I sigh and roll my eyes. "What do you want from me? I spoke with him today, there's nothing left for us. I can't trust him. Words are just words, Ash. He says he loved me ... but then he kept something pretty serious from me. He says he would've walked through fire for me, but he threw me in it instead. My heart can't take anymore. I need a fresh start. I need a new beginning, because all of this," I wave my hand trying to make my point, "Is too much."

She puts her hands up defensively. "Okay, I just didn't want to not tell you we spoke. So what's the emergency that I needed to be home to talk?"

"I got the promotion."

Ashton squeals and starts dancing around the kitchen. "That's amazing! What's the position?"

Here it goes.

"They want me to head up a new satellite office," I pause making sure she's listening, "In California."

Her face falls before she recovers. "Like the state ... across the country? Three thousand miles away?"

"The very one."

"Okay, that's a big move. Head the office though?"

"Yes, I would run the CJJ Public Relations office

in California. I'd hire the staff, get things set up. It would obviously mean a huge raise and title. It's my dream job, Ashton," I say, chewing on my fingernail.

"It sounds fantastic. Are you going to take it?"

That's the million-dollar question. I want this so bad I can taste it. The idea of moving away becomes more and more appealing. A fresh start in L.A. It means leaving behind all my old baggage and allowing myself to breathe again. I can let go of the ghosts that haunt me here. The company obviously trusts that I can do this, and I can. I know I can.

"I think so. I mean, there's only one thing holding me back."

"What?" she asks, clueless that she's the one thing.

"You, you jackass!" I laugh.

Ashton looks at me and you can see the moisture building in her eyes. "I love you, Biffle, but seriously I'm not a factor. You need to take this."

"But I need to know you'll be okay." She's my best friend and I don't want to leave her high and dry. This is our home and I would never put her in a position that would hurt her.

"Hello! You're an ass! I'll be fine and you'll be hanging out with all the famous people. Oh! Maybe you'll become friends with Vin Diesel and you can hook me up. If that does happen, be warned—I'll be visiting monthly. Maybe they need an embryologist out there?" she smiles and pulls me into a hug.

I start laughing and rocking back and forth with her. "Only you would think somehow I'm going to be your matchmaker."

"I'm so proud of you. You're going to be amazing and you'll miss me, but that's normal." Ashton giggles and grabs the pizza, trying to hide the tears I saw in her eyes.

I come up behind her and nudge her hips. "I'm going to miss you."

"When do you think you'll leave?"

"Not sure, but they need my answer by Tuesday. But I think I'm going to take it. I have a shitty relationship with my mother, my father is dead, and you're all I have here. I think this'll be good for me. I mean, running an office. It's huge!" I say and try to reassure Ashton and myself.

"It *is* huge, but seriously you deserve it. I think they've been priming you for this position."

We move to the table and talk through all the pros and cons. The only con we can come up with is her. I'll be making more money, in a gorgeous area, my apartment is paid for, and I'll be running an office. It's a no-brainer.

"I need to ask you this: if you and Jackson were still together—would you go?"

Chewing the inside of my cheek, I try to be honest because my gut reaction is yes, I would. That's the anger though. "I don't know. It would've been a hard choice, but if he didn't want me to go, I probably would've thought more on it. How sad is that, Ash? I would possibly give up my dream job for him." I feel stupid for even admitting it, but I loved him that much. He would've probably been my choice.

"It's not sad. What's sad is that this is where you're both sitting. He's miserable, you're miserable, he's going to Virginia and you're going to California."

That news causes my head to snap up. "What?"

She looks over and shoves food in her mouth.

"Hmmm?"

"What do you mean he's going to Virginia?"

"Why do you care? You're over it, I thought."

"Don't be cute," I say, growing annoyed with her.

Ashton gets up and grabs the plate from the table. "That's not possible. I'm always cute."

"Right now I'd use another word," I grouse, wanting to know what she knows.

She leans in so we're eye to eye. "You shouldn't care if he moves to Siberia if you're so over it." She kisses my cheek and walks out of the room.

She's right though ... I shouldn't care—but I do.

chapter
nineteen

The following weeks fly by. I inform Sean and the other partners I am definitely taking the job. We go over the timeline and they want me in California within the month. Which leaves me three weeks to get everything accomplished.

I was able to give Taylor two options since she was one of my big concerns. She could accompany me and become a publicist in the office with me, or she could stay in New York and take a smaller promotion. She and her boyfriend, well, now fiancé, decided to stay in New York where his job is. I keep catching her crying or refusing to pack up any of the things that are in my office. We're in the process of moving all my accounts over to her until they expire. The clients are already familiar with her, and I'm positive she can handle them.

"There's another delivery here," Taylor says and she brings in a huge bouquet of Stargazer lilies. I don't need to look at the card to know who it's from. I've gotten something to remind me of our time together every few days. "Should I throw these out?" she asks being the ever-supportive friend.

"No, I'll torment myself for a day or two." I smile and return to the emails I have to handle.

"Can I read the card?"

"Sure, I don't plan to," I say turning my chair

around.

I hear her taking short breaths and spin around to see tears starting to form in her eyes.

"Cat, please read this."

My eyes close as the frustration starts to build. He won't stop. It's almost every day I get an email, text, card, or gift. "I can't read it. I leave in two weeks. Please take it," I plead and fight the urge to rip the card from her fingers.

I miss him so much it hurts.

Some days I want to cry, scream, fight, and run back to him. But I've allowed myself to be happy about where my life is going. I got the promotion I wanted and it's better than I originally thought.

I was an open book. I told him about Neil, my father, Piper ... hell, everything I could, but he kept his secrets. That's not the love I want. The love I want is kind, honest, patient ... not deceitful and hurtful. I know in my heart Jackson is nothing like Neil, but I can't help but draw the comparisons here.

"People make mistakes, mistakes don't make the people." Taylor pauses at my desk putting the card in her pocket. "If he didn't love you, or still think of you, none of these would be here." She looks around the room at the various flowers, the game of Battleship, the lighthouse statue, and the letters that sit on my desk.

My heart accelerates as I look at each item silently taunting me, reminding me of the good times we shared. Why can't he just go away? Why can't he let me go? He did this. He severed all the trust I had. Ripped me to shreds and now I've had enough.

Taylor waits expectantly and I grow angry. "So I go back to him and say what? 'Oh, by the way, I'm moving to California.'" I pause trying to rein in the sudden burst of emotion. "No, I'm leaving. I'm getting a fresh start, a second chance. I'm happy about this job and the move," I stubbornly insist and turn in my chair.

"Yeah, you're probably right. Let some other girl have a shot with a guy like him," she rebukes and sits in the chair with her arms crossed over her chest. "I mean, hell, if things don't work out with Quinn, maybe I'll give him a call." Taylor's brow raises and my mouth falls slack.

I look at this sweet girl with a heart of gold whose horns are now showing. I don't know whether to be proud or scared. "This is beneath you."

"What?" she scoffs. "Truth hurts, sister. I never saw you as happy as you were with him."

"Lies!" I burst out suddenly. "God! This is the part none of you are grasping. He *lied* to me! For months I sat by him, slept in his bed—a bed he probably shared with his *wife*." I close my eyes trying to shut out the memories flooding in. "Wife. Say that out loud and let me know how it goes down, because I want to vomit every single time. She has a name. Worse than that, he had other people keep his secrets."

"I'm not saying he was right."

"Then what are you saying? Because all anyone wants me to do is let him explain. But here's the thing, Tay, he can explain all day and it doesn't change the fact that I got this amazing job. I'm moving to California and if I was still with him, I probably wouldn't be. So in the end this is better for me!" I say exasperated.

Taylor stands looking at me with a weary expression. "I'm just worried. I don't want you to run away to California."

"I'm not running. I'm starting over—which I deserve. There's nothing here for me other than you and Ashton. I need to finish up here and then I have some conference calls tonight. Can you make sure the new files are in the box to go to California please?"

She nods and exits the room. I swear I've had this same discussion every day with either her or Ashton.

I look at the stack of letters from the gifts he sent, all unopened by me. Taylor read them when I refused and I can only imagine what they say. He has no problem melting my heart—he never has. It's easy to get swept up in his charms. I don't know if any of it was real. My heart says yes, but my head says it's time to let go. The last time I didn't listen to my head, look where it got me.

Glancing at the clock, I realize I'm going to be late meeting the realtor in Scotch Plains.

"Taylor," I yell out. "Can you text me the agent's number who's handling my father's house please?"

Grabbing my belongings, I rush out the door.

"Sure thing, good luck." Taylor calls out as I head to the elevator.

Thankfully, I drove in to work today, so I can head straight there instead of going home first. I haven't been back to the house since I first was there, but I spoke with an agent as soon as I took the job in California. It'll help financially to sell it, and I don't need anything holding me back here. I want no loose ends. It'll be a clean break.

During the hour drive, I talk to my mother and let her know about the promotion. It's been weeks since we've spoken, but she sounds genuinely happy for me. Which is surprising, but I'm grateful to be leaving on good terms.

Pulling up to the quaint house it looks different. Even though I haven't been back here, I've had some things done to it. The landscapers took care of the overgrown bushes and I had painters do the outside. There are a few minor things I need to have replaced inside, but otherwise it's going to be an "as-is" sale.

I smile as I see Mary peering out at the driveway. I give her a short wave and the curtain closes.

"Catherine?" she calls out and heads over.

"Hi, Mary."

"I thought that was you." Her warm smile shines bright. "I saw the workers here this week."

Her honest concern for the house and for me is heartwarming. I'm sure if I lived here it would seem as if she's nosey, but not having the ability to look after the house myself, it comforts me.

"I hope they behaved."

"Oh, they were very nice to look at." She winks and giggles a little.

I chuckle, "I'm glad."

"Yes, they did beautiful work clearing the shrubbery," Mary notes as she looks at the house. "Hunter would be very happy."

I smile at the idea that he would be pleased, "I'm glad."

"I'm sorry, dear, how are you?"

"I'm doing well. I'm moving to California in a few weeks," I explain and her brow lifts.

"Oh, but you just got here. Why would you move all the way out there?" Mary asks.

We spend the next few minutes talking about the new job and about her grandson who came back from the west coast.

"I'm glad you're happy, dear," Mary says and puts her arm on my shoulder.

Happy? I'm excited about the job. I'm ready to take my career to the next level … but happy? In one aspect of my life, yes. In another … no.

Before I can say anything else, the realtor pulls up and hops out of the car. "Catherine Pope?"

Stepping forward, I extend my hand. "Yes, you must be Mindi."

"Mindi Erickson." She returns the handshake and nods. "Nice to meet you."

I explained the urgency of my move and how the house has to be sold quickly. Not having a mortgage or any debt on the house weighs in my favor. She seems very optimistic and already has a few couples she would like to show the house to.

"How about we go inside?" she asks and I bid farewell to Mary.

After a few minutes of going through each room, we make a checklist of things that would make it easier to sell and what can be the new owner's decisions.

"Do you think it's doable?"

"Yes, absolutely. How quickly can you have everything removed from the house? I think it'll show better."

For a second my breath catches. I didn't think about what I would do with all that's left of my father. While we didn't have any relationship, the last thing I want is to lose any ties I have to him. I don't know why this never occurred to me but suddenly it's as if a boulder is sitting on my chest.

"Oh, ummm, I didn't—" I stop trying to think of how to explain that I never realized I'd need to get rid of everything.

"If you'd rather leave it, we can, but I think if selling quickly is the goal then we should have the house staged. It's well worth the money. You'd need to have anything from here removed quickly. I can have this listed in a day if you tell me you're ready." She explains with a no-nonsense look, waiting for my answer.

"Okay, I just need to make a few calls," I say looking away.

"I'll put the sign up now, and then call me when you're good to go. Here's the number for the company I've worked with. They're fair and efficient." Mindi hands me a card and smiles. "I'm going to take a few pictures of the outside."

I head into the bedroom and look around. There's not much that's salvageable, but these are his things. I grab a few shirts and photos, then enter the office. The box that sits under the desk is empty. Taking a few minutes, I pack anything I might want at some point.

Opening the drawer to the desk I see a VHS tape sitting in the back that says: Catherine Grace.

The office has an old television and VCR. Curiosity gets the best of me and I put the video in and press play. I hear his voice for the first time in almost twenty years.

"Catherine, what does Santa say?" my father says from behind the camera.

I smile at the sight of myself at two years old. I have a pink romper on with pigtails.

"Ho, ho, ho." My mouth forms a tiny 'O' as I walk around saying it repeatedly.

"That's right! And what does Daddy say?"

"No, no, no." Everyone laughs and then my mother appears in front of the camera. "Hunter, put that down and come out here."

The camera is placed on something and I see him. He has dark brown eyes that mirror mine and scruff along his cheek that gives him an almost Mediterranean look. My father looks at me like I'm the sun. His eyes beam and glow when he scoops me into his arms and holds me close.

"My beautiful girl ..." he trails off and the camera flashes to another scene.

I'm maybe four years old lying on his chest asleep. My father turns the camera toward me and him as he rocks in the recliner.

"Hi, baby girl. Today's your birthday and you're sick. Each year since you were born you run a crazy fever and this year is no different. Your Mommy's sleeping so I got up with you this time. I decided I had some things to say while you're lying in my arms," he pauses and presses a kiss to my head and my younger self snuggles deeper.

I sit here and see the man who held me in his arms when I was sick, yet I have no memory other than him walking away. There's a part of me that finds peace, seeing it firsthand, knowing he loved me, and another part breaks because we missed out on so much.

"First, boys are stupid. Remember that. No boy will ever love you as much as I do. When I have to give you away, I'll never really let go. You'll always be Daddy's little girl. Okay, we got that out of the way ... The first time you said 'I love you, Daddy' was a day I'll never forget. To see so much honesty took my breath away. You're so beautiful, sweet, and perfect." My father's eyes shine with unshed tears. "One day, you'll hate me, like every teenager does. I want you to know, even at your worst—you'll always be the best thing I've ever done. You'll be a part of my heart no matter how much you despise me. Nothing in this world will ever take that away. You're a piece of me and I'll always be here for you—even if something happens to me." A tear falls from his eyes and he pulls me closer.

The best thing he's ever done ...

"The next thing is you should know how to change a tire. It's very important you learn this because you shouldn't need a man to fix things. Although ... it's how I met your mother," he ponders that and smiles. "Again, I reiterate the first rule about boys being stupid."

I laugh and watch as he rubs my back and rocks a few moments. It's a glimpse into the man I never knew. I look around at the room that I've packed up. It looks bare and empty, which is how I feel. Clearing out his belongings makes his absence that much more apparent. I've been avoiding this house, his things, because I was focused on Jackson. Now, I'm faced with it head on. The letter was one thing, but hearing him, seeing him, is completely different.

"Tomorrow isn't guaranteed. That may seem like a stupid thing to say, but you should remember it. If your life isn't what you wanted—you can change it. You have the power to make a change. Live the life you want to live. If someone doesn't treat you well ... cut them loose. If you want something bad enough ... go after it. There's nothing in this world that comes easy. Take your life by the horns and don't let go." He stops speaking as I begin to wake.

"Daddy?"

"Shhh, it's okay, Sunshine. Go back to sleep," he

murmurs in my ear.

The screen goes black and it turns back on when I'm eight. It's the time my parents took me to the Jersey shore. I remember this. I watch my father hand the camera off to my mom. They smile at each other but it seems strained. The video plays as my childhood unfolds before me. There are good memories here, where I was safe, secure, and held tight. The last scene ends and I allow myself a moment to reflect.

My entire life I've felt as if I was fighting to be good enough for someone. Watching man after man disappoint and desert me. And my father was the first, but being in his space and seeing the life he lived—is sad. Am I any better? I push against the walls that surround my heart. I keep people at a distance and at what cost? I want to be loved but I don't want to grab life by the horns. Somehow, I always managed to get poked by them.

If only my father had made different choices … if only he had had the courage to come to me before he died. We may have had a fighting chance. I probably would've been angry, but at least there was a shot. My mind drifts to Jackson. Am I doing the same thing?

Not wanting to waste the little time I have, I get up and get back to work. Mulling over all I've learned today. Trying to focus on the task of keeping my walls erect, but catching myself getting teary a few times.

This is much harder than I imagined but I've gone through all of the rooms and made a few piles of things to keep, but most will be donated. I sit on the sofa, exhausted and feeling run down. My phone beeps, but I'm too tired to even look.

I start to doze off and the phone rings. I let it go and try to nap. However, the caller doesn't get the point and calls again. I silence the call and close my eyes. My exhaustion is overwhelming. I could sleep for ten hours. Moving sucks.

My ring tone wakes me from a sound sleep.

"Hello," I ask groggily, turning over, looking at the clock, and seeing it's now nighttime.

"Well, well. If it isn't, Kitty." Mark's voice breaks through my haze and I'm instantly awake.

"Hello, Mark."

My defenses rise since I'm unsure of why he would be calling.

"You don't call, write, or smoke signal. I was beginning to think you didn't find me attractive anymore."

"I'm sure you understand why I haven't be in touch."

He laughs the way only he would, "I know. I told you he was an idiot. I'm not calling about Muffin. Natalie had the baby."

"That's wonderful. How is she? I wanted to call her, but I wasn't sure if I should." My voice is shaky. I became close with her, and we haven't spoken since the break-up. A rush of irritation at myself washes over me. I should've called her. She didn't deserve to be left out because Jackson is a dick.

"She asked me to reach out to you. Nat scheduled Aaron's memorial for next week and asked for you to be there. She said she could use all the support she can get."

"Of course. I'll be there. Where is it?"

"Pennsylvania. In his home town."

"Okay."

Mark takes a second and lets out a long breath.

"Fuck it. I'm going to say this to you because I sure as hell won't say it next time I see you. I'm not going to tell you what to do. I'm not going to ask you to do anything. Just know this … he loves you. In all the years I've known the son of a bitch, he's never looked at anyone like he looks at you."

I start to cut him off, "Mar—"

"You both fucked this up and you're both miserable. Unless you're not?" he questions.

"I'm surviving," I reply, unwilling to lie to him but I don't want to give him any more.

"Isn't that great?" he answers sarcastically. "You're surviving, he's losing his fucking mind, and I'm ready to punch the both of you. This is your life, and far be it from me to give advice because I sure as shit don't do relationships. But I'll tell you this … if I ever felt the way you both did about someone, I'd be breaking every goddamn door to get back to them. I wouldn't be waiting around for shit to magically fix itself, because it won't."

"That's the thing," I pause. "He already broke the damn doors around my heart. I never broke his. He never let me in." My lip begins to quiver as the emotions start to bubble up. "I loved him. He wants to keep secrets. Fine. But I can't have that kind of relationship. You lied for him, his mother lied, he lied. I don't know what's real anymore."

Mark doesn't respond right away. "I didn't lie to you. It wasn't my story to tell and from what I understand—you still don't know it." Mark pauses allowing his words to settle in. "You owe it to each other to talk and at least learn everything. Then you both can go back to being fucking stupid. I'll let Nat know you'll be there and I'll text you the info."

"I'll be there. I promise."

He hangs up without another word.

Next week I'll have to see him. Next week I'll have no choice. And then I can put this all behind me.

chapter twenty

"I'm going to go over the remaining accounts you're taking over and make sure you're all set. The movers come tomorrow to pack, so it's today or never."

"Why do you keep reminding me? Are you part sadist?" Taylor jokes, throwing her arms over her face.

"You know it," I laugh and toss a balled up paper at her. "Oh, please. You're not going to miss me that much. You just got a big, fat raise and a pretty sweet promotion."

"But I'm losing my friend and the only person I like in this office." Taylor's bottom lip juts out.

This is the part that keeps me crying every day. I'm an emotional wreck. I love Taylor like a sister. She's been a part of my daily life for years. On top of that she's a wonderful person—I'm going to miss her desperately. A very selfish part of me hoped she'd come to California with me, and then the other part is happy she chose to stay. She'll shine here and I think if she came with me, she'd have a hard time coming out of the shadows. I want her to succeed and she's ready to take this leap.

"You'll never lose me." I smile and tilt my head. "Here's what I think. When I call you a week after I'm gone, and you're in your new position, you'll have forgotten all about me. You'll be putting Elle's snarky ass in her place, and blowing people's minds."

Taylor turns, wiping at her face, trying to hide the tear I saw falling. "Before I forget, your realtor called. She said everything checks out and the papers will be drawn up. The buyer's ready to close on Wednesday."

"Shit. The memorial is Tuesday. I guess I can go right there after."

"Or you can cancel moving."

"Not likely," I chide.

She throws her hands up and huffs. "Fine. Whatever. Ruin my life. Let's go over the Raven account."

My good mood plummets as I think about having to talk about him. I've been avoiding dealing with Raven up until the last moment. The way we've been handling the account transfers is through conference calls with each client where Taylor and I explain that she'll be their point of contact. Luckily, we haven't had any issues. Most of the clients already know Taylor and trust her. With Jackson though, I know he isn't going to allow it at all.

But the real issue is that I don't want to speak to him. Besides the fact that I don't want him to know I'm leaving.

"I'm going to see him in a few days. I'll go over everything with him then. You know pretty much everything, and at this point we've wrapped most of the account up. Now they should only need us if something catastrophic happens," I say, looking over the file hoping to mask my emotions.

"Right," Taylor says slowly. "I'd like an opportunity to talk to him before you leave. Jackson needs to be comfortable with me as well. You know, in case something catastrophic happens and all. Not like the man has been shot, had his best friend die, or anything major since we've had the account." She gives me a pointed look. "I'm not asking you to share your secrets with him, Cat, I'm just saying he needs to know that I'm his rep. Hell, I don't care if you tell him you quit or were fired."

She's absolutely correct, and I'm being unfair and a bit unprofessional, but these last few days I've been a mess. My emotions are all over the place, from getting excited when I picked out the apartment in California to sobbing when I had to sell my car. Everything feels so much stronger because of all the stress. Ashton keeps looking at me like I'm losing my mind.

"I'll be right back," I say getting up to head to the bathroom.

I'm becoming a chickenshit. This is my damn job and I shouldn't begrudge Taylor. If it were me in her position, I would call the client and handle it. But because she knows everything, she's trying to walk the line of our friendship. Maybe if I tell him I quit and took another job he'd let it go?

Yeah, right.

This is Jackson, the man who runs a security company. He'd track me down before I could even leave the city. I keep my head lowered thinking about what the right way to handle this is and I crash into someone.

"I'm so sorry!" I exclaim and look up to see familiar green eyes and platinum blond hair.

Sure, I can do this now. I mean, it's not like dealing with Piper on a good day isn't bad enough.

"You should be," Piper sneers.

I clench my teeth while balling my fist, ready to

punch this bitch in the face. It's as if she's incapable of being a decent human being. "Why are you in my office?"

She gives her classic smile and I fight the urge to wipe it off her.

"Do you mean *my* new office?" She looks around and waves at Sean who's watching the two of us.

My eyes close and I choke the bile clawing it's way up my throat. I've never been happier about my move than I am in this moment. "You were hired?"

"Yup," she sharply enunciates the single syllable. "Isn't that great? We're going to work together every single day."

I give a half laugh and roll my eyes. "Didn't they tell you?" I lean in conspiratorially, "I don't work here anymore."

Her eyes widen briefly, letting me know I caught her off guard. "You were fired?"

"Fired? No, don't be silly." I pause and smirk. "I was given the California office. I'll be running it. So in a way ..." I tap my chin and trail off.

"Isn't that nice for you," Piper says sarcastically.

"Yeah, it is. Hey, come to think of it, I guess you work for me." I smile when I realize there's a fraction of truth to that statement.

"The hell I do." Piper shifts so she's standing taller.

I've never been an evil person, however at this moment I'm enjoying every moment of her discomfort. She's caused her fair share in my life and I'm all too happy to return the favor.

I let out a dramatic sigh. "Yeah, you kinda do. It's okay though. You probably won't last long here anyway. Our company doesn't take well to lying, vicious sluts who don't know how to be professional."

"Really? Do they take well to sleeping with the clients?"

I rein in my reaction because that's exactly what she'd want. I stand there unwilling to break eye contact. There's no way in hell I'm going to back away from her.

After a few seconds, she sighs and puts her hands on her hips. "Oh, Cat, let's not fight. It doesn't matter anyway because I'll have your job just like I had your man—or should I say men," she goads me but I couldn't care less about the only man she actually has had.

Laughing at her bullshit, I smile and walk away. She's not worth the time.

"Oh, Catherine?" she calls out, stopping me.

Unwilling to make a scene in my office I turn and walk closer to keep my voice quiet. "What?" I ask acerbically.

"I saw your press conference online, I meant to call you but I knew I'd be seeing you soon."

My palms begin to sweat and I feel dizzy.

Piper begins before I can say a word. "You looked great, but I wish I recorded it so I could've seen your face again when you found out about Mr. Cole's wife. That must've been a huge blow. I was really happy to talk to Linda that morning. She's a great journalist and was eager to learn more about his story. How is his wife by the way?"

My stomach plummets and my fingernails are piercing the skin of my palm. "You don't know anything."

She smirks and walks towards me slowly with a gleam in her eyes, knowing she's got me. "Well, it appears you don't either. Such a shame. Another man, another betrayal." She sighs and puts her arm around my shoulder as if we're great friends having a friendly conversation. "I can't believe he never mentioned her to you. It was one of the first things we talked about. You would think considering your high-ranking position, you'd know enough to ask the basic questions. The horror. Just think, you're as bad as me." She laughs and I shrug out of her grasp.

"I'm not anything like you. I don't sleep with men who are knowingly involved with other people. I don't take pleasure in hurting others. And I sure as hell don't get fired from every job I've been at. No, you and I have nothing in common." I turn and walk away.

Fucking Piper. One day, karma is going to throat punch her and I'm going to laugh.

I forego the bathroom and head into my office and shut the door. Taylor jumps at the sound but I don't say a word. I'm sure all the color is drained from my face.

"What's wrong?" she asks concerned.

Is "everything" a good answer? Right now it feels like the floor is falling out from under me. It was bad enough losing him, but to know Piper knew about his wife when I didn't guts me. When are the surprises going to stop hurting? I don't understand how everyone around me seemed to know, but I was left in the dark. Every time I get close to being anywhere near feeling okay, something else slams me in the face about Jackson. The only saving grace is I'm leaving in a week and a half. Thank God I won't have to work with her.

"Piper apparently was hired."

Her mouth falls open. "Here?" she practically screams. "As in this office?"

"Yes, she waved to Mr. Cartright and walked over letting me know she and I would be working together." I groan and flop in my chair. "What in the world could the partners be thinking?"

"She looks good on paper, and in front of a camera."

"She's ugly everywhere else."

"*That* I agree with," Taylor says and laughs. "But you won't be working with her. Only I get that pleasure."

"Are you sure you don't want to come to California with me?" I ask her one last time, hoping I can sway her.

"Unless you want to hire my very sexy fiancé, I would say that's a no. But know I'll be sitting here plotting ways to push her in front of a bus. Accidentally of course," Taylor jokes and we both crack up.

"Yes, because all pushing of evil bitches in front of moving vehicles is accidental."

"I think we'd be forgiven for that one." Taylor smiles and I nod.

Yes, if there's anyone I think a panel of our peers would forgive, it's us for having Piper run over by a truck. She's the devil incarnate.

Taylor straightens up and picks up her notebook. "Okay, what else do we have to get through? I got me a hot date," she drawls, her Midwestern accent peeking through.

"You're a mess," I tease, dispelling the anxiety Piper caused.

"But you love me."

"I do. I do."

We spend the next hour going over what else her new job will require her to do. Since she could've easily done my job, there's not much we have to iron out. Most of the time we laugh or reminisce about accounts we'd forgotten about. There are a lot of memories in this office. Some good, some bad, but Taylor was a part of all of it.

"Okay, tomorrow is packing day. I won't be back in the office until Friday and then next Thursday is my last day actually here."

"I didn't think you'd work at all next week."

"I didn't either, but I need to make sure everything is done. There's a lot to do at home so I'll take some time this week and try to get that stuff straight. This weekend is girls' night out and then Tuesday is the memorial and then my flight is four days after that. You're coming out with us before I leave, right?"

Taylor sighs and stands up to leave. "I'm not sure, Quinn has a work function this weekend and I need to be there for support. Plus, I'll see you at work before you leave. You need this time with the girls."

"I wish you'd reconsider. Ashton and Gretchen won't mind."

"I know." She pauses and looks back at me. "You'll never know how much you mean to me." She smiles and heads out the door.

"Tay?" I call and she peeks her head back in. "Trust me I do know."

She nods and closes the door.

The sun is setting as I look out the window. As the minutes tick by, the exhaustion takes over. I'm run down, overtired, and this is only the beginning of what's to come. Tomorrow, my life will be packed up and sent to California. There are a few things left to do here and then I'll be on my own.

Ashton's already told me I can kiss her ass if I think she'll be home to watch them pack me. We've spent pretty much every night together since I accepted the job. I'm glad we've made time on Saturday for a final night out. I'm going to miss my girls, but they promise to come visit and Sean told me I'd have to travel back to New York for meetings.

I pack up and take the box with all my personal belongings out of my office. I stand there looking at the nearly empty office and my stomach clenches. I've spent my entire career in this building. It's going to break my heart to leave all of this behind, even if it is to follow my dream.

"Ever feel like we're living déjà vu?" Ashton asks, standing in my now empty room. The movers took everything a few days ago. And now it's time for us to spend the night with Gretchen.

"How so?" I ask wondering where she's going with this.

She looks around the room and her eyes harden. "Come talk to me in the living room or something. I can't stare at this shit."

Ashton may seem tough, but this is difficult for her. We've discussed not living together at some point, but I don't think either of us thought it would include a move across the country as well.

I follow her out of the room fighting the urge to laugh because of her face. "Okay, I'm here."

"I hate this, Cat!" She flops on the couch while throwing her hands over her face.

Unsure of what to do, I sit on the table and put my hand on her arm. "I know you do. I hate this too, but I need to go."

She moves her hand and I see the tears threatening to spill over. "No, you're my family. I've never been alone. And Gretchen is saving the world, so I'll never see her. I don't have any other friends. I mean, I'd friend me," Ashton says as she leans back, meaning what she said.

I bust out laughing. "I have no words."

"What? I'm serious."

"That's the sad part."

"People don't understand me." She sits up and wipes the tear from her face.

Moving to the couch I pull her against me. "You're a bit much to handle sometimes, but they just haven't had the privilege of getting to know you. Fortunately, I've been putting up with your shit long enough to know it's how you protect yourself."

Ashton uses her attitude as a shield. I've watched her do it since we were kids. She pushes people away before they ever get close to her. How we ever became friends I'll never know. Sometimes two people who don't look like a good match on paper, work perfectly in real life.

"I'll be fine. I'm just being dramatic."

"As usual," I chide.

"Bite me."

"You'd like it."

"You know it." Ashton laughs and then lets out a long, wavery sigh.

"I've spent most of my life listening to you tell me how I need to do things. Now it's your turn." I pause and when I see her blue eyes soften, I begin, "You have one of the kindest hearts I know, but it's got a steel wall around it. I know you don't let people in because it's safer. But you, my friend, deserve love."

Ashton wraps her arms around me. "Hello, pot ... meet kettle. Your walls are thicker than mine." Her brow raises and she tightens her hold.

"I don't think so. If I had walls, then I wouldn't be crumbling right now."

When the movers packed up my belongings, they found the note from the night Jackson left after the fight with Neil. I held that tiny scrap of paper in my hands for hours and cried. Tears ran continuously as I stared at the words that were my lifeline when he left. I held on to that promise he made during his absence and brush with death. He was everything for me. I wanted a life with him, but in the end, I'm left battered and bruised—again.

"Sometimes you have to crumble because you had cracks and now you'll be crackless."

I laugh and so does Ashton. "You're an ass."

"A crackless ass?" Ash smiles and tries to look at her own ass.

"I think there's a crack in a few places," I giggle and hug her tightly. "I'm serious, Ash, you need to let people in. Let them see the sweet, warm, and caring person you are. You don't always have to be such a bitch."

She pulls back from my embrace and looks at me. "I know. And you ... I've watched you spend weeks pulling yourself together and pretending you're fine. I've seen you get up, get dressed, get promoted, all with a broken heart. You don't have to hide behind your armor but you choose to. I'm not half as strong as you. When Gary left me after college to go live his passions, I lost mine. I don't want to feel that again."

Gary and Ashton were perfect for each other. They met in college and had a whirlwind love. He promised her the world and left her destroyed. Gary was in a band and they had a song hit big. He packed up, left without a backward glance. It was as if she was completely irrelevant. She never cried or fell apart. Instead, she refused to love again.

"If it were me, what would you say?" I ask.

She huffs and stands, "I'd tell you what I always do. But you're different. You have a heart. Mine shriveled up and died."

"Oh, Ash," I stand and envelope her in a hug. "You have a heart. A very big heart."

"Who's going to kick my ass when I'm being a twunt?" she asks earnestly.

I look at her with sad eyes, not knowing what to say. We've both relied on each other and seeing her vulnerable leaves me at a loss.

"I'll still kick your ass, it'll just be from across the country."

"Damn, you've got some long legs," Ashton says in only the way she can. "Okay, enough with the heavy shit. Let's go pretend like you're only going on a business trip instead of leaving me alone and depressed."

I shake my head at her craziness. "You'll be fine. Come on, let's get you drunk, Ashypoo, so I have something to make fun of you about." I loop my arm in hers and we head out of the house. We grab the train and head into Manhattan to meet Gretchen.

Let's hope tonight isn't a repeat of the last time the three of us went out.

chapter twenty-one

"I'm still pissed at you," Gretchen says as she stands outside of the swanky new bar we're meeting at.

"Well, hello to you too," I say laughing at her greeting.

She grabs me and pulls me into a hug. "I can't stay mad at you. It's not your fault you're an idiot. I blame it on you living with Ashton for so long."

I swear, only my friends.

"I resent that!" Ashton exclaims from behind me. "Maybe her stupid rubbed off on me."

"Not likely," she giggles and I wink at Ashton.

"Bitches," Ashton grumbles from behind us as we walk on.

We enter the bar and the music squashes the remainder of their argument. It's a beautiful, new building in the fashion district of Manhattan. I heard about it from a client last week and she got us on the list. She claimed it has the best drinks and hottest bartenders, which was all we needed to hear. I wanted to cancel because of the laundry list of things piling up. But they demanded this was not an optional invitation.

I take in the dark purples and blues, its robust color scheme giving a sexy yet elegant feel. I find myself moving my hips to the bass pumping through the room. But the music is so loud we'll never be able to talk.

"Rooftop?" I ask when we notice it has a VIP rooftop bar.

They both nod and we head over to the bouncer who lets us pass with a smile. I'm wearing a black, strapless, tight dress with my hair down, Ashton's boobs are barely covered, and Gretchen's ass is hanging out. I'm shocked—or not. The three of us are dressed to the nines for our last night out.

Once we reach the bar, we find a couch that's open and grab a seat.

"This is nice," I say and pull my legs up under me while pulling my dress down.

"So, since you skated the question before, I'll ask. Why did you go see Neil after Gretch said you shouldn't?" Ashton asks.

She's got to be kidding me. This is what she wants to talk about tonight? The good mood I was trying to hold on to evaporates.

"The suit never was filed, all is well in the world. Neil is gone. I think I'm much smarter than you give me credit for." I cross my arms and lean back on the sofa.

"Bitchy much?" Gretchen replies and pokes me in the arm.

"Sorry," I say softening my posture. "I'd much rather spend our night *not* talking about Neil. Plus, I'm beat."

"Of course you are! You're moving, you got promoted, you had a month to get it all done, and you broke up with Jackson. It's been a busy few weeks," she says with sympathy laced in her voice.

This is why I love her. She's the ying to Ashton's yang. When one is hard the other is soft. Good cop/

bad cop. But they always seem to tell me what I need to hear. I may not like it, but it's always said with love.

"What are we drinking? It's on me tonight." Gretchen smiles and Ashton whoops, allowing the Neil subject to drop.

We order our drinks and I opt for a glass of wine. If I drink too much, I'll be asleep in the chair. Ashton however is taking full advantage of Gretchen's offer to pay. They're laughing and I'm mostly laughing at them.

"Are we going to talk about Jackson now?" Ashton pipes in.

"Are you trying to piss me off tonight?"

"Better to be pissed off than pissed on," she retorts.

"I'd rather not be either right now," I say, hoping she'll drop this too.

I long for him every night. I've slept with a pillow clutched in my arms just to have something to hold on to. I've cried, thrown things, and memorized that piece of paper to feel close to him.

"Well, I think we should. You've been avoiding saying shit to either of us." She looks as Gretchen for support, who just nods.

I ask myself every day if this job is something worth throwing it away for, but the doubt and lies bring back my resolve. There's no reason for him to have kept this from me, and it leads me to believe there are far deeper secrets he has buried. Then I'm reminded of Piper and how even she knew.

I embrace the rage bubbling up, shoving away the doubt.

"I'm not willing to talk about Jackson, but you two are more than welcome to." I grab my wine and sip it, suddenly wishing it was something stronger.

Sitting here ignoring the two of them, a heavy feeling settles over me. It's hard to breathe and my chest is heaving. All of the energy shifts—it's the same sensation I have whenever Jackson's around. I look around for him as if he's suddenly going to appear. We've never been to this bar, so there's no reason to think he's here, but I feel as if someone's watching me. Scanning the area, I don't see him or anyone I know.

Ashton snaps her fingers in front of my face. "Earth to Catherine."

"Sorry, I thought someone was here."

"I can call him if you want," she says smirking.

My jaw drops as I process what she says. "Seriously?"

Gretchen shifts and taps Ashton's arm. "Enough, Ashton. Okay, let's talk about how I met someone."

Immediately, Ash and I start asking a million questions about the new guy. Gretchen doesn't date. Her job demands her time and she never wanted to put herself through the arguments that come with having to work. My heart is full for her. She deserves love and happiness. Work won't fulfill her forever.

After another round of drinks, Ashton turns her attention back to me. "Okay, I know you don't want to talk about him, so let's talk about how you're about to take over the world with your bad ass self."

"Are you getting excited?" Gretchen asks.

"Yeah, I really am. I'm going to miss you guys, don't get me wrong, but the idea of running an office and getting this opportunity ..." I shrug trying to downplay my emotions.

Gretchen smiles, "I'm really proud of you."

"Thanks. The apartment I found is really amazing. It's a little further away from L.A. than I wanted. It's in San Clemente, but it's close to the beach." I start to let the excitement build. My company believed in me and I'm definitely the youngest in CJJ to ever head an office. Even Sean, who helped start the company, pointed out my age. He said they have absolute confidence I'll be up to the task.

"It sucks that even being here—on an island—we never go to the beach. And when we have two feet of snow you'll be in a bathing suit."

I feign sympathy. "Yeah, that's really going to suck," I pause, "For you."

Ashton slaps my arm and we all start to laugh. It feels good talking with them about everything and allowing myself to really be happy about this opportunity.

"What about your dad's house. Did it sell?" Gretchen asks.

"The realtor said the buyer is good to go and we're going to close the day after the memorial."

"You're going?" Ashton's eyes widen in shock.

I've gone back and forth over the right thing to do. I could skip it but I promised Jackson a while ago, and I promised Natalie. While Natalie might understand, I won't do that to her. It took her this long to do the memorial, so I'm not about to cause any undue stress. We spoke the other day and she sent me pictures of her gorgeous daughter. She said they'd both really like to meet me. So, I'll go.

Biting my lip I look at them both. "I have to. I don't know how the hell I'm going to get through it but I'm going."

"I'll go with you," Ashton says without question.

"Really?" I ask, unsure if she really wants to be there since she never met Aaron or Natalie.

"Of course, Cat. You're going to need me more than you think. You'll see Jackson. You'll be around his friends. I think you've been great at pretending when you don't have to deal with him. In person though ..." She trails off and I suddenly feel nauseous.

My eyes prick when I think about how much this is going to be hard for everyone. "What if he doesn't want me there?"

"It doesn't matter. I do think you should talk to him beforehand though."

That's the last thing I want to do. They're watching me, but I don't respond. My heart says to call, but my head says no. The hairs on the back of my neck raise and I glance around again.

"Why do you keep scanning the crowd?" Gretchen asks looking around.

"I keep getting the feeling I'm being watched."

Ashton stands up and looks around.

"Sit down!" I exclaim and pull on her arm. "I'm probably being silly."

"Or G.I. Joe decided he's tired of being shut out and is coming to get his girl." She leans back with a shit-eating grin, piercing me with her blue eyes.

"Fuck off, Ash. Do you want me angry at you? I'm leaving for California. Even if I could go back to him, it wouldn't work. I'm not about to enter into a long distance relationship that already has issues. Christ, let it go!" I storm off and head to the bathroom before she can reply.

I look up at the mirror and attempt to fix my makeup before going back out there. I know I lost it on her, but I'm tired of everyone and their unsolicited advice. What ever happened to being supportive?

The door opens and a pretty blond enters smiling. She looks familiar, but I can't place her.

Before I can give it too much thought, Gretchen enters. "Cat," she says sympathetically, "You know how she is."

"Yes, I do." I sigh and my head falls back. I get why she's acting like a bitch, but I wish she'd cry it out and move on. "I'm tired, Gretch. I wanted our last night together to be fun, and I don't want to fight. Between work and the move I just want a night to myself. Will you hate me if I head home?"

"Of course not! I'm sure you're exhausted. Promise me you'll find a way to see me once more before you go."

"I'll do my best." I wrap my arms around Gretchen and she kisses my cheek.

"We're being silly girls. But I'm going to miss you."

"I'll miss you more."

She smiles and gives me another hug, "Oh, I meant to tell you ... my lawyer friend, who was going to take on Neil's case, called me. She said since he got back the property he was looking for he no longer needed her."

"Yeah, I think it was really about money."

"I think so too ... anyway, I'm going to come see you, and you'll come back and visit."

"You better," I reply.

Gretchen laughs and grabs my hand. "Let's go, I gotta pay Ashton's insane tab."

We head back out to the seating area and get Ashton. When I turn around to leave, I stop dead in my tracks. Across the room is the figure of a man

I'd know anywhere.

"Oh my God!" I grab Ashton's arm and pull her down.

"What?" she asks looking around to find whatever I'm hiding from.

I keep my head low and try to point to the man making out with the blond from the bathroom. "Look, it's Neil."

She looks and when she spots him, her hand clasps over her mouth and she starts laughing. "Funny, that's not his slut of a girlfriend."

I sit there shell shocked watching him with another woman—who is not Piper. Then it clicks when I see her profile. She's the reporter, Linda, from Raven's press conference. It seems Neil has moved on to one of Piper's friends. My lips turn up at this very interesting turn of events. "Well, this is quite entertaining," I laugh and Ashton snorts.

Pulling my phone out, I snap a few photos of the happy couple. When he turns his head I have the perfect shot.

We sneak out and catch up with Gretchen, showing her the photos. "Well, if the dickface decides to come after you again, we have leverage." She winks at me.

Who thought we'd be here laughing at the fact that he's once again kissing someone else and I had to see it. Last time it destroyed my world, this time I couldn't care less. He has no hold on me and it feels fantastic.

Stick that in your pipe and smoke it, Neil.

I head home as Ash and Gretch continue to another bar. As much as I'd love to go to sleep there's one task I need to handle before I collapse. I need to hire an assistant before I get on that plane. Grabbing the folder of resumes, I thumb for the one I set up to speak to today.

I grab my phone and call. "Hi, is Tristan there?" I ask into the receiver as I walk around my empty room.

Thankfully, this is the last of the interviews I need to do over the phone before I arrive in California. Tristan is the one candidate I'm most excited about interviewing. He has some executive assistant experience along with acting and public speaking.

"This is." His deep voice is gruff and sexy.

Well, hello there. Now that's a voice I could listen to all day.

"This is Catherine Pope from CJJ Public Relations. We emailed and I informed you I'd be calling regarding your application for the assistant position."

"Yes, hi!" Tristan exclaims as he perks up a bit. "I'm very excited about the office opening and was waiting for your call."

"Your resume was great and I'd like to go over a few things." I grab my notepad and sit on the floor. "Is now a good time?"

"Yes, Ms. Pope. Definitely." Tristan's voice is warm yet rough. It reminds me of another man, but I shut that thought process down quickly.

"Can you tell me a bit about yourself and why you're looking to make a move?"

Tristan and I spend almost an hour going over the job, expectations, and possibilities the company has for him. I have a great feeling about him. He's easygoing, articulate, and has a good background for the job. Honestly, he'd be fabulous as a publicist, but for now he'd like to learn as much as he can from me. As long as his references check out, I'll have myself an assistant.

Feeling good about where we leave off, I lie in my bed hoping I can fall asleep, mentally running over the goodbye with my mother tomorrow and the last minute stuff at my dad's house.

chapter twenty-two

Today is the memorial. The day I'll say farewell to two men. One man who meant the world to many. A father, a hero, a husband, and a friend who died leaving a gaping hole in so many people's hearts.

The other is a man who left a hole in *my* heart.

I hate this dress.

I hate this day.

I hate the makeup I'm not able to wear because I can't stop crying.

I woke up this morning a mess. The idea of having to see him has been too much. I received a package last night of more lilies, and this time I allowed myself to open the card and read it.

I've never cried so hard in my entire life, but there's no going back in time.

After my heart was already completely ripped from my chest, I grabbed the other notes he sent with the gifts to my office. I figure I'll get it all done in one fell swoop and allow the pain to take over so I can get it out.

Dear Catherine,

Today, I hate myself. I don't deserve you. It's been less than twenty-four hours since I last held you. One day, and I feel worse than I ever have. I

saw this lighthouse and thought of you. It reminded me of the magic we shared up there. How you made me want to live again. You give me that. I'll tell you everything, just give me a chance.
All of my heart and soul,
Jackson

The tears stream and I sob, but Ashton ignores the sounds of my breakdown if she hears me. I open the next card that came with the Battleship game.

Dear Catherine,
I've lost track of the times I've picked up the phone. I can't sleep in our bed. Everything in this fucking house reminds me of us. Be my anchor, Catherine. I hate myself. I hate what I've done to us. Call me and we can work through it. My heart is yours. It's up to you if it sinks.
All of me,
Jackson

There's no changing the fact that I'm leaving for California in four days. I want to forgive him, to run back to his arms, but it doesn't erase the doubt and the three thousand miles that are about to be between us. I know I should stop myself from reading the rest of the notes, but I owe him.

My Catherine,
Love notes are dumb but I should've written them to you. Then you'd have known what was inside of me the entire time. You wouldn't have questioned anything because it would be there in black and white. My proof to you when you felt doubt and you'd know how much you mean to me. I don't even

know if you read these but if you do ... I miss you. I went to work today and everyone asked about you. I broke two things because I was fucking mad. I'm mad now too. If you love me, how can you walk away so easily? Don't answer that. I'm pretty sure I'm talking to myself. I talked to Mark and my mother today, told them about what happened. I'm sure you can imagine the things I heard. But one thing my mom said that stuck:

"Above all, love each other deeply, because love covers a multitude of sins." – Peter 4:18

I love you deeply. I love you with every breath I take. I've made mistakes. I've fucked up. I know this, but love me.

Don't give up on us.

Jackson

My eyes are puffy, my heart is heavy, and the idea of seeing him has made me sick. I allow myself to read the final letter one more time.

Dear Catherine,

I know now it's over. I know you don't want to talk to me, or hear my side and I respect your decision. I hate it, but I can't push you anymore. I know I hurt you. I don't know how to live without trying to win you back. I can't think. I can't sleep. I hurt so fucking much, Catherine. Every day I look at this godforsaken apartment and I want to sell it and move—but then I'll have lost the only thing I have of you. You were the only woman to ever sleep in this bed. You were the only woman to touch this house. Nothing here matters because you're gone. I'd go back in time and tell you everything. But I can't do that. I can't fix this and it's killing me. I call and you don't answer. I text and you won't respond. I can't fix this without you. I meant every word I ever said to you. I love you and I'll love you until my last breath.

You're it for me.

Jackson

How can someone hurt so much? The depths of my heart are hollow, my eyes are burning from the onslaught of tears. I feel like I've been torn apart and when I was put back together, they forgot some pieces. But I won't quit my job. I can't walk away from this opportunity, and we can't work. So it's my turn to save him. Allow him to move on with a clean break.

I know when I see him today, I'll have to put on the show of my life. If I thought the launch party was difficult, this will be a thousand times worse.

I should've left the damn cards unopened. But I couldn't.

So today I'll somehow handle looking at the man who's no longer mine. The one who forced me to love again, to give my heart to him—then forced me to be alone. He's gone from my life and I can't get him back. I have to let him go—for good.

I'll need a miracle to get through this.

He took everything from me with that damn letter.

CHAPTER TWENTY-THREE

JACKSON

"You ready?" Mark asks from behind me. He's wearing his full dress uniform, white gloves and all.

With a little help I was able to get my dress blues on. The only time I've worn this uniform since I got out was for the last team member we lost a few months ago. I hate how once again I'm putting it on for the same reason. In fact, this is pretty much the only time I wear it. I'm going to fucking burn it after this, and then maybe we'll stop having to go to funerals.

I straighten my belt and huff. I can't do this. I can't bury another friend. "Fuck. I can't do this. Just go without me," I say looking away.

Next thing that registers is his fist connecting with my bad shoulder.

"What the fuck?" I ask while trying to get rid of the stinging in my arm.

"You're going. I'll punch you in the fucking face if you even try to say it again. You shut your mouth and listen. Maybe when you were taking your little nap you didn't hear me, maybe your tiny brain can't retain it, but I've had enough of your goddamn bullshit. You're going! I swear to fucking God you're going today," Mark rages and runs his hand down his face.

I've never seen him so pissed—well, not at me at least. "I don't know what the hell you're talking about."

"Of course not! You weren't the only one in that village, asshole. You weren't the only one who watched Aaron go and handle the issues in Afghanistan that either one of us could've dealt with. *You* didn't fucking go to Natalie and tell her that her husband was dead. No, fucker, I did that. I had to knock on her door, catch her in my arms as she lost it. So kiss my fucking ass."

"Keep it up, dickhead," I warn.

He turns as if I didn't say anything and mocks me, "'I'm not going.' My fucking ass you're not. You're not the only one who's ever lost anyone!" he yells and punches the door. "I fucking lost them too! They were my friends too, Muff. *You* aren't the only one who lives with guilt!" Mark chokes on the last part.

"I know that!" I yell back at him. "But I sent them to their deaths! I live with this every fucking day."

"You *still* don't get it. We were a fucking team. I left the Navy after you did because where you go, I go. I followed because you, me, and Aaron—we're a team." Mark balls his fists up and steps toward me. "You aren't the only one in this team. I've watched every single fucking one of them die. I watched you die too, you son of a bitch." He points his finger and jabs me in the chest. I push him back away from me. And he stumbles.

"Don't fucking push me," I say strained.

"You want to fight me? Today? You want me to fucking lay you out?" Mark says taunting me and throwing his hands up.

"Fuck you!" I don't want to fight him but he's

about to push me there.

"No, fuck you! I'm not sitting around acting like I'm the only person who suffers. It's what the job is. You know this. I know this. When we became SEALs we knew we could die but it's what we lived for. Losing him though—he wasn't supposed to die."

The words I want to say to him won't come out. I want to tell him to fuck off, but I can't. He's lost as many friends as I have. As much as I want to say something, he's right. Mark and Aaron worked together every day. They spent more time together than I did in the last year while I was cleaning up my mess of a life.

After a few minutes of us pissed off with our fists ready to strike, we both take a step back. "He was a brother to me," he says. I look up and he shakes his head. "He was a better man than me or you. He didn't deserve to die."

"I know. It should've been me," I say, feeling devoid of any emotion.

"It shouldn't have been any of us."

"I don't ever want to wear this uniform again," I say, fixing my jacket from the near fight with Mark.

He looks over and grips his neck. "I'm tired of attending these funerals. The next one I plan to go to is my own. And I won't give a fuck what you wear."

There are times when I wish we were back eight years ago, young, dumb, and ignorant to the world around us. We thought we were invincible. Who the fuck was going to bring down a group of SEALs? No one. We lived in this idealistic world that we could live dangerous and not pay for our sins.

We weren't married, no kids, just money to burn and tails to chase. The missions were, in our minds, fun. The deployments were what we looked forward to. I couldn't wait to be away, because Virginia was fucking boring.

"Dude, I—" I start to say but he cuts me off.

"Not today, Muff." He shakes his head. "I'll kick your ass another day, but not today. Come on, let's go."

Today is going to be hard on everyone, but especially Mark.

We get to the funeral site without further incident. I'm able to put pressure on my leg now as long as I use a crutch, but today I won't be using it. I'll stand through the pain because it will be my reminder. I'll fight through the hurt because Aaron deserves it.

There's a tent set up, and Natalie and her family are sitting while the color guard stands guard of the urn. There are a few of the team guys here along with some of their wives. I say hello to everyone and stand off in the back.

Natalie comes over to me hesitantly. "Jackson, thank you for doing all this." She bites her lip and a tear falls.

"Nat, you don't owe me anything."

She gives a sad smile. "Aaron loved you like a brother."

I ball my fists and stand up taller, "I'm sor— "

Natalie puts her hand on my arm and cuts me off. "Don't you dare say it. You didn't kill him. I hate everyone telling me they're sorry because I can bet you a thousand dollars if it were you or Mark, he would wish it was him."

Her mother comes up behind her and hands her Aarabelle. She's a beautiful baby with dark hair and Natalie holds her close. Natalie turns to me while I gaze at the tiny infant in her arms. "I have a piece of him," she says as she rocks back and forth.

I look up and she kisses Aarabelle's head. Mark and I stand there together watching her walk over and talk to the other team guys who are here.

The feeling in the air shifts and my body registers Catherine's presence. My heart pounds harder in my chest as I scan the area looking for her.

"Dude," Mark grips my shoulder and points over at our former Senior Chief as he approaches. "Look, it's Wolf."

I don't respond because I know she's here. Finally, I catch a glimpse of her. She's even more beautiful than I remember. The pictures I have of us don't do her justice. Her hair blows in the wind and I fight the urge to go to her, fall on my knees, and grovel. I want to wrap her in my arms, beg her for forgiveness, and bury myself in her and never leave, but I know it'll do no good. She's made it clear that she's done. Her sunglasses hide her eyes, but the way she's holding on to Ashton leads me to believe she's upset.

I see her nod and look over at the crowd, but she doesn't see me—or at least doesn't acknowledge in any way that she does.

Every part of me is pulled toward her. But once again she shuts me out.

"Cole, it's good to see you. I wish it was under better circumstances," Senior Chief Wolfel says.

I shake his hand. "I agree, Wolf, but it's good to see you as well."

"I hear the company is doing well."

I nod, trying to keep my eyes on Catherine as she approaches with her head down. I'm willing her to look at me, but her head stays firmly downcast and she maintains her distance. "Yes, I'm focusing on growing the firm. Mark and I are looking at doing some bigger bids."

The priest who begins to speak halts our conversation. His voice is somber and the mood within the tent shifts. He talks about Aaron's life as a kid, his heroism as an adult, and the absence his loss brings. There's no comfort because the pain will never completely fade. Sure, it will lessen in time, but Natalie is a widow, Aarabelle will grow up without a father. She'll suffer the loss of a great man and she'll never know why.

I gaze at the woman I lost. She wipes her cheek and her body shakes. My feet move without permission. I can't watch her suffer and not go to her. She's falling apart. One step closer, then I feel Mark grip my shoulder, holding me in place. He shakes his head and I stay where I am, but my eyes stay locked on Catherine.

"Today, we remember a hero who lost his life too soon. We remember the man who fought through wars and protected those who couldn't protect themselves. We remember a husband, a son, a father, and a friend." The priest looks up and I hear Natalie cry louder while people wrap their arms around her.

My shipmates stand off to the side and begin the military funeral honors. The bugle plays "Taps" and the sounds of people crying grow louder. The sound of that song haunts me.

Two sailors accompany our former Senior Chief who's presenting the flag to her. He kneels and says the words every woman never wants to hear. The apology that should never come. A grateful fucking nation my ass. How about telling her we'll kill the fuckers who made her have to hold that folded flag.

Mark and I stand watching her sob, holding the baby to her chest. The echo of her cries breaks our stance. We push forward at the same time and each put our hands on her shoulders. Letting her know she's not alone and we're here. Even with the throbbing radiating from my leg, I refuse to move. Fuck the pain, because it's nothing compared to what she's feeling. Her chest heaves as we stand guard behind her.

I hear the people crying behind me but one sound breaks my hold. The person who matters most to me and the only one I'd be willing to move for. I look over and see Ashton pull her close. I look over at Mark who nods once and puts his hand on Natalie's other shoulder relieving me from my position.

Walking up behind Catherine, without thinking, my hand drifts up her back and rests on the skin of her shoulder. A jolt runs through me from being this close to her. Within seconds, the feelings I'd managed to push away come barreling forward. I need to touch her and feel her against me.

"Catherine," my voice is low and full of emotion.

She sobs, falling forward, and Ashton catches her. She shakes in her arms but I won't move my hand. I can't stop touching her. I won't stop. She's mine and I *will* protect her. Looking at Ashton she closes her eyes and gives a small nod.

It's all the permission I need. I grab a hold of Catherine and pull her into my arms. I hold her once again and my world shifts. Her touch, the smell of vanilla hits me, and I can't fucking breathe. Everything that matters is in my arms and I won't let go of her again.

"Catherine, it's okay," I say softly, running my hands down her hair. I pull her close not allowing any space between us.

She clutches me and pulls me even closer as she buries her head in my chest. This insanity will end. She'll know everything today, and she's not leaving me ever again.

"Jackson," she cries and takes a deep breath. "Please," she pleads, but I don't know what the hell she's asking for.

Catherine starts to pull back, but I tighten my grip and shift on my leg trying to balance. "I'm not letting go. I need you right now," I say unashamed.

She nods into my chest as the funeral goes on. Just her being here gives me the strength I need. It allows me to say farewell to my brother-in-arms.

People filter out, but we stand here clutching each other.

Mark removes his pin from his chest and walks to the urn. He closes his eyes and places it down. The moments pass as he stands there saying good-bye silently. After a few minutes, Ashton walks over and places her hand on his shoulder. He grips her hand and they walk away.

It's my turn. I release Catherine and remove my trident. I grip her face and stare into her eyes. I see all the hurt and pain in her, and I swear I'll never be the cause of that look again. Once she knows every-thing we can move forward.

"I have to—"

Catherine's hand touches my lips silencing me. She leans in and places her lips to mine. I don't want to fucking move. I want to stay with her like this forever. When she leans back, I instantly feel her absence.

Without a word I walk over to the urn. I stand there alone for a moment and tell Aaron everything I need to say.

"I'm so sorry. I'll make sure she's okay. I'll be there for Aarabelle and remind her of the man you were. You'll never be forgotten," I say quietly hoping somewhere he hears me. I'll never break the vow I made to him.

I place the pin next to the other five that lay there from members of our team who came to pay their respects. When I turn to grab Catherine's hand, I see her heading to the car.

The panic sets in. I'm going to lose her.

"Fuck," I say, trying to move quickly.

Ashton stands there arguing with her, and I pray it gives me enough time to stop her.

She sees me coming and grabs the keys and closes her door.

I stop moving and stare at her as she rushes to get away.

"Get your head out of your ass and fix this mess you've created. If you love her, fight like a man. I'm tired of watching you act like a bitch," Mark says and throws his keys at me. "Follow her."

I move as fast as I can and get in Mark's car, ready to chase her. This isn't over. Not by a fucking long shot.

chapter twenty-four

$\mathcal{K}$eep driving. Keep your foot on the gas and don't stop.

I tell myself over and over. Don't look in the rearview mirror because it doesn't matter. It's behind me. I have to keep moving forward and pretend that I didn't allow myself to feel again.

One touch was all it took.

One word crumbled the walls I'd rebuilt.

If I'd stayed there he would've broken me down. I could see it in his eyes. He wasn't going to let me go. So I did as I promised myself before I went—I let him go first. I protected myself from yet another round of heartbreak. Which is all that seems to come from Jackson and I. We hurt each other whether it's intentional or not. The damage is still the same and I've had enough to last me a lifetime.

The drive to the house in Scotch Plains is shorter than if I had to head back to my apartment, so I brought an overnight bag since Mark and Ashton made arrangements for her to get home. As soon as Jackson let me go, I had to get out of there. I needed to get the hell away from him because he'd consume me. The pain remains though.

I wipe the tears that continue to stream down my face. I can still feel him around me, his scent clings to me and I inhale it. I'd give up everything to go back in time and never have given in to him. If I'd saved myself then it wouldn't hurt so damn much right now. There's nothing more I want to do than turn this car around and run back to him. His touch sent my entire world into a tailspin. In his arms I felt it all. The love, the hurt, the agony of our reunion, knowing it was the finale too. It was the last time Jackson would ever hold me, ever touch me, his lips, his face will never be mine again.

I look in the rearview mirror wanting to go back. *Keep driving.*

Pushing the accelerator faster, I fight my heart's wants. It doesn't change the circumstances we're in. My clean start is in California and I leave in four days.

Keep your foot on the gas and don't stop.

I pull up to what was my father's house and drop my head on the steering wheel. Now what? Drawing a deep breath I lean back while the ache washes over me. I remember how it felt to find out everything. How devastated I was during that press release and what it felt like to find out the love I thought we shared was built on lies.

Removing myself from the car, I open the back door and grab my bag.

"I wasn't done," I hear Jackson's voice.

My entire body freezes at the sound of his deep voice and my legs go weak. I grab on to the frame of the door to stay upright. "What are you doing here?" I ask on the verge of sobbing.

He takes a step closer, gripping my wrists, and his voice softens. "No more running. We're going to talk. Now."

I look into his eyes and the storm rages across his face. Allowing myself a minute to take him in.

He's dressed in his dark blue uniform and if I ever thought he was sexy in a suit, this just put that image to shame. I watch as he smirks when he catches me looking him over.

That sexy grin infuriates me. "You don't get it," I say exasperated.

Jackson's hands move up my arms slowly. I start to draw short breaths and shake. Why does he do this to me? Why can't I fight him? I'm weak against his touch.

"I know that I love you," he says as his fingers move against my neck. "I get it, but I don't care about giving you space anymore."

"You don't care?" I push him back and he leans forward, trapping me in his arms. "God, do you hear yourself? Why are you here if you don't care?"

"If we're really done. Why the hell should I care?" His lips graze my ear. "If you don't love me and you're done with me, then I have nothing left to lose." The heat of his breath against my neck causes me to shiver. "So, we're going to talk because I," his lips touch the skin of my neck, "Don't," another kiss, "Care."

He pulls me against him and presses his lips to the base of my neck, lingering and moving slowly while he holds me close.

I melt into his embrace like always. But this is our dance. He breaks me down, and I break more. Only I'm not sure I'll be able to seal the cracks from this one.

"It doesn't matter," I say pulling out of his arms. "None of it matters anymore. You should go."

"I'm sure I should, but I won't. Please, come home. Let's talk." Jackson looks around and takes in the street we're standing on. "Or have you found a new home?"

My eyes close and my heart pounds against my chest. "Not that I owe you any explanations, but no, this was my father's house. Tomorrow I'm selling it," I say as I walk to the door. I need him to go now. "I have a lot I need to do, so please get back in your car and go. Goodbye."

Jackson grabs my arm and I turn to face him, but before I can say a word he slowly presses his lips against mine. His hands grip my neck and hold me at his mercy. Every part of me comes to life. The heart that has been beating out of rhythm just found its cadence. My breath comes easier from one solitary kiss. Needing to be closer, needing this feeling to remain, my hands grip his neck as I pull him closer. Jackson pushes my back against the door and I give myself over to him for a moment. I allow myself the feel of his weight against me. The way he ignites my body because this will be the last time.

Jackson pulls back and his blue-green eyes are solid and he struggles to catch his breath. "There are no goodbyes between us." He grabs the keys and I stand here dumbstruck.

This is not going according to plan.

Jackson fiddles with the keys until he gets the door open. Standing off to the side with his arm outstretched he waits for me to enter.

"You're not staying," I say defiantly.

"I'm not leaving, so either you're coming with me to New York, or I'm staying here until you hear me out. You pick."

"Neither of those works for me. So you can leave or I'll call the cops."

He shrugs, "I'll be right here."

"I'm not kidding."

"Be my guest, baby."

"I'm not your baby anymore."

Jackson takes a step forward and his eyes are steel. "Get in the fucking house. I'm done playing."

I stand there with my arms crossed. He's lost the right to boss me around.

"Always have to do things the hard way, don't you?" he asks before grabbing me around my waist and placing me in the house.

"Put me down!" I yell and he kicks the door shut. "God! You don't have a clue, do you?"

He laughs, apparently finding this amusing, before he winces and grips his leg. "Did you get my gifts?"

"You hurt yourself, didn't you?"

"I'm fine. Answer the question."

"I burned them," I say completely full of shit, but I hope if I can piss him off enough he'll take the hint and leave.

"Mature," he scoffs. "Did you read the cards or did you burn those too?" His brow rises in question.

I blink repeatedly while my jaw falls slightly ajar. I can't lie to him about this. His heart was bared in those letters. "I read them," I say softly.

I read them and fell apart. I lost a part of my heart in those letters, but I won't tell him that.

"But they didn't matter to you?"

"You lied to me, Jackson!" I say infuriated that he continues to neglect this fact. "I told you my deal-breakers. I gave you every chance to tell me about your *wife*." I throw my hands up and start to pace. "I can't have this conversation with you now. I'm not angry, or upset, I'm not going through this again. You promised me. You fucking promised!" I yell and push against his chest. "You promised. Of course those damn letters mattered, but they don't change anything!"

"I know."

"You weren't supposed to break my heart," I say, clutching my stomach.

Jackson pulls me to his chest and his voice is thick with emotion. "You weren't supposed to win mine. I was dead inside. I refused to ever love again, yet here we are."

I look up and plead with him. "Please, let me go."

His jaw sets and he releases me. "I can't. Sit down. No more games, no more lies."

"Jackson," I say drawing a deep breath. "It doesn't matter. Nothing matters. Things have changed."

"Not for me they haven't! I'm fucking dying without you, Catherine. My entire fucking world doesn't make sense anymore. How is that possible? How even after the absolute hell I've lived through does that make sense? Because it does matter. We matter, goddammit." He drops to his knees in front of me.

I look at his face and see it. The bags under his eyes, the pain in his eyes. He's a mess. So am I. I sink to the couch and we continue to look at each other. I ache. I physically ache for him.

"Love shouldn't hurt like this," I say as he grips my hands.

"I was married for six years to a woman named Madelyn."

"Please don't do this."

Jackson continues as if he didn't hear my request. "I met her when I was active duty. I fell in love with her. She was beautiful, alluring, and I was a twenty-two-year-old idiot who thought he was invincible. The world was at my feet. I was a Navy-fucking-SEAL and she doted on me."

I close my eyes wishing he would stop and we could say goodbye.

But he doesn't.

"She was born into a wealthy family. Her parents gave her anything she wanted because she was born with a severe heart condition. I married her after two years thinking it was the next step. Maddie and I had everything even though we couldn't ever have kids. Losing her was pure fucking torture." Jackson looks at me and tears fill my eyes.

"I'm sorry you lost someone you loved." I don't know what else to say.

"I didn't lose her. I was the reason she died," he says as he grips the bridge of his nose.

My jaw falls slack. "I don't understand."

"This isn't going to be easy for me. I know you think you fought feeling anything for me but you have no idea how hard I fought against you. I didn't ever want to love again. There wasn't a part of me that ever wanted to feel this again." Jackson's gaze bores through me. "If I didn't love you, then I wouldn't have to lose you. I wouldn't have to feel the fucking pain and torment again. You were never supposed to get to me."

I look at him as he traces his calloused thumb across my palm. "Jackson, we can't do this to each other."

"Maddie and I enjoyed our life together as long as I kept her needs first. She hated the deployments, training exercises, and most of all she hated how much I loved it. There were times I had to miss her doctor's appointments because of the Navy, but I loved being a SEAL. We knew from the beginning we could never have kids. I was fine with it because I was gone so much." Jackson's eyes glaze over and he grips my hand harder.

"Her family demanded she take over Raven. The Elliotts built it from the ground up. They urged me to leave the service because I should be home to care for Madelyn. After the mission that went wrong, Maddie demanded it too. I wanted to re-en-list, but we barely saw each other as it was, and now she was going to be in New York. She hated being a military wife and I loved her, so I gave it up. We fought and argued, but ultimately her happi-ness came first for me." He looks at me for the first time with tears building in his eyes.

"You don't have to ..." Watching him cry is too much.

"That last mission happened four months be-fore my contract was up. I was on limited duty any-way, so I said fuck it and I quit. She was happy and I thought that's all that mattered. She gained com-plete control of the company and we bought out her brother. I had a lot of money saved from my missions. My only request was that I start the secu-rity company. She supported it—I think she knew there was a part of me that felt dead. I hated the messages from Mark and the guys about what they were doing. I fucking wanted to crawl out of my skin staying in New York, so I made Cole Securities bid for contracts so that I could still use my skills. Of course, it meant I was gone from her again."

"Why are you telling me this?" I ask as a tear falls from my face. I don't want to hear about how much he loved his wife.

"Because I should've told you before. But I was terrified it would make everything real. It was the only piece of me I had left to give you. If you knew about her then you would see how fucking wrecked I am." He trembles as he speaks and another tear falls from his eyes. "I would've sold my soul to have the rest of this story not happen. I was flying between New York and Virginia constantly. We were trying to make it work. She was getting sicker, so I couldn't leave as often and she had to resign from Raven. None of the doctors were sure why her medication suddenly wasn't effective. There was a problem with something in Virginia and I had to handle it ... she begged me not to go. She said she felt sicker than usual, but Maddie was dramatic. She said fine, go, that she'd call her mother. So I left. What kind of man leaves his wife whose heart was starting to fail?" he asks rhetorically before beginning again.

"As much as I knew I shouldn't go, I couldn't stay. I got on the plane and when I landed, I had thirty missed calls. Madelyn had collapsed and was in a coma."

I gasp and he looks up. "See, we couldn't have kids, Catherine. I knew this, she knew this. But she must've come off her birth control or I don't know, but she was pregnant." Jackson's hand covers his heart and he grips at his chest. "Her heart failed because she couldn't carry a baby. I killed her and I killed our baby. Knowing I was the reason she died is beyond anything I can describe." Jackson's tears fall silently as he relives his grief.

He looks up at me and I sink on to the floor with him and wrap my arms around him. He's so broken. My heart drops and I join him with my own tears as

I see the anguish on his face. This isn't what I was expecting. I thought he was divorced, not that she'd died. And he lost a baby too. How much loss can one person handle? He's lost so many people in his life by some form of tragedy.

"I'm so sorry," I say with tears streaming.

"The doctors said she was about four weeks, but the increased stress on her heart was too much and she never woke up. Her family blamed me for being careless and hated me for a long time. But no one can hate me more than I hate myself."

"It wasn't your fault, Jackson." A tear falls down my cheek at how much pain and death he's dealt with. "You didn't kill your baby or your wife. It was tragic and awful, but you didn't know. You didn't do it on purpose."

"In a matter of a year, there was five people's blood on my hands. I was terrified of failing you too, and I did it anyway. I couldn't have you look at me like that. It was my job to protect them and I failed every one of them."

My throat aches and I try to get the words out. "Do you know what I see?" He looks up and then his eyes close. "I see a man who needs to forgive himself for something he couldn't control. You didn't purposely put anyone in danger. Bad things happened, but you didn't kill anyone. You're not capable of doing that."

"I can't lose you, Catherine. I couldn't tell you. I didn't want you to see me that way. I left her, and she died." Jackson's hands cup my face. "I lost my wife and child and the last words I said to her were how I wished I was fucking deployed again so I didn't have to deal with Raven. I vowed after she died I wouldn't ever give myself the chance to hurt anyone else. Then you fell into my lap—literally. I tried not to love you. I tried to keep at a distance, but when I'd see you ... I wanted you more."

"Our entire relationship has been one thing after another," I sigh as his thumbs rub my cheek.

It's been a lot of hurt, but we did have good times with laughter, playfulness, and love. I wish there was more of that because the bad times make those feel minimal. Watching our relationship fall apart has been agony, but Jackson taught me a lot. I learned how to love again when I thought I couldn't.

"In the six years I was married to Madelyn, I never in my dreams imagined loving anyone as much as her—then came you. You make me feel alive. You give me hope that I can be more of a man than I was then. You showed me how to love again. I never felt like I did after you walked away. Doesn't that say something?"

My heart sinks because as much as I understand him, I'm leaving. I move in four days and here is the man that I loved and still love, but now what? Everything's different. Those weeks changed the course of my life and I don't know if I can go back. It doesn't negate the fact that if he'd told me all of this I wouldn't be faced with this choice. Or if I was, we could've navigated this together. If I give everything up for him, then what? If in four months something else happens and our worlds fall apart, can we handle it then? All of the questions swirl around in my head, but I already know the answers.

He looks into my eyes and pulls me close, pressing his forehead to mine. "Give me tonight. Don't say anything, just give me tonight," Jackson says before pressing his lips to mine.

The desperation rolls off of him in waves. He

coaxes my lips apart and I allow him entry. Gently tilting my head, he kisses me deeply and reverently. I feel his hand lower to my back and he lays me down. My brain ceases to exist. I want to feel. I want to have him in my body and my soul because I don't know if I'll ever find a love like this again. And even with all that was exposed tonight, I can't give up everything for him. I can't give up my dreams. So I'll give him tonight, and pray tomorrow doesn't kill me.

chapter twenty-five

*E*very muscle is tight as if someone is pulling me apart from the inside out. He kisses me languidly and ardently. All I want is more. I want aggression and roughness because the tenderness is breaking me. I want to forget. I need to get lost in him and for the world to fade away. No jobs, no loss, no sadness ... only us.

His lips leave mine as he kisses from my neck to my collarbone. "I've missed you so much," Jackson says quietly as he pulls the strap of my dress down, exposing my shoulder.

I close my eyes and memorize the way his lips feel against my skin.

He lowers the zipper of my dress. "We don't have to do this," I say unsure of what I'm feeling. He bared his soul, told me about the loss of his wife and child—it feels wrong knowing tomorrow I have to leave.

Jackson turns me to him, cups my cheeks, and waits for me to look at him. "I need you. I need every part of you. You make me whole."

My chest is weighted by his words because I'm going to hurt him. I know I am and I think he knows it too. "Just for tonight," I say hoping he understands. "You have me."

Without answering he lowers his lips to mine,

stopping all conversation. I close my mind off. If I think about what this is, it'll kill me. The loss that this man has endured, the pain that we've caused each other, is too much. But if he needs this, then he can take from me. I've taken enough from him.

"You're so beautiful," Jackson says letting me know he in no way takes this moment for granted. My dress comes off. He leaves on my heels and I lie here as he admires me while taking off his uniform.

"Let me," I say, sitting up.

Each button that I undo I lose a part of myself—a part of us.

Trust. I trusted him. I trusted us—but we failed.

Another button.

Hope. We shared hope that we would be enough for each other.

Another button.

Security. He made me feel safe, loved, adored.

Another button.

He stops my hands from moving and he removes the tears I try to stifle. "Stay with me."

I nod as his shirt falls. He removes his undershirt and my eyes fall to the scar on his chest. It's no longer red and angry, but it serves as a reminder of how close I came to losing him forever. The scar marks a time that I will never forget. But I don't want to remember any of it because it'll make telling him about the job that much harder. My stomach churns and I struggle to hold it together.

"Jackson, make me forget," I plead. I need to do anything but feel.

His lips crush mine and he lays me down. I relish in the way his tongue dances with mine, volleying for control. When his hands softly graze against my body I shiver. The weight of him on top of me holds me together. His arms press me against him and I'm whole once again.

Releasing me, he never breaks eye contact, forcing me to stay in the moment and not retreat into my head. Jackson's eyes swim with emotion, but he slowly moves his lips to mine while he removes my bra.

"Every part of you belongs to me," he whispers against my lips.

"Take me."

Slowly his tongue glides to my neck as he makes his way to my chest. When his mouth latches on to my nipple, I cry out in pleasure. Jackson's tongue circles it slowly and then he licks his way to my other breast, lavishing it with the same attention.

"I love you," he says as he makes his way to my stomach.

Every part of me wants to tell him how much I love him. Every cell in my body is crying out to give in to him, but I fight it. I resist it because I know it doesn't change the position we're in.

"Please," I beg so he'll stop talking.

Jackson slips my panties down my legs and his fingers brush against my clit and my back bows off the floor. "Jackson," I sigh as he spreads my legs apart and I feel the scruff of his cheek against my thigh. The roughness sets my body on fire. All I want is to stay in this moment forever. Just the two of us tonight, because I don't want this night to end. I want to freeze time and live right here forever.

When his tongue touches me, I grip his hair. He inserts a finger and my body moves of it's own accord. Jackson's tongue enters me and he holds my hips fucking me with his mouth. "Oh, God," I cry breathlessly as his thumb presses on my clit.

He's barely touched me and I'm already teetering on the edge.

Jackson stops and I look at him. "If I only have tonight, we're going to take our time," he says answering the questions in my eyes. "Now flip over."

Again I stare at him, biting my lip, trying to figure out his plan. His hands travel up my body, and when he reaches my hips, he grips them and turns me over. I feel his weight and warmth disappear. Looking over at him, I see him remove the rest of his clothing. He's even more magnificent than the last memory I have.

He returns to my side and I feel his hands on my shoulders, pushing down, working out the tension. "I'm sorry," he says as his lips press against my spine. "I shouldn't have kept things from you."

I close my eyes and attempt to halt the tears. "I know. I'm sorry too," I say.

I'm sorry for the fact that this is where we are. To love someone so much but not be able to be together.

Jackson continues to massage my back without a word, stopping only to place a kiss every few minutes. After he's content with loosening my muscles, he turns me back over. The look in his eyes stops my heart. There's so much emotion in that single moment. The most dominant is despair. He's breaking and I'm already broken.

As we hold each other's gaze, Jackson enters me. It's like coming home. We fit like two pieces of a puzzle. My body welcomes him and he sighs.

"I need you," he says as he slides back and forth. "I hate who I am without you. You have no idea how miserable I am. Please, come back to me," Jackson requests, but I don't respond. "No more secrets."

"I miss you too." It's all I can say because I can't make promises. I'm miserable without him too, but I was living. My life was working out, but now I want to lock myself away with him and never leave.

Jackson grinds his hips and my body climbs higher needing release. I moan and close my eyes.

"I need to see you," he says through gritted teeth. "Let me see you when you come."

I open my eyes and try to keep them on him while he continues to hit the spot that's driving me to orgasm. "So. Close," I gasp in between thrusts. I grip Jackson's face and pull him to me as my tongue delves into his mouth. I lose myself and my body rockets into another world.

Jackson continues milking every ounce of pleasure I'm capable of feeling before he loses it. "Fuck, Catherine. I love you," he says as he orgasms.

We lay here, both spent emotionally and physically.

After we both clean up, I see him in my father's office. "Is this him?" he asks, finding a frame I missed during the packing.

"Yeah, that was my dad," I say looking at the photo.

"You look like him."

"Jackson we should talk," I say softly.

"Not tonight. We've done enough talking. Tonight, I just want to pretend," he murmurs and pulls me against his chest.

I sigh and wrap my arms around him. As much as I want to pretend as he's asked, I know it'll only leave us both in worse shape tomorrow. "I don't want to hurt you."

He rubs his hands up and down my back and sighs deeply. "I know." He places a kiss on my forehead. "Let's go to bed."

My lips press against his scar on his shoulder.

We move into the bedroom and he hands me his t-shirt. A smile spreads across my face as I remember how much he likes seeing me in his clothes.

Today has been overwhelming and heartbreaking. I think about how strong Natalie is, how she lost the man she loves and can't ever get him back. I have the man I love in my arms and I'm going to let him go willingly. I wish I could be mad again. Mad didn't hurt so much. It made leaving a little easier because it was his fault. Now, it's a choice.

Jackson's arm slides under my shoulder and he pulls me against his chest. "Is there anything I can say to change your mind?"

I look up at him and a tear falls. "No."

He nods once and pulls me tighter. "I'm not going to give up. You're mine and I'm going to win you back. I'm just warning you."

"Jackson ..." I start and he brushes the tear running down my cheek.

"No tears."

"It hurts so much."

His eyes stay focused on the ceiling. "I won't hurt you anymore. Nothing heavy, I just want to hold you, talk to you, love you."

"How?" I ask because I don't see how we can pretend.

"Easy. How've you been?" His fingers run up and down my arm as we lie in each other's arms.

This will last a few questions before we find a way back to the conversation we should be having.

"I'm living. How's your leg?"

"Today I overdid it, but it was worth it. I wasn't going to be on crutches for the memorial. Did you get to see Aarabelle?"

I smile thinking about how beautiful that tiny baby was. I promised Natalie we would see each other before I leave for California. "She's perfect."

"Yeah, she is. Natalie asked me and Mark to be her godfathers."

"She told me. I think you'll spoil her and do all the things you're supposed to as a godfather."

My mind drifts to how Jackson would be a father right now. He'd have his own baby to love but he's lost that chance.

"Jackson, this is too hard. It's going to hurt even more in the morning."

"It can't hurt any more than it already has," he says quietly and adjusts himself to be more comfortable. "Go to sleep, baby."

I was a fool to give him tonight. To think I could ever give him one night and it wouldn't ruin me. Allowing him back in my heart even if only for a little bit reminded me all the reasons I loved him. His heart, his hurt, the way he loves are all there buried beneath a lot of guilt and pain. Jackson's lived through hell, yet never let it destroy him.

Tonight I'm in the arms of the man I love. Tomorrow I won't be. Selfishly, I close my eyes and allow the exhaustion to take over so I can pretend tomorrow isn't coming and I can dream of Jackson like I do every night.

I wake up overheated and I can't breathe. Trying to get air, I realize it's because Jackson has his entire body wrapped around me. His legs are tangled with mine and his arms are steel cages around me, ensuring I can't go anywhere.

He begins to stir and I try to disentangle myself, but he shifts and somehow pulls me closer. "Jackson, I can't breathe," I mumble, trying to move him.

"Shhh, it's not tomorrow if we sleep."

"Let me up."

Jackson pulls his leg tighter around mine. "No."

Glad to see he hasn't lost his defiance. "Please, you're smothering me."

"I'll smother you in another way if you want," Jackson says groggily.

"Not until we talk. Now let me up, I need to pee."

He groans and lets me up reluctantly. "I'll be here in case you change your mind about the smothering."

"I've got the closing in a few hours. I need to get up and get ready. But thanks for the offer."

He laughs and gets out of bed while I hop in the shower.

This conversation is happening and time isn't on my side. All I want to do is wrap my arms around him and hold on. My heart aches when I recall everything we shared last night. I hate how his fear of thinking I'd see him at fault kept him from telling me. Our paths might have been different than they are at this moment. My dream job is in California but my dream man is in the other room. I can't give either up but I have to choose.

I clean up in the bathroom and when I come out, I smell coffee. Making my way into the kitchen, Jackson is standing there in his boxers and I can't hold back the appreciative sigh.

The cocky smile spreads across his face when I'm caught admiring him, but he doesn't say anything.

Once I have my cup of coffee we sit at the table. "We should talk," I begin.

"I'd rather not," Jackson says as he leans back in the chair.

"I'm sure, but I need to get this out."

He grabs my hand and laces his fingers with mine. "I need to say something before you start. I never wanted to keep secrets."

"But you did."

"That night Aaron died, when we sat on the couch, I had it all planned out on how to explain about Madelyn." His grip tightens slightly. "Then I got the damn call from Mark. I couldn't think straight. I was responsible for someone else's death. Then I was shot and I wanted to forget about it and be with you. Here's the thing," Jackson pauses and runs his hand through his hair. "Even if Maddie was alive, I don't think I'd be married to her. I resented her for making me leave the Navy."

My stomach rolls as I think about the resentment he talks about. It's how I'd feel about him if I gave up my job. I release Jackson's fingers and sit back in my chair holding my hands tightly.

When I look up, he rubs his hand down his face. "I've really lost you, haven't I?"

Looking at the table, the poisonous word is on my tongue. "Yes."

"I saw it in your eyes," Jackson admits and my heart breaks at the sadness in his voice.

I thought he knew but I wasn't sure. If I could go back in time and rewrite our history I would. I'd do so many things differently, but this is life and love is messy. There's no pretty bow on the box.

"I know yesterday was a lot for you and for me. I can't begin to tell you how sorry I am for all you've lost. No one should have to go through that. I know you weren't trying to hurt me by not telling me about your wife."

"But it doesn't change anything for us, does it?"

Oh, how I wish it did.

"No. Things have changed for me."

"Is there someone else?" Jackson asks and he gets up out of the chair.

"No, there's no one else."

"Then what? Just say it so I can fix it," he says hurriedly.

I close my eyes and say the words I don't want to tell him, "I'm moving to California."

"What? When?" He starts to pace around the kitchen.

"I leave in three days," I say looking down, not wanting to see his face.

Jackson sits back in the chair and doesn't say a word.

"I was offered a large promotion in CJJ. It happened a few days after we broke up. Anyway," I say as the pain lances through my chest. "I was offered to head up the office they're opening out there. It's a huge opportunity for me, and it's what I've dreamed of." I look up and he closes his eyes.

"Funny," Jackson pauses and let's out a shaky laugh. "Here I sit with the shoe on the other foot and all I want to do is beg you to stay with me. I want to say anything to make this not happen, but I can't ask you to give up your dream job. I fucking hate this."

A sob erupts from my chest and Jackson's arms are around me in a moment. "I knew I shouldn't have let you in last night. I knew this was going to kill me today," I cry against his chest.

"I'm not letting go, Catherine."

I grip his shoulders and hold on, not knowing when I'll ever feel his body against mine again. "You have to."

Sure, we could try and make it work long distance, but who knows how long that would last for. Jackson runs two companies and travels, and my job is going to be extremely demanding.

"We'll see," he says and releases me. Jackson stands there for a minute before heading into the living room as he collects his uniform.

I sit here feeling desolate and numb.

When he returns, he pulls me from my chair and holds me one last time. "Can I call you?" Jackson chokes out.

I look up and see the emotion in his eyes. "I'd like that," I say as my heart shatters.

"I love you, Catherine."

The tears stream like rivers down my face. "I love you too, Jackson. So much. I wish ..." I trail off unable to say what I wish because we both know.

"Me too, baby. Me too. I'll call soon."

I close my eyes as our lips meet. He holds my head and we both pour everything we're feeling into each other. Jackson pulls back from my lips too soon. He kisses my forehead once and turns, walking out the door. I hear the door close and I crumble to the floor.

Love is messy and life sucks.

chapter
twenty-six

The house is sold, my things are packed, and I'm finally taking care of some last minute stuff before my last day of work tomorrow. My emotions are all over the place. I'm sad that I only have a few tangible things to hold onto of my father's. I'm excited for the new venture my life is about to embark on. Most of all, I'm broken over losing the love of my life. I go from one extreme to another depending on the hour.

It seems like the only part of my life that I have any control over is my work. Tristan and I have planned out the first week and he's already setting things up with new employees. Already he's proven himself to be valuable and reliable.

My phone rings and it's Natalie.

I swipe the screen to answer. "Hey, Nat," I say with a big smile.

"Hi, Cat," she giggles softly. "Aren't we the rhyming names?" Natalie muses.

I laugh with her, "I'm glad you called me back. I'm so sorry I left so fast."

"It's fine. Honestly, the memorial was a blur. I would've talked to you and probably not remembered. I thought being so far out from his death it wouldn't have been so hard for me."

"I don't know anyone would ever fully get over

it, do you?" I ask.

"Probably not," she pauses. "I heard you're leaving in a few days."

I sigh and run my hands through my hair. "Yeah, I leave in two days."

"The last thing I expected to hear was you were going to California. Why didn't you tell me?" She chuckles but I hear the hurt in her voice.

"Sorry, I don't have any excuses. I didn't want him to know." I feel bad because I didn't want to be deceitful but at the same time I didn't want to risk it.

"I get it. Listen, I'm leaving New York and I'd love to come stop by on my way back to Virginia. Are you around?"

"Yes!" I practically yell. "I'd love that. I have some stuff I need to finish up around here, but I'd love to see you and Aarabelle."

"Great. Text me your address and I'll head over."

I send it off and try to clean up a little more before she gets here. I'm excited to hold the baby and get to spend some one on one time with Natalie. Our entire relationship has been only through phone calls. Then there was the memorial, but it really wasn't the time for a big friendly chat.

The doorbells rings a few minutes later and I rush over to open it.

I swing the door open and she stands there holding Aarabelle. "Hey, come in! Come in." Aarabelle is beautiful. Her pretty pink dress and white frilly shoes melt my heart. You can't help but want to smile around babies.

"Thanks," Natalie smiles and enters the room. It's amazing how someone who just had a baby is already as tiny as she is.

She places the baby in the car seat as she puts her long blond hair into a quick braid. Natalie's bright blue eyes narrow and she looks me over. "You look like I feel," she chuckles.

"That bad, huh?" I ask.

"No, not bad at all, just tired of it all."

We sit on the couch and I fight back the emotions bubbling up. This woman has truly lost it all. The man she loves is gone and she will never see him, touch him, or hear his voice. Jackson isn't dead, but there was a time where that could've been the outcome. I sat there watching and wondering if he would make it.

"I guess you know everything?"

Natalie places her hand on mine and smiles. "We'll talk boys later, let's talk about the job."

"Only if I can hold that beautiful little girl." I grin and she laughs.

"Of course!" Natalie says as she grabs Aarabelle. "I swear, she hasn't been put down once in her life." We both laugh as she hands her to me.

Her tiny frame fits in my arms as I delicately hold her.

We talk a little about the job and the move. Before I finally turn the tables onto finding out about her. "How are you doing?" I ask Natalie.

"Some days are good. Some days are awful. Post-partum doesn't help but she grounds me. She makes me get up and live. Plus, either Mark or Liam, Aaron's swim buddy, call or stop by daily. They drive me absolutely insane," Natalie says with a soft smile as she gazes at her daughter in my arms.

"I'm sure Mark can drive anyone nuts."

"Well, then there's Jackson, who calls me

practically every damn day. I know they're all worried, but honestly, Cat, I knew this was going to be my life. The reality was that one day this could happen. I was built for this. I entered a marriage with Aaron knowing he could die. Does it hurt any less? No, but it was the chance I took when I loved him."

"You're so strong," I say looking at her and then at Aarabelle.

She lies sleeping, oblivious to all the pain in this world. She'll grow up very similar to me. I know what it'll feel like for her to have no father for a father-daughter dance, how she'll feel sad when other girls in her class talk about their daddies. Aarabelle will never know what his hugs feel like, what it's like to have an in-house protector from childhood on. I remember the pain and hurt of not knowing that kind of love. Although this little angel will never really be without a man because of Aaron's military family, but it won't ever be her daddy. When she's ready to give her heart to the man she loves, she won't have him there to give her away.

"Strength isn't measurable, it's inside of each of us and we need to find it when we feel weak. I refuse to break. Besides, I'm no different than you are right now."

Natalie's statement snaps me from my internal pain. "I'm not half as strong as you are."

She leans forward and fixes Aarabelle's dress. "I see it differently. At least from what Jackson explained."

"I'm not sure what he told you."

Natalie smiles warmly and her head tilts to the side. "He told me everything. About how he's an idiot and never told you about Madelyn. How he lied and hurt you. He explained it all."

"I wish he would've told me before."

"When she died, it destroyed him. I've seen these guys low, but he was beside himself. It was like he shut off every part of him that could feel. Plus, if he had told you, you have no idea what path your life would've taken. I think all the choices we make are a road we were meant to veer off onto." Natalie absently coils her hair around her finger. "I loved Aaron more than anything. We were together since we were nineteen. I was there with him when he signed the papers and left for bootcamp. I watched the bus drive away with him on it. I was there the day he graduated and then went through BUDs. My life was always his. Even when he got out," she laughs softly. "My life has never been my own. Everything we did, everywhere we went was always Aaron's choice. Now I have to choose and I don't know what to choose." A tear rolls down her face and she catches it.

"You have so many people who love you and Aarabelle. I know Jackson would help you in any way."

Aarabelle begins to stir in my arms and then settles.

"I know. He's kinda a good guy."

"Yeah. Kinda." I laugh and Natalie joins me.

"Okay, no more heavy crap. I think I've had all I can take. Tell me about California."

We spent the next hour chatting about life, California, and all the things about being a mom. Natalie was stationed in San Diego for years and tells me all the places I need to go. We talk about how much she loved it out there and how she'd love to come visit.

"I'd love to keep chatting, but Aara and I need

to get our butts on the road," Natalie says as she puts Aarabelle in her car seat.

"Thanks for coming over. I know we never really saw each other, but I'm going to miss you."

Natalie smiles and pulls me in for a hug. "If things hadn't happened the way they did, we wouldn't have met," she pulls back and looks at me. "I know he hurt you, but don't give up." I nod and she continues, "I've lost the great love of my life. I know what it feels like to have that taken away. I'm not telling you not to go and follow your dreams, because I think you should go. Sometimes love isn't enough, but sometimes it is. He does love you though, don't ever doubt that."

"I don't doubt his love. And I love him, but our entire relationship has been one thing after another. We've gone from bad to worse to amazing and then plummeted again. I need to rely on myself. I just hate losing him at the same time."

She pulls me back in for a hug, "I'm sorry."

I laugh against her. "I can't believe you're consoling me."

"I'm happy for once I'm not the one blubbering." Natalie laughs and we say our goodbyes.

Unfortunately, this is only the beginning of them.

"Taylor, please come in here!" I ask her once again. My flight leaves tomorrow morning and I don't have a lot of time. She keeps ignoring me and making excuses why she doesn't have time for my "bullshit."

"No!" she yells from outside the door.

I shake my head at her refusal. "Fine. I'll just

keep your present or maybe I'll give it to Ash."

She pops her head in the door. "Present? I like presents." Her eyes brighten.

"Dork. Get in here."

"Give me a second and don't you give that to anyone else!" she exclaims and disappears somewhere.

I don't know how I'm going to get used to dealing with a new assistant. Taylor has been my right hand and sometimes my left. I'm not sure I'm half as good as my bosses think I am without her.

"You got a present too." She smiles as she brings in a huge bouquet of yellow daffodils.

"Wow. You shouldn't have."

"Good, because I didn't," she explains.

"Want the card?" Taylor holds it up smirking.

I walk over to her and take the vase. "Yes," I say putting them down admiring how beautiful they are.

Opening the card from the same florist Jackson used the last time.

Great.

I brace myself for another card like the last.

Dear Catherine,

Did you know there are meanings behind each flower? Like I had nothing else to do today but find one that said what I couldn't say to you. I thought maybe this would win me a few brownie points too since I spent an hour googling flower meanings. Apparently, this flower says you're the only one and some shit about sunshine. I thought you should know that even though you're going to California tomorrow, you're taking my sunshine with you. You're the one for me. I'll miss you and I love you.

Yours Always,
Jackson

I grin and clutch the card to my chest. It's hard to picture Jackson sitting around googling flowers but it means a lot to me. We spoke once and he asked to see me again, but I told him it would be too hard for me, so we've texted a few times. I told him when I got to California I'd call, but it hurts and I don't know if I'll be able to.

"Is he being all swoony again?" Taylor asks, trying to read over my shoulder.

"Isn't he always? I swear it's impossible to resist him."

"That's the truth. He's kinda perfect, isn't he?"

I take a deep breath in and then release it. Yeah, he's pretty damn perfect.

"He loves you, Cat. I have a feeling you two are going to find a way."

"I let him go, Tay. He knows there's no way."

As much as I'd like to believe the words I speak, I know it's not completely true. I don't know that I'll ever really let him go. He found a way to penetrate my soul. Jackson fits me in every aspect and if I wasn't leaving for California, I'd be back in his arms. All our secrets were laid out and we would have been happy and in love. Instead we'll live apart, knowing how much we both wish it was another way.

"Sure. Whatever." She gives me the stink eye and then looks around the room. "Okay, where's my present?"

I pull out the bag from Michael Kors and her jaw falls slack. "No way! Thank you. Thank you. Thank you!" she yells after she recovers.

"I'm going to miss you so much. Promise me you'll call me, and I want to hear all about the new job. Especially if that twunt, Piper, gets hit by a bus." I wink trying to keep from getting emotional.

We give each other a long hug and laugh.

Once we finally get a grip, Taylor asks, "Did you hire your new assistant?"

"Yes, he's starting to get things set up. I think you'd like Tristan."

"Probably, but I'll pretend not to. He better be on his game to handle you."

"I'm not that bad ... well, maybe."

A few people stop by the office and say good-bye while I make sure the files I need for California are in order. I look up when I hear a knock at the door.

"I wanted to wish you a *very* safe flight," Piper sneers.

I smile and tilt my head to the side, unwilling to let this bitch ruin my last day in New York. "Why, thank you, Piper. That's awfully kind of you."

She glares at me, "Did you hear? Neil and I are moving in together." Her brow quirks as she tries to goad me.

Not working, but thanks for playing.

It reminds me that Neil was making out with another blond. I wonder if they're all going to live together or if Piper is unaware of her boyfriend's extra plaything.

"No, I missed that news, but I saw you guys at the bar the other day. Did you see us?" I ask sweetly.

"I have no idea what you're talking about."

"Oh, I swore it was you. I mean, Neil was clearly shoving his tongue down a petite blond's throat." I shrug and return to my paperwork, trying to smother my smile.

I've waited months to hand it back to this bitch and I'm going to enjoy every second. She stands there waiting for who knows what while I ignore her.

"Nice. Glad to see you've come over to the other side. You're so full of shit that it's actually pathetic."

I look up with the smile I can't hide any longer. "I was really sure it was you. I mean, Neil is such a stand-up guy. He would never cheat, would he?" I stand and walk toward her with my phone. "Look, Piper, see for yourself." I open the picture and extend my hand to her.

She glares at the phone, no longer petulant or sure of herself.

Karma.

"It won't bite," I push the phone closer. "How about we take a look together?" I put my arm around her and pull the phone close so we can both see it ... nice and close.

She tries to shrug me off, but she's unleashed my inner Ashton and I'm all too happy to be here to deliver her own worst nightmare.

"Look, that's definitely Neil, but hmmm, that girl ..." I look closer as Piper starts to shake. "Nope, that's not you, but I think she must be a friend of yours. She looks a lot like the reporter that was at the Raven press conference. Strange, right?" I move back and scowl at her.

"Fuck you," Piper replies.

"Nope, fuck you. You thought you were so much better than me. You treat people like they're beneath you, but you're the one who's beneath us all. Once upon a time, you were a nice and decent human being. I don't know what happened to her, but you should work on finding that girl again. In the meantime, get the fuck out of my office and go back to work. I'd hate to have to file a complaint since you're still on your thirty-day probationary period." I return to my seat, ignoring her presence.

I could screw her royally by going to any of the partners and claiming she did something. But I won't because I'm better than her. Knowing that right now she's feeling even an inkling of what I went through is enough. In the end, I'm better off. I got the job and I found real love. I might have lost Jackson, but at least I know what it feels like to really be loved.

"I won't—" Piper starts to say, but I put my hand up and shoo her out.

"I'm done here. I suggest you be smart for once in your life and get out of my sight. I have work to do." I turn my chair and look out the window.

Vindication. Piper deserves to be alone and miserable. After the hell she's caused in my life, I should only be seeking revenge, instead I *almost* feel sorry for her. She's going to live a sad and lonely life. But … not my problem.

I hear clapping coming from outside and when I spin my chair. Taylor is standing there clapping. "Bra-fucking-vo, my friend. That was spectacular."

"She had it coming."

"Ummm, yeah, she did. I wish you would've slapped her."

"Who are you and what have you done with my sweet, Midwestern assistant? The one who would've told me I should just pray for her," I ask.

"I killed her," she winks and walks into the

office.

The text alert pings on my phone and I open the message.

> *Jackson: Did you know a one-minute kiss burns 26 calories?*

I sit and focus on my phone wondering what is going on and why he wants me to know this tidbit of information.

> *Me: I did not know this, but thanks—I think.*

> *Jackson: I think you should come over and burn some calories before your flight.*

I laugh and look at the phone. He's incorrigible.

> *Me: You need help. Thank you for my flowers.*

> *Jackson: I mean it.*

> *Me: Mean what? The card or the kissing?*

> *Jackson: Both.*

> *Me: I'm sure you do. I can't ... I wish things were different.*

> *Jackson: Me too, baby. Call me when you land. I love you, Catherine.*

I put the phone away and Taylor sits there smiling at me. I completely forgot she was there.

"Sorry, it's Jackson," I explain.

"I figured as much. Can I ask you something?"

I already have a feeling it has to do with Jackson, but I allow her anyway. "Sure."

"Do you regret choosing the job?" she asks earnestly.

The question I can't really answer because regret isn't really what I feel—it's sorrow. "No, I don't regret it. I think it's more like I wish we could go back in time. Things would be different, but then again who knows? Because if I was offered the position and I turned it down I would regret that. Especially if things didn't work out between us, and let's face it … my relationship with Jackson hasn't been easy. So maybe us not being together allowed me to follow my dream without having to question what to do about him."

Taylor smiles. "I get that. When I moved here to follow Quinn, I kept thinking what if we broke up once we got here? But then I figured I'd be in New York City and I had the job here so I knew I'd be okay."

"I'm glad we are able to part as friends though. It doesn't hurt any less knowing that we both love each other and can't be together, but at least I'm not leaving thinking there's a wife somewhere. I can think of him and smile instead of wanting to punch him in the junk."

My heart still yearns for him. I don't know if that feeling will ever go away but at least I can have a tiny part of him. If or when he meets someone, I don't know how I'll handle it. The idea of him being with anyone else is too much right now.

"I'm proud of you, Cat."

"Thanks, Mom." I wink as Taylor and I laugh. We finish up packing my office, then it's time for me to leave. I'm having dinner with Ashton and then my flight is early tomorrow morning.

"Okay," I say and take a deep breath. "Be strong. Don't take any of Elle or Piper's shit. My phone is always on and available to you," I say as my lip quivers. I hate saying goodbye. "You're one of the best people I know and I'm so proud of you."

Tears fall from Taylor's eyes and she nods.

"Don't ever doubt yourself, Catherine. You're one of the strongest women I've ever known. I hope you know how much I've learned from you. Thank you for not only being one of the most incredible people to work for, but also one of my best friends. I'm going to miss you so much," Tay chokes out and hugs me.

"I'm going to miss you too but I'll be back to visit." I return her hug and try to stifle my own tears.

"You'll come back for the wedding, right?" Taylor asks.

"I wouldn't miss it for the world."

We embrace again and I leave my office for the last time. When I close the door a part of my heart breaks while another part comes to life at the new adventure I'm embarking on.

Now I have to go home and somehow manage to leave Ashton behind.

chapter twenty-seven

*O*n my train ride home, I think more about Taylor's question. I don't regret anything because it's brought me to where I am, but it makes me sad to think I would've given up an opportunity like this for anyone. I don't believe Jackson would've asked me to, but I probably would've wanted to stay with him. Which I probably would regret later on and possibly would've resented him instead.

When I get home, Ashton is sitting on the couch in her pajama pants.

"Aren't we going to dinner?" I ask.

"Nope."

What in the hell?

"Okay? I thought that was our plan."

She shuts the television off and stands with her hands on her hips. "I'm mad at you, Biffle."

"For what?"

This should be good.

"I don't know. I just want to be mad at you!" Ashton cries out and falls on the couch.

I sit on the couch next to her and lay on her lap. "I'm going to miss you too. This is so hard, Ashy-poo. These goodbyes suck."

Ashton runs her fingers through my hair and her lips purse. "I'm sorry. I know this is hard for you." She puts the mask I know so well up, making sure she protects herself.

After a few moments of silence, Ashton starts up again, only this time her tone is light and playful. "I've decided what I'm going to do with your room."

"Oh, what did you decide? A pottery room or did you decide to make a home gym that you'll never use?"

The first time we talked about what to do with my room I almost peed myself. She had the most insane ideas, but then again, it's Ashton. Last we talked she was leaning toward a meditation room.

"Nope, neither. I'm going to make it into a library!"

"I feel as if you want me to react so I'm just going to say ... okay then, to the girl who doesn't read," I say, shaking my head.

"Jealous much?"

I laugh and snuggle into her. "You're nuts but I love you. Tell me why you look like a homeless person instead of dressed to go out?"

She lets out a long sigh and pats my head like a cat. "I want to spend our last night as roomies drinking wine and eating pizza. You know you won't be able to get Jersey pizza in Cali."

I smile and nod, "I know."

"I still can't believe you're leaving. You're lucky I haven't tied you up so you can't go."

"I might like it."

"You probably would, freak."

"You know it."

"What kind of kinky shit did you and Jackson do?" she asks laughing and sounding slightly scared.

"He didn't need to tie me up." I look up and

wiggle my eyebrows.

Ashton smiles and swats my ass while laughing. "Yeah, I wouldn't willingly leave that man's bed either."

I flush thinking of some of the things Jackson and I did together. The way his body was made for mine, the way he could drive me to the end with his words alone. He was my other half in every way. I miss him already. Every night since the memorial he's starred in my dreams. My mind drifts to him during the day, and then he haunts me in my sleep. I close my eyes and hold my arms over my chest. One day. One day it won't hurt so much.

"Hey," Ashton nudges me. "I'm sorry. Let's enjoy our night with fattening food and then tomorrow hopefully you'll be so hung over you won't be able to fly."

A laugh escapes me at the logic in her plan and I decide I need to keep my thoughts of Jackson at bay. I made my choice, now I have to live with it.

"Okay, let's eat so I can be bloated."

"Deal."

The pizza gets delivered and we spend our night curled up on the couch talking about all the things I have to do in California. She demands that if I meet any Hollywood A-listers she's the first to know. Also if I start dating any of them she's agreed to quit her job and become my personal assistant.

Reluctantly we clean up and return to the couch.

"Let's have a slumber party like we did when we were kids," Ashton suggests.

"Okay," I reply and grab the blankets off the couch.

We turn the lights off and wrap ourselves up. I have to be up in a few hours and Ashton promised she'd take me to the airport.

"I'm going to miss you, Biffle." Her voice is quiet but I hear her.

"I'll miss you more," I whisper, but she doesn't respond.

A few minutes later, right as I'm about to fall asleep, I hear Ashton sniffle as a tear rolls down my cheek.

"Let's go!" I yell to Ashton as she drags her feet. We woke up and had coffee and a lot of tears. But now you'd think she just got out of bed. She's moving slower than normal. I swear she's doing this on purpose.

"I'm coming, Jesus. Calm your tits."

"Well, I'm going to miss my flight if you keep screwing around."

"We have plenty of time." Ashton rolls her eyes and walks away. "I'm gonna grab my keys."

This is the last time I'll be in my apartment. The memories besiege me of when we moved in and I smile remembering us fighting over the paint color. Ashton of course won, which is why we have a blue living room when I wanted brown. I smile thinking of the scuffmark on the floor that we covered up with a rug because we dropped a table. Ashton and I arguing over food, which couch to buy, and so many other things happened right here.

This is my home. It'll always be my home.

I glance at the photos on the wall and my chest squeezes when I see the one of me, Ashton, and Gretchen from high school. I know I'll never find friends like them again and even though there's the phone and internet, it'll never be the same. When I need a hug, or to be slapped around, they won't be able to.

Ashton comes up behind me and tackles me to the ground hugging me. "Don't leave me!" she says in an exaggerated panic and starts to tickle me.

"Ash!" I squirm and try to fight her off, but she holds me tight.

"You can't leave if I hold you against your will," she laughs and sits on my back.

"Get off me, you asshole! What are you doing?" I try to wriggle, laughing while she assaults me.

Ashton starts to bounce up and down, not letting up. "This is a struggle snuggle. Don't fight it—it feels better if you let it happen." She giggles and lies on top of me. "Let it happen," she whispers and pets my hair.

She's lost her mind. That's the only explanation. Girl has completely cracked.

"I'm going to give you a struggle if you don't get off me." I laugh so hard there are tears running down my face. "I'm gonna pee my pants!" I burst out.

She laughs and falls off me, lying next to me on her back looking at me. "Ohhh," she sighs and smiles. "I had to make us laugh or I'd cry again, and we all know that's a bad idea if I have to drive."

My heart warms and I return her smile. There's so much history between us, so many times we've laughed or cried together. I'll miss her more than I can fully express. She's my partner in crime and my world will be boring without her.

"You know you'll always be my better half?" I say as I sit up.

Ashton follows and smoothes her dark red hair

into a ponytail. "Yup. I know, but one day Prince Charming is going to come along and sweep you off your feet," she pauses and stands. "Hopefully he delivers your ass back to New Jersey. Come on, you've got a plane to catch."

She grabs my hand and pulls me up. We head to the car and Ashton suddenly stops short.

"No more stop—" I start to say and freeze when I see Jackson leaning against a black stretch limo smiling.

Ashton turns blocking my view. "This is good-bye, Biffle," her eyes fill with unshed tears. "I'm going to miss you so much. Promise me we'll Facetime every day. Promise that no matter how amazing these people you meet are, they'll suck in comparison to me." A tear falls on her cheek and my chest tightens.

"I promise. They're no Ashton Caputo." I smile and she pulls me in to her.

"I love you. I'm so fucking proud of you, my friend. You're going to kick ass, take names, and be sexy as hell doing it. Don't doubt yourself, Cat." She wipes the tears running freely down her face. "I never have."

"I'm going to be so lost without you and your craziness."

We hug a little tighter and I hear Jackson approach, "Catherine, we have to leave if you want to make your flight."

I nod and pull her close once more. "Goodbye, Ashypoo."

"Bye, my love pie." We both sniffle and break apart.

Jackson grabs my bag and my hand as I look back once more. Ashton stands there holding her middle with tears streaming down her face. He hands my bag to the driver and helps me in the car. Looking out the window at her standing there, my tears fall faster. This is so hard. I want to stop the car and fix my best friend because she doesn't cry. She uses her sarcasm and wit to avoid hurt, but she's hurting.

Jackson's arms encase me and I take the comfort he's offering. Once again, in the back of a car, this man holds me together. Only this time it feels like it's me who died. There's no doubt that this is what I want, this job is everything I've ever wanted for my career—yet the things I feel like I'm losing are ripping me apart. I want it all. The love of my life, my best friend, and this job—but I can't ask them to come with me and I can't stay here.

"I know this is hard, believe me I know, but it'll be okay," Jackson says as his fingers graze the skin on my arm.

I pull myself upright and brush the tears off my face. "I'm so sorry," I say shaking my head trying to dispel the sadness. "You're here."

"Of course I'm here," he says tenderly, drawing me back against him. "You weren't leaving without me seeing you."

My heart sputters and I take a breath inhaling the masculine scent that is Jackson. God, I've missed his smell. It's comforting and arousing at the same time.

"You okay?" Jackson asks, holding me tight.

"I'll be okay until I have to say goodbye to you," I admit. This is only going to keep getting worse. "I'm surprised Ash let me go with you." I look up and he smirks.

"She's known about this for a while, baby. I

called her and let her know I'd be driving you."

With a shaky voice, I say the only word I can, "Oh."

"Don't be so surprised. I told you I wasn't going to let you go."

Jackson leans in and places a kiss against my temple and I close my eyes. Sometimes his gentleness breaks me more than anything. Right now, I want to beg him, plead with him to come with me. Get on the plane and we'll figure out all the shit later, but I can't. Especially knowing how his wife made him give it all up and how much he resented her. I never want to be the reason he gives something up. I want to give *to* him. This is the conundrum we face. My heart wants Jackson and my head wants to follow my dreams with this job.

Two good things and two broken hearts.

"I knew this was going to be impossible."

"It doesn't have to be."

My face pales as I look at him. "How doesn't it? My job is sending me to California. You're in New York. Sure, we could try, but when would we see each other?" I ask, attempting to keep an even tone.

"I don't know. I want to fucking turn this car around and take you home. Do you know how hard it is to drive you right now? Knowing this is the end. I feel like ..." Jackson trails off and grips his neck. "I'm not going to do this to you. I won't be selfish." He looks at me and I see the agony in his eyes.

"I'm no better. I want to beg you to get on that plane and come with me. But you can't and I won't ask you to do that."

"I fucked this all up."

"If we'd never broken up, I might not be going because I wouldn't want to leave you. So then what?

Would I feel like you did about Madelyn?" I wince saying her name.

"I wouldn't have asked you to give it up." Jackson closes his eyes as we have our come-to-Jesus moment.

This is where the truth lies. Nothing would be different, but everything would be. I would either be getting on the plane and feeling the exact way I do now, or I wouldn't and be wondering if I gave up my career for nothing. Jackson's made me strong enough to do this. He's given me the power to get on this plane and while it will practically kill me, I'll survive. I don't know if I would've been able to do this six months ago. If it were Neil, I wouldn't go— and then what? Where would I be? Alone, broken, and jobless.

"How can we want this so much, but not be able to have it?" I ask him, hoping for some brilliant insight, because I don't get it.

"No one said we can't. We just can't right now. But I'm not giving up on you and someday, Catherine, we'll find our way back together."

"I wish today was someday."

"Me too, baby."

"Kiss me," I say breathlessly.

"Any time," he says as his hands encompass my cheeks and he places his lips to mine for a moment. He pulls back and his gaze is locked on mine, and I see my future, my past, and all that could be. Only none of it matters.

We spend the next few minutes of the drive to the airport touching, kissing, and drawing comfort from each other. When the car stops, my entire body locks in place. I can't do this. I can't walk away from him. Jackson grips my hands and I begin to tremble. I knew this would be too hard.

The driver opens the door and a sob breaks through.

Fuck.

I can't do this.

"Come on," Jackson says, brushing my hair off my face with his other hand.

"Dammit," I curse and a tear breaks free. "Dammit, Jackson."

He closes the door and grips my arms. "Look at me."

My eyes slowly lift to his and I see how much this is hurting him, but he's fighting for me.

"I've had to leave more times than I can count. I know what you're feeling. The fear, the excitement, the guilt, and everything in between. But this ... this is worth it. You worked your ass off for this and now you need to go grab it and run. Are you going to miss things? Yes. But, baby, it's all worth it. You're not going to lose the people who love you because *you're* worth it. There are no goodbyes between us. Okay?" he asks and my stomach coils.

Jackson opens the door and we exit the car. I'm splotchy and a mess. His arm wraps around my waist and he tells the driver he'll call him later. I look up in surprise.

"What are you doing?"

"I bought a ticket so I can get through security. I'm staying with you until the last second," he says matter-of-factly.

There's no way he can be any more perfect and completely impossible to resist. I really wish I was still upset with him because then I would get on this plane and not think twice. I'd hold on to the lies and hurt, but it's not there anymore.

We grab our boarding passes and head to the gate. Jackson holds on to me the entire time. He keeps me together while I feel like I'm falling apart. This shouldn't be this hard. I should be excited, but instead I'm totally distraught.

"Why is this so hard?" I ask mostly to myself, but I know he hears me.

Jackson pulls me in his lap, and when I look at him confused, he smiles. "You've been away from me long enough, I need you close."

And my heart melts.

"I don't want to lose you. I've been thinking and maybe we can try this long distance?"

"I don't want this to be it either, but how would that work? You're a busy man, and I'm starting up this office. I'll be inundated with meetings and late nights. You have two companies to run." I shake my head and try to force myself to not get caught up in this idea. "If we weren't on opposites sides of the country ..."

"I have a plane."

"And you have *two* companies."

"I know," Jackson's head falls against my side.

I open my mouth to speak, but they call to begin boarding.

Here is our end. Where there will be our goodbye contrary to what he says.

My eyes close and I tuck my head into the crook of his neck. I feel his pulse, hear his heart beating, and I don't want to move.

"I have to go, don't I?"

"You could stay forever, but I don't think that's in your plan," Jackson whispers from behind me and he helps me stand.

We're eye to eye and I fight hard to form a wall

around my heart to protect me—but it's futile. "Forever is a long time."

"It wouldn't be long enough for us."

His eyes well with tears and mine spill over. They call for the next section to board but I don't move. I'm going to stay every second I can and burn this into my memory.

Jackson leans into me and kisses me worshipfully. His lips move against mine in perfect harmony. I lose myself to his touch. My hands grip his shirt and pull him closer. I want to take him inside of my heart and hold him there. They call for final boarding and Jackson breaks the kiss.

"It's time. No goodbyes."

"This wasn't supposed to be us. We were supposed to be together. This was our time," I say angrily.

"Shhh," Jackson puts his fingers to my lips. He clutches my face and breathes the words into me. "I'll find you again."

I close my eyes and hold on to his wrists, "I don't want to lose you."

The black chill of silence surrounds us. I have to let him go.

Our lips meet again and I taste the salt of our sadness. Unsure of whose pain blurs between us. His tongue glides against my lips and I open to him. With each swipe of his tongue against mine, I break apart from the inside out.

They call once more for final boarding and he draws back and places a kiss against my forehead.

I look up at his turquoise eyes and choke out, "I don't want to let you go."

He's my everything.

"If you love something, you have to let it go. I

love you enough to let you go. Go live your dream, baby."

We kiss once more and I hold on to his hand until the absolute last second. When the tips of our fingers disconnect, my chest tightens so much it physically hurts.

The last image I see when I glance back is the door closing as Jackson's head falls into his hands.

Now I know what it feels like to lose your heart.

CHAPTER TWENTY-EIGHT

JACKSON

I'm a fucking idiot.

That's the only thing that keeps rolling around in my skull. I watch her walk away and do nothing to convince her to stay. It's like someone just shot me all over again. Pure agony. I want her to be in my arms, not on a damn plane. I could've asked her to stay, made her see what her leaving was doing to me, but I told her to go.

I *told* her to leave me, but I didn't think she'd go—or maybe I did.

I'm a fucking idiot.

She needed to choose and I can't blame her. Do I wish she would've stayed for me? Of course I do. She belongs with me. Then again, I've screwed up so many times I'm losing count. So I'm glad she got on that plane because I now know what I have to do.

I lived through her walking out the door once, but I won't live through it again.

Fuck that.

It's time to get her back.

Pulling my phone from my pocket, I call the limo driver to have him swing back and get me.

Then I call Mark.

"What up, dickhead?" he answers laughing.

I don't even have the energy to insult him. I

have more important things to do. "I'm on my way to Virginia. It's time to get shit done."

"About fucking time. I was starting to question the legitimacy of your man card. I thought maybe you liked playing dress up with your little makeup company and I needed to be concerned with how often you might have stared a little too long after the showers," Mark crows in his condescending I-think-I'm-so-awesome-just-ask-me voice.

"You wish. There'd have to be something to stare at. I need to meet with Carter and if that doesn't go well, I have a guy in New York who I can call." The wheels are spinning in my head.

"You know Carter is going to be a prick. I would call your guy now and start the ball rolling."

"I'll handle it."

Mark gives a sarcastic laugh. "Just like you handled everything else? Let's face it, Muff, you've been fucking up left and right. So for once, listen to me. Call me when you land."

"Yup," I say, already forming a plan.

"It's about time you dealt with all this bullshit," Mark says and he hangs up.

Yeah, it is about time.

Two years ago, I went into a dark place. Losing Maddie and the baby was like nothing I've ever felt. When we lost the team guys, it was horrible, but she was my world at the time. I was so pissed at her for constantly riding my ass and needing me to give her more. Even though she told me to leave that day, I never should have. I lost her because I was selfish, and I won't do that to Catherine. When I found out Madelyn died, my guilt was overwhelming.

Once I get in the car, I instruct the driver to go

more than a word here or there. Let's not even talk about the brush off I got the last time we saw each other. I don't know what exactly you expect from me. What's going on?

"I won't bullshit you, so here it is … I want you to take over Raven."

He looks at me and leans back in his chair. This was his family's company and I'd be a total dick if I didn't at least give him a chance at it. When Maddie died, I asked him to take over, but he'd told me to fuck off and fade away.

"When she died, I couldn't imagine going to that office. Now, I have no desire to have anything to do with it. I'm doing well here and I don't want to move Chelsea and the kids."

I give a quick nod and bite my tongue from telling him how I moved because it was what she wanted, but Maddie wasn't his wife. My life was altered more than he can imagine. "I understand. I'll be making some calls today."

"You're just going to walk away from it?" he asks with brows raised.

"I'm making some changes in my life."

"I see. I have a question, since you're here," Carter says as he grabs his drink.

"Go ahead."

"Why did you walk away from the family?"

My eyes widen as I try to decipher the underlying meaning. "I didn't walk away."

"Yes, you did. I reached out to you numerous times. You came to Virginia often, I assume, but you never came and said hi. It was like when Maddie died you disappeared.

"I wish things were different," I pause. "I couldn't see you and the girls. I lost everything. My life was a mess and you hated me."

At her funeral, Carter called me every name in the book. He was distraught and had attacked me. I took it because I understood. It was my baby that killed his sister. It was my fault.

"I didn't hate you." Carter puts his drink down and watches me. "I hated everyone. Her for not being careful. You for leaving her that day. She called me after you left. She was upset, didn't know what to do. She said it felt like she was losing you." He closes his eyes and sighs heavily. "I know you didn't want to leave the Navy and yet you did it for her. I think she knew that too. Anyway, I told her if you loved her, you'd come back. Did you love her?" Carter's question pulls my attention.

"Of course I loved her," I pause. It's about time we have this conversation. "I gave up everything for her, man. I mean, you know how much I loved the Navy. I would've retired from there and even then they would've had to throw my ass out. But Maddie couldn't handle the deployments and the fear of me dying. So I gave it up."

"She used to cry every night that you were gone." He looks up and takes a drink.

I know this. I remember her telling me every time I had to leave.

"We met when I was active duty. She knew what a marriage with me was, but she said she could handle it."

"She couldn't."

"I figured that out. I did right by her so your anger is misplaced, brother. I loved her for a long time, but I didn't kill her. That baby was never planned, and honestly, I wouldn't have let her keep it knowing it would've killed her. I don't know how she got pregnant. We were very careful. *She* was very careful. I know you lost your parents and then your sister, and for that, I'm sorry."

Carter stands and extends his hand. "I'm sorry. I know you lost a wife and a child. That day, I lost a sister, a niece or nephew, and I lost a brother too."

I'm on my feet in a second and I grip his hand and clap him on the shoulder. "I think we both fucked up."

"I'm not proud of how I behaved, but I was fucking livid. At everyone, and you were there to take it."

"You don't have to explain how you handled your grief, but I need to move forward in my life."

Carter nods in understanding and we stand there as the weight of the conversation settles.

I feel like I need to lay it all out. I don't want any misunderstanding in what I'm telling him, and if we can ever move forward, then this will be the deciding factor.

"I'm going to be honest with you. I've found someone, and I can promise you, one day she'll be my wife. She'll never replace Madelyn, but I love her and would like your blessing."

"Is she the girl I saw here last time?" he asks.

"Yes," I reply waiting for him to say something more.

"I think Maddie would want you to be happy, and if she makes you happy then you better marry her before she realizes she can do better." Carter smiles and claps me on the back. He grabs his drink and swallows it quickly, then turns without another word.

"Don't worry, Carter. I'll grab the tab."

He throws his hand up and keeps walking.

Fucker.

I leave the bar and head to the office.

"All right, which one of you dickfaces parked in my spot?" I ask laughing when I enter. Only Mark knew I was coming, so I catch a few of the guys off balance.

"Oh, you work here?" Mark says walking over. "How'd it go with Carter?"

"I need to make a call to Hudson Pierce and see if he'll help me out."

Hudson and I met a few times in New York. If he's not willing, then maybe one of his contacts will be.

"Then what's your genius plan?"

"I'm going to get her back."

"What if she doesn't want you?" Mark asks, taunting me.

"That won't happen, but if it does she's going to find out just how persistent I can be."

He laughs and walks off. "I forgot how stupid you can be."

"I forgot what a jackass you are."

"I never forget that about you." Mark flips up his middle finger and I walk into my office feeling determined.

My phone bings.

Catherine: I landed.

Two words and I could punch a hole through the wall.

Me: I'm glad you're safe.

Catherine: I've got a lot to do in the next few days. I love you and miss you already.

Me: We'll talk soon.

I've got a lot to handle too, and the more time I waste, the more of a chance I have of losing her for good.

chapter twenty-nine

Catherine

*M*y apartment is beautiful, but it feels empty. I feel empty. Around an hour into the flight, the tears stopped and I fell asleep. I was one of those weird girls who smelled her shirt because it made me feel closer to him. When I got off the plane, Tristan had scheduled a car service to pick me up. I couldn't help but think if it were Taylor, she would've been there. Tomorrow morning, we have a face-to-face meeting scheduled, so it's not a huge deal.

I walk around and put some things away. Giving myself a moment to absorb my new home, I sit on the couch and take it all in. The furniture is modern and comfortable. Everything screams upscale, from the cherry floors to granite counters. It has exposed wood beams in the vaulted ceilings and the light paint colors make it feel airy. I open up the windows and inhale the salty sea air. The breeze blows and I let the curtains flap as I walk around into the next room.

Entering the master bedroom, my jaw drops. It has two French doors that open onto a deck. I go out there and hold on to the wrought iron railing. The metal is cool even in the warmer temperature. Going back into the room I look at the huge king size bed that sits against the wall. There's a beautiful fireplace tucked in the corner of the room with light-colored stones that stand out against the deep grains of the wood flooring. As much as I want to love it, it could be a cardboard box for all I care.

I try to make myself feel happy. My choices have consequences and moving here means I had to sacrifice my relationship with Jackson. I knew this, now I need to dust myself off and live. Tomorrow I meet Tristan and we begin getting some staff hired. I need to focus on the task at hand and worry about my lack of a love life later—if that's even possible.

The sun is just now starting to set since I'm three hours behind New York. So while it feels like eleven p.m., it's really only eight here. I see a very early night in my future.

I hop in the shower to wash off the plane and airport smells. When I get out, I throw my hair up in a bun and put on one of Jackson's t-shirts I stole. I feel like I ran a marathon. Even with sleeping on the plane, my entire body is worn out.

Closing my eyes, I sink into the plush sofa, wishing I had someone to hold me close. If I try hard enough I can feel his arms wrap around me, blanketing me with his love and protection. Pulling my shirt up I inhale again, wanting to smell his cologne, but already the smell is fading.

My phone lights up and I smile seeing a text from Jackson on my screen.

> *Jackson: Did you know a female ferret would die if it goes into heat and doesn't find a man to satisfy her?*

> *Me: Good thing I'm not a ferret.*

> *Jackson: If you need some satisfaction, I'm right*

here, baby. I'd be on my plane before you finish talking.

Me: I'm not surprised.

Jackson: You know I'm happy to be of service. I've been known to be equated to God by someone a few times.

Me: She must've been confusing you with someone else.

Jackson: Take it back.

I laugh at the easy banter we have via text message.

Me: Did I bruise your ego?

Jackson: I'm going to bruise your ass if you don't take that shit back.

Me: I'm sorry I can't hear you. Reception is really bad here.

Jackson: Funny, I'll be sure to hold off your orgasm the next time. Or maybe I won't let you come at all.

I begin to respond but I can't type the words. There won't be a next time. Unless I pack up my things and leave right now. And there's a huge part of me that wants to, but that would mean losing what I love to do. Back to square one.

In time, I know everything will fade. The memories, the pain, and eventually our love will cease to exist. It's reality and no matter how hard I fight, our separation in distance will cause a fault in our relationship. I relax into the sofa and hold on to the last touch we shared, hoping we'll find our way back together again. As the exhaustion overtakes me, I close my eyes and see him there in my dreams, waiting with open arms.

"Catherine?" I hear someone calling. "Catherine, are you okay?" I hear a deep baritone voice and open my eyes to a man standing in my living room.

Why is it so damn bright?

Who the hell is in my house?

I leap off of the sofa and shuffle backwards.

His hands fly up and he backs away. "Sorry to scare you, but the door was unlocked. I'm Tristan."

"Oh my God," I grab my throat and focus on breathing. "You scared the shit out of me."

"I called five times and got a little worried that you didn't get here. So I came to check on you this morning. I knocked and then when the door opened, I got nervous," he says slowly lowering his arms.

"I didn't hear anything."

"You should really lock the door at night," he chides as I rub my chest trying to get my heart rate back to normal.

"I don't know if I should thank you or punch you."

"I'd rather the first option if I get a choice."

Tristan smiles and I give myself a second to look at him. He's tall, lean, and has dark brown hair. His eyes are a lighter brown than mine and his smile is mesmerizing. It's obvious that he takes care of himself by the way his clothes fit. The muscles on his arms are impressive. Tristan moves with grace as he looks around the apartment.

"Wow, this place is way better than where I live," he muses.

What time is it?

"Am I late to our meeting?"

"No, I was just worried."

I grab for my phone. Sure enough, I have nine

missed calls—five from Tristan, one from Ashton, and three from Jackson. The men in my life apparently don't think I can take care of myself, and one of them doesn't even know me.

"Sorry, I was beat. I must've passed out. Thank you for checking on me though."

He smiles warmly, "Taylor called me and gave me very strict instructions and informed me if I screwed up she'd make sure I paid for it."

A smile paints across my face as I imagine my cute, little, Midwestern friend threatening Tristan.

"She's all talk, but I appreciate it. I'm gonna get changed real quick. We can grab some food and then get to work."

"I'll meet you in the courtyard," he says as he heads out of the apartment.

Looking myself over in the mirror, I'm deeply embarrassed. This definitely wasn't the impression I was hoping to give. I have the lines from the throw pillow across my cheek, my hair is knotted and sticking up in random directions. Quickly, I brush my teeth and hair. Throwing on my capris and a cute top, I hope for 'gym cute' or maybe 'hobo chic,' because right now all I see is 'hot mess.'

Tristan takes me to the restaurant down the street. We grab some coffee and a few things we can eat in the office. The drive from my apartment into the L.A. office is around forty minutes, but I was adamant that I wanted to be close to the ocean and not living in the city.

Once we reach the office, we settle in and start to make a plan. Some of the clients we already secured will be meeting with us this week. There's a lot to do to ensure the space is ready. Tristan already ordered some of the furniture and it'll deliver in the next few days.

"So, how did someone as young as you get so high up?" Tristan asks as we start to put some files away.

"Well, I busted my ass. I started as an intern while I was still in college, then I got hired full time. From there I made sure I was always on top of my game. I worked extra hours, helped without being asked, and became invaluable. At least that was my plan."

"I'd like to be a publicist after I prove myself."

"I'm sure you will." I smile at how he was able to let me know his goals without being uncomfortable about it. "I had a fantastic assistant in New York and she's now running accounts on her own. I don't believe in holding anyone back." As the words slide out, I'm brought back to Jackson. One day I'll be able to talk without somehow circling back to him.

"Must suck though, not really having time for anything other than work."

"I made time for friends and life outside of work. But yes, being a workaholic comes at a price."

A very great price for me.

"So there *is* a guy?" Tristan's voice rises in surprise.

"There was. What about you? Anyone special?"

"Are you asking me out?" he asks smirking, and then laughs.

I blink repeatedly and shake my head. "No, no, I was—"

"Catherine, relax. I'm kidding. You're missing a key part to my engine, if you know what I mean."

"Huh?"

Tristan pauses waiting for me to catch up.

"Oh!" I say as it clicks. "Sorry, the coffee and

time difference are slowing me a bit. Well, he's a very lucky guy. Have you been together long?"

"Two years, and I'm sure this is going to floor you, but he's an aspiring actor."

I sit here enjoying how I can feel comfortable around him and not have to worry about a sexual harassment suit. It was one of the things Taylor warned me about, since there were plenty of times I had to have her come over late at night, or we were traveling alone.

"Is this something I'm going to hear a lot?"

"This is L.A., honey. You're going to be shocked when you don't hear it. Now tell me about this guy you gave up."

The next week passes without incident. Tristan and I work extremely well together. He's funny, smart, witty, and it's as if we're lifelong friends. Ashton and he spoke on the phone last night and she's in love with him. I'm pretty sure he feels the same.

Today the rest of the office starts work, and I'm both excited and nervous. There's a lot we need to do and I heard from Sean letting me know they'd be coming out later this week to see the set up.

"Cat, there's a delivery for you," Tristan says strolling through the door.

"He's never going to stop," I say more to myself than anyone.

Sure enough, Tristan is carrying in a large photo wrapped in brown paper.

"Is this from my favorite sailor?" he asks, trying to peel the paper back.

I slap his hand and start to open the gift.

"Probably. He's been texting me and calling, but with the time difference it's really hard."

I rip the paper off and start laughing so hard I have to hold my stomach.

"What is that?"

Jackson sent a huge photo of my time from the obstacle course. However, in true Jackson fashion he added one question across the top: REMATCH?

"It's a long story, but let's just say Super SEAL lost and apparently isn't over it."

I pick up the phone and dial his number.

"Hello, baby." Jackson's deep voice vibrates through the line and I fight the urge to sigh.

"Hello, Muffin."

Jackson chuckles, "Oh, we're going to play that way?"

"Whatever do you mean, my dear?" I say playing coy.

"So what do I owe the honor of your phone call, Kitty?"

I purse my lips at his jab toward the nickname I hate so much.

"I got your present," I say looking at it while Tristan tilts his head as if he'll find some hidden meaning in the photo.

"Did you now?"

"I did."

Jackson clears his throat and muffles the phone, "I only have a minute, babe. I'm about to head into a meeting."

My lips turn down. This is the exact problem we'll face if we tried for anything other than friendship. "It's fine. I have a really busy day too. My client is due here in a few minutes."

"I miss you," Jackson says and my chest tightens.

Tristan comes back in and taps his finger on his wrist letting me know we have to go. I pull the phone from my ear, "Okay."

"Okay?" He sounds instantly pissed.

"Not you. I was telling Tristan okay," I explain.

"Who the fuck is Tristan?" Jackson's voice no longer holds any tenderness.

"Jealous much?" I taunt him playfully. After a second of his silence I realize he's upset. "Relax, Muff. He's my assistant."

"You hired a guy?" Jackson doesn't sound any less pissed than before.

I huff and organize the file on my desk. "I did. And if I remember correctly you have women who work for you."

"Yeah, but they're old or ugly."

"Danielle isn't either of those," I gently remind him.

"Is *Tristan*," Jackson sneers his name, "old or ugly?"

"Well, he's definitely not old," I joke and he growls.

Jackson smothers the phone but I can still hear him. "Hold the fuck on, dude. I'm dealing with a pain in the ass on the other side of the country."

"Jackson," I call but he doesn't answer.

"Jackson!" I yell and I hear the phone clear.

"You can hold on too."

"Jackson we're not together and I don't have time to ex—"

"Don't. It's been a week and a half, Catherine. I'm fucking miserable and you're hanging out with some tool."

I roll my eyes as Tristan taps his foot letting me know I really need to go. "As much as I'd love to argue with you, I have to go. Apparently I'm late. Thank you for my present and you can forget about any kind of rematch. I'll never run that shit again. I love you, always," I say and I hear him grumble as I disconnect the call.

Tristan smirks playfully when I approach. "That was like watching a one-sided tennis match. I can only imagine what you just did to him."

I jab him with my elbow and we start walking to the conference room where our first Hollywood client is waiting. "He can handle it."

Tristan elbows me back. "Muff?"

I laugh at how someone who doesn't know Jackson or Mark would hear that word and insinuate what it means. "Not that kind of muff. Come on, we've got clients to sign."

After the meeting, I feel terrible about the way I handled the call. The entire time I wondered how I'd feel if the shoe was on the other foot. If he walked away from me and then taunted me about another woman, I'd be hurt.

I grab my phone and call, but it goes to voice-mail.

"Hey, it's me. I'm sorry about before. Thank you for the gift. Give me a call when you get a chance if you want to talk. Miss you."

I set the phone down and feel even worse.

chapter thirty

"Hey, want to hit the beach?" I look up at Tristan standing at my door smiling. It's still warm and sunny even though it's fall.

"When?" I ask.

"Now? I have this amazing boss, who loves me. And she wants to stare at my luscious body." Tristan's eyes sparkle with mischief.

"I'm pretty sure you crossed about a hundred lines of inappropriateness, but I *am* amazing. Is the schedule clear?"

"Yup! Go home, grab your suit, and I'll meet you at your apartment."

Tristan and I have been spending a lot of time together since he's funny, sweet, and actually cares if I take breaks. Plus, he tells me that Taylor calls him to threaten his life daily.

I still haven't heard back from Jackson, which has been weighing heavily on my mind. I send him a quick text while I'm on my way home.

> *Me: Hey, I'm sorry if you're upset.*
>
> *Jackson: I'm not. I'm really busy. There are some big things going on that I'm handling.*
>
> *Me: I understand.*
>
> *Jackson: We'll talk soon. I love you.*
>
> *Me: I know, I love you.*

Sometimes you can love someone so much, but it isn't enough. It's been two weeks and already whatever I thought we had is dissolving. There is a part of me that knew all of this was going to happen. Loving someone doesn't mean that it'll work out. Plenty of times I thought love was going to make me whole. Neil for one, I loved him and he showed me how sometimes love is blind, and not in a good way. I loved my father, but that love couldn't conquer his guilt or reasons for staying away.

Then I have the good love. The people in my life who reciprocate love: Ashton, Taylor, Gretchen, and many more. Love shouldn't come with a price. It shouldn't take from you and make you miserable, because then what would you be left with? If I gave up everything for him and it didn't work out … then what? No matter what the future holds, I know I'm strong enough to handle it.

I get changed and meet Tristan outside my apartment. The beach is within walking distance, so we head toward it on foot. The sun warms my skin and I draw a calming breath. The sounds of the seagulls above and the waves crashing soothe my soul.

"Do you miss Jersey?" Tristan asks after we find a spot and get comfortable.

I close my eyes and soak in the vitamin D. "I don't know. I miss some stuff but it's fall now and I'm at the beach … that's pretty amazing. I don't miss the cold."

"So I won't be worrying about you skiing in Tahoe?" he laughs and I join him.

"Definitely not. I will be parked right here until the last beach day possible." I smile realizing I have no clue when that will be. I could get the beach for a lot longer than I even realized.

"Sweetheart, you're going to be a California girl sooner than you planned," Tristan teases.

We laugh and he promises to take me around L.A. and we plan a tourist day. The day passes and when I check my phone, I'm brought back to the small piece of me that won't let go of the east coast.

Jackson: Today, I miss you more than should be allowed. Today, I hate California. Today, I want to hold you, kiss you, love you. Today, I found one of your shirts.

I type out my response but delete before sending ... *Me: Tomorrow, you'll be okay.*

Instead I send:

Me: I miss you too.

Today marks a month since I've left New Jersey.

As much as I long for certain things, I'm growing into my new life. The office is now at a functional level, we have some new clients signing on. There are two publicists that work under me and we're in the process of getting the marketing team in place. Tristan is my lifeline. He's fast become my best friend out here. We spend so much time together, he's almost like a little brother—only not.

The only real dark spot in my life is Jackson. Since our last phone call, I haven't spoken to him but we've had an occasional superficial text. I spoke with Natalie last week and she said she hasn't heard much either. Thankfully, she and Mark still keep in touch. I also get random cat texts from Mark, but it makes me smile. I sent him a Twilight picture the other day and I got a nice text back: *Fuck you.*

Tristan is on his way over to have dinner and keep me company. He said we had to celebrate my one-month open office anniversary with wine and man-candy. I'm a little worried about what he means by the man-candy, but I'm going to go with it.

I'm sitting on my couch going over the proposal letters the new publicist I hired is sending out, when my computer pops up with a video call from Ashton.

"Biffle!" I yell as I accept the call.

"Hello, my gorgeous friend," she smiles and I want to reach through the screen and hug her. "How's my California girl?"

"Eh, you know," I shrug.

"Nope, I sure don't, because you *never* call me, twunt."

"I've been busy and this time difference really makes it hard. Tell me about your life? Miss me?"

I figure if I can get her to talk about herself maybe she'll back off me.

"I made some babies, met some guys, dumped them … you know, typical day."

"Still breaking hearts. What about Mark?"

"Pffft. Mark is in Virginia." She waves her hands in the screen. "Hello! I mean, you dumped your ridiculously hot boyfriend because you were a few states away."

I roll my eyes and huff. "I think you need to go back to geography if you think New York to California is a few! It's not even a few hours. It's a damn near six hour flight." I throw my hands up and give her the stank-eye.

"You're being dramatic," she smirks knowing

she riled me up. "Miss me yet?"

"Not right now I don't." I give a forgiving smile. She knows I do and I know if there was any way I could make her come here I would've done it already.

"Tell me about the new clients." Ashton practically bounces in her seat wanting juicy details.

I laugh and talk to her about the office, how much I'm decorating. All to which she waves her hands telling me to move it along. She should know better than to ask me about my clients. Of course I can't resist taunting her a little bit.

"The new one we should sign this week you would die over."

"Oh my God, Cat! Tell me! I'm dying here."

"Now, you know I can't do that, but I will tell you I'm really happy!"

"Bitch! Show me the apartment and what it looks like outside," Ashton requests and her eyes glow.

"Okay." I smile showing her how close I live to the beach.

We talk about the location and how I've found a few cute shops. In all honesty though, I'm doing well. I've become close with Tristan and his boyfriend, Logan, and one of the girls in the apartment next to me and I had drinks last week. I make sure to rub in the warm weather when she tells me how it's starting to get cooler—but other than that I miss Jersey. The food, the friends, and him—all there.

"I think that's normal," she says with pursed lips. "You spent your whole life here, but it's been a few weeks now. I think you're doing really well. Have you heard from the Muffin Man?"

"No, after our last talk where he got insanely

jealous over Tristan, we haven't spoken."

Leaning on her elbows she comes close to the camera. "Wonder why! You know he's all sad you left his ass crying at the airport. Then not even two weeks later you're joking about a guy. Stupid ass. I bet he'll get his shit together though."

"I don't think so. It's why I said it wouldn't work."

"Details, my friend. Well, have you guys spoken at all?" she asks curiously.

I huff and lean back. "I called and left a message, then a text, but I only got a quick text back. I miss him but I'm happy for the most part here. I don't know that I'll date anyone any time soon, but I have the beach, the sun, and I love being the boss."

"You never know, you may meet someone. Just leave your heart open. For fuck's sake, the man has done some pretty big shit. I can't see him sitting around New York giving up," Ashton says with a raised brow.

"I don't—"

I hear a thud at my door. "Caaaaaat," Tristan whines at my door. "Let me in."

"Speak of the devil. Hold on, you can *officially* meet Tristan."

I jump up and answer the door, letting Tristan in. He looks better than he did this morning, but I take pity on him. "Come on, want to meet Ashton?"

"She's here?" he instantly perks up.

I laugh and grab his hand pulling him into the living room. "No, but she's on the computer."

"Tristan!" Ashton squeals when she sees him. "Holy shit! You're hot!"

I giggle and he puckers up to the screen. "You're pretty sexy yourself. What do they feed you girls in

Jersey? On T.V. they sure as hell don't do you any favors."

"Do not get me started," Ashton says irritated by his comment. "I hate those stupid reality-my-ass shows. We are not like that. Fuhgeddabout it," she says in her best Sopranos imitation.

"You don't want to get her started." I laugh and shake my head. "However, Ash, growing up we did think your dad was in the Mafia."

"Yeah, I'm still not sure what he does for living," she shrugs and we all laugh a little.

Tristan, Ashton, and I talk for a while and it's the first time I think I've laughed this hard. The two of them would drive me absolutely insane if we lived close. Between Tristan's flirting and Ashton constantly telling him she could flip him I've almost peed myself twice. After a few more minutes Ash has to go since it's midnight her time and she has to be in the lab early. Since Logan is filming a movie in Seattle, Tristan's been over here more. Might as well be lonely together.

"Movie?" Tristan asks after we go over a few things we need to get done this week.

"Sure, you pick something. I'm going to grab some popcorn and candy—and pee." I hop up and head into the bathroom while Tristan looks for a movie.

"Someone's at the door," he yells to me.

"Can you answer?"

"Sure thing, hot stuff."

CHAPTER THIRTY-ONE

JACKSON

Knock.

"Someone's at the door," I hear a fucking dude's voice say.

No motherfucking way.

"Sure thing, hot stuff."

I'll kill him.

My whole body locks up ready to beat the ever-living fuck out of whoever is in her house. I don't give a fuck if she's happy with him. He's done.

Time's up.

He opens the door and I puff myself up taller. His eyes widen as he looks up.

Yeah, that's right, douchebag. Now test me. I fucking dare you.

"Can I help you?" He smiles and I push forward through the door. "Hey asshole!" He calls to me but I couldn't give a shit.

"Catherine!" I yell and he grabs my arm.

Without a second thought, I grab him and push him up against the wall. Holding him there with my forearm.

"Where is she?" I ask and he holds on to my arm trying to make sure he has access to air.

"Can't. Breathe. Dying," he barely gets out.

I lean in and my voice is cold as ice. "If I wanted you dead, you'd be dead. Where the fuck is

Catherine?"

"Fuck you," he says and I push harder on his neck.

The questions swirl in my head. Did he see her naked? Has he seen her face when she comes? Has he known what it's like to sink into her and bury yourself so deep you don't know where you begin and end?

My eyes narrow into slits as he tries to push against my arm.

"Jackson!" Catherine calls out and is already at my side trying to pull me off. "Put him down! Now!" she screams and pushes me.

"You're fucking kidding me." I let go and he slumps to the floor, gasping for air.

"You idiot!" She pushes me and goes to his side. "He's my assistant!"

Ohhh, so this is her "not old" assistant, Tristan.

I stand there seething, ready to punch something, someone. I can't fucking believe this. It's been *one month*. One. Not a year, but a month and she's already moved on. She's already fucking someone else.

"Seems you moved on pretty easily."

I'm too late.

"Unreal. You're unreal," Catherine says as she stands up after checking on him. "I haven't moved on, you asshole!" She pushes me forward and her touch wakes every part of me. "He's my assistant. Not my lover. You haven't called, or anything, in weeks, and then you show up and almost kill my only friend here."

"There's a fucking guy in your apartment! What did you expect me to think?" I ask as she pushes me back again. I stumble, walking backwards, as the rage practically steams out of her head.

Nice. I'm retreating from a five-foot-two woman. I'm a pussy.

"Wait, this is Jackson?" the *assistant* says from the floor. He's not a small guy by any means, but I'll lay his ass out if he touches her.

Catherine glares at me and turns to him. "Tristan, can you give me a minute with my *friend?*"

"Can I watch?" he replies but his eyes stay fixed a beat too long. My fists flex unconsciously.

"No!" Catherine yells.

"Damn, he's hot. Be careful, hot stuff, and call me in the morning." Tristan kisses her cheek and I growl.

This woman is going to be the death of me.

Tristan smiles at me and then looks at Catherine. "Logan's going to love this story." He turns to me and extends his hand. "I'm Tristan, by the way. Her assistant. Her very gay assistant."

Motherfucker.

I suddenly feel like I'm going to be laid out.

Or she's going to kill me.

I extend my hand and grip a little too tight. I may have figured out what an idiot I am, but that doesn't mean shit. "Jackson. Her ..." I trail off not knowing what to call myself.

"Dead ex-boyfriend," Catherine replies and glares at me.

"Nice to meet you." Tristan looks me up and down, but I'm smart enough to keep my mouth shut and nod.

She walks him out the door while I stand there waiting for the wrath to begin.

Five.

Four.

Three.

Another two heartbeats pass and I anticipate her fury.

But instead she stands there with her back against the door. Waiting for God knows what.

Not sure if I should speak or keep my fucking mouth shut, I just wait.

"Want something to drink?" she asks sweetly lifting her brow.

I'm so fucked.

"No, I'm fine. Look ..." I start to backtrack. "Think about how this looked for me."

"Hmmm," she says as she pours herself a glass of water.

"You've been gone a month. I fly here and some guy opens the door." I keep going because if my foot is this far in my mouth, I might as well lodge it all the way in. "He's calling you 'hot stuff' and I snapped."

"Mmmm hmmm," Catherine hums as she puts the glass to her lips and looks at me over the rim.

I start to make my way over to her. There's no way I can keep standing here without touching her. "You would've lost it if I was with another woman."

"Would I?" she asks, standing her ground as I stalk her.

I smile at this game we're playing, stepping forward. "I think you would."

Her lip slips between her teeth and I'm instantly hard. I need to get it under control.

"Why are you here?" she asks and her eyes drop to her glass.

Moving quickly, I'm in front of her in an instant. My finger pulls her chin up and my world stops. She doesn't see it.

"For you."

"Jackson," she sighs and tries to step away, but I grip her and pull her closer. I breathe her in, and when her hands grab my arms, I feel her tremble.

"I had this speech planned out but nothing with us ever goes as planned." I chuckle and she looks up.

Her brown eyes pin me and I need to touch her, taste her. I crash my lips to hers.

They mold to mine and I kiss her like a man dying of thirst. I need more. My hands move up and hold her neck in place. She sighs and my tongue delves into her mouth.

Heaven.

Every piece of her is heaven.

Catherine moans and I forget about everything but her. The sound she makes leaves me desperate for more. I want to taste her skin and sink deep inside her. I want to make love to her for hours until neither of us can move and then do it again.

She breaks the kiss and pulls back. "I can't do this again. I can't go through losing you anymore."

Good, because that's not happening ever again.

"I'm here for you. I'm not leaving."

She looks up and narrows her eyes, "I haven't heard from you in weeks."

I walk towards her as she takes another step back. She's not running from me ever again.

"I couldn't hear your voice and not hop on a plane. So I'm here now and I'm not leaving. I love you."

I need her. Right now. Lacing my fingers in her hair, I take hold of her again. I push her back and lift her onto the counter. When her legs wrap around me, I feel her heat and I lose it.

Every part of my brain detaches and all I can think about is feeling her. Her small hands glide up my arms as my lips press against hers. I graze my tongue at the seam of her perfect mouth, waiting for her to let me in. She opens them slightly and it's all the permission I need. My tongue pushes against hers and I pull her closer to me as she whimpers.

I pull back and nip at her ear. "I fucking need you. Tell me you want this." She has to tell me before I fucking erupt.

"I-I," she stutters, and my mouth covers hers again, pushing her to give me the damn answer I need. If I can keep her from overthinking, we might be able to get through this.

"Do you want me, Catherine?" My lips brush over hers, and every part of me is rock hard.

Her breathing increases and I take my tongue and sweep it across her lips. Per-fucking-fection.

"Jackson," she moans my name and I cover her mouth with mine again.

Fucking hell.

"Answer me. Do you want me?" I kiss her swollen lips, needing her again. "To keep going?"

"Yes!" she cries out as my hand finds its way up her shirt where I find she doesn't have a bra on. *Nice.*

"I'm not going to stop, so you better be absolutely fucking sure, baby." I don't know how or why I'm still talking.

She grabs my shirt and our eyes lock. Her pupils dilate and the fire burns through them. "You better not."

Hell yes. Don't have to tell me twice.

As much as I'd love to tease her and make her beg, I don't have the patience for it. I want to claim her. I want to feel her wrap her perfect legs around me and fuck me until all I can see, hear, feel, taste, and smell is her. I hope she's ready because I sure as shit am.

Releasing her perfect tits, my hands glide down her sides and pull her shirt off. I tease her with my tongue before sucking her nipple in my mouth as she writhes in my arms.

"You missed me, baby? Want me to fuck you now?" I know how much it turns her on when I talk dirty to her.

"God, yes."

I break away and smirk. I'm a cocky bastard but I can't help it. "I told you I was compared to God."

Her head falls back and she laughs. When she looks back up, she smiles. "Your humility is astounding. Now," her eyes harden, "Do you want to talk or do you want to show me how much you missed me?" She winks and pulls my head close.

There's my sex kitten.

Catherine takes hold of the kiss and I give her the control for a minute. She needs to feel the power and I'm willing to give it up for her. Plus, it's hot as hell when she gets aggressive. Her fingers weave in my hair and she pulls—hard. I almost blow my load right there.

I pull back and her eyes are liquid. I lift her and slide her shorts and thong off. I'm completely unprepared when she hops off the counter and backs me against it.

She's completely bare and she hooks her finger in my belt loop and pulls me against her. My hands glide across her delicate back to her round ass and I grip it roughly, lifting her up. Her hands fumble with the button and my jeans fall around my ankles.

With her mouth fused to mine, I shake my jeans off and grind down against her as she tries to line herself up with my dick.

"Not yet, baby," I manage to choke out as I try to find the bed or a couch.

"Hurry," she moans and then pushes her lips to mine.

Not able to see where the hell I'm going, I walk into the table.

Perfect.

"I'm going to fuck you so hard right now, but I promise I'll be sweet next time." I give her warning because the very thin thread is about to snap and I can't control myself.

Her hand wraps around my dick and I almost drop her. "I don't need sweet. I just need you."

Jesus Christ that feels fucking amazing.

"You've got me, baby."

She glides her hand up and down and I'm harder than I've ever been.

"Promise?" she asks, placing a kiss on my neck.

"Oh yeah, I promise." I lay her on the table and pull her hips close.

Before she can say another word, I push inside her.

Home.

I'm home and I don't plan on leaving again.

Her eyes close and I lift her hips and sink deeper. Wet, hot, and mine.

She moans and I wrap her legs around my back and lift her up. I can't get deep enough. I want her to feel me everywhere. I'm like an animal needing to possess her. There will be no doubt when we finish how I feel.

"Catherine," I say through gritted teeth. "Look at me."

When her deep brown eyes meet mine, her hands cup my face. "Take me."

I snap. The words I need to hear from her. With her back on the table, I take this time to plunge into her again. I ride her in and out, allowing her to milk my cock as I lose my fucking mind. She's every breath I breathe, every beat of my heart, and I never want it to stop.

"Fuck. I'm losing it."

Needing her to come, I put my thumb on her clit and rub in circles. I feel her clench and I have to bite my tongue to stop from finishing right then. Her hands find my arms and she holds on while I pound her relentlessly. Each thrust I lose myself in her. I claim her each time I slide in and out. The need to protect her, keep her safe, and ensure she never runs from me again surges through my body.

"I fucking love you. You're mine."

My fingers press harder into her clit and I feel her thighs tighten around my hips. I fuck her harder and as her eyes stay locked on mine, I can feel her get closer, her nails digging into my forearms. She scrapes them down my arms as she falls apart. I can't last much longer.

My hands grip her thighs roughly and she screams my name over and over.

"Catherine!" I call out as I slam against her harder and lose myself over the edge while her pussy squeezes around my cock draining every ounce of me until I'm empty.

My head drops and rests on her breasts as our breathing calms.

That was intense.

I close my eyes and focus on her heart beating beneath me. Catherine's hands slide slowly up and down my back when she lets out a deep breath.

If she pulls away, I'm gonna lose my shit.

"How long are you here for?" she asks, already sounding defeated.

"Forever."

She huffs, "I don't think that's funny."

"I wasn't kidding."

Why does everything with this woman need to be so damn complicated?

"Jackson, be serious."

Standing up, I put my hands on her sides and look at her. I need to make sure she sees everything in my heart when I get this out. Considering she seems to need me to spell it out, it's best I give myself little room for misinterpretation.

"I sold Raven."

Her eyes go wide. "You what?"

"I sold it. It's gone."

"Why?" Catherine's mouth falls open.

"Because I love you. Because a life without you isn't the life I want. Because every day I think of you. Every moment I want to be with you. So you being in California and me being in New York isn't working. The day you left me, I made a choice."

"But, Jackson, you can't."

"I did."

"This is crazy," she says and starts to shift under me.

"Goddammit, Catherine," I say, growing frustrated as I pin her down from getting away.

She tries to slide out from under me and can't. Trying to hide from me, she puts her hands over her face.

Here we go.

"Why don't you get it?" I ask pulling her hands away.

"Get what?"

I take her hands in mine and pour my heart out. "I'm not leaving. I choose you. You're it for me. I love you—infinitely."

"But you can't give everything up for me. You'll resent me."

I rub small circles on her tiny palms. "Catherine, I didn't give everything up *because* of you. I gave it up for me. For us. I loved you enough to let you go, but I love you enough to give up everything *for* you. You didn't ask me to do this. I did this because my life without you doesn't work. This is your dream and I won't ask you to choose, but you, you are my dream."

She gasps as tears fall from her eyes. I've laid it all out for her. I let her up, and she sits on the table as I wait.

"I guess the question is, do you feel the same?"

Her beautiful eyes lock on mine as the word I want to hear falls from her perfect lips. "Yes."

"Yes?" I ask needing her to tell me again.

She hops down and wraps her arms around me. Her eyes glimmer and are filled with love. "You're it for me. Always have been and always will be."

EPILOGUE

Seven years later

"Okay, you ready?" I ask her with that glint in her eye as she stands there with the timer.

"No cheating this time. I swear," she vows. I glance at Catherine as she smiles.

Yeah, I know that look. She's already scheming.

"Mommy, push the button!" Erin yells as she starts jumping up and down.

"I thought you were on my side?" I ask the little traitor. She looks up with her big brown eyes and bats her eyelashes quickly. Her dark brown hair is in pigtails that she keeps making slap her in the face when she turns.

"Sowwy, Daddy. Mommy said we could have ice cream if she wins. If you win, we have to eat spinach. Yuck!"

Her puppy dog eyes melt me. Damn girls.

I look at my wife who shrugs with a shit-eating grin on her face. I make note to wipe it off later.

"Kennedy, whose side are you on?" I ask the other half of the demon spawn. Her blond hair is covering her face as she tries to do the same thing her sister is. She may only be three, but surely she wouldn't leave me for ice cream. She's honorable.

"Mama!" she calls out and puts her hands up.

Or not.

Catherine walks over as we stand in front of the obstacle course in California. "What's the matter, Muffin?" she asks coyly. "You ready to lose to the girls today?"

"My ass, Kitty."

"Butt," she corrects me but lets the nickname slide. I'm sure she'll punish me later—which I might like.

Erin spins in circles in the sand pit and Kennedy runs over to her sister. "They can't hear." I grab her waist and pull her against my side. "Besides," I whisper in her ear and she shivers. "You know I like your ass and I know you like it when I swear. You had no problem telling me to fuck you harder last night."

My dick stirs at the images, how hot she looked when she fell apart in my arms.

"You may want to get yourself ready since I'm about to kick your butt—*again.*"

"Over my dead body." I snake my hand up her back and run my tongue along her neck.

"Girls!" Catherine calls over and they come running.

"Low blow, Catherine."

"No blowing anything, baby. Other than you're about to get blown out of the water," she says as her fine ass starts to walk away.

"I'd rather you blow something else." I give her a knowing look.

Her head whips around and she smirks. "You'll pay for that."

"I'm sure I will."

She knows the three of them rule my world. Kennedy looks just like her mother—she's tiny and has the biggest brown eyes I've ever seen. Her pout can melt me, and I'm pretty sure she's figured out all she has to do is turn her lip down and I'll cave. She has the same tiny cleft in her chin, which is why most people say she's her mother's child. I think it's her feisty attitude and quick wit.

Erin, on the other hand, is pretty much all me. She's tall and slender but has her mother's facial features. I love that I can look at any of them and see Catherine. They ground me and give me a love like I've never known.

Even with Catherine running her own P.R. firm and my traveling, we find a way to make it work. When we fight, we have a lot of fun making up. When I found out Catherine was pregnant, I was obsessive over everything. What she wore, what she ate, if she took her prenatals, doctor's appointments, pretty much everything she did I was on top of. Needless to say, she really hated me by month two, but she understood. With Kennedy we were much more re-laxed. I actually enjoyed my very horny wife.

"Daddy, we're ready to run the os-tickle course," Erin calls, clearly screwing that name up.

I think my cadets need a little extra training.

"Fall in, girls!" I command and they all stand there giggling.

Fine. We'll do this the hard way. I lift each of the girls and put them in line. Kennedy starts to draw in the dirt while Catherine crosses her arms and covers her mouth trying not to laugh.

"Kennedy, you need to stand at attention." I huff as she shakes her head back and forth.

"This should be good," I hear Catherine from behind me.

"Zip it, woman."

"I'll give you 'woman.'"

I turn and wiggle my eyebrows and she rolls her eyes. Some things haven't changed and I hope they never do.

"Okay, Muffin. Let's see how a SEAL loses to his wife—who doesn't exercise—and his two daughters under the age of five," Catherine taunts. "This time if I win, I want something big."

"How big? I've got a big prize for you." I raise my brow and she slaps my chest.

"Idiot. Well, first I want to hear your terms."

My cadets are now doing ring-around-the-rosey. I need a full out boot camp for these two. "Girls … you're killing me. Killing me." I look back at Catherine and I need to kiss her.

So I do.

I feel someone little pulling on my shirt. Looking down, I see Erin. Little cock blocker. "Is Uncle Mark coming? He always lets me win."

"No, because he doesn't want to lose to your amazing daddy!" I say a little too excitedly.

My beautiful, sweet, perfect daughter laughs at me. "Daddy, you're silly. Uncle Mark always wins."

"Do you want to ever get a present again?" I ask her. "Because I'll make sure you never see another Barbie." I purse my lips and she laughs harder.

I swear I was drunk when I wished for girls.

"Are you done threatening the kids with things they know you'll never do and ready to lose?" Catherine asks from behind me, holding Kennedy in her arms.

Arguing with her is a full-time job. "Sure, baby. Let's set the terms so we're crystal clear on what I get when I win."

"Let's hear it."

I steeple my fingers and try to make this good. When I win, I want to be sure I really come out with what I want. After the fucking play from hell, I still had to send her to a spa in Napa when I moved out here—and fly Ashton out. It's payback time.

"I want a guys' golfing weekend. In Bermuda. With Mark, Tristan, and Logan."

"So you want to take all my help?" she asks.

"Fine, you can keep Tristan. He sucks at golf anyway."

Tristan and Logan live down the street from us. Logan had a breakout role in a major film and now Catherine represents him. Tristan stays home and does ... well, nothing.

"Okay," she agrees.

Immediately my spidey senses kick in. She agreed way too easily.

"That was too quick. What did you do?" I look around and put my hand out. "Give me the stop-watch, dear."

Catherine's eyes widen and she smiles. "Here ya go, pumpkin," she says sarcastically. I almost prefer "Muffin"—almost.

I look at the timer but it's still at zero.

"I don't trust you," I narrow my eyes before turning around. "Erin and Kennedy," I call them over, "Did your mommy do something?"

They both smile and shake their heads no.

"Fine. You ready to watch me teach your mommy how it's done?"

They both give me a blank stare.

"Okay, good."

"Ready, Muffin?"

"Sure thing, cupcake."

"Go!" Catherine calls out and I sprint off. I get over the logs and halfway to the tunnel when I hear Kennedy start screaming hysterically.

I stop immediately and rush to her. When I get there, she stops and looks up at Catherine. "Like that, Mommy?"

Catherine looks up and tilts her head to her shoulder.

"You're using the kids?" I ask incredulously. This means war.

"A girl's gotta do what a girl's gotta do. You should probably get back to it, old man."

I growl, "I'll show you an old man." I turn and run faster hoping she doesn't try anything else. I leap back over the logs and get through the tube quickly.

Ha! I'm not even breaking a sweat.

I climb the rope, but when I get to the top of the wall, Erin is sitting at the bottom where I would land.

"Catherine!" I practically snarl her name.

I look at my oldest and give her a knowing look. "Sweetheart, can you move so Daddy doesn't crush you?"

"Sorry, I was told I would get to go to Toys R Us and pick out anything I want. Grandma Nina also said if I stayed extra long she'd send me money."

"What? She's in on this too?"

They're all out to get me. Next thing Reagan will somehow be involved.

I leap onto the other side and hear Catherine yell out, "That's an extra minute, babe. You're clearly cheating."

I get through the next four parts of the course and make it down the tower.

Now it's time for my wife to pay for her transgressions.

"What was so important that you wanted to win? You know I'd give you everything."

She smiles and places her hand on my chest.

"You already have."

"Does this involve a play? Because I really don't want to sit through that horse shit again."

"No, but you will get to star in it." She smiles and my mind starts to race. "I have conditions though."

"Of course you do," I shake my head and already regret this.

Catherine smirks and wraps her arms around my neck. "Yes, I don't want anymore presidents. I just want one thing."

Now she has me thoroughly confused.

"And that would be, my love?" I question while kissing the tip of her nose.

"A boy."

The End

Letter to the Reader

There's no words to fully express my gratitude for reading these books. I truly hope you enjoyed Jackson and Catherine's story as much as I enjoyed writing it. If you could take a few seconds and leave a review on Amazon, Goodreads, iBooks, or Barnes & Noble it would mean the world to me.

You can pre order Consolation and Conviction on iBooks.

Thank you again!
Corinne Michaels

beloved bonus

CHAPTER TWENTY-EIGHT

JACKSON

*O*f all the times I wish I'd never answered my fucking phone! I get here, we finally talk, we fuck, and then I find out Aaron's dead. How much more am I supposed to take? Natalie's pregnant... and now Aaron's dead. She's a widow and the baby has no father. All because I stayed here to handle the company I never wanted.

I have to get out of here.

The plane leaves soon for Afghanistan. I need to leave here and fix this mess I've created. Maybe I can find some answers and give closure. Maybe this is a fucking dream and none of this is happening. And maybe there are magical unicorns and gold at the end of the goddamn rainbow. None of this is a lie. Once again, Jackson Cole took someone's fucking life.

I need to go. *Now.*

"Talk to me. What happened?" she says in a voice I barely hear. "Hey." Catherine's hand lifts my chin but I can't look at her. I don't want her to see the hate and anger raging through me. I won't let her see the blackness that consumes me. It will overtake her too.

I push away, needing to get the hell out of here. I've killed another person. Another wife will bury her husband because of me. I sent him there. I signed his death certificate and I'll have to live with that.

I'm done.

Checked the fuck out. Catherine stands before me and I know it. She will die. And then I'll never live with myself. I have to save her the only way I know. Give her a chance to not end up as another victim of my tragic decisions.

I close my eyes so I won't see the hurt when I break her. "What happened?" I echo. I hate myself because I have to hurt her. But this is it. "I'll tell you what happened—I did it again!" I allow the rage to consume me. If I'm angry, hopefully it won't destroy me when I do this to her.

"Did what again?" She asks. I can hear the fear in her voice. It obliterates any hope I had of being able to make it through this. I remind myself to hang onto my self-hate.

I throw my hands up and pace. "I fucking knew it." That statement has so many meanings. I knew this is where I'd be, that someone else would suffer and now I have to do the same to her. I'll devastate her and ruin myself in the process. I didn't want this. I didn't want to open myself up again. *Fuck!*

"I don't understand. What did you know?" How could she know or understand. She's not a killer. She's perfect.

"I'm no good for you." There is it. The truth.

Catherine looks hurt already. If only she knew. "Why would you say that?"

"Don't you get it? Everyone I love dies!" I want to comfort her—go to her. But I stop. If I touch her

I'll never walk away. "I can't let you be next. I'll die before I let that happen."

"Jackson, talk to me." Her hand touches my arm and the current that made me desperate for her burns me. I break from her touch. "Don't push me away. I'm trying to understand," Tears form in her dark brown eyes. Tears that I'm putting there. The last thing I ever want to do is make her cry.

I'll sacrifice my happiness because I don't deserve it. I don't deserve her. Catherine is beautiful and smart. She's stronger than she knows and she'll get over this. She'll find a way to love again and this time it will be with someone worthy of her.

"I'm not pushing you away. I'm saving you!" Where the fuck is my phone? I have to get the hell out of here. I have to stop her questioning. "I won't let it happen to you too!"

"Let what happen? You're not making any sense!" Fuck my phone, I'm leaving. "Stop! Talk to me!" She pleads but it's too late. I've made up my mind.

I stand here looking at her as she fights me—I know what will happen if I stay. I have to break her. I have to hurt her so fucking much that she will never come for me. She has to hate me and I have to be the one to do it. I have to lie.

"How many more tattoos do I have to get? Huh? How many ways do I have to mark my mistakes? I'm protecting you, Catherine. I won't let you love me," I say with disgust for myself evident in my voice. She'll think it's at her but it's not. I couldn't hate her. I hate me. I'm a fucking pussy and I can't take another second.

"Too late."

I lose it. I see red. She can't love me. "Don't!

Don't say that!" Her eyes fall as I yell at her. I watch every part of her start to shut down.

Catherine's eyes fill with hurt as my heart fills with hopelessness. "I will say it because it's true. What did you think was going to happen? I knew I was falling for you. Then you told me…you told me I was it for you! Don't walk away. Don't give up on us." I did know. I just can't let it happen anymore.

She breaks me. I love her but I have to say good-bye. I have to find a way to stop destroying everyone. I lift my hand and swipe one of her tears with my fingertip. I can't stop myself. I have to touch her—comfort her. Catherine pulls that from me. She makes me want to be better. Someday, maybe I can be. Right now though, I have to go. I press my lips against her temple and pause. I inhale, taking in her warmth and the way she smells like vanilla.

"I'm not giving up. I'm giving you a chance."

Watching her try to be so strong breaks a part of my resolve. I want to stay but I can't. I have to go. Why is she fucking fighting me so much? Why doesn't she see the black that eats at me? I hold her in my arms one last time. Savoring the way she feels against me.

"Jackson, I love you! Give *us* a chance." Her voice breaks at the end.

I can't fight the need to protect her. All I want is to never see another tear fall from her gorgeous face. I want to be the reason she smiles—not cries. I take her fragile frame in my arms and hold her close. Her arms wrap around me like vices. She's trying to hold on so tight and I wish it were enough. If things were different I'd stay here and we'd make love, we'd laugh and I'd tell her everything. Life sucks and things aren't different. I'm not the man she needs. I've sent a man to his death, sentenced a child to be fatherless. I've broken families, people, and by that I've condemned myself into this life.

I look down at her with resolve.

"No..." her voice cries out.

It's not enough to keep me here. I'm already gone.

I start to walk to the door and hear her whimper. I can feel the pain in the room. The despair is suffocating. I just have to keep walking.

"Jackson." Catherine's voice is pleading. I know she thinks I'm what she wants but I know I'm not what she needs.

The bottom line is I do love her, and leaving her like this is tearing me apart. I know I'm the cause for the hurt she'll feel. My feet are rooted to the ground.

"You said I shouldn't run." Her voice morphs from sadness to anger. "You lied to me! You're doing what you promised you wouldn't—leave." I stand unmoving because I did promise and I have to go back on my word. Shit's changed. "Fine. Be a coward! Go! Walk away just like they all do."

She has some fucking nerve. Both of us are like time bombs and either of us will blow. It's just a matter of who will be first. I'm doing this for her.

I turn and glare at her. "Coward? I'm fucking saving you. The only thing I'm afraid of is losing you."

I'll never live with myself if something happened to her.

"I can't do this again, Jackson. Please don't walk out that door after I've told you how I feel." She pleads with me and I battle my own wants and needs.

Right now, I could end this. I could take her in my arms and let her heal me. I could touch her, hold her, make love to her. Or I can walk out the door and ensure she never feels the pain I somehow manage to bring. My head shakes back and forth as the decision clashes on. "I can't lose you like that. I'd rather walk away."

"You're going to listen to me goddamnit! Four days ago, when we went into that lawyer's office, I was falling apart. Everything in my life felt out of control. It was you who held me together."

And then I fucked her world up that night.

She continues on, "I drew on your strength to get through that fucking day from hell. But after everything else, I was terrified. You could hurt me so much."

Well, I'm going to live up to that fear.

"I was falling in love with you weeks ago, but that day I saw it all vanish. I ran because I was so afraid you'd let me go. I thought if I pushed you away before you got rid of me, it would be better. But it wasn't!"

I look at her and she seems so sure that her speech will change me. Any other day it would've. I'd smile and go back to her, tell her how cute her attitude was. Today, things are changed. Life smacked us both in the face and there's no going back. "I'm not running, Catherine." I let her know I'm done with this conversation. "Aaron is dead. I'm going to collect his fucking body and deliver it to his pregnant wife." That's the fucking situation. That's the bottom line. "Guess whose fault it is again? I give up trying to fight a war I'll never win."

I'm drained from this entire last half hour. If I don't get out of this apartment I'm going to cave.

"It's not your fault," she whispers.

My entire body goes ramrod straight. Not my fucking fault. She's blind and I'm angry. I won't listen to this. "Try telling Natalie that." I point my finger and step forward. "I leave for Afghanistan to get his body and bring it home. I'm done arguing with you. I'm just ... done."

Catherine is relentless. She's fighting and I'm caving. "I'm ready to fight for you. For so long I thought it wasn't my choice if things worked out or not with any man. But with you—it's different. You told me I was it for you. Well, same here. I love you." I stare into her insistent soft brown eyes as she pours her heart out.

My Catherine.

The woman who wouldn't agree to a date. The one I had to push and push to open up to me is begging me. I need her like the air I breathe. I don't know if I can keep going.

"So you choose, Jackson. You tell me now if you want me to walk away. You walked through my door today. It's up to you to keep it open. I'm not talking about going to do what you have to do. Please, don't close the door on us."

Again she uses my own pleas against me.

I stand silent but when her head falls forward in defeat it becomes too much. I grip her chin and lift her eyes to mine. I can't give her what she's asking but I can't watch her cry.

"Say something, dammit!" she yells as I stare in her eyes. My hand falls because I know I can't walk away if I'm touching her.

"I've said it all already. You're not listening."

"That's your answer?" she asks with the look of already knowing the answer.

I let out a deep breath and my resolve strengthens. "Everyone I love or care about dies. I'm protecting you."

"No. You're protecting yourself. People die, Jackson. It's tragic, but it happens."

I push the hair off her face and my fingers stay clasped against her head. This moment is the last we'll have. This will be the last time I touch her. I look at this woman I love and wish I were dead. "You know that night we met in the restaurant? It was so intense." I recall how instantly I needed to talk to her. I came up with anything I could just to keep her around. "I'd never felt so connected to someone so quickly. You walked away. Then, by some miracle ..." I cup her face and my eyes close. I commit this moment to memory. I focus on how warm and soft her skin feels against my fingers. The way her dark brown hair slithers over my hand like smooth silk. When I lift my lids I see the fear evident in her stare. "You found your way back. I won't allow anything to hurt you. Including me."

My hand falls and she steps closer to me. "The only thing hurting me is you leaving."

I need some fucking divine intervention because good God, this woman is not giving up. She begs me and no matter how many times I say I'm leaving, she continues. Needing this to stop, I do the only thing I can think of.

I crush my lips against hers. I hold her close and give her all I have. There's no letting up. Each second I savor her touch and hunger for more—but there will be no more. She gives it back to me and I wish it were enough. I don't want this kiss to end and I can't pull away from her. She's the air I breathe and I'm about to suffocate.

Catherine pulls back and her chest heaves. "Don't kiss me if you're going to break my heart."

When my eyes meet hers, she knows. I close my eyes and can barely speak. Somehow, I force the words from my mouth. "Good-bye, Catherine." I turn and walk out the door, leaving my heart and lungs behind. I have no use for them anymore.

I've just broken us.

acknowledgements

This is always the hardest part. I have so many people who make this journey what it is. The book wouldn't be what it is without the help of those who are close to me. Whether you helped me work through a scene or you just messaged me to say "hello", you were a part of this. If I leave you out please forgive me, I literally hate this part.

To my readers, thank you isn't enough. You took a chance on a debut author and the love and support was beyond anything I could ever imagine. Thank you for leaving reviews, messaging me, joining the group, and spreading the word. You'll never know the difference you've made in my life.

Mandi Beck- my sweet, supportive, amazing, and fantastic friend. You're the glue that keeps me together. There's not a word you don't read, or a call you decline. Your love of Jackson has never waivered, even when you were pissed at him. I don't know how I would've made it through this journey without you.

Jennifer Wolfel- as much as you scare the crap out of me, I couldn't wait to send you the next chapter. You push me. You make me work hard on every paragraph, sentence, and word. Your wisdom made me fight through the scenes and the fact that I made you cry...makes me happy. I love you and thank you immensely.

Melissa Saneholtz – there are people who come into your life and make things brighter. That's you. I can call you anytime I need you, trust your guidance and you keep me in check (which is no small feat.) Thank you for the countless hours you spend with me, the laughs we share, and your friendship. I couldn't imagine doing this without you!

My betas: Roxana Madar, Megan Ward, Linda Russell, and Ninfa Maisano – Thank you for taking the time to read over and over and give me all your feedback. My early readers: Alison Manning, Lara Petterson, and Susan Rayner – you're the first people to see it and give me the best idea on how it flows. I can't thank you enough.

Christy Peckham – You my Stabby Jr. are so important to me. You'll never know how much I love and appreciate you!

Stephanie, Ninfa, Julie, Carla, Melissa, Jennifer, Amy B., Jillian, Debbie, Tanya, Jessica, Annette, Robin, Michelle, Sherry, Mindi, Amy C., Laura, April, and Wendy... You are my lifeline, my friends, and my heart.

Pam Carrion – I'm giving you a face right now... did you smile? You've been a saint! A godsend! No matter what crazy idea I came up with you were there to help. You're an amazing blogger and I'm fortunate to have you as a friend.

Linda Russell – Woman...no freaking words. Just THANK YOU! You were the first person to read Beloved and I'll never forget the way you rallied behind me. This book wouldn't have been half of what it became without you.

Sharon "Satan" Goodman – Oh, my love. You are so far from being Satan...you're more like an angel...that might be pushing it. I love you so much.

Thank you for keeping me on track by being afraid of Maleficent and not allowing us to have tangents. You're one of the best people I know.

Crystal Pugh – My giant pain in the ass. If it weren't for you the cover wouldn't have happened. Thank you for being my friend. You know the ugly and you still find the beauty. Thank you for driving me insane but then turning around, making me laugh, and offering to make out with me.

Laurelin Paige – You're constant support is invaluable. You keep me grounded and make me laugh when I need it. The world is a better place because of friends like you. If you never encouraged me, this would've never happened. Thank you for changing my life.

Claire Contreras – You'll never know how much your friendship has changed my life. You're an inspiration to women and me. #FYTTMCC except I would say #ILYTTMCC.

Katie Stankiewicz – My graphic slave. You come through for me every single time and I don't know how I'd do it without you. You're not only an amazing artist but you're an even better friend. Thank you for everything. Love you!

FYW – I'm so blessed to have you all in my life.

Lisa, my editor, thank you to for fixing my words and your endless support. You forced me to dig deep and fight hard to give them the story they deserved.

SG4L – You are my sisters, my friends, and I can't imagine life without you.

Bloggers, without you I wouldn't be here. You always give your time, thoughts, and support. Thank you for taking a chance on me and telling your readers. You are truly some of the best people

I know. Thank you!

Danielle and Alex – You made this cover more beautiful than I could've imagined. Thank you both for in the midst of your move doing the photo shoot and gracing the front of this book.

My family, thank you all for supporting my dream and encouraging me. Even if most of you will never read, I still appreciate you. To my mother: Without you, none of this would've been possible. You'll never know how much I love you and appreciate all you've done for me.

My husband, a long time ago I fell in love with you. I pushed you, pulled you, and sometimes I ran from you...but you were always there. You love me no matter what and I can only pray our children find a love like ours. Thank you for putting up with my crazy and showing me I'm enough.

My children, you're my biggest cheerleaders and I love you more than my own life. You both make me smile at your praise (even though you'll never read.) I love that you tell your friends parents to read and you are the best things I ever did.

about the author

Corinne Michaels is an emotional, witty, sarcastic, and fun loving mom of two beautiful children. She's happily married to the man of her dreams and is a former Navy wife. After spending months away from her husband while he was deployed, reading and writing was her escape from the loneliness. Beloved and Beholden conclude The Belonging Duet and she's currently working on three spinoffs.

Connect with Corinne

Connect at https://www.corinnemichaels.com

Connect on Facebook
https://www.facebook.com/CorinneMichaels

Connect on Twitter
https://twitter.com/AuthorCMichaels

Connect on Goodreads
https://www.goodreads.com/author/
show/7753662

20469364R10399

Made in the USA
Middletown, DE
27 May 2015